PENGUIN BO
From London w

Jemma Forte has worked for many years in the television industry, including five years at the Disney Channel, as well as presenting on BBC, ITV and Channel 4. She lives with her husband and two children in London. This is her second novel. Her first novel, *Me & Miss M*, is also published by Penguin.

From London with Love

JEMMA FORTE

PENGUIN BOOKS

For Lily and Freddie

PENGUIN BOOKS

Published by the Penguin Group
Penguin Books Ltd, 80 Strand, London WC2R 0RL, England
Penguin Group (USA), Inc., 375 Hudson Street, New York, New York 10014, USA
Penguin Group (Canada), 90 Eglinton Avenue East, Suite 700, Toronto, Ontario, Canada M4P 2Y3
(a division of Pearson Penguin Canada Inc.)
Penguin Ireland, 25 St Stephen's Green, Dublin 2, Ireland (a division of Penguin Books Ltd)
Penguin Group (Australia), 250 Camberwell Road, Camberwell, Victoria 3124, Australia
(a division of Pearson Australia Group Pty Ltd)
Penguin Books India Pvt Ltd, 11 Community Centre, Panchsheel Park, New Delhi – 110 017, India
Penguin Group (NZ), 67 Apollo Drive, Rosedale, Auckland 0632, New Zealand
(a division of Pearson New Zealand Ltd)
Penguin Books (South Africa) (Pty) Ltd, 24 Sturdee Avenue,
Rosebank, Johannesburg 2196, South Africa

Penguin Books Ltd, Registered Offices: 80 Strand, London WC2R 0RL, England

www.penguin.com

First published 2011

1

Copyright © Jemma Forte, 2011

The moral right of the author has been asserted

All rights reserved

Without limiting the rights under copyright
reserved above, no part of this publication may be
reproduced, stored in or introduced into a retrieval system,
or transmitted, in any form or by any means (electronic, mechanical,
photocopying, recording or otherwise), without the prior
written permission of both the copyright owner and
the above publisher of this book

Set in 12.5/14.75pt Garamond MT
Typeset by Jouve (UK), Milton Keynes
Printed in Great Britain by Clays Ltd, St Ives plc

A CIP catalogue record for this book is available from the British Library

ISBN: 978-0-141-04963-2

www.greenpenguin.co.uk

Penguin Books is committed to a sustainable
future for our business, our readers and our
planet. This book is made from paper certified
by the Forest Stewardship Council.

Prologue

Two parents, that much we all have in common, at least at the point of conception anyway. Nothing's guaranteed after that, of course, though thankfully most baby makers are keen to stick around to look after and enjoy the fruit of their loins. After all, the word 'parent' is a verb as well as a noun.

Parenthood, it's the club that's easy to get into (fertility permitting) and yet such a privilege to be part of. The club which doesn't offer money back, a trial run or any guarantees but entices us with the promise of untold joy and fulfilment. And which, for that reason, will always have people on the waiting list.

One day, back in 1984, movie stars Edward Granger and Angelica Dupree didn't know it yet but they were about to come off the waiting list and become fully paid-up members themselves, any second now . . .

The famous couple were in London celebrating the royal première of Edward's latest outing as James Bond and with two weeks to go until their due date they had the world at their feet (not that Angelica had seen hers for months). They were excited and nervous about the birth of their first child in equal measure, though admittedly Angelica was looking forward to getting the 'shoving it out' bit over and done with. After that, however, the couple assumed the rest would be plain sailing. Why would it not?

They were rich, gorgeous and hugely successful at everything they did. The timing was a little off, but millions of people looked after babies every day. How hard could it be?

'Are you all right, my darling?' Edward asked Angelica. 'Not too uncomfortable on that stool?'

'I'm fine, just tired. Can we go soon?'

'Of course,' he replied, placing a protective hand on her burgeoning belly.

Just then, Jill Cunningham, his agent, sidled up to them, breaking the spell. 'The critics love you,' she drawled with greedy relish. 'This time tomorrow we'll have signed another two-movie deal.'

'Wonderful,' replied Edward agreeably and was just about to ask what she wanted to drink when an excited-looking woman came charging into their eye line.

Barging her way through the crowd, she looked overcome with excitement. 'I can't believe it's really you,' she squealed, clamping her hand over her mouth. 'James Bond in the flesh and . . . oh my God! Sorry, it's just I didn't see you at first. Angelica Dupree! You're even more stunning than in your pictures and . . . you're expecting!' she gabbled, pointing out the obvious.

'Lovely to meet you,' said Edward chivalrously, sliding off his stool to greet his fan. 'And what might your name be?'

'Anita,' she said coyly. 'Or should I say, "Fletcher, Anita Fletcher".'

Edward flung his head back and laughed as though this was the most original thing he'd ever heard. Angelica smiled to herself.

'So tell me, Anita Fletcher, what did you make of the film?' Edward was saying now.

'Loved it, really loved it. In fact, me and my sister who's . . . somewhere . . . anyway, we're huge Bond fans and we won a competition to come tonight, and it was just brilliant. The baddie was excellent and we loved the Bond girl . . . though she wasn't as good as you were in the last one,' she added hurriedly to Angelica.

'Don't be silly,' placated Angelica, despite the fact that a slightly sore point had been touched upon. Getting pregnant now, when she was on the cusp of a glittering career, hadn't exactly been the plan. 'Bond's supposed to have different girls and, besides, I wouldn't fit into my bikini at the moment anyway – though hopefully I'll be back into it in time for the next one.'

Jill Cunningham was dying to interject at this point, but held her tongue. As Edward's agent, she'd always hated how ambitious his young wife was and wished she'd stop trying to compete.

Anita Fletcher stared back gormlessly. She wasn't sure where to look. Angelica's silk maternity dress plunged into a low V, showing off to full effect her incredible bosoms and perfect décolletage. 'You're carrying beautifully,' she said eventually. 'What do you think you're having? Apart from a baby obviously . . .'

'I don't know,' interrupted Angelica.

'Really? Gosh, when I was pregnant with my Paul, I knew it was a boy from the beginning. Didn't stop kicking, for one thing.'

'Right,' Angelica replied faintly.

'And what would you have called him if he'd been a girl?' asked Edward politely.

'Lorraine.'

The smile faded from Angelica's face. '*Mon Dieu,*' she wailed in her first language.

'Lorraine's not that bad,' Edward said.

'No!' cried a mortified-looking Angelica. 'I've had an accident, look.'

Edward followed her gaze downwards. A huge wet patch was emerging through the pistachio silk of her dress. 'Angie darling,' he said, blue eyes twinkling 'That's not wee. I think your water's have broken. We're going to have a baby.'

Angelica stared blankly at him for a second and then she gasped, and in years to come Edward Granger would always remember that moment. For it was the moment his life changed for ever. The moment that marked both a joyful new beginning and a sorrowful end, and the last time Edward would feel absolutely sure about anything for a very long time to come.

Twenty-Six Years and Three Months Later (To Be Precise)

I

Jessica Granger was sitting behind her desk at work, trying to figure out what on earth was going on. For nearly a month now she'd been working as a receptionist at one of the most prestigious art galleries in Los Angeles and, while manning the phones wasn't the most stimulating of jobs, she liked it. It was something to get up for in the morning and lent a comforting sense of normality to her otherwise abnormal life.

The vast white space, located a few blocks from Rodeo Drive, was a magnet for wealthy residents and tourists alike and Jessica's desk was situated right in the middle, at the back. The atmosphere inside the air-conditioned gallery was sombre, quiet and still, and – as in a library or a church – visitors spoke in hushed, reverential tones. Though in the case of the current exhibition, if they'd run from the building screaming Jessica wouldn't have blamed them.

On the walls was the work of a hip new German artist. The show comprised eight huge canvases, which were smothered in fluorescent blotches, bright splatters of primary-coloured paint and speckles of gold and silver. Not content with the cacophony of colour he'd created, the artist, for some reason Jessica had yet to grasp, had also smeared the finished pieces with buffalo dung. So they smelled, as one would expect, very unpleasant. To be more precise, they smelled of shit.

Having lived with the paintings for the last few weeks, Jessica had grown to hate them. They made her feel anxious, gave her a headache and offended her senses. Passers-by recoiled in horror as they took the full impact and when one of her colleagues described them as offensive Jessica couldn't have agreed more. But then what did she know? Christopher, their boss, obviously thought they were good enough to grace the gallery's walls, and now, as it turned out, he wasn't the only one.

'It's amazing, isn't it?' said financial controller Nick, one of several members of staff who had gathered round Jessica's desk to gaze in wonder at the red dots that were stuck next to every single piece.

'Unbelievable,' agreed Jessica wholeheartedly, as she looked around the room warily, half-expecting Ashton Kutcher to spring out from behind a pillar yelling 'You've been Punk'd!'

Just then, Christopher himself arrived. 'Morning everybody, and good morning Jessica, how are you today?' he enquired, striding in triumphantly.

'Er – great, thanks, Mr Starkey,' Jessica replied, surprised to have been singled out.

'Look,' he said dramatically, 'sold, sold, sold.'

'Huge congratulations,' said Kate, who as head of sales was immensely relieved she could finally stop risking her reputation by pretending to like them. 'So who bought them then? Did they all go to the same client?'

'Yup,' said Christopher, grinning smugly, his eyes flitting to Jessica once more. She blushed, panicking in case someone had told him what she'd said about the paintings.

'Was it Stevie Wonder by any chance?' laughed Kate, confident that now the paintings were finally off their hands, a joke might be permitted.

Several people spluttered with laughter. Unfortunately Christopher wasn't one of them. 'Well, thank goodness not everybody shares your narrow view of what is, and what isn't, great art, Kate,' he snapped, before storming off to the back offices, leaving an embarrassed silence in his wake. One by one, everyone shuffled back to work, but Kate marched after Christopher, looking like she wanted to pick a fight.

Minutes later, however, she reappeared. 'I may have been wrong about these paintings, you know?' she said tentatively, hovering round Jessica's desk. 'They're really pretty amazing when you think about the amount of work that's gone into them.'

Jessica looked up from the mailing list she was updating and tucked her fair hair behind her ears. 'Um . . . sure, I suppose.' Privately, she was disappointed by Kate's lack of backbone. Just because one insane individual had decided to buy the paintings didn't mean anything had changed. They were still an eyesore.

Still, at least Christopher's mood had reverted to one of friendliness and joy, and when he reappeared a little later he even offered to pop to Starbucks to get Jessica a coffee. On the one hand she was delighted her conscientiousness and eagerness to please was finally being recognized; on the other, it was unnerving. Then, when he laughed like a drain at something she said as if it was the funniest thing he'd ever heard, a sixth sense suddenly made her feel horribly wary. As soon as he'd left again Jessica dialled best friend Dulcie's number.

'It's me,' she whispered into her headset. 'I'm having a really strange day so I need you to tell me that I'm going crazy for having the thoughts I'm having.'

'Tell me in a second because I'm so glad you've called,' came the reply. 'I've just booked my next dress fitting, so put July twentieth in your diary and, oh my God, you will not believe who Kevin wants to invite . . .'

Five minutes later and Jessica was beginning to regret calling. Her friend was in full bridal flow, she hadn't got a word in edgeways and there was a call coming through that she needed to answer.

'Dulcie . . .'

'. . . anyway, it's such a relief about the chairs, I knew you'd be pleased, and next time I go to check out the venue you should come because –'

'Dulcie . . .'

'That way we can decide together –'

'DULCIE!'

'What?'

'I've got to go.'

A few minutes later, Rob, the gallery technician, turned up complete with ladder.

'Morning, Jess,' he said. 'Just to let you know, the new paintings for the next exhibition have arrived and Christopher said to feel free to look at them in the viewing room.'

'Right,' said Jessica, who didn't know quite what to make of that. 'That's cool of him.'

'I guess,' said Rob.

Jessica watched thoughtfully as he climbed the ladder, which he'd positioned underneath one of the lighting rigs. 'So, only a couple of weeks to go and we don't have to see these any more, eh?' she said conspiratorially.

From his lofty position, Rob looked at her with a bemused expression. 'You mean because we'll see them somewhere else?' he said and then he winked.

Jessica's hackles immediately went up. 'Who bought the paintings?' she asked impulsively.

'Don't know,' said Rob quickly. Too quickly. He was lying.

Thinking swiftly, Jessica changed tactics. She had a hunch, a hideous one that she simply had to eradicate. 'It's all right,' she stage-whispered, going for a bluff. 'I know.'

'Really?' he replied, concentrating just a little too hard on his light bulb.

'Yeah,' said Jessica in a blasé voice, which belied the fact that her pulse was accelerating by the second.

'Who told you?' asked Rob as he climbed back down.

'Oh, you know,' said Jessica, as if he ought to.

'It's just that Christopher said we shouldn't say anything,' he replied, looking flustered, 'because I think he thought you didn't want us to know about who . . . you know . . . though I have to admit,' he said, looking pained, 'I've been feeling really bad ever since I found out. I want you to know that when I called them monstrosities the other day I was only joking.'

Jessica's heart fell into her stomach. 'Oh, sure,' she said weakly. 'Anyway, don't worry about it. Obviously I know that he . . . my –' She stopped, still hoping she might have got it wrong. Maybe she was being paranoid, fishing in the wrong pond?

'Your . . . dad?' offered Rob hesitantly.

'My dad . . .' Right pond then.

'O-K,' said Rob, suddenly looking anxious in case he'd said the wrong thing. 'So, anyway, I need to go out now, Jess, but . . .'

'What?'

'Don't take any notice of what anyone else thinks, yeah? At the end of the day, art is entirely subjective,' he added kindly.

Jessica nodded faintly and forced a smile. She didn't know where to begin so she just didn't bother and as she waved goodbye to Rob she suspected she was waving goodbye for good, because how could she possibly stay at the gallery now? She sat there despairing for a while, feeling utterly humiliated and more than a little stupid. Yet another job had just hit the dust, been taken away from her, and now she needed some lunch, to resign and to work out what on earth to do about her interfering dad, only not necessarily in that order.

2

Jessica was anxiously nibbling on a breadstick when her phone vibrated.

'Dulcie,' she muttered, 'I can't talk. I'm at Spago waiting for Shawn.'

'Don't worry about it,' said Dulcie, 'everyone talks on their phones there. What did you want to tell me earlier?'

Jessica glanced around the Beverly Hills restaurant. 'Well . . .'

'Actually, before you tell me, Jess, I need to pick your brains about which magazines to approach about the wedding. I mean, they're going to be interested, right?'

From nowhere Jessica found herself battling with an overwhelming urge to scream *'NO ONE IS INTERESTED! Even I, your best friend, would rather impale myself on a rusty sword than see or hear anything else about your wedding right now because, as astounding as this may sound, I actually have other things to think about. And, by the way, who are you and what have you done with my friend?'* This flood of pent-up emotion took Jessica quite by surprise. Until this very second, she hadn't realized just how much Dulcie's perpetual wedding chatter had been bothering her. Still, she opted for a less controversial reply.

'I'm sure they will, Dulcie, I'm sure they will.'

'Yeah, I think so. I mean, between me and Kev, there are going to be a lot of well-known people there and . . .'

There was only one thing for it. Jessica cut her off, before wearily placing her head on the table for a quick despair, which she was actually quite enjoying until her phone bleeped, signalling a text. She turned her head to the side and brought up one hand to press the view button.

**THINKING OF HAVING
'PRE-HEN' DRINKS SOON.
WHAT DO YOU RECKON?**

Jessica 'reckoned' there were twelve whole months to go until the wedding next May for crissakes and that there were only so many times a girl could say 'Yay!' A silent scream unfurled in her belly as she sat up to text back a reply.

YAY!

Now she was relying on Shawn to help her figure things out, something which didn't fill her with a great deal of hope. Especially considering he wasn't actually there yet which, come to think of it, was really annoying.

Feeling like her scrambled brain was in need of a break, Jessica reached over to the adjacent table to pinch a discarded copy of the *Los Angeles Times*. She flicked through it, eventually settling on a piece on page seven about British culture and traditions, and which aspects of it did and didn't appeal to Americans. The history, the royal family, much of the pop, art and TV culture all got the thumbs-up and then it went on to dissect what the US weren't so sold on. Bad dentistry, the cuisine, all the usual suspects were there, as were more left-field examples such as funny spelling that incorporated far too many vowels and Simon Cowell's dress sense.

Jessica smiled. She'd been born in England, had lived there for the first seven years of her life, in fact, so felt a strong connection with the place. Having an English father and a French mother was something she was proud of and her peers had always been fascinated by her European heritage. However, the truth of the matter was that her memories of actually living in England were pretty hazy these days, though she'd never forget being a pupil at Parkhurst.

Parkhurst Abbey was one of England's most prestigious and traditional girl's schools, set in stunning rural surroundings. As a confused five-year-old it may have taken her a while to settle in, but when she had it had been like living in an Enid Blyton book. Until, of course, Edward's time as James Bond came to an end, at which point Hollywood had beckoned and moving Stateside became inevitable.

Jessica scanned the restaurant briefly, looking to see if Shawn had appeared yet. As she did, she suddenly vividly recalled — for the first time in a long time — how much of a wrench it had felt to leave England behind all those years ago and how, back then, it had been the place she considered home. A strange thought, given that these days she felt like a Californian chick through and through and was so totally used to her sun-drenched way of life.

Of course, over the years there had been many trips back to England, but returning as a tourist had never felt quite the same somehow. Whenever Edward had a movie to promote, or simply fancied a dose of home, she'd usually gone with him and had often wondered what it would be like to return to Britain as a separate entity one day. To view the country through the eyes of an independent adult, as opposed to a child's, had always been something she was keen to do at some point. Obviously she had dual nationality so whenever that time came it would be easy to organize and . . .

At that instant Jessica experienced a strange surge of excitement and found herself staring with renewed interest at the accompanying pictures of Buckingham Palace, fish and chips, Cat Deeley and red buses. A warm flood of welcome nostalgia washed over her as she recalled one particularly happy trip to London during which she'd spent lots of time with her auntie Pam, Edward's sister. Maybe it *was* time for a long vacation of some description? To get away and rediscover her British roots would be fantastic and being away might just provide her with some much-needed answers and ideas. After all, what was keeping her in LA? Apart from her friends, her boyfriend and her own foolish reluctance to ever make a go of anything in case it didn't work out.

Five minutes later Jessica finally spotted Shawn, looking irritatingly unflustered about the fact that he was late. Though he soon looked less smug when he casually tried to barrel straight through the gate and the doorman prevented his entry with a large, unimpressed arm. Feeling weirdly detached, Jessica watched him bluster and protest for a while, but then he must have mentioned her name because the doorman's entire demeanour changed and Shawn was swiftly ushered in. She sighed, feeling thoroughly underwhelmed to see him.

'Hey, baby,' he said in an overly loud voice as he swaggered over to their table. 'Look at you with your *LA Times*. You hiding a copy of *In Style* underneath?'

What exactly was he trying to say? 'Actually, I've just been reading an article about England, which has kind of given me an idea,' she replied, trying to perk up but hating how Shawn's eyes were flitting around the restaurant, busily scanning for famous faces. He didn't have to look too far.

'And what might that be?' asked Shawn, not looking remotely interested but at least doing her the honour of swivelling his eyeballs back in her direction. There was no denying he was a good-looking guy but today Jessica hated how contrived everything about him looked. His T-shirt was so . . . ironed. His dark, longish hair had been slicked back into a rather creepy ponytail and his nails looked suspiciously like they might have been manicured. She was sure he hadn't been anywhere near this groomed when she'd first met him, but then again, she had met him at the beach. She opened her mouth to reply but closed it again when she noticed the approaching waiter.

'Good afternoon, Miss Granger,' he said, greeting her like an old friend. 'If I may say, you are looking very lovely today, very much like your father.'

Jessica blushed. She was an attractive girl but nowhere near as extraordinary-looking as either of her parents, and she lived in permanent dread of the inevitable comparisons.

'Speaking of which, how is he? I've not seen him for a while.'

'Oh . . . he's fine. Busy as always, but great . . . thanks,' mumbled Jessica, omitting the part about him being desperately annoying.

'Please send my regards,' the waiter replied, whipping

Jessica's napkin off the table and placing it across her lap with a flourish. 'Now, what can I get you?'

'*We* need a couple of minutes,' said Shawn brusquely, making it clear that his fragile ego didn't appreciate being ignored.

Jessica waited a beat. For weeks now Shawn had been getting on her nerves. Any of the original charm he may have possessed when she'd first met him seemed to have evaporated completely. 'Actually, *I've* been waiting ages,' she said eventually. 'And I'm starving. So, the chicken Caesar salad with extra anchovies and some iced water would be great, thank you.'

'Jeez, what's wrong with you today? Since when was waiting twenty minutes such a big deal?' Shawn said petulantly. 'OK, I guess I'll have the same, but make my dressing low cal and hold the anchovies. Can't stand the fishy fuckers,' he said, delighted by his hilarious alliteration. 'Fish breath is so not a turn-on.'

Jessica made a quick mental note to eat every scrap of anchovy on her plate and then breathe all over him first chance she got. The waiter finished scribbling and walked away.

'Anyway, what's up, sweetie?' said Shawn, misinterpreting her frown. 'How come it was so urgent we meet for lunch?'

Briefly Jessica toyed with the idea of keeping what had happened to herself, but the need to confide was too great. 'Oh, Shawn,' she began. 'I've had an awful morning and, to cut a long story short, I've resigned.'

'Why? Were you bored?'

'No,' said Jessica impatiently. 'I left because I found out

that . . .' She swallowed, as the extent of how hurt she was caught up with her. She blinked and looked at the ceiling for a moment. She needed to start at the beginning. 'You remember how I told you that Christopher was always pretty grumpy? Well, today he was in a great mood because the show had sold out, and he started being really nice to me –' Shawn rocked back on his chair and cocked one eyebrow skywards, which Jessica tried not to let bug her as she carried on – 'which only goes to show how naive I must be, because Rob let it slip that the person who bought the *whole* exhibition – you know the one I'm talking about? The paintings you said looked like alien puke. The ones with shit on them. Anyway, the mystery buyer who bought the entire lot was . . . my dad.' Jessica looked down at her hands. 'Everybody at the gallery knows, so they all think I had something to do with it, which is hideous on so many levels. Though I think what I'm most upset about is the fact that he's gone behind my back again, even though I expressly asked him not to interfere.' Having finished, she waited for some sympathy.

'Cool,' said Shawn, nodding and grinning enthusiastically. Then, as her face dropped, 'Aw, come on, Jess, don't look like that. Who cares if your dad wants to help you? You should be proud of your connections – though personally, if I were you, I'd forget about working altogether and take some time out.'

'Time out from what?' asked Jessica quietly, feeling baffled, dismayed and not a little frustrated. How could he not get it? She gave up, cross with herself for having expected anything different from Shawn. There was no point explaining anything to him. He was simply too moronic to understand. At that moment Jessica realized this probably wasn't a great thing to be thinking about her own boyfriend. She cleared her throat. 'Look, let's just forget about it, all right. I'll sort it out with my dad later,' she said, suddenly keen to move on.

'Hey, you're not exactly being fair, Jess . . . oh, hang on a minute, I need a beer,' said Shawn, and then he actually clicked his fingers at a passing waiter.

In that instance, the many niggles that Jessica had been experiencing about her 'boyfriend' seemed to solidify. It occurred to her that she didn't just find Shawn annoying, but that she loathed him, which said less about the flakiness of Jessica's personality and more about how tenuous their relationship had been in the first place. After all, what was an amazing torso without a personality to go with it?

The waiter turned slowly, bestowing a smile upon Jessica before eyeballing Shawn as threateningly as possible, given the customer/waiter dynamic.

'Can I help you?' he enquired frostily.

'Don't know. Can you?' chuckled Shawn. 'Get me a beer and make sure it's ice cold.'

It's over, thought Jessica resignedly, not feeling much apart from mild relief.

Shawn was off again. 'Listen, you get all cagey when we talk about your dad, but how can you expect me to say the right thing when I haven't even met him? We've been dating, what, three months, and we still haven't set up a time for me to meet your folks.' As Shawn swung back on his chair his face clouded over with an expression that looked suspiciously sulky. 'It's like you're ashamed of me or something.'

He probably had a point.

'Why are you so obsessed about meeting my parents anyway?' she asked wearily, even though she knew the answer. 'Most guys would be grateful not to have to meet their girlfriend's family. I've told you how busy Dad is and you know I hardly ever see my mom myself.'

Shawn struggled to come up with a rational argument, but it was too big a task so he gave up and reached for a breadstick, which he gnawed on like a huffy chipmunk. Jessica gazed into the middle distance. Not only was she furious with herself for letting the relationship get this far, she was also sick and tired of feeling like her entire life was defined by one thing, and one thing only. That she was the daughter of Edward Granger and Angelica Dupree, otherwise known as James Bond and Heavenly Melons, the sexiest Bond girl of all time.

Suddenly she remembered what she'd been considering earlier. 'I was telling you before that I'd had an idea. Do you want to know what it was?' she asked her sullen-looking, soon-to-be ex-boyfriend, her tone almost daring him to say no. All she wanted was for someone, anyone, to be remotely interested in what she had to say, just for once.

'Go ahead,' said Shawn magnanimously.

'Right,' said Jessica quietly, fighting to hold back the tears that were suddenly threatening to slide down her face. 'Well, I was thinking that, what with everything being such a disaster here, maybe it was time for a trip. I was thinking about England, actually, London.'

Shawn stared hard at her and for a fraction of a second Jessica thought he might be about to show some proper interest. 'Cool, count me in. Didn't you say your mom was in Europe? We could go see her at the same time.'

And there it was. That famous last straw.

'Shawn,' Jessica said calmly, folding away her paper and standing up, 'that wasn't an invitation. It's over. I'm sorry, but I can't go out with someone who only likes me for my parents any more.'

And with that she left, although not as abruptly as she'd intended.

'Excuse me,' said a man in a suit, springing up from his table and blocking her escape from the restaurant. 'You're Edward Granger's daughter, aren't you? I hope you don't mind me introducing myself but your father and I go way back. I'm Billy, Billy Jackson, and I've got a script here that I'd love him to take a look at. The part of Steven has been written specifically with him in mind and I was going to send it to his agent, but if you could give it to him directly it would be so fantastic and –' He broke off, misinterpreting Jessica's horror at the situation entirely.

'Oh, I'm sorry, honey, I'm being rude. Are you an actress too? Because I'm sure we could come up with a part to accommodate you. In fact, if you get this to Edward for me then we could even write one in especially for –'

Jessica shook her head vigorously. 'I'm not an actress.'

'You're not?' replied Billy Jackson. 'Well, what are you then? What do you do?'

Squirming inside, Jessica shrugged. Everyone was staring. 'I'm not sure,' she muttered, before grabbing the script and fleeing the restaurant as quickly as she could, leaving Billy Jackson scratching his bald pate, the other diners with something to talk about and Shawn with the bill.

As she waited on the sidewalk for the valet to bring her car round, Jessica Granger made a decision. It was time to leave LA, go somewhere she could be herself and find out what on earth that might be like. That way, the next time someone asked her what it was she 'did', she might know what to say.

3

Across the pond in London, Mike Conner, executive producer of *The Bradley Mackintosh Show* for the BBC, was sitting in one office, well aware of the fact that his entire team were waiting for him in another. He insisted on punctuality for the weekly meeting but then liked to keep everyone waiting, just a bit, to remind them that he was an incredibly busy man.

He sipped his latte. Compared to being at home, the office was a luxurious haven of calm and he suspected it might continue to feel that way for some time to come. Thank God he wasn't Scandinavian, he mused, for he seemed to remember reading somewhere that Swedish men were allowed to take a full year of paternity leave, which the journalist had written as if it were a good thing. As far as Mike was concerned, two weeks of keeping his toddler daughter Grace entertained while Diane, his teary, lactating wife, got to grips with feeding the latest addition to their family, had been plenty. Not that he didn't love them. He did. Adored them, in fact. It was just that recently, according to Diane, everything he did was wrong, so it seemed easier to stay away. Hence why this morning, despite not really needing to start work until ten, he'd invented a completely imaginary nine o'clock meeting. Something he'd be doing more of in the future. During that first quiet hour before the office had filled up he'd watched *Sky News* and read the paper cover to cover. Bliss.

Still, he'd have to be careful. His wife would take serious umbrage if she were to find out that he was purposefully absconding from the morning chaos otherwise known as family life.

While he had a minute, Mike decided to email everyone on the team to say that next week, due to something terribly urgent having cropped up, the production meeting would have to be cancelled for one week only. An agent had invited him out for lunch and he intended on getting stuck in. He certainly wouldn't want to have to rush back.

Mike pressed 'send', then scrolled through the rest of his emails, squinting as he did so. His eyeballs felt gritty, due to lack of sleep. Last night he'd been able to hear baby Ava screaming even from the sanctuary of the spare room. Maybe later he'd hold his calls, lock the door and put his head on the desk for a twenty-minute power nap. Not that he'd tell Diane. He wouldn't dare, for fear of being stabbed. His wife was so wild-eyed with exhaustion at the moment that the mere mention of anybody getting any sleep at all was enough to set her off on a jealous rant, and while he understood and appreciated it wasn't easy for her, Diane didn't have a stressful job like he did.

Still, his recent 'time off' had served as quite a vivid reminder that by choosing to stay at home Diane wasn't exactly having the life of Riley, drinking coffee and watching daytime telly as he sometimes liked to imagine. In fact, if he were completely honest, he didn't know how she did it day in and day out.

He turned his attention back to his in-box just as an internal message arrived. It was from David Bridlington, the controller of light entertainment, who also happened to be his father-in-law. (A double-edged sword in many ways and something Mike was incredibly paranoid about.) As he read it, a vein of worry flowed through him. The contentment he'd been feeling was abruptly replaced by an unwelcome shot of stress. Bloody ratings were the bane of his life and this week they'd been lower than expected. He clicked on the next email just as a rap on the door made him jump.

'Come,' he shouted authoritatively.

Kerry, his feisty celeb booker, poked her head round the door. 'Hi, Mike,' she said. 'It's gone two, just in case you hadn't realized.'

With the door now open, Mike could hear that the natives were getting restless, but he didn't like the feeling that he was being told what to do by a member of his team.

'Yeah, thanks, Kerry, I'm well aware of the time, but sometimes things come up that I have to deal with right away – unless, that is, you want to risk us not getting on air this week?' he said, not even looking her way and concentrating instead on the screen as if what he was reading was a matter of vital importance. In fact, he was quickly scanning a reminder from M&S that there was twenty per cent off the Autograph collection as of Thursday.

Having taken the hint, Kerry closed the door and Mike was left to ponder firstly whether to go for the V-neck or the crew-neck sweater and, secondly, how to handle his boss's misgivings about last week's show.

Suddenly he felt a bit sorry for himself. There should be more passion and excitement in his life than he was getting at the moment. The strong, sexy career woman he'd married had disappeared and been replaced by someone who resembled early woman and who seemed to have forgotten how to shave her legs or give a blowjob. And now, instead of grabbing forty winks later, he'd probably spend the rest of the day feeling uneasy about the prospect of a meeting with David, who was always on his case about something. Mike knew he felt compelled to justify his huge salary, which was fine, but David was also aware that he and Diane had just had a baby and that things were a bit tough at home at the moment, so surely 'Granddad' could back off for a short while?

Still, there wasn't time to dwell on all of that now. It was time for the meeting, even though he knew the majority of his team resented having to down tools in order to listen to him vent his spleen. He knew because he'd heard them say as much, but he didn't care. The meeting would remain a regular fixture (unless he had a lunch), whether there was anything important to convey or not, so he could remind everyone exactly who was boss. So if they didn't like it, they could go fuck themselves. This burst of vitriol finally jet-propelled him into action. He leapt out of his chair and started gathering together what he needed for the meeting. It was seven minutes past two, time to get the show on the road.

4

Edward Granger let his script drop to the ground and reclined on his lounger, letting the afternoon sun's strong rays shine fully on his face for a few lazy moments. He didn't start shooting for months, so there was plenty of time for learning his lines anyway. He inhaled deeply, savouring the tangy aroma of Pacific Ocean salt that hung in the air, taking the edge off the extreme heat and refreshing the atmosphere, making it just about the healthiest lungful one could enjoy in California.

From where he was sitting he had a perfect view of his magnificent, colonial-style mansion, sprawling landscaped gardens, enormous infinity pool and portion of beach that was exclusively his; one of the most sought-after pieces of Malibu real estate. Yet despite having been successful for over a quarter of a century now, his fame and fortune still never ceased to amaze him, a by-product of years spent struggling before landing his big break. When he had finally won the role of 007 he'd been pronounced an overnight success, the irony of which hadn't passed him by. There was nothing overnight about the bars he'd worked in, the years spent labouring on construction sites, or how long it had taken to persuade his family that there was nothing 'poncy' about wanting to be an actor.

Belching softly, Edward adjusted the waistband of his khaki sailing shorts, easing them off his distended stomach slightly. He'd had a delicious lunch but had eaten far more than his recommended calorie intake, even allowing himself a glass or two of fine Merlot to wash it down with. He felt rather guilty about this rare venture off his strictly managed culinary piste. In terms of getting back into shape for his next movie, he was cutting things fine. Then again, if you couldn't indulge occasionally when approaching the age of sixty-five, frankly, what was the point? The roar from the ocean in front of him was immensely soothing, as was the feeling of the sun warming his bones, and soon he felt himself sliding towards a lovely soporific afternoon snooze.

'Honey,' squealed a voice, dragging him back to the here and now. Maybe if he ignored her she'd get the hint, he thought wistfully, knowing full well she wouldn't.

'Honey, put the umbrella back up. You know you shouldn't have the sun shining directly on to your face and I bet you're not wearing protection,' chastised wife Betsey, who was undulating across the lawn towards him, ruining the moment completely.

He sighed inwardly.

'Are you even listening to me?' she asked, bending over him, her tanned, pneumatic breasts in his direct line of vision, hoisted inside one of her many sports bras. This one was hot pink.

'I could hardly not,' Edward replied, but with enough affection in his voice for her to know he wasn't angry. Betsey bent down and ruffled Edward's thick thatch of silvery hair, which still possessed the faintest trace of blond. Then she picked up some lotion that was lying nearby, squirted some into her hand and proceeded to slather it on to his face, probably a case of too little too late given that he was already brown and weathered from years of outside shooting. The crinkles around his piercing blue eyes were another giveaway; not that they detracted from his handsome looks particularly, a huge and horrifically unfair advantage of simply being male. Edward blinked – Betsey had managed to get some lotion into his right eye and now it was stinging. Unaware of her husband's discomfort, Betsey enthusiastically straddled him until she was sitting directly on his groin. He groaned, but only out of discomfort.

'It's day fifteen. My eggs are ripe and ready for in-se-mi-na-tion,' she purred, oblivious to the fact that the second she'd mentioned her 'eggs', any chance she'd had of turning him on had vanished. 'Come on, honey,' she persisted, her bossy manner reminding Edward, not for the first time, of Miss Piggy. 'Let's go make love.'

With the eye that wasn't blurry and stinging like hell, Edward surveyed his second wife's cleavage and silently grieved for the breasts they'd once been. She'd previously had a beautiful set of medium-sized, natural breasts which he'd only had to look at to feel blood flowing to the appropriate area. Yet Betsey had insisted on going under the knife and was now delighted with the results, presuming Edward was too, though, in truth, her new assets held zero appeal. He regarded them now, trying his best to summon up desire but failing miserably. They were perfect orbs, having been transformed from bosoms to tits, and nuzzling into them had somehow lost its appeal.

'Well?' said Betsey.

Edward swallowed. 'Maybe later, darling? A lie-down

sounds wonderful, but I've just finished eating so I should probably digest... and I need to learn my lines,' he added hastily.

Betsey's incredulous expression spoke volumes and Edward didn't need to be told how middle-aged he'd sounded, yet rather begrudged having this held against him given that middle age had passed him by long ago. He sighed again, only too aware that Betsey was wondering how a red-blooded man could turn down sex on a plate from a nubile woman nearly half his age. He could see the all-too-familiar disappointment and frustration showing in her green eyes. Then he spotted his housekeeper, making her way towards them from the house across the lawn.

'Ah, Consuela,' he yelled gratefully, practically tipping Betsey off his lap and on to the grass. 'You're a mind-reader. Jill's coming over later with my contract. Would it be OK if she joined us for dinner?'

'Not a problem, Mr G. I was just coming to see if you wanted coffee,' she replied, as a sulky-looking Betsey stomped past her in the opposite direction, pert, lycra-clad behind positively bristling with resentment, muttering loudly to herself, 'Digest... I'll give you freaking digest...'

Edward exchanged a long-suffering look with his loyal maid, who chuckled and rolled her eyes heavenwards.

'Coffee would be great. I'll come and get it in a bit,' said Edward. Consuela headed back to the house.

Alone once more, Edward sat up and fiddled with the parasol. His previous good mood had vanished, for he knew he couldn't blame this lack of interest in what was once his all-time favourite occupation squarely at the feet of Betsey's bosoms. His legendary sex drive had been on the wane for a while now, but if before it had been staggering about like an old drunk, then it had finally been knocked out altogether when, from nowhere, Betsey had done the most enormous about-turn on their original joint decision not to have children. She'd announced her change of heart six months ago, as casually as if she was talking about buying a new lipstick, and it had come as a terrible shock. Why on earth would she want to be impregnated with his ancient sperm?

Since then, Betsey had become obsessed. Not a day went by when Edward couldn't tell you what day of her cycle she was on, what her temperature was, and whether or not her discharge resembled egg white, all of which he found baffling and faintly repulsive. Meanwhile, she seemed determined to continue ignoring his protests, as if his words were a mere buzzing in her ear. At times he felt like a fly trapped in a room, repeatedly banging itself against a window pane.

Feeling irked, Edward retrieved his reading glasses from the table next to him, picked up his script and found the next scene. The dialogue was terribly banal, which only depressed him further; especially when he realized that here was yet another scene that required him to take his shirt off.

'Dad!'

Edward shaded his face with his hand just in time to see his beloved daughter coming round the side of the house towards him. One interruption at least that was more than welcome. His heart swelled with affection as it did every time he set eyes on her. Today she was wearing a denim skirt, with a plain white vest and flat, jewelled sandals, a silver bracelet on her wrist her only jewellery. She looked divine.

'Hi, Dad,' Jessica panted, having run the rest of the way across the lawn, so desperate was she to cool off in the pool. She was already pulling off her skirt and shoes, until she was wearing only her top and underwear. 'You don't mind, do you? It's just I'm so hot, I can't be bothered to get my costume.'

'Don't mind me,' he said smoothly in his quintessentially English voice. 'You're home early, aren't you? I thought you were working at the gallery today.'

But Jessica had already flopped into the pool. Small air bubbles came to the surface as she swam a length underwater, and when she reappeared at the other end she swept her hair off her face and blew water out of her nose before replying. 'I was supposed to be, which is what I need to talk to you about. Where's Betsey?'

'Working out,' Edward replied, glancing over to the house where he could see her through the glass doors, contorting herself into the most alarming positions as she practised her yoga.

Jessica resurfaced from the bottom of the pool again and gasped for air. 'She's exercising a lot at the moment, isn't she?' she asked before swimming to the side, where she pulled herself up and clambered out.

'Mmm,' murmured Edward vaguely, peering down his pale pink shirt at the small pool of sweat that had gathered in the middle of his chest. It was true; the more frustrated Betsey grew sexually, the more she exercised. What a shame he couldn't hire someone in to see to her needs, he thought ruefully, a wry smile spreading across his handsome features as he even considered such an outrageous idea.

Jessica grabbed one of the numerous white fluffy towels that were piled up on a table by the pool and dried off her legs, which, like her father's, were covered in freckles. With her fine blonde hair, looks-wise Jessica was the polar opposite of her sultry mother. She was very much her father's daughter. It was his fair skin she was wrapped in, his blue eyes she'd inherited and his features she wore on her face, though they didn't fall into their place quite as effortlessly as his did. What looked handsome on a man looked slightly more ordinary on a girl and Jessica had also inherited his robust frame, though she kept her figure trim with plenty of exercise.

'Anyway, what did you want to talk about?'

Jessica drew up one of the loungers, making a huge puddle on the cushions as she did so, and plonked herself down. Searching for the right words, she frowned. 'Dad, I found out you were the "mystery" buyer at the gallery who bought the entire show,' she said evenly and only then did her face display the betrayal she was feeling.

Edward's jaw dropped. Then, realizing he'd been well and truly rumbled, he opened his mouth to begin explaining. Jessica cut him off. 'Don't. I know you only do these things because you love me, but you will never understand how stupid I felt knowing that everyone at the gallery knew except me.'

Edward was maddened to feel himself blushing. Damn it. How the hell had she found out?

'I told you from the start I didn't want anyone to know who I was and that I wanted to do things on my own for once, so why did you do it?' his daughter demanded, her voice cracking.

'Because you were miserable?' offered Edward rather feebly. 'You said your boss was really grumpy so I thought I'd help.'

'But I wasn't miserable,' said Jessica in frustration. 'I was freaking elated. I couldn't believe that someone *was* being grumpy with me because no one ever is, and if you must know it made me feel excited that here was an opportunity to win someone round simply by working hard.'

Edward swallowed. He'd never seen Jessica this vexed before.

'And besides,' she said, wringing water out of her vest, 'you make it sound as if I was asking for your help, when I wasn't. I was just telling you about my day, which clearly I'm going to have to stop doing in case you muscle in again.'

'Bloody James bloody Bond to the rescue again, eh?' said Edward jokily.

'Exactly,' said Jessica, sounding more sad than angry, 'which is how it's been pretty much my entire life. I was actually thinking about it on the way over here, about all the times you've waded in to "save" me. Do you remember when we first got here and I was struggling to make friends at my new elementary school?'

'Y-e-s,' replied Edward nervously as he tried to recall what parental crime he may have committed all those years ago.

'So, rather than just letting me make friends in my own time, you insisted on inviting the whole year to a Christmas party at our house, and spent I don't know how much money on turning it into a Winter Wonderland. Suddenly I had more friends than I knew what to do with, which as far as you were concerned was problem solved. Only most of them weren't my real friends, they just wanted to come to my house again. Then, at high school,' Jessica ploughed on, not giving Edward any opportunity to defend himself, 'I must have mentioned that I was a bit disappointed not to make the cheerleading squad and what happened next?'

Edward shrugged meekly.

'That's right – you donated a huge amount of money to the school for new sports equipment, flew back from wherever you were shooting at the time, turned up to school in your Aston Martin and flirted like mad with my teachers. Then, hey, by some miracle I made the squad. But that's the thing,' said Jessica, realizing that the floodgates had now been opened and that she was powerless to prevent years of hurt and embarrassment hurtling through. 'While all these things you do are really sweet and generous, they also leave me no room to do anything for myself, like most people have to. My life isn't a film, Dad, and without sounding horribly ungrateful I'm afraid the only thing I really want or need saving from is you.'

Edward recoiled.

'OK, I don't mean that,' said Jessica, instantly regretting the harshness of her words. 'But you are the ultimate embarrassing parent.'

'Really?' said Edward doubtfully.

'Really,' replied Jessica firmly. 'I'm not like Dulcie or Paris or Nicole. I hate the limelight and, to be honest, would love, just for once, to have a chat or a job for that matter, without James freaking Bond *always* having to come into it.'

'Right,' said Edward, feeling like a prat and nowhere near as slick as he did in his films. 'Well, I can see why you might feel that way.'

'I'm not happy,' Jessica said tentatively and suddenly Edward didn't want her to get to the point.

'Not happy?' he said jovially, gesturing to their luxurious surroundings, the azure blue sky and the jug of iced tea that was sitting in front of them, willing itself to be poured, but Jessica ploughed on.

'All this is because of you,' Jessica said cautiously. She looked Edward squarely in the eye. 'I've never had to do anything on my own, Dad, but it's time I did because otherwise how am I ever going to figure out what it is I want to do in life, or what I'm actually capable of? At the moment I just don't have any real purpose and every time I try and do something, either it's come about because you're my father, or if not, you get involved anyway, which makes it all feel a bit . . . pointless.'

Edward studied his daughter's earnest face and his heart swelled with a pang of painful love. Jessica was such a good girl, always had been, despite a rather unconventional upbringing. Still, as much as he wanted to keep her close by for the rest of his days, to protect and look after her, that obviously wasn't what she wanted any more.

He considered his next move very carefully. 'That fundraiser last month?' he began steadily, his deep voice masking how disconcerted he was feeling. 'Jen Petersen said your organizational skills were remarkable and that without you they never would have raised as much money or got so many young people involved.'

Jessica's response to this was to give Edward a look he couldn't quite decipher. Then, to his dismay, her eyes filled with tears. 'Dad, don't you get it? The only reason I was of any value on that committee was because of who I am. If I wasn't Edward Granger the movie star's daughter, I doubt your wealthy friends would have contributed so generously. And, besides, I can hardly bask in the glow of Jen Peterson's praise. She's been trying to get you into bed for the last twenty years.'

'Has she?' replied Edward, looking chuffed before swiftly realizing this was hardly the point. 'OK, maybe not the best example,' he said. 'And I admit I never should have bought those paintings. I should have trusted you to deal with that horrid man on your own . . .'

Exasperated, Jessica shook her head. 'Just because he didn't fall over himself to be nice to me doesn't mean he's "horrid". He's just a guy who hadn't sold anything from his latest exhibition so was feeling stressed.'

'I'd be stressed if I had to shift that lot of crap too,' remarked Edward drily.

Jessica cracked a despairing smile. 'Er, the fact you hate the paintings doesn't exactly make me feel better about the situation. Look, I know I've let myself be mollycoddled in the past but maybe that's because . . . well, Mom not being around much . . . I don't know . . .' Sitting in the shade of the umbrella in her soggy underwear and vest, she was starting to feel chilly. She stood up, hair plastered to the side of her face, and moved into the sun. It was time to break the news.

'I want to go back to England . . . on my own, and not just for a vacation. Nobody knows who I am there, so I may as well join them seeing as I don't either, and when I arrive I want to live under a different name. That way I can try and get a normal job and see if I can achieve anything on my own merit. I have to do this and I want to do it with no financial help from you. I'll take a couple of thousand dollars to get myself started and that's it.'

Edward abandoned his lounger and, in an attempt to reclaim the upper hand, stood up to his full six foot four inches. 'Sweetheart, I see your point and maybe it is time you had more independence, but let's not get carried away. England is out of the question,' he added with a nervous laugh, placing his hands on her shoulders.

Jessica wriggled out of his grasp, exasperated beyond belief. 'You're not listening. I'm not asking if I can go, I'm telling you.' And with that she raced towards the house.

Edward sank wearily back down on to his lounger. All the women in his house had gone mad. Was just a little bit of peace too much to ask? Reluctantly he got up to follow after Jessica, and as he did so he cursed his first wife, more out of habit than anything else. If only Angelica hadn't abandoned him all those years ago, he wouldn't be left to work everything out on his own as usual. Then something occurred to him. Hadn't Jill mentioned that Angelica was supposed to be in England for much of the summer? Suddenly Edward felt a bit panicky and picked up the pace a little. Was there more to this trip than met the eye?

5

Paul Fletcher, chief comedy writer for *The Bradley Mackintosh Show* at the BBC, strolled into the packed production office. He scouted the room, looking for best mate Luke and the girls, namely Kerry, Natasha, Isy and Vanessa. They were gathered in the far corner, so in order to join them he had no choice but to circumnavigate the entire room, the rest of the team and their bags.

''Scuse me, sorry, thanks . . . sorry . . . Right, breathe in then, Kerry,' he instructed until Kerry was the last thing left between him and a bit of empty floor space.

'Bloody hell,' she gasped as Paul squeezed himself past her enormous bosoms, wedging them both against the wall in the process. 'Don't mind me or anything.'

'You love it,' joked Luke. 'That's more action than you've had in ages, isn't it?'

'Paul should be so lucky,' interjected Natasha, a pretty blonde who had once had a bit of a thing with Paul.

'If it makes you feel any better, Kezza, I'm wearing a condom so you're definitely not pregnant,' said Paul, unabashed.

Natasha, Isy and Vanessa giggled.

'Oh, don't you worry,' said Kerry ruefully. 'Pregnant is one thing I know I'm not. The way my love life's going, I wouldn't be surprised if I'd sealed up completely.'

'Sealed up?' asked dark-haired Isy, looking worried. The junior researcher was sitting on the floor near Kerry's feet and was wearing more accessories than Mr T, even managing to carry off a strange, boater-style hat, which was no mean feat. 'That can't actually happen, can it?'

'Christ,' said Paul indulgently. 'No, Isy, it can't. Now, where's that penis Mike? He's even later than usual, isn't he?'

'I went to give him a nudge,' replied Kerry, plaiting the front of her curly dark hair and going boss-eyed as she did so, 'but he was busy on his computer.'

'Oh, I forgot. Mike's such a busy man,' said Paul, deadpan. 'He was probably ordering some slacks from the Next catalogue, rearranging his nostril hair or chatting on the phone to his pals, arranging a bit of buggering for the weekend.'

'You've really got it in for him, haven't you?' said Vanessa, her strong Liverpool accent as pronounced as ever. 'What's he ever done to you?'

'Bored me rigid. Kept me waiting when I could be writing links. Reminded me at least fifty times that he went to university and I didn't. Been crap at his job but never been pulled up on it because he's married to the boss's daughter,' fired back Paul rapidly.

'You're mean,' said Natasha slyly. 'Mike's all right and at least he's easy on the eye.'

Paul glanced at Natasha as nonchalantly as possible, trying to glean if this comment was for his benefit or not. The two of them had been an item for a few months last winter until Natasha had dumped him cruelly, with no warning and by text (the part that had really stung). For a while (though he would rather have died than admit it), Paul had been fairly cut up.

Now, Natasha's heart-shaped face and big green eyes

were the picture of innocence, and though Paul knew he'd appear jealous if he said anything, he felt compelled to do so anyway. 'Well, I'll never get what you girls see in Mike. He's been driving me mad ever since he got back from paternity leave. I've never known so many pointless script changes and, frankly, I can't wait for him to piss off on holiday so we can have a break from him again. The man's an arse.'

None of the group paid much attention. The way they saw it, as far as Paul was concerned, Mike had never been able to do right and it didn't take a genius to work out why. Paul fancied Natasha, Natasha fancied Mike, Mike fancied himself.

'Who's on seven minutes?' called out Luke suddenly.

'I am,' yelled Penny, the production assistant, her unmistakeable gin-soaked voice booming across from the other side of the office. 'Who's on seven and a half?'

Robbie, head of make-up, perused the sheet he was clutching as he paced around, stepping over people's legs and bags. 'Oooh, that's me! Right, come on, Mike, let's be having you.'

'Well, I think if you heard what Mike has to put up with at home, you might be a bit more understanding,' said Kerry darkly, fishing a bottle of nail varnish out of her bag and giving it a good shake. 'Honestly, his wife's always moaning at him. In fact, I'd say she phones pretty much daily to check he's not going to the pub and the other day –'

But she never got to finish what she was saying because just at that moment Mike himself finally walked into the room. Twenty heads immediately turned to look at the clock on the wall, which said eight minutes past two. Robbie stopped pacing, glanced from the clock back to his notes and up again to be met by a sea of expectant faces, at which point he mouthed for all to see, 'Congratulations, Hassan.' Hassan puffed up with pleasure, but everyone else looked pretty fed up. The production accountant always seemed to win the sweepstake.

'Hi, guys,' said Mike, trying to sound as flustered as possible. 'Sorry I'm late. It's been so bloody frantic this week that at one point I thought I wasn't going to get away. But somehow I've managed it, so let's crack on.'

Paul rolled his eyes so witheringly, it made Isy giggle out loud.

'Right, first on the agenda,' Mike began. 'Tomorrow I've got a meeting with David Bridlington to talk about our ratings. So, Kerry, remind me who we've got booked for the next few weeks, please?'

'Oh, right,' she said dolefully, starting to look through her notes. The subject of ratings never boded well for her. 'OK, so this week we've got Jamie Oliver . . .'

'Great,' said Mike.

'Jane McDonald.'

'Mmmnah,' said Mike.

'And Juliette Binoche. However, I am having a bit of a mare with the week after. Hopefully I've got Michael Sheen, but the other guests I had booked have pulled out.'

'Well, that's a major worry,' said Mike, looking furious. 'I hope you've got a back-up plan.'

Kerry wondered if maybe she shouldn't have bothered trying to defend Mike earlier. She stared back at him defiantly. His rumpled white shirt was rolled up at the sleeves displaying tanned forearms and, with one button too many undone, it was easy for her to tell that his chest must be brown and smooth with just a suggestion of hair. She'd probably fancy him if it weren't for the fact that A/ he was married and B/ would never be interested in her in a million years. Still, his attractiveness was diluted somewhat by his rather 'Boden' dress sense and his front teeth, which had an unfortunate tendency to rest on his bottom lip whenever he was deep in thought or cross. Like now.

'My "back-up plan" is to book the best guests I can get,' she answered. 'I've put feelers out everywhere so I'm hoping that —'

'So you're telling me I have to convince David that ratings aren't going to be a problem, and yet in a fortnight's time we haven't got anyone confirmed,' stated Mike.

'Sure "Daddyo" will understand,' muttered Paul to Luke, earning himself a frown from Mike, who could tell he was being talked about.

'Well, yes, but only because of unforeseen cancellations. It's not easy finding people week in week out, you know,' said Kerry. Sometimes her job felt like a thankless task. 'I may have one of the best sets of contacts in the business, but I don't have a magic wand, plus I do all the booking myself, which is practically unheard of on a show this size.'

'Woooooh,' crowed Luke.

'Oh, don't be such a tit, Luke,' Kerry snapped.

'All right, all right,' said Mike. 'Look, I get where you're coming from, Kerry, but at the same time we *have* to have big names every single week or we're doomed. So if you really think you need help in order to make that happen, well then, let's have a meeting and talk about getting you an assistant. Although I can tell you now, there won't be much in the budget for it.'

'There definitely won't,' piped up Hassan. 'There are bigger priorities that need paying for at the moment.'

Something inside Kerry snapped. She'd been busting her gut for this show for a year and a half now and when ratings were sky high and the guests were amazing, no one seemed to thank her or give her any credit. Yet when things weren't going so well, it always seemed to be her who was hauled over the coals and she was sick of it. To her horror she realized she was about to burst into tears, not a nice feeling when you're at work, so she grabbed her bag and bolted from the meeting. The team gazed open-mouthed at her departure.

'I was only saying,' said Hassan, shrugging defensively.

'Mm, that's not like her, is it?' said Mike, gathering his wits. 'Maybe it's the time of the month?' he suggested, pausing to give everybody the opportunity to laugh out loud at his hilarious gag. 'You know, perhaps she's got the painters in?'

An eerie silence greeted him, however, and slowly the grin slipped off Mike's face as he realized no one was laughing. Maybe he'd got that one a bit wrong.

'Shall I go after her?' offered Isy.

'Er, yes please, Isabel, if you wouldn't mind,' said Mike, clearing his throat. 'Right . . . moving on.'

In the ladies' loos, Isy hugged a tear-stained Kerry.

'Are you all right now, babe?'

'Yeah, I'm fine,' said Kerry, who did feel like a cry had got a lot out of her system. 'And if Mike's serious about me getting an assistant then I'm going to bloody well take him up on the offer. I've been asking him for one for the last year.'

'Yeah,' mused Isy, idly examining her split ends. 'Hey, when you legged it, Mike made a joke about you having your period. How out of order is that?'

'Sexist idiot,' sniffed Kerry.

'I know,' said Isy indignantly. 'Have you though?'

'Er . . . obviously. Now, let's get out of here. I need to find Hassan and once I've forced him to stop being such a tight bastard I shall be *telling* Mike that I *am* having an assistant, whether he likes it or not.'

6

Deep in thought, Edward Granger plodded up his grand staircase. Upon reaching the top, he paused for a moment. Then suddenly, just for the hell of it, he flattened himself against the wall and with one arm out to the side, the other brandishing an imaginary gun, staked out his spacious landing. At the end of the corridor the door to his luxurious bedroom was open, tempting him to forget about everything and go for a nap. Still, Betsey would probably view this as an invitation to jump his bones. Exhaling loudly, he lowered his weapon. Right, he'd just have to do what he'd always done when delicate parenting skills were called for, suck it and see.

He knocked gently on Jessica's door, but she was playing music so he knocked again harder. 'Jess, let me in, will you? I know I can be a bit overbearing sometimes, but only because I care and, darling, I can't apologize enough about the paintings. It seemed like a good idea at the time, but I was wrong and . . . I'm sorry.'

Jessica opened the door. She'd changed into a cotton sundress and had a towel wrapped round her head like a turban. She gave him a small, slightly wobbly smile of encouragement. 'Right,' she muttered. 'Well, in case you were thinking of doing your "breaking down the door" joke, you'd better come in.'

'You used to love that when you were little,' said Edward,

following her into the room where he could see she'd been rummaging through her things and had even got a suitcase out. For an odd moment he realized the scariest thing about Jessica going away was the fact that he'd be left on his own with Betsey. As he plonked himself down on the small white sofa at the foot of her bed, Jessica grinned. 'What?' said Edward, glad to see her smiling.

'Nothing, it's just the song,' she said, motioning to her iPod before pulling the towel off her head and rubbing her hair with it. 'It's the Pet Shop Boys, "What Have I Done to Deserve This?"'

'Ha bloody ha,' replied Edward. A comfortable but ponderous silence ensued while they both figured out what to say next. In the end it was Jessica who found the right words first. Discarding her damp towel on the bed, she began to talk.

'Dad, I know I'm incredibly lucky and you are the most amazing father a girl could ever have. You do know that, right?'

Edward nodded and tried not to get emotional.

'But I'm twenty-six now, so I have to spread my wings a bit. I mean, when you were twenty-six you'd left home and were working two jobs while struggling to get your big break. And by the time Mom was twenty-six she'd starred as Heavenly Melons, got married, had me and was about to file for divorce, and yet here I am, and so far my lack of achievement is a bit pathetic really.'

'That's a bit strong,' countered Edward. 'Most people don't have everything figured out by the age of twenty-six, for goodness' sake, and you can hardly hold your mother's example up as a beacon of success. Is she still seeing that hairy idiot Graydon Matthews by the way?'

'Not that it has anything to do with anything, but yes, she is. Anyway, the point *is*,' she said in frustration, 'is that, good or bad, at least Mom was *doing* stuff, whereas unlike most people I don't *have* to do anything. I'm in this amazingly privileged position that would let me get away with turning into a total airhead who did nothing but shop and party, which isn't who I want to be.'

Edward tried to remain diplomatic. 'Take it from me, struggling is hugely overrated.'

'I'm sure it is, but isn't that something I deserve to find out for myself?'

To this Edward really had no answer, so he changed tactics.

'Has this got anything to do with Dulcie? Vincent mentioned she's been very taken up with the planning for her wedding and I've noticed she's not been around much lately.'

Jessica flopped on to the bed. 'This has got nothing to do with Dulcie . . .' she said, pausing just long enough for Edward to suspect maybe this wasn't entirely true. 'It hasn't,' she insisted. 'Admittedly, Dulcie has gone a bit . . . crazy about the wedding, and at times I do wonder why she's leaping into getting married so quickly, but me wanting to go away has nothing to do with her.'

Jessica's best friend, Dulcie Malone, was the daughter of celebrated recording artist Vincent Malone, the twenty-first-century's answer to Barry White, only slimmer, who also happened to be Edward's best and oldest friend. Having grown up together, the two girls were more like sisters, and yet there were certain things they felt very differently about, having a famous father being one of them. This contrast in attitude had first been highlighted a while back when they were asked to star in a reality show called *Daddy's Girls*. Jessica had flatly refused to even consider it, which Dulcie had felt deeply resentful about, viewing it as a missed opportunity. Since then, what neither of them had said out loud, thus making it real, was that disagreements that had once seemed like easy hurdles to get over were beginning to feel insurmountable.

Edward, who'd been studying his daughter's thoughtful face, got up from the sofa and came to sit down next to her on the bed. 'OK,' he said. 'Firstly, Jess, you have to understand that this idea about going to England has been rather sprung on me. So if my first reaction wasn't the one that you were after, I apologize, though you must appreciate I'm still trying to get my head round it.'

Jessica shrugged, but allowed Edward to put his arm around her and nestled in.

'Secondly, I only want you to be happy, so if this desire to go to England is something that won't go away, then so be it. Though I'd like to know more about your plans. Where were you planning on staying, for instance? Because, if I may make a suggestion, why don't you stay with your auntie Pamela until you get settled? I could ring her now before she goes to bed. Sound her out. I know she'd love to have you and it's high time you caught up anyway.'

Jessica couldn't resist a smile. She loved her auntie Pam, whom she'd missed over the years. Pamela had a phobia about flying so as far as she was concerned there wasn't a sleeping pill strong enough that would ever get her to the States. Still, staying with her wasn't the answer.

'I don't think so, Dad. As much as staying with Pam sounds great, I don't want to take the easy option. I meant it when I said I wanted to do things properly so I'm going to do what normal people do when they go away.'

'What's that then?' asked Edward, struggling with a vision of his daughter in a shitty bedsit or residing in a travel tavern.

'Stay at a hotel. I'll make a reservation at the Dorchester. Only not the penthouse, just a regular room,' she said firmly, standing up and crossing the bedroom to skip the next song on her iPod.

'Er, right,' replied Edward faintly. 'Well, I guess that would keep things "normal" . . . I mean, if that's really what you want to do?'

'It is.'

'OK,' said Edward, concentrating hard on not looking amused. He hoped she was planning on taking her credit card. 'So when were you planning on going?'

'Soon. Tomorrow maybe?'

'Tomorrow?' spluttered Edward. 'Are you bloody joking? Jesus, Jess, when did you suddenly become so gung-ho?'

Jessica didn't know, but after months and months of malaise it felt so thrilling to have a plan that she just wanted to get on with it. She shrugged, trying to repress a grin.

'Christ, what about all your friends – don't you want to say goodbye?' Edward continued, running his hands through his hair and rubbing the back of his neck, something he always did when he was stressed. 'I know you two have had a tricky time lately, but Dulcie especially would be really upset if you just buggered off.'

'OK, OK. Dulcie's having "pre-hen" drinks anyway, so I should probably stay for those,' said Jessica, trying not to giggle. Her dad seemed really rattled, which proved he was taking her plan seriously, which meant it was actually going to happen, which in turn made it all feel suddenly real and very exciting.

'And what about my birthday party?'

'That's not until September, which is four whole months away, so obviously I'll come back for that. But there is one other thing,' Jessica continued, the smallest trace of defiance in her voice as she prepared to talk about something delicate.

'What's that?'

'I think Mom may be in London soon.'

'Right,' replied Edward steadily.

'And I know I didn't see her that long ago, but it might be good to see her on neutral territory for a change.'

'Is that why you're going?'

'No,' replied Jessica immediately. 'Not at all. In fact, I only realized she'd be there just now when I checked her schedule. But seeing as she *is* going to be there, I thought – as long as you're cool with it, of course – I should hook up with her. Though if you'd rather I didn't then . . . you know, I don't really care either way.'

Edward swallowed. Watching his daughter struggling to seek permission to see her own mother made him feel so deeply sad it was as if the sun had just gone in behind a dark cloud. 'Darling, you can see your mother whenever you like. You're a grown woman and you don't need to check with me anyway.'

'But I want you to be OK about it,' mumbled Jessica, torn as ever.

'I am. I'm more than OK, I'm pleased,' he added for good measure, though it practically choked him to do so.

'Sure?' checked Jessica suspiciously.

'Completely,' replied Edward, wondering how things had ever got to this point.

'OK,' said Jessica, trying to sound blasé. 'Well, we'll see.'

Just then Betsey poked her head round the door.

'Hi,' she said, bestowing Jessica with a quick, fake smile before turning to Edward. 'Honey, could I see you for a few minutes . . . in our room?'

As she said this, she raised one eyebrow and beckoned him to her with a long pink talon.

Oh, gross, thought Jessica, as she tried not to retch. She knew full well what her stepmother was after. Despite having spent the last twenty-six years yearning for a little brother or sister, she wasn't sure she was ready for the spawn of Betsey, especially when she could see a mile off how reluctant her father was. Still, it was nothing to do with her and she didn't want to be caught up in his personal life any more. Another good reason to get away.

'In a minute, Betsey,' replied Edward forcibly, causing his wife to flounce out in a rage, slamming the door behind her in frustration. Edward seemed to deflate before Jessica's eyes, suddenly looking crestfallen and rather old. She went to give him a hug. She'd miss him terribly.

As Edward hugged his daughter back, he cleared his throat. 'So if you're not going to be Jessica Granger in England, what name are you going to use?'

Jessica grinned. As the daughter of an A-list movie star she had learned the art of discretion from a young age. 'I thought I'd use your real last name. Meet Bender, Jessica Bender,' she said cheekily.

'Right,' mused Edward. 'Well, just to warn you, Bender's not the easiest name to get by on in the UK. It has slightly different connotations over there.'

But Jessica wasn't listening. She was too busy prancing around her room and, besides, she really didn't care what name she used, so long as it wasn't Granger.

7

One transatlantic flight and several days later, Jessica opened first one sleep-filled eye and then the other. Waking up from a deep night's sleep meant she was groggy and not entirely sure where she was, until gradually things swam into place and started making sense. Of course, she was in her room, at the Dorchester, in England.

She stretched. She loved this hotel. It might not be quite as 'rock and roll' as somewhere like the Sanderson or the Mayfair, but it was quintessentially English and unapologetically luxurious, harking back to the glamour of the twenties which was reflected in the art-deco-influenced interior. She'd never stayed in one of the regular rooms before, which wasn't as spacious as the suites she was used to. There was barely enough wardrobe space to fit in all her luggage, but the bed was unbelievably comfy and the view of Hyde Park was amazing. In fact, the only thing making her stay less than comfortable were the prickles of doubt and guilt that kept needling her. As soon as she'd arrived it had struck her that the majority of the hotel's clientele were either much older than her, blatantly wealthy and/or on business, which had made her wonder if staying here really was quite such a 'normal' thing to do after all.

She recalled the novelty of having flown economy, something she'd insisted upon to demonstrate how serious she was about eschewing her privileged lifestyle. As the wheels had been lowered ready for landing, she'd gazed out of the window at the unseasonal blanket of grey, rain-filled cloud that was waiting at Heathrow. The impending gloom had made the other passengers feel like getting on the first plane back out the minute they landed. Jessica, however, had been flooded with undiluted excitement and the feeling that this adventure was absolutely the right thing to do. It wasn't just her dad she needed a breather from, but Los Angeles too. LA was an unforgiving city, all about 'making it', so if you hadn't worked out which ladder you wanted to climb, let alone got a foot on the first rung, it was a tricky place to be. In London, though, nobody but herself would be in charge and the albatross of her identity could be unwrapped from around her neck. She'd already felt as though she were chipping away at the years of guilt-ridden privilege that was stuck to her like lime scale. Though, admittedly, she'd missed the leg room . . .

It was just a shame she hadn't been able to tell Dulcie face to face that she was leaving. She'd tried on numerous occasions, but simply hadn't managed to get a non-wedding-related word in edgeways, even at her 'pre-hen' drinks. Their friendship had definitely taken a weird turn for the worse and, though it made her miserable, Jessica didn't know what she could do about it; short of tying Dulcie to a chair and forcing her to listen. Not something she wanted to resort to. No, Dulcie would have to find out she'd left the hard way. Next time she phoned Jessica for a quick bore, she'd be getting a foreign dialling tone.

In the meantime, first and foremost she needed a job. London was proving to be a tougher nut to crack than she'd anticipated. She'd applied herself to finding a job with zeal, but so far hundreds of phone calls and emails to temping agencies and recruitment companies had yielded nothing and she wondered if her scattergun approach was to blame. Still, she was determined not to give up, so today she and Pam (her moral support) would be hitting the streets to find a job that way. As soon as she'd had breakfast. Reaching one arm out from under the covers, she picked up the phone. 'Room service, please? Hi, can I get an omelette, some coffee, the fruit plate and some orange juice? It's room number . . . oh, you know. OK, thank you.'

Forty-five minutes later, Jessica left her room and headed for the elevators, ready to face the world, feeling confident in her black trouser suit that she looked presentable, smart and, above all else, employable. Punctual as ever, Pam was waiting for her in the lobby. Jessica smiled as she strode purposefully across to greet her.

'Morning, love, you look nice.'

Jessica grinned and took her by the arm. 'So do you. Thanks so much for saying you'd come with me.'

'Ooh, pleasure, treasure.'

May was drawing to a close and as they emerged from the hotel into warm sunshine Jessica felt grateful, not for the first time, of Pam's company. Her aunt was every bit as warm and lovely as Jessica remembered, and provided her with a comforting sense of home in a foreign place. In fact, from the minute they'd met at the airport it had struck Jessica that here was where the majority of her genes derived from. Their resemblance to one another was something she must have been too young to have appreciated before, but now it came almost as a relief, as if a mystery had been cleared up.

Pamela was what one would describe as a handsome woman. She exuded a smart kind of glamour, aided and abetted by a good quality wardrobe, and today was wearing a lilac skirt suit, Russell and Bromley navy shoes and a matching handbag. Her nails were painted in her trademark shade of pink and her silvery hair was blow dried and immaculate as ever. It glinted in the sunshine as they hit Park Lane. The combination of a husband who had left his affairs in order before he died, and a well-off and generous brother, meant Pam hadn't had to worry too much about money. Just as well, for when Bernard had passed away she'd been too grief-stricken to do much more than merely function.

'Right, where to?' Pam asked as the doorman lifted his arm to hail them a taxi. 'What's first on the agenda?'

'It's OK, thanks,' said Jessica to the doorman. 'Today we're doing things the London way and walking,' she added, feeling really buoyed-up and positive. 'So we'll just keep going till we see somewhere that we like the look of.'

'Right you are then,' Pam said pragmatically. 'I suppose that's as good a plan as any. Somewhere we like the look of.'

Two hours later, however, as Jessica emerged from yet another shop, tired, dejected and disillusioned, her enthusiasm was waning. Pam, who was waiting for her outside on the pavement, raised her eyebrows questioningly. 'Well?'

Jessica just shook her head.

'Right,' said Pam, pointing at a coffee shop. 'In there.'

'Can we give that one a miss? I bet they don't have any jobs going and I need a break,' said Jessica.

'And I need a latte and a big fat Danish pastry,' puffed her aunt.

'Oh,' replied Jessica, dolefully following after her.

With two rejuvenating cups of coffee in front of them, Jessica and Pam regrouped.

'I'm just not convinced that aimlessly wandering the streets is the right way to go about finding a job, love,' said Pam. 'Maybe you need a bit more of a proper game plan, as it were.'

'I guess I was naive,' said Jessica, 'but I didn't expect people to be so dismissive. The man in that café was horrid and there was me thinking everybody in London would be really friendly. Those girls who worked in that clothes shop were so bitchy about my name too.'

'Well, you had that coming,' laughed Pam. 'Why you've gone and saddled yourself with the name Bender I shall never know. When I met my Bernard I was so happy to get shot of it. Bernard Anderson, I thought. What a perfect name. And it was, until that wretched *Baywatch* came out, at which point being Pamela Anderson took on a whole new meaning.'

Despite her mood, Jessica couldn't help but grin. Pam regarded her niece thoughtfully.

'Look, it's tough times out there at the moment, love, so you shouldn't be too surprised not to have found a job yet. Without your dad here to help you it's going to be a lot harder for you, but think of the freedom you have now to try and work out what you really want to do.'

'But that's just it,' said Jessica helplessly. 'This is why I needed to get away from LA in the first place, precisely because I don't *know* what I want to do. I kinda hoped things would be different here.'

'And they will be,' said Pam convincingly, 'but you have

to give fate a helping hand. Bernard always used to say that "you get back from life what you put in", so don't go giving up, love. Stick with it and something will crop up eventually. And, in the meantime, having you here has been a tonic. It really has.'

Jessica managed a smile. She knew her aunt wasn't just saying it, so at least she was doing something right. 'I wish I could remember Bernard. He sounds like such a lovely man.'

'He was,' Pam answered simply.

A silence followed and the two women were left to their own thoughts while Pam made inroads into her pastry.

'Dad ringing every five minutes to find out if I've got something yet isn't exactly helping,' said Jessica eventually.

'Oh, I know,' agreed Pam vehemently, dabbing icing sugar off her mouth with a napkin. 'He rings me every day to make sure you're OK, usually when I'm trying to watch *Come Dine With Me*. Honestly, I can see why you needed to get away, love – one parent does far too much interfering, while the other one doesn't do nearly enough.'

Jessica flinched at this rather barbed reference to her mother and her mind started working overtime as she debated whether or not to mention to Pam that she had in fact arranged to meet with the object of her contempt for breakfast the next day. Probably best not to. Judging by Pam's expression, it would only give her indigestion.

8

The next morning Jessica walked into the hotel's opulent dining room where breakfast was served every day, though this would be the first time she hadn't taken it in her room. Angelica was due to arrive at nine thirty and Jessica automatically found herself looking around at the other guests. How many of them would react when her mother walked in? How many would whisper behind their hands? How many would be bold or interested enough to approach her at the table? Questions she'd been asking her entire life.

'Good morning, Ms Bender. Table for one?' asked the head waiter.

'Er, no, actually I'm meeting my . . . I'm meeting someone at nine thirty.'

'Very well,' he replied, 'then perhaps you would like this table over here next to . . .' He trailed off, distracted by the sound of a huge commotion that was coming from the lobby.

Jessica followed his gaze. 'That'll be my guest now,' she said resignedly. She could only imagine that the paparazzi must have spotted Angelica's arrival and caused a disturbance big enough to have spilled into the hotel. Why couldn't breakfast ever just mean breakfast?

'Sorry, madame,' the waiter continued. 'I'm not sure what's going on out there, but if you'd like to take your table then I'll –'

Once again he failed to finish, for just then a cluster of hotel staff appeared in the doorway, making a huge fuss of whomever was in their midst. Eventually, one by one, the staff members were dismissed by the person they were flapping over and gradually they all seemed to melt away until only the cause of all the fuss remained. By now everyone in the dining room was straining to see what was going on. It was an entrance and a half and, as ever, Jessica couldn't blame anyone for staring.

At forty-eight years old, Angelica Dupree was still extraordinarily beautiful. Her hair tumbled down her back, still brown and lustrous, elegantly highlighted with copper hues to cover the inevitable grey (hair dye was one of Angelica's few concessions towards trying to prevent the ageing process). Despite immense pressure to do so, she'd never gone down the surgery route. No needles had ever touched her exquisite face either, which ultimately looked all the better for it. It was certainly more expressive, which may have had something to do with how well her acting had been received recently. Now, as she strode into the dining room looking eagerly around for her daughter, stunning as ever and dressed immaculately in a white silk blouse, a skirt made of the softest caramel suede and cream Jimmy Choo boots, Jessica felt a strange mixture of pride, misery and something akin to awe.

'Jessica,' Angelica gasped, having finally spotted her standing awkwardly in the corner, half-hidden by a potted palm in a Chinese vase. 'It's so good to see you,' she said, hurrying across the dining room, a touch self-consciously. Even the most blasé guests were gawping at her, the men relishing this unexpected sighting of Heavenly Melons, the women scrutinizing her for signs of ageing which they could later dine out on.

'It's good to see you too, Mom,' Jessica replied, feeling frumpy by comparison in her jeans and simple cotton shirt. Angelica kissed her warmly on both cheeks. She was eager to sit down and didn't want to be stared at longer than was necessary, so was glad when they were swiftly shown to a table.

'Graydon Matthews will be joining us,' Angelica informed the waiter in her French-accented voice. 'So please keep an extra place setting, thank you. Now, how are you, Jessica? Tell me everything. I want to know what you've been up to.'

Jessica tried to keep any feelings of hurt at bay. She hadn't seen her mother for ages and yet she had to bring her awful boyfriend?

'What's the matter?' asked Angelica, having picked up on the sulky expression that had clouded over her daughter's face.

'Nothing. Where is Graydon anyway? Didn't you come together?'

'He had to use the bathroom. You don't mind that he's here, do you? It's just that when I said I was meeting with you he was so excited about seeing you.'

'Right,' said Jessica, though she didn't believe a word of it and suspected he wanted to keep an eye on Angelica. Jessica had always got the impression that Graydon was vaguely controlling of her mother, in a passive-aggressive kind of way that was hard to pinpoint.

'Maybe I shouldn't have?' Angelica continued, her French accent more pronounced than ever. 'I'm sorry if it has annoyed you, Jessica, but I would just love you to get to know each other better.'

'Why?' asked Jessica, somewhat disingenuously.

'Why do you think?' replied Angelica lightly. 'Look, I know you don't like getting attached in case things don't work out, but I think this time they will. I hope so anyway. Most people consider Graydon to be a pretty good catch, you know. He's hard-working and he really looks after me. He is a good man.'

'Is he?' her daughter replied, aware of how much her mother wanted her approval, yet still not convinced. Taking advantage of Graydon's absence, she couldn't resist adding, 'It's just I never see you having much fun when you're with him.'

'Well, I laughed my way through one relationship and look how that turned out,' joked Angelica bitterly. 'Sorry,' she added more gently. 'Look, I know Graydon's not funny like your father but he has other strengths that are probably more important.'

Like the ability to grow hair out of every orifice, yet still be balding?

'He is very dependable.'

'Right,' said Jessica.

'Anyway, enough of all that, I want to know how you are,' said Angelica, desperate not to get off on a bad foot. 'How long do you see yourself staying here? I have to admit I was a little sad that I had to find out about your plans to come to England from Jill.'

'Er, isn't that a bit hypocritical? You've been in Morocco for ages,' said Jessica. Angelica had been filming a low-budget French movie in Morocco for the past couple of months and it had been a bad period in terms of contact even by her standards.

'Yes, but you always had a number for me, so you could have rung. In fact, I only assumed you didn't because . . .'

'Because what?'

Angelica sighed. As ever, her daughter held the moral high ground. She really had no right to assume anything or to expect anything from her. She'd given up that right years ago. 'I'm sorry. Let's start again, shall we? Tell me what made you decide to come here.'

'OK,' replied Jessica, feeling stressed. 'Well, I suppose initially I just needed to get away from LA. Stand on my own two feet for a while, if you know what I mean.'

'Of course,' nodded Angelica.

'Plus Dulcie's getting married and she's so taken up with the wedding and everything . . .'

'Well, it's a big day for her, *non*?'

'Yes, but you have to ask yourself why she's going ahead with it when she's only known him a year.'

'Maybe she loves him?' suggested Angelica.

'I'm sure she does, for now,' retorted Jessica, 'but does that mean she should be rushing into an institution that's doomed from the start?'

'Not for everyone.'

Jessica stared at her mother in frustration. How could a woman who wasn't even on speaking terms with the father of her child, and who was seeing someone who clearly didn't respect her, think she was in a position to dispense advice? 'Anyway,' she said, deciding to change the subject, 'it's got nothing to do with that. I just felt like I needed to come here and live more normally for a while.'

Angelica couldn't help it. An entirely reflex action, she looked around, her gaze encompassing their luxurious surroundings.

'What?' said Jessica, irritated by her mother's reaction. 'It's not like I've taken a suite or anything, and they've given me a discount and stuff.'

'I didn't say anything,' soothed Angelica, 'please calm down.'

Jessica didn't reply. She knew she was behaving abominably. Despite the London setting, it seemed this encounter was going to be like every other time. Honestly, nobody had the ability to transform her into a truculent teenager like her mother did. 'I know this is a plush hotel, but I am trying. Pamela and I even took to the streets to try and find a job yesterday. Not that we had much luck.'

'Pamela? You mean your aunt Pamela? Edward's sister?'

'Yes, we've been hanging out. She's really sweet actually.'

Angelica tried to look enthusiastic as she nodded her head in agreement, though in truth she herself had experienced another side to her sister-in-law all those years ago. Back then, Pam, just like everyone else, had cast her as the villain and made sure she knew it.

Jessica narrowed her eyes. 'What? What have you got against Pam?'

'Nothing,' replied Angelica swiftly.

'There's something. I can tell,' Jessica persisted.

'It's nothing . . . really, it was all a long time ago now,' said Angelica. 'Anyway, you are right, she is a nice woman so I'm glad you're getting to know her better. I remember she and Bernard wanted children very badly. Did she ever have any in the end?'

Jessica shook her head.

'That's a shame. She would have been a great mother, I'm sure.'

This remark seemed to hang in the air between them.

'I'm even using a different name here,' said Jessica, manfully trying her best to dispel any awkwardness. 'I'm really serious about doing things on my own.'

'I'm very proud of you, Jessica, really I am. And what name are you using?'

'Bender.'

'Oh,' said Angelica in surprise. Hearing her ex-husband's real name after all these years was a bit of a shock. It was a name they'd worked very hard to bury, so it seemed terribly ironic that Jessica had brought it back from the dead.

The waiter approached the table. 'Can I get you anything, ladies, or would you prefer to wait for Mr Matthews?'

'That's fine, we can order now. I would like two poached eggs, please,' said Angelica, 'and some wholegrain toast with butter and black tea. Jessica?'

'An omelette, please, and some herbal tea.'

The waiter scribbled down the order.

'Where is Graydon anyway?' asked Jessica suddenly. 'He's been ages.'

Angelica looked faintly embarrassed and seemed reluctant to answer until the waiter was out of earshot. 'He'll be along soon,' she muttered.

'But didn't you say he'd gone to use the bathroom? He's been such a long time.'

Angelica sighed a little tensely. 'Just drop it, Jessica.'

'What?' she asked in all innocence.

Angelica tutted then waited a beat to make sure no one

could hear before answering. 'Come on, Jessica, I told you about Graydon's little *problème*, didn't I?'

'Er . . . no,' said Jessica, not sure she wanted to hear about it now either.

'Really? I didn't tell you about his toilet . . . issues?'

'Issues?' Jessica asked blankly.

Angelica looked Jessica directly in the eye, as if weighing up how much to reveal, then leaned across the table. 'Actually, I am at my wits' end about it. Graydon has an "issue" about "going" in public places.'

'O-K then,' said Jessica, hoping she'd leave it there, but now she'd started, Angelica wasn't in such a hurry to drop the subject.

'I'm completely serious. He's had it since he was a child. Then, when he does feel able to go, he has these rituals, you know? He has to be completely naked. It's quite bizarre.'

'I'm sorry?'

'He has to take every scrap of his clothing off, even his watch, before he can . . . perform, which is fine when he's at home, but when we are out it can present real problems.'

Jessica was aghast and for a second wondered if they were talking about the same thing. 'Are you serious? Are you trying to tell me Graydon has to take all his clothes off in order to take a shit?'

'Ssh,' flapped Angelica. 'Don't be like that, Jessica. It really is a terrible affliction for him. His therapist says he suffers from genuine anal retention.'

Jessica's face crinkled in a mixture of amusement and disgust.

'If you're going to be immature about it then let's not discuss it,' said Angelica, regretful that she'd bought the subject up. 'Let's talk about something else. How is your father?' she asked, her tone changing so imperceptibly that anyone other than Jessica would have missed it.

'Fine,' said Jessica, still smothering the desire to laugh.

'Is he doing anything for his birthday?'

'A party.' Whenever talking to either of her parents about the other, Jessica had learned that it was best to keep detail to a minimum. A monosyllabic art she'd perfected over the years.

'Oh, well, that will be nice,' Angelica replied unconvincingly. In reality she looked like she hoped a plague would visit it. Then, 'I've really missed you, Jessica . . .'

Jessica tried to say 'me too' but it was as though her tongue was suddenly glued to the roof of her mouth. 'Well, you know where I am now,' she said lamely.

'And I really didn't mean to have a go at you about – ah, look, here's Graydon now.'

Jessica looked over and, sure enough, there he was, looking as self-important and studiously macho as ever. Graydon Matthews was a powerful businessman from New York who ran the marathon every year, played squash three times a week and started each day with a cold shower. Despite these and many other macho pursuits, he was also a fastidious man who couldn't bear mess or for anyone, or anything, to look less than perfect. At times this resulted in him coming across as a little 'queeny' or precious, an image he most certainly was not trying to project. Unless he was working out, Graydon always wore suits, along with specially made shoes with built-in lifts concealed inside them. Graydon Matthews's height did not match up to the scale of his ego and the day he'd realized he was never going to be more than five foot eight had been the worst of his life, surpassing even the death of his father in terms of the pure grief he'd experienced. His favourite actor was Tom Cruise.

Despite all of this, his burly, hirsute yet slick presence commanded a certain amount of respect from those around him, although now Jessica knew he'd been freaking out in the toilets for the last half hour, naked, while trying to take a shit, she wasn't sure she'd ever see him in quite the same light again.

'Ladies,' Graydon said smoothly, kissing Angelica on the cheek before ruffling the top of Jessica's head. Jessica noticed that all his fingers possessed an individual patch of black hair, just below the knuckles. She hoped he'd washed his hands.

'Great to see you, Jessica. Are you well?'

'Fine, thanks,' she replied robotically. 'You?'

'Not bad, actually. Though very glad your mother's finished filming in Morocco. It was far too hot for me over there and I wasn't terribly keen on the food.'

'I can imagine,' agreed Jessica. 'I bet you had to be careful not to get an upset stomach?'

'Ah,' said Angelica swiftly, 'breakfast is here, wonderful. I'm starving.'

'Eggs again, darling?' said Graydon as the waiter placed the plates in front of them. 'You really must stop ordering them all the time. They're so bad for your cholesterol and fattening too. You know what it's like, I'm sure, Jessica. A girl's got to watch her figure, especially when it's such a pretty one, eh, honey?' he said, reaching under the table to do who knows what to Angelica.

'Right,' Jessica said weakly.

'Well, hopefully in my new movie people might be able to look past my figure for once,' Angelica said slightly testily.

'Oh, of course,' said Graydon. 'No need to get all touchy now,' he said, giving Jessica a conspiratorial little wink, which had the opposite to the desired effect and made her want to slap him.

'Oh!' exclaimed Angelica suddenly. 'I totally forgot, Jessica. I have a little gift for you. I was sent this the other day, but I don't think I will be able to go because I'm off to LA in a couple of days. I've just found out that the studio want to do a few pick-up shots and –'

'You didn't tell me that,' whined a dismayed-looking Graydon. 'When?'

'Soon, but just for a bit,' Angelica explained.

'But I won't be able to come,' he protested. 'You know I have that big deal coming up and I have to be in New York to tie it up.'

'Well, that's fine,' said Angelica impatiently. 'Anyway –'

'But I want to support you,' he persisted.

Jessica sat on her hands.

'You do support me,' said Angelica, smiling at Graydon reassuringly while clearly wanting to focus on Jessica. 'But if you can't come then *c'est la vie*. I will survive, I'm a big girl, now . . .'

'Well, I just think I should be there for you, darling. For one thing, I'm not too sure I like the cut of that director's jib and also I –'

'Maybe you could discuss this later,' Jessica heard herself suggesting coolly. 'It's just I haven't seen my mom for such a long time.'

'Oh, gosh, of course,' said Graydon, looking wounded. 'Am I being a terrible hog?'

'Anyway,' said Angelica, looking utterly mortified by how things were going. 'This is for you,' she said, retrieving a thick cream card from her clutch bag and handing it across the table.

Jessica looked at it without much enthusiasm. It wasn't that she wanted to be rude, it was just that, no matter how old she got, liking her parents' partners as much as they did was an impossible task. You might not be able to choose your family, but at least the freaks you were related to came from the same gene pool. When her parents split up, however (as if that wasn't hard enough to deal with), random strangers sporadically joined the family. To the point where sometimes she felt like she was playing a lottery, only one she hadn't been asked if she'd like to buy a ticket for. Over the years she and her dad would be ticking along quite nicely, thank you, then suddenly, bam, he would meet someone else. The next thing she knew she was expected to break bread with, go on holiday with or (possibly the most stressful scenario) spend Christmas or Thanksgiving with a person she was hardly acquainted with. On the rare occasions she did take to someone it wasn't worth it anyway, because the next minute the relationship would be over. As a result, she'd stopped bothering. In fact, these days the only thing she knew about her parents' partners for sure was the uncomfortable truth that they were having sex with her mom or dad. Jessica shuddered.

She often thought it would help somehow if she could remember what her parents had been like when they'd been together. If she could remember them making each other miserable, as they inevitably must have, maybe it would be easier to appreciate why their new partners suited them better. As it was, she'd seen plenty of old video footage of Edward and Angelica together, but in it they looked passionately and happily in love. Then again, so did lots of famous couples who behind closed doors, she knew for a fact, hated each other's guts.

Finally she registered what her mother had just given her. It was an invite for a private shopping session at Jimmy Choo. Though in this case 'shopping' was a euphemism for 'take whatever you like for free'.

'Thanks for this,' she said half-heartedly.

'I thought you'd be excited,' said Angelica. 'The current season is wonderful, one of their best yet, but because I can't make it I phoned and told them to expect you instead.'

'Is someone being a little ungrateful?' interjected Graydon, entirely unnecessarily.

'I'm *very* grateful, thanks,' said Jessica tetchily. *He* should be grateful she hadn't asked him how his shit had gone. 'I shall look forward to . . .' She trailed off. A lady had just charged into the dining room and if she hadn't known better she could have sworn it was her auntie Pam. Oh, gosh, it *was* her auntie Pam.

'Jessica,' the older woman yelled, having spotted her. 'Yoo hoo, it's me, they said you were in here. I rushed over in a taxi because I've got some news . . .' As she approached the table, however, it was her turn to trail off.

'Oh,' said Pam, looking shocked as she finally registered who was at the table. The woman she hadn't seen for twenty-three years. The woman who'd broken her brother's heart and abandoned her own child. The woman she'd never forgiven.

'I didn't realize *you* were going to be here,' she said stiffly, as two spots of colour appeared on her cheeks.

'Hello, Pamela,' said Angelica softly, shame flitting across her face, and something else, something that was far harder to read.

'Jessica,' said Pam, ignoring Angelica completely. 'I'll leave you to it. Why don't you give me a ring later when you're free?'

'I don't think that's necessary,' said Graydon, standing up and pushing his chair back. 'Come on, Angelica, we should leave Jessica to it, she obviously has important things to discuss and we need to get going anyway. Besides, I have that meeting soon.'

'But I would rather stay a bit longer. I haven't seen Jessica for –'

At this point Graydon shot Angelica a pointed look and Jessica couldn't help but think that he'd been waiting for an excuse to escape all along. Her mother instantly backtracked. 'You're probably right. OK, well, we'll speak soon, darling.'

Jessica couldn't believe how quickly her mother was bailing. She opened her mouth to protest, but before she'd had time to even form a sentence, Angelica had already kissed her on both cheeks, gathered up her things and scarpered, Graydon holding on tightly to her elbow in a way that made Jessica more than a little uncomfortable. He was ushering her out so fast they didn't even notice the person who was trailing behind them, clearly after an autograph.

As they disappeared from sight, Pam's frown was thunderous. Jessica gulped and then blinked, hard.

'I'm so sorry, love,' said Pam, sounding grave. 'If I'd known she was here I never would have come. I know you haven't seen your mum for ages and now I've ruined things.'

'It's fine,' said Jessica over-brightly.

'It's not,' said Pam, shaking her head. 'Honestly, every time the going gets tough, she can't help herself, can she? She just takes the easy option and runs. And who's that gorilla she was with?'

Jessica didn't answer. She just stared hard into the middle distance, trying to ignore the feeling that she'd been abandoned. Pam's heart twanged with sympathy and regret. 'Sorry, love, that was rude. Look, let's forget about her, shall we? I came here to tell you some good news anyway.'

'Really?' said Jessica, trying hard to shrug off her knee-jerk reaction to the whole experience, which was to immediately seek out a therapist and book in for multiple sessions. 'What is it?'

'Well,' said Pam, lowering herself into the seat that Angelica had previously occupied. 'I spoke to my friend Jean last night and I may have mentioned about how you were looking for work. Anyway, she phoned this morning and apparently her daughter's friend has got a niece who's looking for an assistant. She's called Kerry, I think she said, and she works on *The Bradley Mackintosh Show*. Anyway, I've got her direct line,' said Pam excitedly, 'so you can give her a call and try and get an interview.'

Jessica let the carrot of possibility dangle for a couple of seconds before making a grab for it. 'Do you mean the show that was on the other night? The one I thought Vincent had been on before?'

'That's the one,' said Pam eagerly. 'Obviously the pay would be appalling and you might hate it, working with all those media types . . .'

'Oh.'

'But it's a job, a proper one, and if you could just get an interview then I bet you'd get it, love.'

Her enthusiasm was infectious and Jessica started to feel hope and excitement bubble quietly in her belly then spread throughout her like an injection of positivity. She wasn't going to let her disappointment in her mother ruin this opportunity.

'Oh my gosh, thank you so much, Pam,' she said, as the news sank in. Then, without stopping to think about it, Jessica got up and walked round the table. Reaching Pam, she bent down, grabbed her and pulled her into a great big hug, which took her aunt quite by surprise. These days her friend Jean was the closest person to her, but hugging and the like wasn't something they went in for a great deal.

'Love you,' said Jessica into her aunt's large chest, breathing in her Guerlain scent.

'Love you too,' said Pam, feeling really quite moved. 'Now, let's make that call.'

9

The next day Jessica sat on the tube, armed only with an *A to Z* and the new Oyster card her aunt had recommended that she buy. She felt proud of herself. If only her mother could see her now, she thought, travelling towards White City on her own, having managed to navigate the route without asking anyone, all the way from Green Park tube. It felt like a real achievement, though she had to ignore the usual side dish of pain she felt whenever her thoughts turned to Angelica. She banished her mother from her mind and thought of her father instead, emotionally a far easier point of reference. He, too, would be proud. In LA, she'd never taken public transport anywhere, so it felt doubly impressive somehow, and for the first time in her life she felt a real sense of independence.

As the carriage trundled along its tunnel, Jessica decided the tube was the most fabulous place to people watch. In LA, only the lowliest members of society – gang members, people with live chickens under their arms and illegal immigrants – dared to get the buses. Here, however, it seemed a complete cross-section of society chose to get around the city by public transport, which was quite liberating, as was the fact that there were obviously no hard and fast rules about how to dress here either. In LA her friends tended to all wear variations on the same unimaginative themes. Jogging bottoms, jeans, Ugg boots, sneakers or flip-flops by day, taking it up a gear by night, but with the aim still being to look as if they weren't trying too hard – the reality being that they would have spent at least three hours on grooming that week alone.

Almost before she was ready for the journey to end, the train glided into White City. Here she was and, the minute she left the station, there *it* was. The BBC.

Jessica gulped. Working in television might not be her heart's desire, but if it was the only job she could find for now then where better to start? The BBC was world famous and, as she took in how vast the circular-shaped building was, she could feel her heart beating harder than it probably should. Feeling very nervous, she crossed the road, remembering just in time to look right first. She entered the building via glass revolving doors that led her into a huge reception area and approached one of the desks.

'Can I help you?' asked a woman in uniform.

'Yes, please. I've got an interview at eleven with Kerry Taylor on *The Bradley Mackintosh Show*.'

'And your name is?'

'Jessica Gr– Bender.'

'Grebender?'

'Bender.'

The woman gave her a look that could only be described as wary and called through on the phone. 'Hello, I've got a Miss Bender in reception to see Kerry? Take a seat,' she said, not bothering to look up again.

'Thanks,' said Jessica, going over to the black leather seats in the middle of the space and picking up a copy of *Ariel*, the BBC's in-house magazine.

The reception was full of people coming and going, and after realizing that *Ariel* was of no interest to her whatsoever, and that even if it had been her nerves were preventing her from reading it, Jessica busied herself watching all the comings and goings instead. Briefly she worried whether she might be dressed too smartly. She was wearing flat pumps with tight, dark denim Capri pants and a navy-and-white striped fitted T-shirt, so nothing over the top, and yet compared to some people who were brandishing their passes at the security guy and striding in she looked downright 'put together'.

Just then, a woman who clearly wasn't letting size be any obstacle for the clothes she chose to wear appeared within her eye line.

'Are you Jessica?' she asked.

'Yes,' said Jessica, leaping to her feet and pumping her hand enthusiastically.

'Nice to meet you,' the woman said less enthusiastically and extracting her hand. 'I'm Kerry. Do you want to follow me?'

'Sure,' Jessica said eagerly. 'It's really nice to meet you. I was so pleased when you said you'd see me. I guess you've probably seen a lot of people?'

'Er . . . yes,' replied Kerry. She knew the girl was only being friendly but she had indeed been seeing people all morning, so didn't want to talk more than was strictly necessary.

Nerves racing, Jessica followed after Kerry through the maze of corridors that wound themselves around the building until they reached a bank of lifts. As if to make up for her earlier dismissal of Jessica's attempt to engage with her, Kerry spoke up suddenly.

'So, you said on the phone that you don't have a great deal of experience in TV.'

'I don't,' she agreed sincerely. 'Though I guess most people who can afford to work for so little probably don't, right?'

'Um, kind of,' replied Kerry, who was a little thrown by this comment. Though, in fairness, what Jessica had just said was pretty close to the mark. Quite a few of the people she'd seen so far were graduates with names like Hugo and Fenella, who clearly had parents well off enough to support them while they started out on a pittance.

'Still,' went on Kerry, 'with no experience, I'm wondering what drove you to apply. You don't want to be a presenter, do you?'

'Gee, no,' said Jessica emphatically. 'Actually, I couldn't think of anything worse.'

Kerry nodded. Well, that had to be a point in her favour. The last candidate, a hideously bubbly girl called Bonnie, had bought her showreel with her. Kerry didn't do bubbly and she certainly wasn't going to accommodate anyone who'd be treating the job as one long audition. Bonnie had been shown the door quite quickly.

'To be honest,' said Jessica, keen to fill the silence that had descended again, 'I've never particularly dreamed of working in TV, but I just really like the idea of working in an office.'

At this, Kerry looked taken aback and deeply unimpressed. 'Do you know how many people would love to be seen for this job?' she demanded to know. 'Or have any idea what an amazing opportunity this is? Just because

I don't want some wannabe working for me doesn't mean I don't want someone with an interest in the business.'

'Oh, right, of course,' said Jessica, blushing red as the lift finally arrived. They got in. 'I don't know why I said that, actually. What I probably meant was that I would enjoy the challenge of being organized and helpful.'

Kerry was overwhelmed with irritation. She'd spent the last fortnight or so whittling down thousands of CVs to what she'd thought was going to be a promising pile. Yet, so far, she'd spent a crappy morning talking to idiots, all of whom were totally wrong for one reason or another. Too earnest, too ambitious, too inexperienced, too shy or too annoying. Now, this American chick (who knew someone who knew her aunt or something) was acting as if she was so cool that she wouldn't be even a little bit excited about the people she would meet should she get the job. There was a balance, surely?

As they travelled upwards, Kerry tried to decide what to do. Should she just tell this strange American pretender to piss off and stop wasting her time? Then again, could she really afford to spend more time trying to find people to interview? Due to the paltry budget she'd been given, it wasn't as if she had hundreds of great experienced people clamouring to earn no money. Maybe she should just bite the bullet and have a chat with this girl. The two of them eyeballed each other grimly, both wondering what their next move should be.

'Right,' said Kerry as the doors glided open. 'Here we are then, so I suppose you may as well come and have a chat, though you might want to at least pretend you're vaguely interested in TV or we can just call it a day now. Personally, I really don't care much either way.'

Jessica gulped.

'Seriously,' said Kerry, gathering steam. 'I know the pay's a bit crap, but we are talking about one of our flagship light entertainment shows so if you can't be arsed then just say so, because frankly I'm teetering on the edge of telling you to do one.'

Wow. Nobody had ever spoken to Jessica like that before in her life. Bizarrely, she'd quite enjoyed it. Maybe she was the employee equivalent of a masochist?

'I am interested,' she said calmly. 'Really I am.'

'Come on then,' said Kerry. 'But no more bullshit, right?'

And with that she turned left down the corridor, Jessica following meekly. Before long they came to a door marked THE BRADLEY MACKINTOSH SHOW.

'Here we are then,' said Kerry more warmly, before shoving open the door to reveal a very average-looking office filled with lots of busy-looking people, who were all occupied with their computers or chatting to one another.

'We'll go to Mike's office. He's out, so we won't be disturbed,' said Kerry, and as Jessica followed she found herself wondering what she'd got herself into and how on earth people with no connections ever coped in interviews without bursting into tears.

Meanwhile, Paul Fletcher was about to send the final version of that week's script through to Bradley Mackintosh, as he did every Tuesday, the theory being that the nation's favourite interviewer could then spend all of Wednesday familiarizing himself with his links in time for Thursday's recording. In reality, Bradley was such an old pro he was usually confident enough to have his first quick read sat in make-up, while having beige foundation smeared all over his face and his bald patch sprayed with hair in a can. Yes, there is such a thing. Paul pressed 'send' and then rubbed his face with his hands. Time for a cup of tea.

He rolled his chair, which was on castors, away from his desk just in time to see Kerry walking into the office. Behind her was an attractive blonde girl who was wearing a stripy sort of nautical-looking top with tight jeans. She was unfeasibly healthy-looking. Yes, healthy, decided Paul. Her skin was all . . . glowy . . . and her limbs looked toned and despite the fact that her bum was a decent size it looked as though it wouldn't wobble if you squeezed it. Paul grinned. New blood in the office was always an interesting proposition. He carried on rolling in the direction of the kettle and started to make tea, but by the time he got back Kerry and the girl had gone into Mike's office so he couldn't be nosy any more.

Inside Mike's office, Kerry had got her notepad and pen out and was in full interview mode.

'So, actually, what's your full name again?'

'Jessica . . . Bender.'

'Ooh, Bender. Unlucky,' said Kerry sympathetically. Still, sympathy made a change from sarcasm or laughter.

'OK, Jessica, what do you think of the show?'

Jessica swallowed. 'I think it's great. I caught some of it the other night and it was really fun.'

Kerry sighed. 'I'm not being funny, but you can't turn up to an interview with no opinion on the show you've come to work on. Don't you have any notes?'

'Well, no, though I would have done had I known earlier

that I'd be meeting you. It's just that when I watched the show I wasn't really concentrating because I was at my aunt's house and we were having dinner and —'

'Great,' said Kerry sarcastically. 'I hope it was tasty.'

'I thought the job was to help book guests,' said Jessica, who was growing a little tired of the way Kerry was talking to her. It was almost as if she wanted the interview to go badly.

'Ye-ah?'

'So surely my opinion of the show wouldn't ever really be required?'

Kerry looked surprised by this reasoning but not necessarily put off. It seemed she responded well to straight talking.

'Kerry, I'll level with you,' Jessica continued. 'I've only just recently come over from the States —'

'No shit, Sherlock.'

'So I'm not all that familiar with the show yet. Though, having said that, I get that it's a big deal and that it would be a privilege to work on it. I'd even heard of the show in the States. In fact, I'm pretty sure Vincent Malone was a guest once, right?'

Kerry nodded, slightly bemused.

Jessica recalled Vincent telling her about it. She seemed to remember him saying that the host was well known for being irreverent with his guests, and that you either loved or hated him. 'Yes, I remember hearing about it — in the press. But, anyway, I'm really keen, I'm a quick learner and when it comes to the world of celebrity I do have a bit of experience having ... worked around a few ... in the States.'

'Where?'

'I was an intern at . . . Fox Films,' Jessica improvised, though even to her ears her reply sounded more like a question.

Kerry regarded the girl in front of her. 'To be honest with you, Jessica, I'm looking for someone who really knows the show and who can come up with great ideas for future guests. That someone also needs to be able to help me actually book the guests, which in turn means someone who can speak to very high-powered agents and publicists. In other words, the person I need would have to be comfortable dealing with people who would gladly negotiate their own grandmother for a better rate, and I'm just not sure you're that –'

Thinking fast, Jessica cut her off at the quick. 'Agents like Dolores Rainer? Jill Cunningham? Or Max Steadman?' said Jessica, spouting the names of just a few of Hollywood's biggest agents, all of whom she knew personally. Her mother's, her father's and Vincent's.

Kerry's jaw dropped to the floor, but she recovered quickly. 'Blimey, well at least you made the effort to do *some* research, even if you have aimed rather high. I do try to get one stellar, international guest every week, but sometimes it's simply not possible. Although this coming week we've got a great line-up, actually, especially seeing as we're getting into summer when it's harder to get good bookings. We've got the presenter Jeff Bates, Kate Templeton, which is obviously brilliant, and Alan Carr.'

Jessica nodded enthusiastically, even though she'd only heard of one out of three. Kate Templeton was huge at the moment, the darling of the US box office and even giving Jennifer Aniston a run for her money. Edward had played a cameo part in one of her films and spoke of her fondly. Apparently she was lovely, though her manager was reputedly a fierce old dragon.

'Sounds awesome and I guess a show like this is only ever as good as the guests, so your job must be really tough.'

Kerry was flattered. It was what she'd always thought deep down, but it was lovely nevertheless to hear it said by someone else.

'Is there a DVD I could watch?' Jessica asked, spotting the machine in the corner. 'That way if you really do want to know my thoughts, for what they're worth, I can tell you.'

'Er, yes,' said Kerry, feeling quite wrong-footed by Jessica's dramatic U-turn from annoying and clueless to perceptive and straightforward. 'You can watch one from a couple of weeks ago. It's one I'm quite proud of, actually. Michael Sheen was our big guest and also Dawn French – as in French and Saunders? Vicar of Dibley?' she tried again, having noted Jessica's blank expression. 'Forget it. Anyway, enjoy, and while you're watching I'll find someone to make us a cup of tea.'

'Oh, I'm fine, thanks,' replied Jessica. 'I'm not really a big tea drinker.'

Bloody yanks, thought Kerry, but as she left Jessica watching the TV she found she was smiling to herself. Fancy her having pulled those agents' names out of the bag.

Fifteen minutes later Kerry returned to Mike's office with a mug of tea and Paul and Luke in tow. They'd persuaded her to let them come and meet the potential new addition to the team.

'How are you getting on?' Kerry said, barging open the door to Mike's office with her shoulder in order to avoid spilling her tea. 'This is Paul and Luke.'

'Hi,' breezed Jessica happily. 'Good to meet you both.'

'And you,' said Luke. 'Kerry tells me the name's Bender . . . Jessica Bender,' he quipped, though he wished he hadn't when Jessica whipped round in surprise, looking like she'd seen a ghost.

'You all right?' asked Paul, bemused.

'Yeah,' said Jessica, blushing madly and looking flustered. 'Fine.'

'So what do you think?' asked Kerry, gesturing at the screen.

'Oh, gosh,' Jessica exclaimed, still feeling thrown by Luke's comment. 'Um, well, that lady, Dawn French, she was hilarious. It was just brilliant the way she embarrassed Bradley Mackintosh like that by slapping him on the fanny.'

'On the what?' asked Paul, unable to suppress a smirk.

'The fanny,' repeated Jessica. 'It was awesome,' she continued hesitantly, 'really funny.'

'Should have seen it before the edit. Then you really would have laughed,' interrupted Kerry drily, trying to drown out the sound of Luke who was killing himself laughing.

'Oh, really?' said Jessica, looking nervously at Luke.

'Yeah,' said Paul, pulling a disbelieving face at her before turning to Luke and adding so only he could hear, 'You total nutter.'

'Shit, man, I hope you get the job,' Luke snorted. 'There are hours of fun to be had.'

Kerry tutted at him disapprovingly and gave both boys

the filthiest look she could muster. She'd decided Jessica deserved a chance. There was something about her apparent lack of cynicism and lack of guile that appealed. It was quite refreshing, quite sweet. Besides, if everybody reacted to the show with such enthusiasm then life would be a lot easier.

'Well, I'm glad you enjoyed it,' she said.

'I did. It's a great show.'

'And, just for the record, over here the word fanny doesn't mean bum.'

'Oh . . .'

'You're American,' stated Paul.

'Half British, half French actually, but I moved to the States when I was seven,' replied Jessica shyly, wondering what the word fanny did mean over here.

'Well, that explains it then.'

Now Jessica looked from Paul back to Kerry, her eyes wide and questioning.

'Bit more prone to PDEs over there, aren't you?' said Paul.

'PD what?'

'Public displays of enthusiasm.'

Seeing Jessica's unsure expression, Kerry decided it was time to intervene.

'Right, well, thanks, you two, but I'd like to talk to Jessica alone now, so I'll see you later,' she said bluntly, half pushing them both back towards the office. Luke was first through the door, at which point he yelled, 'Who can I hit on the fanny?' to the entire office.

'Don't mind them,' Kerry said, shutting the door behind

them. 'They're like schoolboys when they're together, which is a lot. They share a flat,' she added, by way of explanation. 'You probably won't believe this now, but Paul is actually considered to be one of the most talented writers at the BBC. Anyway, I just need to get a few more details from you because, frankly, if you can handle agents like Jill Cunningham, you'll be worth your weight in gold, which is more than your wage packet will be, I'm afraid.'

'Oh, right . . .'

'So what I'm trying to say is, as far as I'm concerned, if you want the job you can start on Monday. Truth be known, you're the only person I've seen so far who seems up to the job and like someone I might get on with.'

'Oh my gosh,' replied Jessica, reeling from the speed at which everything had just happened. What a strange day. On the one hand she was pretty sure she'd just been vaguely humiliated by that guy Paul and his friend Luke. Yet, on the other, someone who had no way of either knowing or caring who she was had just offered her a job. Albeit a terribly paid job, which involved working on a show that centred on famous people, one of the very things she was trying to get away from, but a job nonetheless. In England. At the BBC. Though how she'd ever cope with it, she didn't know. Suddenly she felt absolutely drained and quite overcome.

'Are you up for it then?'

'Oh, yes please, I'd love it, thank you,' replied Jessica, running her middle fingers underneath both of her eyes to wipe away whatever havoc her eye make-up may have wreaked and smiling weakly. She was telling the truth. She was definitely up for it all right. Of that much she was certain. What worried her was whether she was up *to* it, another matter altogether, and if the last ten minutes were anything to go by, one she suspected she'd be getting to the bottom of pretty damn quickly.

10

That evening, Jessica returned to her room after a long workout in the hotel gym. It had been such an eventful and exciting day that she'd needed to run some of it out of her system. She smiled. Pam's delighted screams were still ringing in her ears from when she'd phoned earlier to tell her she'd got the job. She was such a sweetie and Jessica would seriously be considering her most recent offer to move into her house in Hampstead. She'd been expecting her wage to be low, but when Kerry had informed her of the exact amount she'd be getting paid as her assistant, certain truths had finally hit home. In one week she'd be earning less than she was currently paying for a single night in the hotel.

She flicked on the TV. Now that the adrenaline she'd been surviving on all day had run out, she felt exhausted and not a little fearful of what she'd be facing on Monday. All the doubts that had first emerged at the BBC about what she was getting herself into had risen to the surface. How was she going to pull this off? She'd never had a job like it before in her life and the people seemed downright scary. For the first time ever she wouldn't be wearing the armour of her identity and it had taken that interview for her to fully comprehend how much it usually protected her. No one ever wanted to upset her dad, so they didn't upset her.

She stared at the screen. An English soap called *East-Enders* was just starting. She'd caught it a few times since arriving and found it fascinating. The tempo of the show was fairly slow and everything and everyone in it appeared to be either a shade of grey, brown or pale green, and yet the combination was strangely soothing. By the same token, watching such ordinary-looking folk going about their day was almost more surreal than the outlandish characters and plots one found in the colourful, high-octane American soaps she was used to.

Ten minutes later and Jessica had decided that *EastEnders* was doing nothing to dissipate her nerves. If anything, some of the more bolshie female characters were reminding her of Kerry, so she switched off the TV and picked up the phone to ring her dad. She fancied hearing his voice and it would be fun to tell him that she'd found a job. Not that she'd be telling him what show she was working on, or where it was, otherwise faster than she could say 'intruding old fart' she'd probably have a promotion and a pay rise.

'Hey, Dad? It's me . . .'

Half an hour later, in Malibu, Edward replaced his receiver, feeling better than he had in ages. Chatting to Jessica for so long had been wonderful and he suspected that the job she'd got could be her ticket home. He knew what it was like being a lowly assistant in TV. It was bloody hard work and with a bit of luck she'd soon appreciate how good she had things here and come home. He hoped so; he really missed her.

Putting thoughts of Jessica to one side for the moment, though, he stretched before bounding upstairs to start getting ready for his big day. Today it would be nice to feel like Edward Granger the movie star again. It had been a while. Feeling chipper, he strode into his bedroom only to find Betsey lying provocatively on the bed, wearing a black negligee and very little else. His heart sank.

'Hi, honey,' she purred. 'Come and get me.'

His first reaction was to start making excuses about not having enough time, but once he'd had a second to think about it a spot of sex didn't seem like the worst idea after all. What the hell. She did look pretty hot in that black thing she was wearing and it would get her off his back for a while.

A few minutes later, however, his back wasn't the only body part Edward was wishing Betsey would get off. Meanwhile, Betsey was trying hard to lose herself in the moment. To be fair, she was hugely grateful it was happening at all, having spent days nagging Edward for sex, but was disappointed that the only thing (or things) that were stirring up any real feeling of desire were her own boobs, which she was enjoying watching in the mirror as they jiggled up and down. A flash of grave concern for her marriage almost overwhelmed her for a second, but she quickly quashed it. Making love brought couples closer together, babies even more so. It was a well-known fact.

'Oh yeah,' she panted. 'Oh yeah, oh yeah, oh yeah.' She threw her head around a bit, emulating someone in the throes of passion, hoping that by doing so she might start feeling it for real. Briefly, she opened one eye to check what Edward was doing and for a second they made eye contact, which rather ruined the moment and only served to remind her how disconnected they were. Dismayed, she snapped it shut again, having seen enough to know that

Edward's expression wasn't one of desire. His face looked the same as it did when he was putting on his socks or plucking his nostril hair.

Betsey upped the ante. 'Oh my God, oh my God, oh my God,' she screamed, riding her husband as vigorously and as determinedly as a cowboy on a bucking bronco. Again, as her head flailed around, she opened one green eye for a peak. Fuck it, now his expression was less enraptured passion, more alarm, horror, terror. Clearly, the quicker she got this over and done with the happier they'd both be.

One and a half minutes later, Edward was standing stark bollock naked at the foot of the bed, watching his suits glide by inside his remote-controlled hi-tech wardrobe.

'Er, how was that for you, darling? Was it . . . good? Did you . . . you know?'

Betsey, who couldn't stand it when Edward got all coy about things, pulled the sheets up under her armpits and deliberated for a while before answering. 'No, but it doesn't matter. I'm just glad we finally got round to doing it. I was starting to think you were avoiding sex altogether.'

'Don't be ridiculous,' said Edward, not particularly convincingly. With a bit of luck that might be his conjugal duties over and done with for another month, he thought hopefully.

Plucking one of Savile Row's finest from the rail, he swung round to face Betsey, who couldn't help but notice that his balls swung round with him, only a split second later. She averted her eyes and fixed them on his face instead, as Edward lifted the suit up for her to see. 'What do you think? This, or I could just wear my blazer with some beige slacks?'

What Betsey *thought* was that she couldn't believe she was married to a man who could, in all seriousness, utter the words 'beige slacks'. She also wished to high heaven that, whatever he chose to wear, he'd hurry up and put it on because the harsh sunshine pouring through the window was rather unforgiving. As a result she was being forced to confront the fact that, handsome though her husband still was, he had most definitely passed his prime and was starting to look less fillet steak, more scrag end.

'The suit would be better, honey. It's much more your image than a blazer and slacks. Leave that to Roger Moore,' she said pointedly.

'You're the expert,' said Edward, sounding more cheerful than he felt. He pressed another button, which caused the top rail to start moving so that he could pick a shirt out from the hundreds he owned.

Betsey sighed and rolled on to her side. It was probably time for her to get up and get changed too. Today was a big day and while her marriage might not be everything she had once hoped it would be, it was important to remind herself how lucky she was to be married to her very own movie star. James Bond, no less. Today her husband was being awarded a gold star on Hollywood's walk of fame and she would be by his side, playing the part of the beautiful, loving wife. She slid out of bed and went to the chair where she'd already laid out the outfit she'd bought especially for the event.

Five minutes later, Betsey was examining herself in the mirror. She'd chosen her outfit with a great deal of care, but with hindsight probably wasn't really a Chanel kind of gal. She looked at least five years older than she was, though maybe subconsciously that was what she'd been aiming for all along. Recently she'd been feeling horribly aware of the twenty-seven-year age gap between herself and her husband.

'You look beautiful,' said Edward, sidling up to her and putting an arm round her waist. He wasn't just saying it either. His young wife looked much more elegant than usual. The Chanel suited her.

Touched by her husband's clearly genuine compliment, Betsey turned to give him a hug. Not a grope, or a lusty grab, but a hug, and for a second everything felt right between the two of them. A calm descended and in that moment the couple felt closer than they had in a long while. Edward was pleased. Maybe he could even forgive her for the Roger Moore jibe. As they pulled away, Edward smiled down at his wife, and in a manner that would have had his legions of female fans swooning, proffered his arm for her to take. 'Shall we?'

'Yes,' she said softly, taking his arm. 'It's a good thing I'm not wearing any knickers, otherwise I really would be feeling like Barbara Bush in this get-up,' she had to add though, which ruined the moment completely.

Edward sighed wearily and, as Betsey made her way downstairs, he stopped to check his appearance in the landing mirror one last time. 'Nothing wrong with Roger's style anyway,' he muttered to himself as he adjusted his cuffs. 'One of the most stylish men I've ever met, I'll have you know.'

11

Jessica's first day as Kerry's assistant dawned a bright and sunny beautiful June day. She knew this for a fact because at dawn she was already running in Hyde Park. Of course, in LA there was nothing particularly unusual about this kind of early morning, active behaviour. However, later, when Jessica happened to mention to Kerry what a great run she'd had, judging by how her new boss reacted she may as well have said she'd been out on a casual killing spree.

'Right,' said Kerry, looking at her as if she'd offended her sensibilities. 'Well, each to their own.'

Today Kerry was wearing black three-quarter-length leggings with a rather shapeless, baggy tunic dress over the top, a wide belt slung round her hips. Her hair was unkempt, but suited her that way, and she had a chunky wooden bangle on her wrist.

'OK, let me show you where you'll be sitting. You're next to me and then – ah, here's Natasha, our researcher. Tash, this is Jessica, my new assistant.'

'Hi,' said Jessica shyly.

'Hello,' said Natasha, putting her bag down on the desk and slipping off her denim jacket. She gave Jessica the once-over with her discerning eye for fashion but there was nothing much to disapprove of. Jessica's short khaki skirt, ballet flats and long-sleeved T-shirt might be boring but they smacked of good quality. Natasha raised one eyebrow while wondering what her male colleagues would make of this new girl. She was pretty, but not as pretty as her, so that was OK. 'I like your skirt. Where's that from then?'

'Um, I'm not sure,' said Jessica, who knew full well that Angelica had bought it for her in Paris, from Comme des Garçons. 'I think it's Gap,' she bluffed, not really sure why she was bothering to lie.

'Right, come and meet Mike,' Kerry interrupted, saving Jessica from any more sartorial scrutiny by ushering her through the office towards the room where they'd had their interview. She rapped sharply on the door.

'Come.'

'Mike,' Kerry said, poking her head round the door. 'Have you got a minute? I want you to meet someone,' she said, shooing Jessica in. 'This is my new assistant, Jessica Bender.'

'You're such a bitch,' exclaimed Mike, taking both Kerry and Jessica by surprise.

'Sorry?' said Kerry.

'There's no need to take the piss out of the girl on her first day,' said Mike, who was sitting at his desk and had immediately struck Jessica as rather good-looking, despite the fact she had no idea what he was on about.

Kerry did though.

'No, no, Mike,' she said, shaking her head vigorously while widening her eyes to try and alert him to his mistake. 'Bender is actually her name.'

For a split second Mike froze. Then, 'Course it is,' he said swiftly, but the tell-tale red patches that had appeared on both cheeks were a giveaway. 'I knew that, I was just saying, you know, don't be a bitch, like you sometimes . . . can be. Anyway, Jessica, welcome to the team.'

'Thanks,' she said, mildly horrified by how things were going so far. 'I'm really pleased to be here, and I loved your show the other week with Michael Sheen. He was such an awesome guest.'

'He was very good, wasn't he?' said Mike, giving Jessica the visual once-over. 'So whereabouts are you from in the States then?' he asked, pleased that Kerry's new assistant was so attractive. She was by no means beautiful, but had something about her. Plus you could tell she took care of herself. Nice toned legs.

'LA,' she replied hesitantly. The less she talked about home, the better.

'Very nice too. Can't imagine why you'd want to leave really. Which part of LA? I know it a bit,' said Mike, leaning back in his chair and chewing idly on a biro.

'Um, Santa Monica,' she said, blushing to her roots. Lying wasn't something that came particularly naturally to her, but the truth would only provoke more questions. If he really did know LA a bit then he would also know that only the very rich, or the very rich and famous, lived in beachside Malibu mansions.

'Actually, while I've got you here, Kerry,' said Mike, with the distracted air of a man with a lot on his mind, 'have you had confirmation from Will Smith's people for August?'

'Yes,' said Kerry. 'We're on, and unless something unforeseen happens we should be good to go. Obviously I've guaranteed that Bradley will talk about the movie, and that we'll show a clip.'

'Cool. *The Pentagon* is going to be huge. The effects are amazing,' said Jessica enthusiastically. It was weird hearing something familiar mentioned when so far away from home. Will Smith was a friend of her dad's and she'd already seen quite a bit of *The Pentagon* because Vincent had written two songs for the soundtrack. Kerry shot her a puzzled look just as Jessica was realizing she may have said too much, but Mike didn't seem to have noticed.

'Good stuff. That'll be a great show and, with the line-up looking so good this week, we should be back on top.' As Mike finished speaking he let out the most enormous yawn. 'Sorry, do excuse me.'

'Baby still keeping you awake?' enquired Kerry.

Mike nodded.

'Oh, wow. Do you have a baby?' asked Jessica, fascinated.

'Mmm, two actually. Grace is three and a bit and Ava's about seven weeks now. Knackering business, but still — all good, you know.'

Jessica didn't really know at all but thought how terribly exciting it must be to have a tiny baby in your life.

'Well, hopefully you'll have a nice rest on holiday,' said Kerry.

Mike forced himself to resist snorting with disbelief. He had a sneaky suspicion his holiday was going to be far from restful and was almost regretting having booked it, but all he said out loud was, 'Hopefully. If the office doesn't run amok while I'm away.'

'Sure it won't,' said Kerry, signalling to Jessica that it was time to leave the boss to it.

'Oh, hang on a sec,' said Mike absent-mindedly, having already turned his attention back to his in-box. 'Speaking of holiday. Do you think it would be cheeky of me to ask one of the runners to water our garden a couple of times while we're away? Diane, my wife, reckons this hot weather might be here to stay.'

'I'm not sure,' said Kerry, who was really. Personally, she thought it was a bloody cheek to ask the poor runners who were on such a shit wage to give up their precious time just to go and water his garden.

'You're probably right,' said Mike quickly. He could tell Kerry didn't really approve. 'I'll see if I can get a neighbour to do it.'

'Isn't your sprinkler system working?' asked Jessica, sounding disarmingly sincere.

'Er . . . we don't have one,' said Mike, looking bemused.

'Really?' said Jessica, thinking that maybe here was a fabulous window of opportunity to show her new bosses just how keen she was to muck in. 'I could do it,' she offered, and Mike and Kerry both looked at her questioningly, wondering faintly if she was taking the piss. Realizing she was serious, Kerry shook her head as forcefully as she could without Mike seeing.

'Honestly, Kerry, I really wouldn't mind,' said Jessica, misinterpreting her completely. 'It would be an honour.'

Kerry groaned. What the hell was she talking about?

'Really?' said Mike. 'Well, that's certainly very kind of you. Where do you live? I'm in Chiswick.'

'OK, well, I'm in . . .'

As Mike and Kerry waited for an answer, Jessica panicked. Where should she say? Not the Dorchester, that was for sure. She tried to remember the name of the place where Pam lived but her mind had gone blank. She plumped for the first place that popped into her head.

'I'm in Walford.'

'Walford?' repeated Mike. 'I'm not sure I know where that is, though it certainly sounds familiar.'

Kerry (*EastEnders*' biggest fan) was looking very doubtful, while Jessica was praying Mike wouldn't make the connection to the soap. Why the hell had she said Walford? She wasn't even sure the place actually existed.

'Anyway,' she said now hastily, 'I'm sure I could get to Chiswick really easily so I'd be happy to do it. I wouldn't mind at all. I don't have much on at the weekends and I love getting the tube, so –'

'Now you're really taking the mickey, aren't you?' interrupted Kerry who, plain-speaking as ever, simply had to find out.

Jessica blinked, confused. 'Er, no.'

Kerry shook her head again. Who in their right mind liked getting the tube? And how . . . weird to both suck up to the boss and take the piss out of him, all on your first day.

'OK, well, let me talk to Diane, and thanks very, very much, Jessica. I really appreciate the offer,' said Mike, giving her his most dazzling grin. Jessica puffed up with pleasure, feeling enormously smug that on day one she'd already managed to ingratiate herself with the boss by appearing helpful and hard-working, like a normal girl who was ready to pull her sleeves up and get stuck in, something which would surely curry favour with Kerry. When they left the office, however, Kerry shot her an extremely odd look.

'What?' asked Jessica, dismayed. 'Have I done something wrong?'

'Not wrong, just . . . you don't really like getting the tube, do you?'

'Oh, yes,' reassured Jessica. 'I love it. It's just wonderful for people watching.'

'Right,' said Kerry, in a tone that made Jessica's heart sink. 'And what the hell was all that Walford stuff about? I admit it was quite funny, but don't get too clever on your first day, will you?'

'No,' said Jessica, shocked once again at being spoken to so bluntly. 'I won't, I really wasn't meaning to –'

'Don't worry about it,' said Kerry. 'Like I said before, each to their own, but we should get on with some work now, if that's OK? I want to talk you through the next couple of months' shows, who I have and haven't got booked and confirmed at this stage. Then I'll show you my contacts list and we can discuss some ideas. Good?'

'Good,' said Jessica, determined not to say anything else that might annoy Kerry.

'Did you meet Mike then?' asked Natasha casually as they approached their desks. She was busy typing away.

'Yeah, he seems like such a nice guy,' said Jessica.

Natasha stopped typing and looked up, her gaze drifting between Jessica and Kerry. 'Do you mean nice as in nice-looking?' she asked, the picture of innocence.

'Oh, gosh, no,' said Jessica blushing. 'I meant nice as in nice. As in, he seems like a really nice person.'

'Who's a really nice person?' asked Paul, who was passing, and Kerry felt her buttocks tense.

'Mike,' said Jessica. 'He's even letting me water his plants while he's away on holiday.'

Kerry cringed and briefly considered clamping Jessica's mouth shut with her hand. Positivity didn't go down well in this office. Instead the three 'sms' were the order of the day: pessimism, cynicism, sarcasm.

Paul stopped in his tracks and, as if by magic, Luke and Julian the director appeared, having sensed that something more interesting than work was happening over in this corner of the office.

'Get this,' said Paul in a voice dripping with disdain. 'You'll never guess what Mike's done. He's been so kind, he's actually letting Jessica here – it is Jessica, isn't it? He's actually letting her water his garden for him while he pisses off on holiday for a fortnight, leaving us all in the shit. Isn't that good of him?'

Luke flung his head back and laughed. 'Seriously?' he said to Jessica. 'He's got you watering his plants already? I hope he's giving you something extra for your troubles.'

'Leave it out,' tried Kerry.

'Oh, no,' said Jessica, having concluded wrongly that they all thought she was getting paid extra to do it, in which case they might think she was being devious or money-grabbing, which wasn't how she wanted to appear at all. 'I was saying to Kerry that I only offered because it would be a real pleasure to help and I love getting the tube so . . .'

'Yeah, well, you probably use an imaginary station that's far better than the ones I'm used to,' said Kerry.

'What?' asked Paul, clearly intrigued.

'She told Mike she lived in Walford,' said Kerry flatly.

Paul laughed. 'As in *EastEnders*? Why did you do that?'

'I don't know,' admitted Jessica. 'I guess it just popped into my head and –'

'So where do you really live?'

This time, thankfully, the name of the place where Pam lived came to her. 'Hampstead,' she said, sounding terribly proud when in fact she was just relieved.

'Figures,' Paul replied. He should have known she'd live in one of the smartest parts of London, but there was no need for her to sound so smug about it.

'Meaning what?' asked Jessica, who was seriously considering jacking the job in already. She half felt like walking out and not stopping till she got to Heathrow.

'Meaning nothing,' said Paul, not nastily but wearily. 'Christ, I'm not sure I can handle these American babblings on a Monday morning. Day one and you've signed up for extra curriculum activities with Mike already. You'll be cheerleading next. Give us an "M", give us an "I", et cetera.'

Jessica's face fell. She chewed her lip as the awkwardness she was feeling gave way to outrage. Who was this creep? How dare he judge her for being American? And since when did he think American-bashing was all right? If he were talking about any other race it would be deemed racist.

'I thought the English were supposed to be polite,' she said quietly, a steely edge to her voice that Paul didn't seem to hear.

'You'll be making some of the other Mike fans in this office very jealous if you're not careful,' a man who Jessica hadn't yet been introduced to added drolly. He looked like he was only half listening as he scrolled through the messages on his BlackBerry. 'I'm Julian, the director, by the way. Oh my God, you'll even have access to Mike's pants drawer while he's away. I'm betting he's a jockey man myself.'

'Oh, gee, er – I'm really not doing it because I'm a fan of his,' floundered Jessica.

Luke got up from his desk and, for the benefit of his watching audience, swaggered over to Natasha, walking like a cowboy. 'You might not be a fan of his, Miss Bender, but someone else around here is,' he said in a ridiculous voice, loaded with innuendo.

Natasha, who was thoroughly enjoying the whole scene, burst out laughing. 'Does it bug you, Paul?' she said, batting her eyelashes coyly. 'Does it upset you that our new girl fancies Mike too?' she finished, knowing this would piss her ex off.

At this, Jessica stood rooted to the spot feeling horribly embarrassed and unsure as to how her efforts to appear hard-working had been so wrongly translated. She could feel all the various undercurrents swirling around her and yet had no idea how to navigate them.

Paul's face rearranged itself into a scowl.

'Oh, shut up, you two,' said Kerry. 'Give Jessica a break, will you? It is her first bloody day after all and you haven't even bothered to say hello properly.'

'Yes, I have,' squealed Natasha indignantly. 'Haven't I, Jess?'

Jessica nodded emphatically, already wary of this pretty blonde who seemed to have a complicated but not very well-hidden agenda.

'You're right, Kezza,' said Paul, the scowl disappearing from his interesting face. Jessica couldn't figure out whether he was incredibly gorgeous or incredibly off-putting. He had very dark hair and a long lock of it kept falling sporadically into his green-blue eyes. He was of average height and had typically English skin, pale with a hint of sunburn. Yet there was something very charismatic about him that elevated what could sound average on paper into far better in the flesh. He also had a slim but strong-looking body.

'We're being rude,' he said, formally offering Jessica his hand to shake. 'Welcome to *The Bradley Mackintosh Show*. It's very nice to have you on the team, even if you have already fallen under the spell of Mr Mike Connor. In fact, we're all having drinks later, so why don't you come and we can fill you in on a few things? Drum some of that eagerness to please out of you?'

'Um, well, maybe,' said Jessica, unsure how to respond, but relieved that Paul, who was obviously a main player in the office, had decided to be nice to her after all. At this rate, she was pretty sure the only thing she'd be able to face after work was her bed, so didn't want to commit. 'I'll see how I go, though I tend not to drink much really.'

Paul rolled his eyes and shrugged at Kerry before strolling off, as if to say 'I tried, but what can you do?'

Jessica sighed. She had a lot to learn and if she was going to survive in this office she'd better start learning it quick. So far, her two very brief encounters with Paul had made her stomach churn, and not in a good way. In a way that was warning her to steer clear of him and his quick-witted tongue. He clearly didn't suffer fools gladly, something that, due to the cultural differences between her and her new colleagues, she was probably appearing to be. This she could cope with, but if he ever teased her again about being American she'd have to say something. Still, he was obviously fond of Kerry, so maybe he was OK. Maybe he just did a good impression of being an asshole.

'You going to Sue's drinks later?' asked Luke nonchalantly, to no one in particular.

'Who, me?' said Kerry, and Luke nodded, shrugging at the same time.

'Course I am, why?'

'Just wondered,' said Luke. 'Thought you might have some more Internet dates lined up, that's all.'

Kerry looked daggers at him. 'Don't you bloody start. Even if I did, I'm hardly likely to give you any more rope to hang me with. I'll leave that to my new assistant, thanks.'

Jessica looked up, startled.

'Joking,' said Kerry quickly. 'Anyway, if you must know, I'm giving up on all that malarkey for a while. I've decided to let true love find me.'

She winked at Jessica as she said this, indicating that she might not be telling the entire truth and Jessica giggled. Luke nodded and walked away, looking as if he'd hardly even registered the answer, but Jessica noticed that the back of his neck had gone pink. Suddenly she wondered if the intuitive Kerry might not be quite so perceptive after all, or at least not when it came to reading signs that were pointing her way.

'Right,' said Kerry, her manner switching to businesslike and efficient. 'Can we *please* get on with some bloody work?'

12

That evening Jessica returned to her room after yet another long workout in the hotel gym. As anticipated, her first day had been so gruelling that the last thing she'd felt like was going for a drink. Still, given that she'd never even met 'Sue', it wasn't like she'd be missed and, besides, she needed to make the most of the gym before she moved into Pam's at the weekend, something they'd now definitely agreed on. She headed for the shower.

A short while later Jessica emerged from the steamy fug of the bathroom to find her cell phone beeping away at her. She had four missed calls, though before she'd had time to check who they were from, it rang again. 'Hello?' she answered.

'Jess? It's Dulcie. Where are you? I've been trying you for ages. Edward told Dad you've gone away. Why didn't you tell me you were going?'

Finally, Jessica thought. Finally she'd stopped yabbering long enough to realize she hadn't seen or heard from her 'best friend' in nearly three whole weeks.

'I did try to tell you, a few times actually.'

'Well, where are you?' Dulcie huffed.

'London,' she replied, unable to prevent a happy grin from spreading across her face.

'What are you doing there? Are you having a vacation? I thought you hated shopping trips?'

'I'm not on a shopping trip,' stated Jessica firmly, reaching over for the fluffy robe that was hanging on the back of the bathroom door and manoeuvring herself into it, before lying down on the bed and wriggling into the big, square pillows. No matter how strange things with Dulcie had been lately, she was excited to finally be able to fill her in on what was happening in her life. 'I'm actually hoping to be here for a while,' she began. 'Remember at your drinks how I told you I left my job at the gallery and split up with Shawn? Well, all in all I really felt like I needed a change. To be honest with you, I'd been feeling unhappy for a while and –'

'Can I ask you something?' Dulcie interrupted.

'Sure.'

'Has you leaving got anything to do with me marrying Kevin? Because if it has, I would understand. I mean, it would be natural, right?'

Wrong, thought Jessica, experiencing familiar stirrings of irritation. Since when did everything have to come back to her getting married? And she hoped Dulcie wasn't suggesting she might be jealous, because she couldn't be more wrong. Marriage was something she never planned on doing, given that she was completely against the whole idea of it.

'My trip has nothing to do with you getting married. Honestly. Though what I will say is that I think we want different things from life these days.'

To this Dulcie said nothing, and Jessica felt like screaming with frustration.

'What? I swear to you I am not jealous,' she said, spelling it out.

'Oh, I'm still focusing on the "what we both want out of

life" comment,' Dulcie said, 'which is interesting because ever since you screwed up our one chance to be something by turning down *Daddy's Girls* I've been waiting to find out what better idea you might have. But if running off to England and abandoning me right when I need you the most is it then, frankly, I'm a little disappointed. I mean, you're supposed to be my best friend but ever since I told you I was engaged you've been acting weird.'

'That's not true,' said Jessica.

'Is so,' retorted Dulcie. 'You obviously have something against Kevin and I just wish you'd admit it.'

'I don't have anything against Kevin,' replied Jessica truthfully. 'But maybe I don't get why you feel the need to get married so young. You've only known him a year, so how do you know you're doing the right thing?'

'Because I love him!' screamed Dulcie, somewhat hysterically.

'Oh, well, that's OK then,' said Jessica, who was starting to feel scared she might say something that would be hard to take back. She swallowed. 'Look, all I'm saying is why the rush? Is being in love really enough? Look at my parents, for crissakes. Everyone seems to be of the opinion that they were madly in love and look how shitty that turned out.'

'That's what it always comes back to with you, isn't it?' stated Dulcie, sounding disappointed and fed up. 'Don't you understand? Of course nothing is guaranteed one hundred per cent. No one knows how anything is going to pan out. Kevin could turn round and tell me he's gay. I could get run over tomorrow. Or we could get married and be very, very happy, but how will we know unless we take a chance?'

'It's not just that,' said Jessica. 'You've changed, Dulcie. You've gotten so obsessed with the wedding you seem to have completely missed the part about how unhappy I've been. And *that's* the reason I'm in London, only you've been too wrapped up in freaking napkins and tie pins to notice.' Jessica scrunched her face up in an effort not to cry. This was horrible, but she had to stay in control of what she was saying. 'I miss you, Dulcie, and I am happy that you're getting married, but what's happened to you?'

'Nothing's happened to me,' she said quietly.

'Look,' Jessica said, 'if I haven't been totally supportive then I'm sorry. Kevin's a lovely guy and I really hope it does work out for the two of you. At the same time, though, your wedding isn't the only thing going on in the world and you can't expect everyone to put their lives on hold till the big day.'

'But I'm not asking *everyone*,' insisted Dulcie and in that awful instance Jessica could tell that her friend had started to cry.

Jessica sighed and, blinking back her own tears, tried to make head or tail of what was going on here. There had to be more to this than met the eye. 'OK,' she said patiently, rubbing her face vigorously. 'I've admitted that I've been a bit freaked out about things, so now it's your turn to tell me what's going on. Because I know you can't really have transformed into some awful clichéd Bridezilla-type person. So, please, just talk to me?'

And finally, after months and months of strangeness, Dulcie did.

'Oh, Jess,' she gulped down the phone in a tone so heartbreaking it quite took Jessica's breath away. 'I miss my mom. I miss her so much and getting married without her is so, so hard,' she finished, now breaking down completely, sobbing her heart out.

Loretta had died when Dulcie was twelve, a terrible day that Jessica still found hard to think about even now. Despite a long illness leading up to it, none of them had been even remotely prepared for the end. When it had arrived Vincent had been utterly devastated, completely floored, and so wrapped up in his own grief that he'd found it hard to be as present for Dulcie as she'd needed him to be. As a result the two girls had ended up clinging to each other more than ever during those tricky teenage years. They'd lived in each other's pockets and now, partly through her own hang-ups, Jessica felt she'd let her down. Not just as a friend, but as a sister, or even a mom of sorts. God, relationships could be so complicated.

Jessica felt dreadful. Suddenly everything about Dulcie's recent behaviour wasn't just explained, it was also excused. Not having her mom around to help pick out her dress, and to decide everything with, must make what should be such a happy time so horribly bittersweet.

'Oh, Dulcie,' said Jessica, wishing she was back in the States so she could give her friend a much-needed hug. 'I'm so, so sorry.'

'That's OK,' wailed Dulcie down the phone. 'It's not your fault, it's mine. I've been putting so much pressure on you to be something you're not. It's just, I suppose you're the closest thing I've got to a sister, or in some ways . . . you know . . . you look after me, Jess. And I know I'm young to be getting married, but I just want a family of my own.'

'I know,' said Jessica, who by now was crying just as hard as her friend. She cleared her throat and took a deep breath. There were some things in life that were simply more important than finding out who you were. 'I'll come home. I could fly in the morning and be back by tomorrow.'

'No,' said Dulcie firmly. To her own surprise she started to giggle, spluttering through the tears. The relief of finally having said out loud what she'd hardly dared to admit even to herself was overwhelming. 'Of course you have to stay, silly. I want you to and I want you to have an adventure. You deserve one and, besides, I need to pull myself together . . .' Her voice cracked again and Jessica's heart felt like doing the same. 'I love you, Jess, and I'm really sorry if I've been a bitch.'

'You haven't,' said Jessica. 'Slightly nutty perhaps, a bit OTT about things maybe, but not a bitch and, besides, you've had good reason.' A stray tear escaped, which she wiped away, still feeling guilty.

'Hey, if you're going to be there for ages "finding yourself" maybe I should come and see you in London? Have a break from thinking about the wedding all the time?' said Dulcie suddenly in an inspired tone Jessica knew only too well.

She swallowed, instantly filled with unease. This was her trip and she felt rather possessive of it. Like a small child who didn't want to share.

'OK, you're so obviously not into that idea,' said Dulcie.

'No, no, I am,' rushed Jessica, desperate to avoid another row. 'But maybe give me a while to settle in, yeah? I just really want to see if I can do things on my own for a bit, you know? I think it would be good for me.'

'OK,' agreed Dulcie. 'But once you're settled I am so there, just try and stop me.'

Jessica grinned as she realized that having her best friend there for a bit would actually be fun. 'Great, and we could even make your visit into a hen weekend, one just for you and me,' she suggested.

'Cool,' agreed Dulcie.

Then Jessica couldn't resist adding, 'I flew here economy, you know.'

'No way!' exclaimed her friend, shocked to the core. 'Are you OK?'

'I survived,' laughed Jessica.

'Hey, you'd better make it back for your dad's party, by the way. Dad said Mr G's climbing the walls without you.'

'Of course,' said Jessica, making a mental note to tell Kerry as soon as possible that she needed time off in September while feeling thankful that at last it seemed she had her friend back.

13

Jessica's second day in *The Bradley Mackintosh Show* office continued in much the same vein as day one. That is to say, it was scary, nerve-racking and a struggle to keep up with what was going on as she tried to acclimatize to her workmates' way of doing things. Making head or tail of their quick-fire banter required all her concentration and that, coupled with having to be on guard about everything she said, meant that by lunchtime she felt like she needed a holiday.

As a result, when everybody set off for the canteen Jessica decided to hang back for a minute so that she could email Dulcie, gather her thoughts and take a literal deep breath.

Had she known that by doing so she was providing her workmates with the perfect opportunity to have a good gossip about her, she might not have bothered.

'There's something about her that doesn't quite ring true,' Natasha was saying to the group.

'What are you on about?' said Vanessa in her thick Scouse accent. 'You just don't like her because she's an attractive girl and you don't like the competition.'

'It's not that,' insisted Natasha. 'She's not all that anyway. Or at least she wouldn't be if she wasn't so . . . shiny.'

'What?' said Kerry. 'Jessica's got great skin; it's not shiny at all.'

'I'm not talking about her skin,' said Natasha, struggling to find the words to express what she did mean. 'I'm talking about her overall persona, I suppose. She just looks a bit too fresh to me, sort of "done" in the same way that certain celebs do, but only because you know they have a team of people whose jobs it is to make that person look and feel their absolute best. In the same way Jennifer Aniston looks like she wouldn't be capable of having BO no matter how hard she exercised. Or have greasy hair. I mean, has anyone else noticed how expensive her clothes are?'

'They aren't that flashy,' interjected Luke, who was more engrossed in flicking bits of rice salad up Kerry's sleeve.

'I know she's not "flashy", but her T-shirts aren't exactly Top Shop's finest and I know for a fact her jeans cost well over a hundred quid.'

Vanessa rolled her eyes.

'What?' said Natasha indignantly.

'Even if you are right, and she's got a bit of money, why should it bother you? I reckon you're just pissed off because our Paul told Luke she's got a nice arse.'

'Bollocks,' snapped Natasha before clamming up, because just then she'd spotted Jessica herself waving over to the group as she entered the canteen. Natasha at least had the good grace to wave back, albeit unenthusiastically, before turning back to Vanessa to say something else.

Over the other side of the room, Jessica sighed. She got the distinct impression she was being discussed, but knew how desperately important it was to ingratiate herself with these people in order to survive. She armed herself with a plastic tray. She felt like she was back in high school, the only difference being that back then *she* was the one people wanted to impress, not the other way round.

As she stood in line she noticed Paul Fletcher strolling casually into the canteen, hands in pockets. She smiled across at him, but her smile soon faded when she realized that, unlike everyone else, he wasn't intending to get to the back of the line (or 'queue' as the Brits liked to call it). Instead he bypassed the long, slow-moving line completely, grabbed a sandwich, a drink and a packet of crisps from the section near the till and barged ahead, seemingly unconcerned that people were tutting at him. Only as he was paying did he spot Jessica.

'All right?' he called over to her. 'What are you having?'

'Not sure,' she answered truthfully, having completely lost her appetite. Of all her workmates, he was the one who made her nerves most jittery.

'Oh, well, come and sit with us anyway,' offered Paul magnanimously, in a way that made her feel rather patronized.

Feeling about as clunky and inept as she ever had in her life, Jessica nodded feebly while wondering what to do. In the end she gave up on lunch altogether, deposited her tray back where she'd found it and followed him across the room.

There wasn't much space round the table, but Paul squashed in next to Kerry. 'Budge up, fatty,' he said playfully.

'Fuck off,' said Kerry, her mouth full of lamb curry. 'I need comfort food after the date I had last night. I'm only just about getting over the stress of it.'

Jessica had reached the table by this point, but there was no room and she felt too shy to ask anyone to move up, so ended up hovering in the background, hoping that someone would eventually notice and let her in.

'Thought you'd given up on dating,' said Luke.

'A girl can change her mind,' she said, giving him a ridiculously over the top wink.

'Tell Paul what he was wearing,' said Natasha, who had spotted Jessica but didn't feel particularly inclined to include her, so didn't.

'What?' said Paul. 'What could the poor bastard possibly have been wearing that was quite so terrible?'

Having already been regaled with the facts, Natasha, Vanessa and Isy giggled in anticipation.

Kerry swallowed her mouthful of curry before announcing: 'Cufflinks in the shape of wine bottles.'

The group all laughed and Jessica wondered how to react given that she was standing awkwardly on the outskirts of their conversation. Joining in felt absurd, but not as ridiculous as standing there like a self-conscious lemon. Thankfully at that moment Luke noticed her.

'Oi, girls, let Jess in,' he said. 'She hasn't got a seat.'

'Oh, sorry, babe,' said Kerry immediately. 'Here, squeeze in next to me. Vanessa, move your ruddy great big bag out the way.'

'Thanks,' said Jessica, grateful to them both. When Vanessa flashed her a warm smile she felt borderline tearful. She hated feeling so pathetic but when you're used to being in the inner circle, becoming the outsider was an alien experience that was tough to get used to and frightening to boot.

'So is the line-up still the same for this week?' asked Paul, slurping back his drink.

'For a change, yes,' replied Kerry. 'I think it's going to be a good show, actually, and with Mike away there won't be anyone breathing down my neck either.'

'Thank God,' said Paul with feeling.

'Anyway,' said Kerry, 'guess what I've got in my handbag, everybody?'

'Two severed hands and wrists, complete with naff, wine-bottle-shaped cufflinks?' asked Luke.

'Better than that,' she declared, bending down to rummage in her bag. 'This week's copy of *Heat*!'

The other girls all whooped with delight, flinging themselves across the table in order to get a better look with such enthusiasm that, for the first time that day, Jessica's laugh was completely natural.

'Ooh, fantastic, look at her,' said Vanessa with relish, her hazel eyes dancing as she studied some unfortunate, vaguely famous person who'd been snapped looking pale and dishevelled. 'Doesn't she look a right bloody state?'

Jessica's face fell ever so slightly as she tried to make head or tail of what Vanessa had just said, so strong was her accent.

'To be fair,' piped up Paul, 'she has just walked out of hospital; I can't say I'd appreciate a camera being shoved in my face straight after an operation.'

The girls ignored him. Bitching over the latest copy of *Heat* was a pastime you weren't allowed to partake in half-heartedly.

'She's pretty,' said Isy, pointing at a picture of a haughty but beautiful-looking young heiress stumbling out of a nightclub.

'Pretty stupid,' said Paul, getting into the spirit of things. 'I'd love to see her doing a proper day's work and see how special she thought she was then.'

'Well said,' agreed Vanessa. 'Life's bloody unfair, isn't it?'

'Hang on a minute,' said Kerry, laughing at how decisively Paul had dismissed the girl as being useless. 'I know she's had a jammy start in life, but it's not her fault, is it? Just because her dad's loaded doesn't automatically make her a bad person.'

'No, but I bet you it makes her a spoiled, stupid one,' said Paul.

'Well, that's just such a knee-jerk reaction,' said Jessica forcefully, before she'd had a chance to even register what was about to come out of her mouth. Everyone fell silent, looking to Paul to see how he would react.

'I don't think so,' he said calmly, regarding her coolly.

Jessica blushed to her roots but felt compelled to push her point. 'You don't even know her, so all you're basing your opinion on is what you know about her father.'

'Her father who is a multi-millionaire,' retorted Paul.

Jessica looked to Kerry, who was listening intently but clearly didn't plan on getting involved. Everyone else was suddenly taking a keen interest in their food. Jessica swallowed.

'But so what if her dad's rich?'

'So it doesn't take a genius to work out that, judging by the way she's staggering out of that club, she's led a pretty pampered, cosseted existence. *So* I happen to think I can imagine exactly what she's like, and while I would love to live in the idealistic world you clearly inhabit in Hampstead, I don't. I live in the real one.'

'Meaning what?' Jessica asked hotly, outraged by how rude he was being.

'Meaning that Helena Davies will undoubtedly have been spoiled by daddy so will have turned out a right horror, which might not be her fault but is just the way it is.'

'You're very judgemental, aren't you? I mean, you haven't even seen where I live in Hampstead.'

'I can imagine.'

'I'm staying with my aunt,' Jessica continued, wondering why she cared quite so much what Paul thought anyway, 'and as it happens her house is very ordinary; very nice, but ordinary.'

'You don't have to justify your existence to me,' he replied.

Jessica opened her mouth to argue but something about the way Paul's eyes were glittering prevented her from doing so.

'Still, Helena Davies is wearing great shoes,' added Isy, giving Jessica's knee the slightest squeeze under the table.

'Guys, it's nearly two,' said Natasha, who remained unmoved by the exchange. 'We'd better get going.'

Reluctantly, the group began to clear up their debris and one by one got up and dragged themselves in the general direction of the lifts and *The Bradley Mackintosh Show* production office two floors above. Jessica hung back. She was still reeling from Paul's outburst and felt humiliated and regretful about picking a fight. From now on she'd be avoiding him as much as possible, seeing as every time he opened his contemptuous mouth she ended up feeling incredibly uncomfortable.

'Sorry about that,' she apologized to Kerry, who was the last to gather up her things.

'Don't be silly,' her new boss replied kindly. 'You're entitled to say whatever you like, and don't worry about Paul, his bark's worse than his bite. He's actually a lovely guy when you get to know him.'

Jessica nodded, not at all convinced. From what she'd seen of him so far, he was a judgemental dick. Her stomach grumbled. She'd never make it through the day on an empty stomach so she'd have to risk salmonella and purchase one of the limp salads no one else had liked the look of. She trotted off to find one.

Meanwhile Kerry went to fold up her magazine and, as she did so, the small bit of writing that accompanied the photograph of the rich heiress caught her eye.

> Helena Davies looking somewhat worse for wear after celebrating raising over half a million pounds for aid work in Namibia. Her father, property developer Damien Davies, has allegedly threatened to cut her off without a penny if she gives any more of her inheritance away to charity. Her leopard-skin shoes are Olivia Morris.

Kerry decided to find out if Helena Davies had an agent straight after the meeting. Ironically, she might just make a very good guest. As she packed away her magazine and followed her colleagues out of the canteen, Kerry gave a wry smile. She'd met enough celebrities to know by now that Paul was wrong. If you only took people at face value you were making a huge mistake. People were never how you expected them to be when you only had an impression of them via the media, and were only equipped with a handful of facts. Besides, in Helena's case, she could hardly be blamed for who her parents were, surely one of the few things in life no one has any control over.

No, like Jessica she knew that you should never judge a celebrity, or indeed anyone else, by their cover. Unless their cover incorporated wine-bottle-shaped cufflinks, of course, in which case it was probably fair game.

14

Wednesday started off grey, cloudy and chilly enough to need a jacket, though such inconsistencies in the weather were still a huge novelty for Jessica who had woken up eager to crack on with her working day. Being part of the rat race was exciting, being part of the British rat race even more so, and she got a huge kick out of travelling into work with the masses. Just an ordinary girl. As soon as she sat down at her desk, however, she was reminded that in many ways she was far from ordinary and that pretending she was might be hard to keep up.

'Morning,' Kerry chirruped as soon as she walked in the door. 'We're going to have to bump off one of this week's guests to another week because I got a call this morning and someone fantastic has become available.'

'Great,' said Jessica enthusiastically. 'Who?'

'Leonora Whittingston! You know, the comedy actress? You must. She's huge in the States.'

Jessica blanched and froze to the spot. Was this a joke or a test? Had they found out who she was already?

'What's the matter?' asked Kerry. 'Why do you look so freaked out?'

'Morning,' said Paul, barging into the office, saving Jessica from having to answer and providing her with a much-needed moment to gather her thoughts.

'Morning, Paul. You're going to hate me because you'll

need to rewrite a few links. I've just booked Leonora Whittingston for tomorrow's show,' announced Kerry proudly.

'Oh, she'll be great,' said Paul, sounding impressed, 'but you're right, I do hate you, especially if you drop Jeff Bates, whose introduction I love.'

'Even if you do say so yourself,' said Luke.

'I think I'm going to have to,' replied Kerry apologetically. 'Obviously I can't drop Kate Templeton and I really don't want to get rid of Alan Carr because I've been trying to get him on for ages, so that only leaves Jeff Bates. Though I reckon he's a bit of a twat anyway.'

'He is,' agreed Isy. 'I was at his birthday party at Movida the other night and I don't reckon anyone there was actually his mate. It was full of freeloaders . . . like me.'

The words 'birthday party' reminded Jessica that she needed to ask Kerry about getting time off in September. It was three months away, but the earlier she got it sorted out the better. Maybe she should ask if she could have tomorrow off too while she was at it, so she didn't have to see Leonora?

'Um, Kerry,' she began, feeling mildly panicky about everything, 'can I have a quick word?'

'Go for it,' Kerry said, winding her curly hair up on top of her head and securing it with a biro. Several sets of ears tuned in – a huge downside to an open-plan office, though at least most tried not to look like they were listening. Unlike Natasha, who stopped typing and sat back in her chair with her arms folded.

'I need to go home for a week in September. Is that OK?'

'Er, I don't think so,' said Kerry, looking surprised. 'You've only just started and because the show's rolling, time off has to be booked massively in advance. We can't have loads of the team away at the same time, which is why Mike gets to go away now while other poor sods have their summer holidays in November. Besides, I think there are a couple of people already going away in September for the Ibiza closing parties,' she finished, clearly assuming their discussion was at an end.

Jessica felt like she'd been slapped in the face. The day was going from bad to worse. How could she not go to her father's party? It would break her dad's heart if she wasn't there. Plus she had to see Dulcie. This was a nightmare. 'Right,' she said, feeling vaguely nauseous. Being told she couldn't do something was a strange sensation, as was not automatically having her own way. Funnily enough, in all the jobs she'd had over the years, all of which her father had got himself involved with, time off had never been a problem.

'So when does Mike get back again?' she asked, trying but failing to sound casual.

'Monday after next. Why? Thinking of asking him yourself?' said Kerry, finally registering Jessica's dismayed expression. 'I mean, you can give it a go if you want, but I don't think you'll get a different answer. Was it something special you were going back for?'

'My dad's sixty-fifth,' she replied, hoping that would sway things.

Kerry looked sympathetic, but only mildly. 'Oh, well, not such a big deal then. God, poor old Julian – you know, director Julian? He missed his sister's wedding because he was working on a live show and in order to be able to do the series he had to commit to doing every single one.'

'That's awful,' said Jessica, aghast.

'That's showbiz,' Kerry said bluntly. 'Now, let's get on. We need to figure out what we're going to do about our unwanted guest. Delicacy and diplomacy are the order of the day, I think.'

Not half as much as they will be tomorrow, Jessica thought, when Leonora Whittingston, her mother's best friend and her very own godmother, was due to be appearing on the show.

An hour or so later, Jessica was just starting to debate which disguises she might be able to get away with (a yashmak and a crash helmet being her front-runners), when Leonora changed her mind about coming on. Kerry was livid but Jessica was over the moon and wanted to hug her godmother. In fact, she would next time she saw her. Now all she had to do was to help Kerry find someone else to fill in.

'Bloody flaky bastard celebs,' ranted Kerry, her mood deteriorating rapidly. 'Do they know how much hassle they create by changing their infuriating minds all the time? What am I going to do if I can't get someone at this short notice? Now precious Jeff Bates has got his knickers in a huffy twist and can't be persuaded to grace us with his dull presence either, so at this point any suggestions are welcome,' she announced to a slightly scared office.

Jessica racked her brains. She desperately wanted to help, but having already put the word out to every agent under the sun she was pretty sure there wasn't one decent possibility left in town, apart from her godmother. Short of phoning Leonora herself and begging her to reconsider as a favour, there wasn't much she could do, and that simply wasn't an option.

'How about Helena Davies, the heiress from the magazine?' Jessica suggested hesitantly. 'You saw the stuff I found out about her yesterday. I reckon she'd be amazing and you've already sounded out her agent.'

'Mmm,' mused Kerry, and Jessica could tell her mind was working overtime. 'She's not really a big enough name. Then again, she'd be a damn sight better than an empty sofa and there's no way we can eke the others out for an entire show. I'll think about it,' she said, verbally dismissing Jessica so she could mull over the implications of such a big gamble.

Taking the hint, Jessica got on with some work and only looked up when a sixth sense told her someone was staring. It was Paul and when she returned his gaze he got up and padded over to her desk.

'Trying to make a point?' he said lightly, his eyes almost daring her as usual. They were such an amazing blue-green colour. In certain lights they almost looked silver.

'What do you mean?' she said, her stomach churning. This, it seemed, was her default response to him.

'I mean, I don't think you're doing Kerry any favours by persuading her to have Helena Davies on the show, when all anyone knows about her is that she's a socialite with a rich daddy. Our viewers deserve a bit more credit.'

'But we did some research and actually —' began Jessica.

'Look, it's not really any of my business,' he said, looking over Jessica's shoulder at her screen. 'I just don't want to see Kerry get into trouble, especially when you've got an email there from Lisa Wright's agent.'

'She's the soap actress, right?' questioned Jessica, unconsciously inhaling. Paul may have been deeply aggravating and volatile but he smelled gorgeous.

'Yes. Not a very interesting one, but at least people have vaguely heard of her.'

'I haven't,' she protested.

'Er, well, you wouldn't have, would you? Given that you're from the States,' he pointed out before strolling off.

'What was he on about?' asked Kerry, looking up.

'Nothing,' said Jessica, whose heart was pounding. Why did he have to be so spiky?

'OK,' said Kerry, leaning right back in her chair and stretching. 'I'm officially starting to panic now, so if we don't hear from anyone else soon, I think I will book Helena Davies and just pray your hunch about her is right. I'll ring Mike first though. Then if it backfires at least I can say I warned him.'

'Good idea,' said Jessica, her mind performing somersaults. She knew she should mention Lisa Wright's availability, for it was probably up to Kerry and not her to decide if she was a better option or not, and yet for rather shadowy, ulterior, proving-a-point-to-Paul-type motives, she chose to keep quiet, watching mutely as Kerry picked up the phone.

'Mike, hi, it's Kerry here. Can I pick your brains for a second?'

'Kerry, hi, what can I do you for?' answered Mike, who had only arrived at his Tuscan villa twenty minutes previously but was already wishing he was back at work. It was boiling hot, Diane was spoiling for a fight, the baby was screaming, his toddler daughter was demanding he blow up her water wings and he was naked but couldn't find his trunks.

Unable to hear what Kerry was saying over the children's din, he shooed his daughter away and signalled to his wife to take the baby.

Seething with resentment, Diane frowned. She'd literally only just off-loaded Ava and had wanted a minute to find everybody's flip-flops. Grace hadn't stopped whinging for the last hour and Mike was doing bugger all to help. It had been a long journey and Diane felt sweaty, intensely stressed and desperate to air her swollen feet. She'd been really looking forward to having an extra pair of hands to help on this holiday, but if those hands weren't going to do anything except check their ruddy emails on their sodding iPhone there was a chance she'd lose the plot. They all needed to plunge into the pool and cool off, but she couldn't find everything and see to two children at the same time. Did Mike really have to take a work call the second they'd arrived? Wanting to avoid a fight, Diane took a deep breath and retrieved a wailing Ava from her naked husband, just in time to see her screwing up her face in concentration. The smell that followed was horrific.

'Muuuummy. Want go pool now,' whined Grace. 'Hurry up.'

'Just give me a minute, will you?' snapped Diane. 'I can't do everything round here. I need to change Ava's nappy, so wait until your father *gets off the phone*.' She mouthed this last bit in Mike's direction, who flapped at her as though she were an annoying mosquito – at which point Diane experienced a strong desire to knee her husband in his dangerously exposed balls.

'Well, I can't pretend I'm one hundred per cent happy,' he was saying, pacing around, hand on hip, just as if he were in the office. 'And, frankly, if this Helena Davies turns out to be anything other than a blinding guest, it'll be your neck on the line, Kerry, not mine.'

Back in London, Kerry gulped but, sticking to her guns, spent a further few minutes reassuring him it would all be fine before concluding their conversation.

As Kerry recounted what had been said to the entire office, Jessica listened intently before quickly deleting all the emails from Lisa Wright's agent from her in-box.

Now Helena Davies simply had to be a great guest because, apart from anything else, Jessica couldn't bear the thought of Paul Fletcher saying 'I told you so'.

15

Angelica Dupree was in a quandary. She was in LA for the week filming pick-up shots for her new film. Word on the movie grapevine had got out that her most recent performance was fabulous. The word 'Oscar' was even being bandied about. Yet right now work was the furthest thing from her mind.

Picking up her cigarettes and lighter, she slid open the glass doors that led out on to the balcony of her penthouse suite. Surveying the sun-drenched Beverly Hills landscape, she tried to relax but it was no good. Recently Graydon had started dropping hints about taking their relationship to the next level, which had triggered an unexpected but urgent desire to speak to her ex-husband. She hadn't spoken to Edward directly in years, having always made arrangements concerning Jessica via his agent Jill Cunningham, but with marriage looming it felt like the time had come to set things straight with husband number one.

She'd never forgiven Edward for not replying to the hundreds of letters she'd written him after she'd left, but she wanted to lay the ghost of their relationship to rest. Before getting married again she needed closure. So, after days of procrastination, she'd finally decided she was damn well going to ring him. In a minute. Happy to have reached a decision, but slightly confused by how she'd got there, Angelica dragged hard on her cigarette.

Meanwhile, not far away at his home in Malibu, Edward was just finishing up a meeting with agent Jill, his assistant Clare, and Brendan, the producer from his upcoming movie *Soldier*.

'Well, it's been enlightening, Brendan, and thanks so much for coming all the way out here,' Jill was saying as she saw him out.

'I'll be in touch,' said Brendan, halfway out the door already, squinting in the bright sunshine. 'And I just hope Edward comes to his senses about our leading lady,' he added quietly, so only Jill could hear.

'Oh, he will,' she said firmly, waving goodbye.

Edward stood scowling in the background and as Jill shut the door his assistant, Clare, decided to make herself scarce. 'If you don't need me, I think I might just go and type up these notes,' she told Edward.

'Good idea. Thanks, love,' he replied as she scuttled off.

Jill took a deep breath. Now Brendan had left the building, she could tell her oldest client was about to give her a rocketing.

Sure enough . . .

'Is he out of his fucking mind?' Edward blustered. 'I simply cannot and will not act opposite a twenty-one-year-old love interest. Juliana – whatever her name is – is five years younger than my own daughter, for Christ's sake. I'll look like Gary bloody Glitter.'

'Calm down,' said Jill, following Edward as he strode angrily through the hallway in the direction of the kitchen.

'Juliana Sabatini is going to be huge and, I'm telling you now, in a few months' time you'll thank me for standing my ground over this one. I agree she's a bit young, but they wouldn't have cast her if they didn't think you could pull it off. And, besides, would I ever let you look foolish?'

'No,' conceded Edward huffily, though he was still fuming inside. 'But even you have to admit, Jill, the script's a heap of crap. Trite at best. Ah, Consuela, there you are,' he said, marching into his vast kitchen. 'I'm peckish. Any chance of one of your legendary lobster sandwiches, preferably with lots of mayo?'

'Coming right up, Mr G,' she replied.

'Why don't you have a nice egg white omelette instead?' suggested Jill bravely, ever mindful of the ten pounds she'd promised the studio her client would drop before shooting began.

'If I fancied a plate of something deeply pointless and unsatisfying I would have it, but I don't,' said Edward angrily, fetching himself a can of Coke from the fridge.

Ignoring Consuela, who was trying not to laugh, Jill stared at Edward reproachfully.

'Oh, for God's sake,' he said wearily, holding his hands up in a gesture of surrender before exchanging his can of Coke for a Diet Coke instead and going to sit at the breakfast bar.

'Look,' said Jill, taking in his sullen expression. 'I know you're not happy with every aspect of this movie, but you have to trust me. Remember how concerned you were about the script for *Fifty Guns* and how did that turn out in the end?'

'Pretty well,' muttered Edward.

'That's right, so try not to worry. Leave Brendan to me. By the time I've finished, the script will be up to scratch, I promise. As for the Juliana issue, this is Hollywood, where a handsome man like you can be with whomever he likes. In fact, the younger and prettier the better as far as the audience is concerned. Even if we all know that in the real world a man's far better off with a more mature woman,' she finished, a touch flirtatiously, just as Edward let out the most enormous gassy burp, having knocked his soda back far too fast.

'Sorry about that,' he said, not registering what she'd said as his phone had just started ringing.

Consuela had heard, however, and as she delivered Edward's sandwich to him, her shoulders were heaving. Jill's cheeks flamed red.

Oblivious to everything, Edward answered the phone crossly, irritated that a phone call was coming between him and what looked like a triumph of a sandwich.

'Hello?'

'Hello, Edward,' said a familiar and yet distant voice from the past that he instantly recognized and yet couldn't quite comprehend he was really hearing. 'It's me . . .'

For a few seconds Edward simply stared gormlessly into space before sitting bolt upright as if he'd been stung. Then, offering no explanation to either Consuela or Jill, who were both staring at him, he leapt down from the breakfast bar, abandoning his snack altogether in order to take the call in another room.

'Hang on a minute,' he managed as he raced through the house towards the privacy of his study, holding his phone aloft and staring at it in the same way Superman might regard a lump of Kryptonite. Finally, upon reaching his study, he locked the door behind him and cleared his throat. 'Angelica, is that you?'

'*Oui, c'est moi,*' came the reply and Edward was instantly transported back in time, overwhelmed by memories, both good and bad.

'How are you?' he enquired, immediately feeling ridiculous for having done so.

'I'm . . . OK,' said Angelica. 'How are you?'

'I'm fine, I suppose . . . but . . . look, what do you want?' he asked bluntly, changing tack completely. Exchanging social niceties with someone who had caused him so much pain simply didn't feel appropriate or natural, so he cut to the chase.

'To talk . . . I don't know, I'm sorry. I just wanted to try and talk about . . . everything.'

Hearing her voice, something he'd once longed for, was agonizing and Edward felt as though someone had just lobbed a hand grenade into his life. Why now, he wondered, as his brain whirred away? Why after all this time was she ringing out of the blue when he'd prayed that she would do so for years and years?

Just then, someone knocked hard at the door. It was obviously Jill coming to find out what was going on, but he ignored her. He swallowed, wishing he'd had some kind of warning that Angelica was going to ring. That way he could have figured out what to say, how to be. As it was, he felt utterly thrown. 'Well, I'm not sure we really have anything to say,' he stuttered. 'I mean, it would have been nice to have talked about, ooh – twenty-odd years ago, but I think the moment may have passed now, don't you?'

'But at least I tried to . . .'

'Tried to what?' he demanded to know.

'I should go,' said Angelica, her voice almost a whisper and Edward felt an instant jolt of emotion. He didn't want her to go, which was horribly unnerving given that he'd spent the last couple of decades convincing himself he loathed her. Yet suddenly it didn't feel like that at all. In truth, it was unbelievably good to hear her voice. More than good. It was like coming home and reminded him not just of everything they'd once had together, but of everything she'd thrown away. What he had thought were old feelings of grief and rage began to unfurl in his belly and now he knew they'd never really gone away. All the hurt and regret had merely been lying dormant inside him, like a sleeping dragon, and he didn't know if he was strong enough to handle dredging up all those feelings again.

Jill banged on the door once more. 'Edward, open up.'

'I don't think we can talk until you've reconciled things with Jessica properly,' Edward said eventually. 'She's grown up not knowing why you left, but deserves to know, Ange. She deserves to know but only you can tell her.'

The familiarity of him calling her 'Ange' made Angelica's heart expand and contract as she experienced a dull ache of longing for the whole sorry situation to be different, but she understood what he was saying. What she didn't understand, however, was why he himself couldn't have helped their daughter to try and make sense of things. 'OK,' she said simply. 'I will talk to Jessica. You are right.'

'Right,' said Edward, blinking furiously. 'And then, you know . . . maybe . . .'

'Maybe . . . what?'

'You know – we could speak . . . maybe . . .'

'Goodbye,' said Angelica before putting down the phone.

Edward shut his eyes, inhaled deeply and put everything he was feeling into a little box somewhere deep inside him. He would be having a good look at it all later on, but not while Jill was there, demanding to know what was going on.

'Edward, what's happening? Let me in.'

As he unlocked the door, an irate Jill practically fell into the room. Having taken one look at Edward's ashen face, however, her tone switched from affronted to one of concern.

'What is it? Tell me, Edward.'

'You won't believe who that was.'

'Try me.'

'Angelica.'

Jill gasped. It was a shock all right and yet, funnily enough, she could believe it only too well.

16

Jessica had always known her first show day would be a big day to get through, but could never have anticipated quite how much would be riding on it. It was half tempting not to show up at all, but she knew she would, if only to avoid letting Kerry down. Though if Helena Davies was a disaster, she might be on her way home whether she liked it or not. However, this was still only her fourth day of gainful employment so she sincerely hoped not because she wasn't done yet. Not by a long shot. She willed things to go well.

Kerry had decided on the running order for the day. Alan Carr would be on first, followed by Helena Davies and finally Kate Templeton.

With Mike away, it was especially important that the day ran smoothly and by three o' clock in the afternoon, when all the guests had arrived and were ensconced safely in their dressing rooms, it was starting to look like it might. Helena Davies had turned out to be far more beautiful in the flesh than she was in photographs and Kerry had already commented that underneath the lights her fantastic bone structure, porcelain skin and auburn hair should make for a pretty devastating combination. Having spent time chatting with her and briefing her about the show, Kerry and Jessica were also delighted and relieved to confirm that, as suspected, there was a lot more to Helena Davies than met the eye.

In the studio, which had been a hive of rehearsal activity all day, they were finally ready to shoot Alan Carr's segment. The four cameramen had their headphones on and were manning their cameras, which meant the director, vision mixer, engineers and sound guys were all in position in the gallery, the nerve centre where it all happened. Once the audience had been revved up into a frenzy by the warm-up man and floor manager, the show got underway. The first interview went very smoothly. Alan Carr was hilarious and as Jessica got into the swing of the day she was surprised to find herself enjoying the chaos. It was only when she suddenly found herself on her way to fetch and escort Helena back to the studio that her nerves returned.

As they walked down the corridor together, Jessica smiled reassuringly at Helena, pleased to see how remarkably calm she looked, though when she went to look again she noticed that her hands were clenched tightly into fists. Paul walked past just at that moment, on his way to the gallery. Without prior warning he tapped Jessica on the shoulder before pulling her towards him so he could whisper in her ear: 'How's Lady Muck then?'

Jessica replied with a filthy look and prayed even harder that Helena Davies would acquit herself well. Paul whispering into her ear in such an intimate way had evoked another feeling too and if she didn't know better she would say she'd got some kind of cheap thrill out of it. She gave herself a shake. It had been a while, that was her problem.

They reached the set with minutes to spare and soon Jessica could hear in her headphones that cameras were ready, Julian was ready and Bradley Mackintosh was good to go. The floor manager started signalling for the studio audience to cheer, which they did with gusto, and then Bradley started reading the introduction that Paul had penned for him.

'And now to my next guest. You will all have heard of course of Damien Davies but you may not be so familiar with his daughter Helena... I'll take it from that awkward silence I'm right, so let's get her on so we can ask her where on earth she's been hiding and what it's like to be the only daughter of one of the richest men in the country. It's a tough non-job but someone's got to do it. Ladies and gentlemen, please welcome Helena Davies.'

Jessica just had time to wish Helena 'good luck' before it was time for her to stride on to set to be judged and assessed by millions of people. Kerry rushed over to join Jessica so they could watch her performance together on a monitor behind the set.

'So, Helena, welcome to the show,' began Bradley once the applause had faded. 'And firstly, may I just say that you are a very beautiful young lady, not that I mean to sound surprised, but if we can just get a picture up of Helena's dad, please?'

In the gallery, Penny, the vision mixer, pressed the appropriate button to bring up a particularly unflattering picture of Helena's father.

Helena laughed. 'Aw, that's a bit mean, Bradley.'

'I know,' he agreed. 'It's not the best, is it? And he's a proper ginger, isn't he, whereas you appear to be more auburn, but then you probably colour your hair a bit, don't you? In fact, I think many of our viewers will be wondering what you do *apart* from go to the hairdressers.'

This got a cheap laugh from the audience, which only

encouraged Bradley further. 'Obviously there's manicures to fit in and probably facials too but, let's face it, other than your "charidee work" you don't actually do anything, do you? Not that I would if I were you either!'

Helena blushed but heroically managed to continue smiling, though Kerry was fuming and Jessica felt equally horrified. Fortunately, however, Helena — having spent her whole life defying expectations — could look after herself.

'Actually, I have been to the hairdressers,' she replied, 'but only because I knew I was coming on telly for the first time ever. Also, I've spent so much of the past year in Africa that my hair had the longest split ends known to man, so it was kind of necessary.'

Jessica exhaled. Now surely Bradley had no other choice than to at least enquire about what she was doing in Africa? She hoped so because Helena was looking like she was seriously regretting coming on at all.

'Right,' said Bradley. 'Africa, of course. Tell us about that then.'

'Well, as you mentioned earlier, I do work with a charity, which probably sounds as if it's a little hobby to give me something to do, but actually it's much, much more to me than that so I just wanted to talk about Namibia and what's going on there really,' she said almost apologetically.

'And we will,' said Bradley. 'It does sound really interesting, and it will probably project you into the limelight. If it does, would you fancy becoming a reality TV star and if so what kind? Could we be seeing you in the jungle soon, or ballroom dancing maybe?'

Helena laughed, albeit through gritted teeth. 'Neither,

thanks. I've never wanted to be on telly. I'd be totally rubbish and not entertaining at all.'

'We-ell . . .' said Bradley, intimating that she wasn't exactly being riveting right this second and getting another cheap laugh out of the audience.

'Look,' said Helena resignedly. She'd already had enough of the vacuous direction this interview was headed. 'I know what people probably think about me. That I'm a spoiled airhead with nothing to say for myself who has never had to work or struggle for anything, but my dad is a down-to-earth northern man who has done his best to keep me grounded. I get the fact that receiving an amazing education and growing up in the lap of luxury is a huge privilege, but I honestly don't want to be on TV just for the sake of it. I really don't.'

Jessica felt a strong pang of empathy for her and prayed that Bradley would start giving her some credit.

'OK,' said Bradley, holding his hands up. 'Maybe you should tell us why you're really here then.'

Helena took a deep breath and Jessica noticed her unclench her hands for the first time since the interview had begun. 'I'm here because the first time I travelled to Namibia I spent the first four days crying so much I could barely think straight. Then, once my initial shock at the poverty and disease I was witnessing had subsided, I realized maybe I should stop feeling guilty about everything I was born into and start trying to do something with it. So that's why I'm here, to raise awareness so that as much money as possible can be raised, specifically for a charity who are trying to reduce the mortality rate of mothers and their newborn babies. It's literally a case of the more people I can reach, the more money we can raise and the more lives we can save.'

Her passionate tone seemed to have won Bradley over and, as he nodded seriously, someone in the audience started to clap slowly. Then someone else joined in and before they knew it the whole front section was wolf-whistling and cheering loudly.

'Wow,' said Bradley. 'So tell us more about this charity of yours then.'

'Well, three years ago, much to my dad's utter horror, I decided to get involved with this charity full time so I moved to Namibia for nine months of the year to live in a village where . . .'

As Helena got into her stride you could have heard a pin drop, both on the studio floor and in the gallery. Kerry breathed a huge sigh of relief before turning to Jessica to give her a conspiratorial wink, at which point she was dismayed to note that her assistant was filling up.

'You OK?' said Kerry.

'Oh, ignore me,' said Jessica, determinedly keeping any tears at bay by blinking hard. 'I'm just being a softie.'

'She is bloody amazing. I can see why she's got to you.'

However, Jessica wasn't so sure she could, for she was feeling both deeply humbled and utterly impressed by Helena Davies. A girl who, like Jessica, had been born into wealth, and yet, unlike Jessica, had chosen to spend both her time and money doing something positive, inspiring and downright useful with it. Yes, Helena Davies had certainly given her a lot to think about, though such introspection would have to wait, for at that moment Jessica noticed Paul lurking in the wings, along with her opportunity to get one up on him. Quickly she composed herself, then headed over in his direction.

What she didn't know, of course, was that Paul, who had already spotted Jessica marching towards him with an unmistakeably triumphant glint in her eye, was also experiencing a pang of something that felt a bit like guilt, only his was for having judged Helena so harshly.

'So,' Jessica said, as she strode up to him, trying hard not to look too victorious. 'Slightly ruins your theory, eh?'

'What theory?' he said, flashing her a reluctant grin.

'The theory that if someone has a rich dad, they must automatically be a dreadful person.'

Paul wrinkled his nose before appraising Jessica coolly for what felt like an age. 'She was a good guest and no one's more surprised than me. Is that enough, or do you really want to make the most of your victory?'

'So it *was* a battle then, was it?' asked Jessica.

Paul opened his mouth to reply, but just then Kerry appeared. 'She was bloody brilliant, wasn't she? Now, Jessica, I'm going to see Helena to her car and then I'll go and make sure everything's OK with Kate Templeton.'

'I'd better leave you guys to it,' said Paul as he sloped off.

Jessica felt rather sorry to see him go. 'So how's Kate?' she asked Kerry, still watching him leave. 'Is she nice?'

'Surprisingly nice, actually,' said Kerry.

'Oh, she is,' said Jessica. 'I mean, people say she is . . .' she added hurriedly, having realized what she was saying.

'Right,' said Kerry, grinning. 'Well, in my experience, actresses are often lovely until something goes wrong, which is when you discover what they're really all about, so let's hope everything continues to run smoothly.

Jessica kept quiet. There was no point in reassuring Kerry that Kate Templeton was definitely one of the good guys. Her dad had described her as a sweet girl who could hardly believe her own luck at having made it. 'Why don't I see Helena off?' she suggested. 'Then you'd be free to go back and see Kate.'

'Brilliant,' said Kerry. 'I keep forgetting I have an assistant. You do make life a lot easier for me.'

Jessica blushed at the compliment.

'OK, well, I'd better dash,' said Kerry, breaking into an urgent sprint.

'No worries,' said Jessica, trying to smother a smile. What could possibly have happened to Kate Templeton in the last ten minutes that her PA and manager couldn't handle, she wondered? And why did everything have to be communicated with such an air of panic? Kerry was by no means the only offender. At one stage she'd heard Luke saying (and for once he wasn't being sarcastic) 'Running all the way' as he'd raced down to the studio floor from the office with some new script pages. While Jessica appreciated that in TV and film time was precious, she could never work out why crews got so worked up about the smallest of things, something she'd first noticed as a child, when visiting her dad on set. One minute she'd be mentioning casually to her dad, or nanny, that she wanted a glass of milk and suddenly the most unbelievable game of Chinese whispers would ensue, with people barking into their Motorolas, panicking. 'Mr Granger's daughter wants some milk. Can we get some milk to set ASAP!' She was still enjoying this unexpected memory when suddenly her own walkie-talkie started going berserk.

'Jessica, come in, Jessica, can you go to channel three please, it's Kerry.'

'Hi,' said Jessica cheerfully, having switched over to channel three so that they could speak in private without the whole crew listening. 'Go on.'

'We've got a bit of a situation here. Can you come straight away?'

'On my way,' replied Jessica, before hurrying the short way through the corridors to Kate Templeton's dressing room where some kind of drama was clearly occurring.

Kate Templeton had brought her own make-up artist with her for the day, a skinny, frantic-looking woman in tight jeans, an oversize Stella McCartney T-shirt and Converse trainers, who was rifling through her huge canvas professional make-up kit bag in a manner that suggested she'd lost something.

'Ah, there you are,' said Kerry. 'Jessica, this is Ali, who does Kate's make-up, and this is Vivienne, Kate's manager,' she said, indicating a livid-looking woman who was immaculately dressed but looked like that could change any time soon when she ripped off her blouse and turned into The Hulk. 'Anyway,' Kerry continued, looking tense and widening her eyes in an attempt to convey to Jessica how grave the situation was, 'I need you to phone the car firm *right away*, please. Poor Ali here thinks that some of her products must have slipped out in the back of the taxi, one of them being Kate's absolute favourite lipstick. I need you to get that car back here asap. Kate's in hair at the moment so we've got a bit of time and I thought I could make up some excuse about why she needs to have her briefing before make-up.'

'No worries, I'll call now,' said Jessica calmly, who had only just noticed Paul standing in the corner, clearly getting ready to brief Kate Templeton. 'But, Kerry?'

'Yes?'

'Are you sure Robbie hasn't got the same lipstick in his kit?'

'Checked already,' hissed Kerry out of the side of her mouth.

'Checked what?' said an instantly recognizable voice. A coiffed Kate Templeton had just snuck into the room, looking lovely even without a scrap of make-up.

'Nothing,' said Ali, looking as though she was having a mild coronary.

'Kate, let me introduce you to our chief writer, Paul Fletcher . . .' said Kerry.

Jessica slunk out of the room and into the corridor, shaking her head briefly, so amazed was she by the histrionics, before quietly phoning the car firm.

'Hello, I was wondering if you could help me . . .'

Five minutes later and Jessica had managed to glean that the driver had found the lipstick but had knocked off for the day and was on his way home to Brighton. If he turned round he'd be late for his own ruby wedding anniversary. Jessica immediately said not to worry. It was a question of priorities, after all. Let's face it, they were only talking about a lipstick. She went back to the dressing room where Kate Templeton was chatting away with Paul. Jessica noticed primly that he suddenly seemed to be at his most charming.

Just then Kerry spotted her and started miming thumbs-up signs at her to find out how things had gone, but Jessica saw no reason not to address things head on. A stupid lipstick had gone missing and, from what her dad had said about Kate, no one had any reason to feel nervous as one might with certain other Hollywood divas.

'Um, excuse me, Kate,' Jessica said confidently. 'Hi, I'm Kerry's assistant. I'm afraid on the way over here your favourite lipstick fell out of Ali's kit bag into the car.'

'Oh,' Kate said, looking mildly perturbed and very surprised at being addressed directly by a stranger – something that had ceased to happen ever since her first couple of movies had been such a success.

'So I rang the car firm and . . .' At this point she noticed Kerry's face had gone an alarming shade of puce. Jessica turned a fraction to see how Vivienne was doing. Her expression was one of pure rage. For the first time she wondered if she was doing the right thing. Maybe she should, in fact, be riding a horse bareback to Brighton to get this lipstick as a matter of life and death? She tried to keep things in perspective. Tried to remind herself that Kate was only human.

'. . . the driver could come back . . .'

'OK, great,' said Kate.

'But he was already halfway to Brighton for his ruby wedding anniversary, so I said not to worry.'

Everyone in the room except Jessica and Kate seemed to hold their breath. By now Kerry was positively wide-eyed. Paul looked bewildered. Vivienne looked like she wanted to kill someone with her bare hands. Everyone waited to see what the actress would say.

'Oh, good for you,' Kate said finally. 'That would have been crazy. It's only a stupid lipstick. I mean, it is my favourite, but I bet your guy here's got hundreds. Why don't you go and have a look, Ali?'

'Right,' said Ali, looking relieved and like she might be about to cry.

'Great,' said Jessica matter-of-factly. 'Now, can I get anyone a fresh drink at all?'

'But what were you thinking?' Kerry demanded to know later, once filming had wrapped and they were back in the office having a quick debrief.

'I just figured she wouldn't want to ruin someone's day because of a lipstick,' reiterated Jessica. 'I knew she would be cool about it and, if she hadn't been, I had Plan B to fall back on.'

'Which was what?' Kerry spluttered, looking across to Luke and Paul for support, but they weren't taking a great deal of notice. Kerry tutted. She didn't know whether she should be telling Jessica off or giving her a pay rise. It had been very confusing watching someone so inexperienced deal so calmly with one of Hollywood's biggest stars.

'If she'd freaked out I would have offered her some free Jimmy Choo stuff,' Jessica explained. 'Actresses love getting stuff for free.'

'Where did you say you worked again in LA?' piped up Paul. He hated to admit it, but he was horribly impressed by the new girl's no-bullshit attitude.

Jessica blushed for the first time that day. 'In an agent's office.'

'I thought you said you interned at Fox Films?' said Kerry.

'Oh, yeah, I . . . did,' she mumbled, kicking herself inside.

'Look,' said Kerry, 'the bottom line is, you really helped me out today, which I absolutely appreciate. However, in future tread carefully with these people because another actress might not have reacted quite so reasonably. I know it's hard to comprehend but they don't exist in the real world like we do. I mean, had that been someone like . . . Caroline Mason, for instance, she would have hit the roof. Aren't I right, Paul?'

'Yes,' he agreed, nodding his head.

'Still, thanks for what you did. You were kind of brilliant, as was Helena, which was also down to you,' said Kerry grudgingly. 'Though I'm not sure my heart can cope with the stress of wondering what you're going to do next week.'

Jessica grinned. She could tell deep down Kerry was pleased with her and that she may even have impressed Paul slightly, possibly an even more satisfying feeling.

'One more thing,' said Kerry, before going to leave. 'Don't even think about offering celebs free stuff, because when you can't produce the goods we'll just look stupid. Besides, if we really could get our hands on free Jimmy Choos, Natasha wouldn't let anyone leave the building till she'd got her own hands on them.'

'Right,' said Jessica warily, feeling drained and grateful that show day only came around once a week. What a day. 'I'll bear that in mind.'

17

The next day, Friday, was one of those unusually hot, gorgeous, sunny afternoons in London when the city's workforce pray their boss will let them leave work a bit earlier than usual. Luckily for the production team of *The Bradley Mackintosh Show*, their boss wasn't around to enforce, allow or veto anything. So the majority of the office had decamped to the pub by four. Their early arrival at The Boaters by the river in Hammersmith meant they'd nabbed some outside tables and the weekend was getting off to a great start.

'On days like this,' Isy said thoughtfully, looking so relaxed that unless you'd spotted her mouth moving you'd be forgiven for thinking she was asleep . . . or dead, 'you can understand why London's got so much going for it in terms of culture.'

'What are you on about?' said Natasha, pulling down the straps on her vest top as she basked in the afternoon rays, face turned to the sun.

'Well,' said Isy, 'if it was hot like this all the time, then nobody would ever feel like doing anything, you know? Whereas when it's cold and raining you can't avoid thinking, can you? Your brain doesn't melt and you can be arsed. I mean, right now, I feel like a hot, lazy, fat sloth, who wants to sleep in a tree and drink beer.'

'Do sloths drink beer?' asked Luke, managing to ignore the fact it was baking hot by continuing to dress the same way he did all year round, in black jeans, a white shirt, a mod-style, single-breasted grey jacket and a black trilby. Thankfully he wore this trademark combination completely unselfconsciously so looked good, as opposed to like he was trying too hard.

'Dunno,' said Isy, closing her eyes and drifting off into a sun-induced stupor. 'But I'm a sloth for sure and I love beer.' Then, in an action that somewhat startled the rest of the group, she flung herself forward, her plan being to rest her head on the small, round aluminium table that they were all crowded around outside the pub. 'Fuck,' she said as head and table made contact, instantly hurling herself back again while clutching her head and pissing herself laughing, all at the same time. 'Flipping table's boiling. I've burnt my forehead.'

'Doofus,' said Luke, lighting a cigarette before offering the packet around.

Vanessa and Paul accepted one immediately, but Kerry hesitated. 'God, I'd love one to wash down this spritzer, but I've been so good . . .'

'Oh, don't,' beseeched Jessica quietly. She was perched next to Kerry and up until now had been happy just to sit and listen to the group's banter. 'You'll regret it later if you do, you really will.'

Natasha sneaked a look at Vanessa, but Vanessa – who genuinely liked the new girl – refused to be drawn in.

'If you're a sloth then, Isy, what sort of animal am I?' asked Luke, dragging deeply from his cigarette.

'Koala,' she answered like a shot, while rubbing her

forehead. 'Natasha's a wolf, Vanessa's a lizard and Paul's a bear, a grizzly one.'

'Freak,' said Paul good-naturedly. 'Hang on, what about Kerry?'

'Dog,' said Luke. Kerry kicked him hard under the table.

'She's not a dog,' said Isy indignantly, as if Luke had just uttered the most nonsensical thing she'd ever heard in her life. 'She's a woolly mammoth.'

'Give me strength,' said Kerry, not really perturbed at all. The sun had zapped any real strength of feeling about anything.

Meanwhile, Paul was in a great mood. Yesterday's show had gone brilliantly and had managed to run completely smoothly without Mike's presence. He knew it was wrong to take such a delight in this but he couldn't help his feelings towards the man. When you'd worked as hard as he had to get to where he was in life, it was somewhat galling to work for someone who, as far as Paul was concerned, had had less of a helping hand up, and more of an arm and a leg.

He supped his cold pint, considering whether or not to cash in on his great mood and ask Natasha for a date. She'd been her usual self this week, a bundle of increasingly mixed messages, but unless he put himself on the line he'd never find out for sure if she regretted ending things between them. She was complicated, but then, wasn't everybody? He knew his best friend and flatmate Luke would disapprove, but Natasha was gorgeous and, as far as he was concerned, unfinished business. What was the worst that could happen? She could say no ... actually, that would be pretty dreadful now he came to think about it.

He looked across the table. Kerry and Luke were deep in conversation so the new girl had been left to her own devices. Yesterday she'd turned out to be a bit of a revelation, so unfazed was she by the celebs. At the time he hadn't known whether her direct approach with Kate Templeton was incredibly brave or incredibly stupid, but it had worked out, so he guessed she'd played it just right. Jessica was very pretty too. Not quite as pretty as Natasha and yet there was something about her he was drawn to. He probably shouldn't have been so quick to dismiss her as a Californian airhead. She definitely had things to say for herself.

'All right?' he said now, and quite sweetly she blushed. They should ease off her a bit. He knew she was intimidated by him and Luke so it wasn't really fair to tease her so much. 'So did you enjoy yesterday? You looked like you did.'

'Yeah, it was really great, thanks,' replied Jessica, pleased to have been asked. She meant what she'd said too. Being a part of yesterday's organized chaos had been a real buzz.

'I must say, your approach on how to treat celebrities surprised me, though to your credit I'd say you helped prevent a three-act opera unfolding there. I think being spoken to so logically was quite the novelty for Kate Templeton.'

'I know,' agreed Jessica. 'It's kinda sad when you think about it, because she seems pretty down to earth.'

'I still say you were lucky,' said Kerry, butting in. 'Like I said before, if that had been someone less reasonable you could have ended up with egg on your face.'

'Sure,' agreed Jessica, 'but Kate's awesome so I don't know why anyone would be intimidated by her.'

Natasha narrowed her eyes. 'And I don't know why you wouldn't be.'

'I know what you mean, Tash,' said Kerry thoughtfully.

Jessica looked away. She'd have to be careful. For her to continue being a 'normal' girl, an experiment she felt like she was finally starting to get to grips with, even to enjoy, it was essential her identity remained a secret. She could only imagine the fuss the truth would cause and she was enjoying being taken at face value for a change.

'Who did you sound like when you said "awesome"?' mused Vanessa in her strong Scouse accent.

Jessica frowned. She desperately wanted to decipher what Vanessa had just said, but it was no good – her accent was just too pronounced. All she could make out was a load of 'k's and other guttural sounds emanating from the back of her throat. She may as well have been speaking Urdu.

'I beg your pardon?' she asked hesitantly. Asking Vanessa to repeat everything was starting to get embarrassing.

'I said, who do you sound like when you say "awesome"?' repeated Vanessa slowly.

Jessica started to sweat. 'Sorry?'

'WHO DO YOU SOUND LIKE WHEN YOU SAY "AWESOME"?'

No. Still no clue, but she couldn't face asking her to repeat it again so took a gamble. 'Er, yeah, I guess,' she tried hopefully. To her horror, Vanessa looked perplexed. Paul chuckled.

'She sounds like Britney Spears or someone,' Kerry suggested helpfully. 'That's who you sound like when you say "awesome".'

'Oh, right,' Jessica said, wondering if that was a good thing or a bad thing, and whether she would ever be able to understand the nuances of her workmates' banter. Still, at least she'd figured out that their constant bickering wasn't meant in an aggressive way.

She looked at Paul. She had yet to have a conversation with him where she didn't feel like she was being assessed, but he was certainly charismatic and very clever. In fact, she found herself gravitating towards him more and more. There was something about him that . . . fascinated her and when he smiled his eyes crinkled up in such a sexy way. In fact, she'd found herself constantly striving to say something he found interesting or entertaining for one of these smiles alone. She could certainly tell why so many of the girls in the office liked him. Vanessa blatantly had a soft spot for him and she suspected Natasha had him on her radar too, though it was hard to know for sure. Still, Jessica had already decided there was no point fancying him herself. He would be far too much like hard work. Plus there would be no point, given that a fling with him could never amount to more than a holiday romance. Though she would love to know if his legs looked as strong as they appeared through his jeans and when he'd leaned over to get something yesterday she'd caught a glimpse of an eye-wateringly flat, muscular stomach.

Jessica gave herself a little shake, blaming the sunshine for making her mind and indeed her libido run away with itself, refusing to consider that she'd never had the same problem at home in LA, where it was sunny every single day . . .

'I'm going to get another round,' said Paul, standing up.

'Let me buy you a pint, Jessica. Watching you drink fizzy water makes me nervous. It doesn't seem right on a day like this.'

She laughed. 'Thanks, but remember I said I don't drink beer.'

'You've said lots of things,' he replied. 'Most of them nuts, but it's been five whole days now, so it's high time you got to grips with our culture, which means drinking beer.'

'I'd rather not,' she said, feeling bullied. 'I'm going for a run in a minute so I'll stick to water, thanks.'

'You're going for a run now?' exclaimed Isy, her jaw slack with amazement.

'Yeah, actually I'm going to run home, because I couldn't go for one yesterday, it being show day.'

'Wow,' said Isy loudly, looking as deeply impressed as if Jessica had just told her she'd won gold at the Olympics or climbed Everest in her lunch break.

Luke half choked on a mouthful of lager. 'You're bloody priceless, Bender. You're going to run home? To Hampstead?'

'Um, well, actually just into town to . . . meet my aunt,' Jessica improvised, not that she saw what was so funny about her running anywhere. She just didn't want them to find out that home, until tomorrow, was still a hotel. She looked down at her trainers, suddenly feeling very tired. It was exhausting having to have your wits about you the whole while. It was time to go. She needed to pack up her stuff to take to Pam's tomorrow and she wanted to phone Dulcie too, who seemed to have disappeared off the radar the last couple of days.

'Well, if you're still here in the winter, let's see if you're quite so keen to get your running shoes on then, shall we?' said Vanessa.

'Do you think you will be?' asked Paul, suddenly curious to know.

'What's that?' asked Jessica, who was still trying to work out what Vanessa had just said.

'Here in the winter.'

'I hope so,' replied Jessica politely. 'I like London, it's a nice break from —'

'Sunshine?' said Luke.

'Beaches?' suggested Julian from the next table.

'Beautiful people?' offered Vanessa.

'What do you actually do in LA anyway?' asked Natasha, who was still busy sun-worshipping, though the sun was just about to disappear behind a cloud. 'Who do you live with?'

'My dad and my stepmom,' Jessica replied, gathering up her backpack and wriggling into it. Definitely time to go.

'So where's your mum?'

'She left when I was three.'

Natasha didn't react but it was obviously an uncomfortable moment and everyone knew she'd be feeling bad for asking one question too many.

Paul felt a sudden rush of sympathy for Jessica and empathy too. Maybe they weren't so different after all. He watched her now as she bent down to make sure her laces were tied properly on her trainers. Then she took a hair band from the pocket of her denim shorts and tied her fine blonde hair back.

'What are you up to this weekend? Are you going to be

all right?' Kerry asked, genuinely concerned. She got the sense that Jessica didn't do much with her spare time, apart from hang out with her aunt.

'Not sure yet,' replied Jessica, who was actually looking forward to a couple of peaceful days to digest everything. 'I'll probably water Mike's garden at some point and, you know, bits and pieces.'

Kerry, who couldn't comprehend anybody having anything less than a hectic social life, felt a pang of something approaching pity. 'OK, well, I'm off to a spa this weekend but next week some of us are going clubbing so you should come. Don't feel you have to or anything, it's just that seeing as you said you liked music so much . . .'

'Do you?' said Paul, who was a music nut.

'That sounds great,' said Jessica, deliberately pretending not to hear Paul. The last thing she felt like right now was being grilled on her musical tastes. 'It would be great to check out an English club.'

'I can't believe you've only just mentioned that you're going to a spa,' interrupted Vanessa enviously. 'You're such a cow, Kerry, I'd bloody love to go to one of those.'

'Me too,' said Isy, draining the last of her Bacardi Breezer. 'I'd have my claws cut and my paws rubbed.'

'Yeah, well, I am looking forward to a bit of pampering,' said Kerry, who having worked with Isy so long was oblivious to her strange turn of phrase, 'but I'm going for a family friend's hen night. To be honest, I'm slightly dreading all the wedding chatter,' she finished rather tellingly. Kerry was only thirty-four, but Jessica could sense she felt ready to meet Mr Right.

'What's everybody else up to?'

'Sleeping,' said Isy.

'Clubbing,' said Luke.

'This and that,' said Natasha, stealing a glance at Paul in a way that made Jessica feel inappropriately bothered. 'What about you, Pauly? You going home to see Mummy?'

Paul didn't rise to the bait. He had his reasons for going home to his mum's house in Staines as often as he did, but they weren't ones he felt particularly comfortable talking about. Even when he'd been going out with Natasha he hadn't opened up to her much about his life. Luke was the only person at work he trusted completely, and trust was something Paul valued greatly.

Kerry looked at Jessica, who was hovering, backpack firmly on, clearly waiting for a gap in the conversation to say goodbye. 'OK, hon – well, have a good one and don't worry too much about Mike's bloody garden, will you? I'll see you on Monday at ten and thank you so much for all your hard work. It's been brilliant having you here this week.'

Jessica swelled with pride. 'See you then,' she said before giving a little wave and setting off at a fairly energetic pace down the path.

Everybody stared after her, fascinated by what was largely considered to be fairly dubious behaviour. Why would anybody in their right mind want to run anywhere on a day like this, especially when there was cold lager to be drunk?

'Run, Forrest!' yelled Luke suddenly at the top of his voice, 'Run!', which made everyone giggle like mad, including Jessica. Now a large speck in the distance, she turned round briefly to wave over her shoulder again.

As they all watched her disappear down the path, Natasha was the first to speak. 'Do you think she'll go round the corner and get the bus? I bet she does.'

'I bet she doesn't' said Isy, who was still looking completely awestruck. 'She's amazing. If she was an animal, she'd be a gazelle.'

'A gazelle with slightly thick ankles,' retorted Natasha nastily, and at that moment Paul wondered if he really did still want to take Natasha out.

18

On Saturday Jessica moved into her aunt's house in Hampstead, having long since realized how misjudged her original decision to reside at the Dorchester had been. How much more normal to stay in an ordinary house that was comfortable, yet basic and tiny compared to what she was used to. Pam told her it had been built in Victorian times, over one hundred years ago, a fact that astounded Jessica, though also explained why the house felt so quintessentially English and quaint. The decor clearly hadn't had a facelift since the eighties, which only added to the house's charm as far as Jessica was concerned; although she'd been baffled beyond belief to discover there was no laundry room in the house. Just a solitary machine in the kitchen, which Pam claimed both washed and dried clothes. Incredible.

On Sunday Jessica woke up glad not to have any real plans for the day. Her workmates' brand of humour took no prisoners and constantly trying to decipher who was and wasn't being sarcastic made her brain ache. At least she was starting to remember people's names though and she also felt like she was making headway with a couple of the girls. Kerry, in particular, and Isy.

'Je-ess,' her aunt hollered up the stairs, interrupting her thoughts.

'Yeah?'

'There's someone here for you, love.'

'Pardon?' cried Jessica, not sure she'd heard right.

'There's someone here for you.'

Jessica sat up. Who could possibly be here? Angelica was in LA; not that they'd spoken since Graydon had dragged her from their breakfast. No one from work would turn up unannounced on a Sunday morning, so it had better not be Edward. She'd be furious if it was. Suddenly she could hear feet thudding noisily up the stairs in her direction so she quickly hopped out of bed, feeling horribly nervous. What the hell?

'Surprise!'

The door to her room was flung open and there, standing in her doorway, was none other than Dulcie.

'Dulcie!' exclaimed Jessica. 'What are you doing here?'

'Same as you, sweetie, ripping it up in London town. How are you, baby?'

'I'm . . . I'm totally in shock. Oh my God, it's so good to see you but I –'

'Oh, shut up and give me a hug, will you,' ordered Dulcie and Jessica, who didn't have a better plan, did as she was told.

'But when did you get here?' asked a still-staggered Jessica. She wished she could get more excited, but her overriding emotion at this precise moment was a nagging annoyance that Dulcie should have told her she was coming.

'Last night. I flew in, went straight to the Berkeley where I've been sleeping like a baby ever since. Soon as I woke up I got my driver to bring me here.'

'But I thought you were going to give me some warning

about when you were coming,' said Jessica, through faintly gritted teeth. 'How long are you here for anyway?'

'Just a week,' said Dulcie.

'But you know I have a job now, right?' said Jessica, feeling panicky. 'So I won't be able to hang out with you every day.'

'Hey, quit stressing, will you? I'm sure we can come up with some great excuse for your boring old job. Anyway, who cares about that? We're here to have some fun.'

'But . . .'

'No buts, now come on, get dressed, my driver's waiting and I have an appointment at the bridal section of Harrods in forty-five minutes.'

'OK,' Jessica whimpered, already missing the sense of independence she'd experienced for such a brief time. 'I'll come, but seriously, Dulcie, we need to talk. I'm so happy to see you, but I also want to spend some time with Pam today and I am telling you now that I *can't* miss work on Monday, or any other day. I've only been there a week for crissakes and, anyway, this is the first time in my –'

'Chill out, will you?' admonished Dulcie. 'Pam's fine and I'm not going to make you miss work if you don't want to. I know you're on some mission to wear a hair shirt and be really poor and miserable and bored like everyone else, so who am I to stop you?'

'Idiot,' said Jessica, but she was laughing.

'Though I hope you've sorted out coming home for your dad's party. Mr G's pining for you and he'd never forgive you if you weren't there.'

'Of course I have,' Jessica lied, making a mental note to sort that out as soon as possible . . . somehow. 'OK, give me five minutes to get dressed and washed properly, will you?'

Dulcie nodded happily and went to sit on Jessica's bed, pulling her iPhone out of her Vuitton bag so that she could text someone, looking ridiculously glamorous in her Pucci dress and Prada wedge heels.

'What is this job you're doing anyway?' she asked idly.

'It's pretty cool actually,' replied Jessica, wriggling out of her pyjamas and wrapping herself in a towel. 'I mean, it's not what I want to do for the rest of my life, but Kerry, who I work for, is awesome. Then there's a girl called Isy who's kinda crazy but very sweet. Vanessa, who I *think* is lovely, though I can't understand a word she says. Then there's Mike, who's away at the moment, but who's really good-looking and friendly. In fact, there's only one person I'm not sure about and that's this guy Paul, who can be so nice at times and then, at others, really confrontational and opinionated.'

'Sounds like someone's got a crush,' said Dulcie, still texting busily.

'Who, Mike? No way,' protested Jessica. 'He's married and not my type at all.'

'Not Mike, Paul.'

'Don't be ridiculous,' said Jessica, frowning. 'You obviously weren't listening.'

'Whatever,' grinned Dulcie, not convinced. 'So you haven't said what it is you actually do in this office of yours.'

'I assist the celeb booker on *The Bradley Mackintosh Show* at the BBC,' said Jessica, halfway out the door by now and headed for the bathroom.

Dulcie immediately stopped fiddling with her phone.

'You what? You're kidding me? Why didn't you say that before? I love that show. I watch it on BBC World all the time. Oh my God, Jess, you've got to get me on. My dad went on it years ago and his album sales practically doubled the next day. This is just the exposure I need.'

Jessica's heart sank. Damn it. Dulcie could be like a dog with a bone when she got an idea in her head, and this was one of the most terrible she'd ever had.

Later that evening a rather subdued Jessica and a faintly hostile Dulcie got the tube over to Mike's house. The appointment at Harrods had been surprisingly fun, but what hadn't been so enjoyable was Dulcie's incessant nagging to get her on the show.

By now her bottom lip was wobbling dangerously, as for the life of her she couldn't see what harm it would do to simply ask the question. However, for Jessica, the words 'Can my friend who's ever so slightly famous in LA, only not in her own right and not for anything in particular, come on the show for no reason other than she's marrying a guy who was runner-up on *American Idol*?' weren't ones she ever wanted to utter.

'But why can't I just phone your boss directly?' whined Dulcie in a last-ditch attempt. 'That way you don't even have to get involved.'

Jessica sighed heavily with frustration. 'Because the answer will still be no, and if it wasn't, which it would be, she'd probably end up finding out we know each other and the game will be up.'

'Fine,' said Dulcie, knowing that when Jessica had really

made up her mind about something there would be no budging.

'Fine,' repeated Jessica grumpily, staring out of the window as they approached leafy Chiswick and Turnham Green station. 'We're here.'

They got off the train and by the time they were at the ticket barriers Dulcie had clearly decided to try and make amends. In fact, she'd changed her tune completely and for once seemed content to admit defeat.

'I'm sorry, Jess,' she said. 'I promise not to bring it up again, OK? I can tell this job is important to you so I won't ask again, all right?'

'OK,' said Jessica, feeling relieved, though not entirely convinced that this would be the end of the matter.

'And thanks for forcing me to take the subway,' added Dulcie. 'It was quite fun, actually. A little unhygienic but OK,' she said, pulling out some antiseptic hand gel from her Vuitton bag and smothering her hands in it. When she started to pat it on her face, as if she were a man putting on aftershave, Jessica's sense of humour finally returned.

With the aid of Jessica's *A to Z* the two girls managed to find Mike's house fairly easily, though when they did they were surprised by how normal it looked. In LA successful producers lived in enormous, palatial homes, whereas Mike's house was a similar size to Pam's.

'This is it?' said Dulcie incredulously, voicing exactly what Jessica herself was thinking, only in such a way that made her feel ashamed for doing so.

'Of course,' said Jessica firmly. 'What were you expecting? Not everyone can live in a palace like the execs we know.'

Dulcie rolled her eyes behind her friend's back and waited patiently while Jessica carefully let herself in with the keys that Mike had given her. The second the door opened the alarm started to beep ominously and the two girls squealed and shrieked with panic until Jessica had keyed the correct numbers into the pad. Once it was off and it was clear that they were safely in, they both giggled with relief before making their way through to the back of the house.

'Oh my God,' said Dulcie, her nose wrinkling. 'It's so tiny, it's like a freaking doll's house.'

'Shut up,' said Jessica, slapping her friend on the arm affectionately. 'You sound like such a snob. Anyway, it's not that tiny – it's only a bit smaller than Pam's place.'

'I am not a snob,' retorted Dulcie. 'I'm just saying.'

Jessica unlocked the French windows in the open-plan kitchen then went outside. She found the hose at the side of the house and switched the tap on.

'Can I have a go?' asked Dulcie.

'Sure,' replied Jessica. 'But in a minute, it's my turn first.'

Taking it in turns, the two of them gave the thirsty, lawned, forty-foot garden a satisfying soak, both enjoying the simplicity of a task that neither of them had ever done before. The grass revived before their very eyes, the dry soil lapping up the water gratefully.

Job done, they made their way back through the house, Jessica having made sure she'd locked everything behind her. As she did so, a framed picture in the kitchen caught her eye. She went over to get a closer look and Dulcie followed, curious to see what she was looking at.

'Is that Mike?' asked Dulcie.

'Yeah,' replied Jessica. It was Mike and an attractive-looking lady who Jessica presumed must be Diane, his wife, and a cute little girl with curly but scraggly ringlets framing her cheeky face. The three of them looked incredibly happy and Mike's wife looked lovely. She had long, dark-brown hair and a beaming smile. She was wearing a pretty floral dress and was tanned, so they were probably on holiday.

'His wife's kind of fat, isn't she?' said Dulcie cheerfully.

Jessica frowned.

'Oh my God, look at your boss's dick,' exclaimed Dulcie and Jessica's eyes travelled downwards to see that the T-shirt Mike was wearing only just covered what looked like . . . oh my word . . . small, almost indecently tight trunks that left nothing to the imagination. Embarrassed to have seen the outline of her boss's testicles, Jessica averted her eyes.

The two girls travelled back to Hampstead in comfortable silence, only this time in Dulcie's chauffeur-driven car, which Dulcie had summoned to meet them. (As far as she was concerned, the tube was an experience not worth repeating.) Jessica's mind kept returning to the picture they'd seen in Mike's kitchen and not just because of Mike's tight trunks.

'They looked so happy,' she said suddenly.

Dulcie answered straight away, without even needing to ask what she was referring to. 'She's a lucky little girl. They sure do look like the perfect family.'

Later that night the weather became oppressively hot and muggy so Jessica was not surprised to wake up on Monday to the sound of thunder roaring across the sky. As she snuggled back under her sheets, she realized how pointless their watering expedition had been, given that right now Mike's garden was getting a complete drenching. For a fraction of a second she felt rather envious of Dulcie who, in her luxurious suite, with no responsibilities, could wake up any time she liked with the day spread before her to do with as she pleased.

Still, once she was up and showered, having negotiated the temperamental plumbing in Pam's guest bathroom, Jessica was raring to go, although the novelty of catching the tube was starting to wear off a bit. In fact, that morning's was one of the most tiresome journeys yet. She had to stand the entire way, so was pleased to be greeted at work by some positive news.

The ratings for last week's show were in and it was confirmed. Helena Davies had been an inspired booking and an utter triumph.

'I'll have to buy you a drink, Jess,' Kerry was saying across her desk as Paul walked through the door.

Jessica's heart sort of twanged in her chest when she saw him. He was wearing jeans and a grey sweatshirt, so nothing special, but for whatever reason he looked really good. Oh, great, she thought dolefully, remembering what Dulcie had said. Developing a crush on someone so unpredictable was not what she needed.

'Hi, Paul,' said Kerry. 'Good weekend?'

'Fair to middling,' he replied enigmatically. 'What about you, fatty?'

'It was OK, thanks,' said Kerry, tapping away on her

keyboard. 'The spa was lovely anyway. The hotel was a bit "travel tavern" but you get what you pay for, I suppose.'

'Well, you look . . . exactly the same as you did before,' he laughed, hopping away as Kerry took a swipe at him with a magazine.

'I'm just on Facebook, actually,' she said good-humouredly. 'I'm changing my status to *"Kerry Taylor has still got spa face"*.'

Isy, who was busy putting Bradley's various autograph cards into separate piles, started to laugh. 'What the hell is spa face?'

'Well,' said Kerry, 'my hair was covered in oil and, as you know, it's a bugger to control at the best of times, so I looked like the Medusa. I had red lines on my face from where I'd been lying with my head through one of those hole things and I was dribbling.'

'You paint an attractive picture,' chimed in Luke from across the office. 'Wish I could have been there to see it.'

'Attractive I definitely wasn't,' retorted Kerry, picking up her coffee mug and realizing it was empty.

'I don't get the appeal of Facebook,' interjected Penny, the vision mixer, who had come into the office to catch up on her paperwork and was sitting at Julian's desk. 'I mean, why do you feel the need to tell everyone you know about your weekend?'

'God knows,' said Kerry, 'but it's a laugh, I suppose. In fact, are you on it, Jessica? Where are you? I'll add you as a friend and then you too can benefit from my hilarious status updates. After you've made us a cup of coffee that is.'

'Oh, yes,' she said, still distracted by the sight of Paul rolling up his sleeves and flexing his fingers as he prepared to type. He had lovely forearms, she thought, as she crossed the office to put the kettle on. 'I'm in the group LA LA Land and listed as Jessica Gra–' Just in time, she thought about what she was saying. 'Actually,' she said quickly, spooning Nescafé into a mug and selecting a herbal tea for herself, 'I've just remembered. I'm not on Facebook any more. I stopped it before I came away.'

'Thought you weren't,' said Paul distractedly.

'How would you know?' said Natasha, as quick as anything. 'Did you look for Jessica on Facebook, Paul?'

Paul, who had but didn't really know why, refused to rise to the bait. 'You know me, Tash. I'm a nosy bugger. Didn't look for long though. Do you know how many Jessica Benders there are on Facebook? Bloody hundreds.'

'Well, I'm not on anyway,' Jessica said, feeling flushed. She made a mental note never to check her page while at work. Apart from anything else, people might be surprised to see that Leonora Whittingston was one of her 'friends'.

'But why come off now?' asked Natasha, screwing up her eyes suspiciously. She could be irritatingly persistent. 'What with you being away from home, I would have thought you'd want to keep up with your mates.'

Jessica just shrugged and looked away, stirring Kerry's coffee more vigorously than was strictly necessary.

'Look, can we forget about all this Facebook bollocks, please?' said Kerry. 'As much as I'd like to revel in the glory that was last week's show, we've got another one to think about now and we're a guest down . . . again.'

The office settled down and a relatively peaceful morning's work ensued. Later that afternoon, an hour or so after everyone had returned from lunch in the canteen,

Jessica was so engrossed in an email which Kerry had asked her to draft to an agent that when at first she heard a familiar voice it took her a moment or two to register it was one that didn't belong in the office.

'Hi, hi there, how are you today? Do you know where Jessica sits? Actually, scrap that, I see her . . . hi . . .'

Jessica spun round in her seat as if someone had just poked her with a hot iron. 'Dulcie!' she hissed. 'What the hell are you doing here?'

She could hardly believe her eyes. Her best friend was standing in the middle of the room, looking like a peacock that had lost its way. She was dolled up to the nines, resplendent in a mixture of Versace, Alexander McQueen and Marc Jacobs. The most subtle thing about her outfit was her nail varnish and that was fluorescent orange.

'Hi, honey, surprise . . . again,' she said, an infuriating lack of caution in her voice. 'I thought I'd pop in and see how you were doing. You were being so strict about not taking any time off so I decided to come to you.'

Jessica was furious. How dare she jeopardize everything? She couldn't even say anything because every single person in the office had downed tools to have a good stare. Including Paul. There was a chance she was about to hyperventilate.

'Who are you?' asked Kerry, giving Dulcie a very thorough once-over.

'Dulcie Malone. Friend of Jessica's,' said Dulcie, swaggering over to greet her. 'And you are?'

'Wondering what you're doing here,' Kerry answered in a flash, completely deadpan.

'I'm so sorry, Kerry,' said Jessica, desperate to gain

some control of the situation. 'I did tell my friend that she wasn't supposed to come here,' she said between gritted teeth. 'That I was working...'

'So you're Kerry,' said Dulcie. 'Oh my God, Jess has told me so much about you. You book the guests, don't you?'

Instantly Jessica understood very clearly what this visit was all about, which only made the desire to scream at Dulcie even stronger.

'Yes,' said Kerry, looking at Dulcie with barely concealed contempt, while Natasha just looked downright suspicious, as if a rather large penny was about to drop. Horrified, Jessica was propelled into action.

'Dulcie, can I talk to you outside for a second? People are trying to work in here and you're being very distracting,' she said, leaping up to manhandle a startled Dulcie through the office. 'Let's catch up out here,' she hissed, shoving Dulcie out of the door and into the corridor. 'I'll literally be a minute, Kerry,' she called over her shoulder. 'I'm very sorry, back in a sec –'

In the corridor, Jessica let rip. 'What the hell do you think you're doing? You know I don't want anyone here to know who I am. How selfish can you be?'

'I'm sorry,' said Dulcie, looking a little regretful for the first time since she'd arrived. 'I just thought if I came here myself, I could make your boss see that I would be the perfect guest. You were so ... closed off about helping me. Isn't this the best way to get what we both want?'

'No,' hissed Jessica. 'It isn't, and what I want is to try and cope on my own for once, with none of the baggage of who I am getting in the way, which you know. So you're completely out of order because now people will suspect that something's up. Look at you. You look like you're going to the freaking Emmys or something.'

At this point Dulcie had the good grace to look mildly shamefaced. 'I'm sorry, OK,' she muttered. 'I didn't realize the office dress code would be so casual and I didn't mean to upset you. I guess I didn't really think it through.'

'No, you didn't,' agreed Jessica.

'Is my outfit really too much?'

'Aaerrrugh,' wailed Jessica and Dulcie looked properly worried for the first time.

'OK, OK, what should I do?' asked Dulcie. 'It'll look weird if I just disappear.'

Jessica shrugged, feeling utterly defeated. She slid down the wall in a crumpled heap of despair.

'Oh, don't be like that, Jess,' rallied Dulcie. 'You're giving up. Now come on. We can make this work. Just leave it to me and try to remember . . .' she stopped for a dramatic pause.

'What?' snapped Jessica.

'We're AmeriCAN, not BritISH.'

And with that she swept back towards the production office.

Jessica willed herself not to cry. She knew she should get up but felt too immobilized by the dread of what Dulcie might do next. Still, leaving her unattended wasn't an option either. Taking a deep breath, she got back on her feet and willed herself back into the office, where her fate was about to be sealed, one way or another.

'So, anyway . . .' she could hear Dulcie saying to Kerry as she walked through the door. Her heart sank as she saw that Dulcie was perched on the corner of Kerry's desk in a presumptuous manner she just knew Kerry wouldn't be appreciating.

'... not only is my dad Vincent Malone, but I'm also marrying Kevin Johnson. You know, the guy who was runner-up on *American Idol* last season? He was the guy who everyone thought *should* have won. So, on top of my own talent and project, I would have so much to talk about.'

'Can you get off my desk?' asked Kerry, sounding highly irritated.

'So how exactly do you know Jessica then?' asked Natasha, who was swinging back in her chair, observing the whole scene like a lion who'd spotted a lone impala at the watering hole.

'Ah,' said Dulcie, turning to Jessica and giving her what she obviously thought was a reassuring wink. 'I was just coming to that. You see, her dad is . . .'

'Oh, be quiet,' interrupted Jessica in a flash. 'No one wants to hear about my boring old dad. Boring old *Mr Bender*,' she emphasized.

'Oh, I don't know,' said Natasha. 'I think it all sounds fascinating.'

Luke was clutching his sides as he tried not to laugh out loud. Paul wasn't quite so amused by the whole scene.

'If you'll just give me a chance, Jess,' said Dulcie. 'I was about to say that your dad, *Mr Bender*, is my dad's chauffeur, which is how Jess and I know each other. And just because he's a chauffeur doesn't make him boring,' she finished, looking terribly pleased with herself at this extra ad lib.

Help, thought Jessica sorrowfully.

'Your dad drives Vincent Malone?' said Kerry. 'You didn't tell me that.'

'You didn't ask,' replied Jessica weakly.

'Is that how you knew about him being on the show?'

'He's been his driver for years,' said Dulcie, getting on a roll. 'Have you seen the film *Sabrina* with Audrey Hepburn? Jessica's life is a bit like hers. We've kind of grown up together, yet we're worlds apart.'

At this point Luke got up and excused himself from the room, shoulders heaving. Natasha was the only one who looked slightly impressed, though her cool demeanour prevented her from showing it. Besides, she wasn't just impressed, she was also consumed with jealousy to discover that Jessica was friends with someone so glamorous and that her life overlapped with proper Hollywood stars.

'I like your dress,' she said now, casually. 'McQueen, isn't it?'

'Yeah,' confirmed Dulcie enthusiastically.

'Thought so,' said Natasha. 'I've seen it in *Elle*.'

Paul rolled his eyes and grimaced in Dulcie's direction. Jessica could tell she was his idea of hell. Too awful even to bother taking the piss out of. Today she almost agreed with him. Somehow, in this environment, Dulcie was coming across far worse than she ever would at home.

'Well,' said Kerry, contempt oozing from every pore, 'while I can only imagine how lovely it must have been for Jess to grow up in such close proximity to yourself, Ms Malone, in answer to your request to be a guest, the reply is no. You're not our sort of guest, I'm afraid, and we only have people on who have something to talk about that involves themselves. Not just their dads.'

'Are you sure about that?' said Paul sarcastically. 'Scarlett O'Hara here might make for some good old-fashioned car crash telly.'

'Excuse me,' said Dulcie indignantly, and Jessica briefly considered leaping from the window. 'I don't know who you think you are, but I am in the room, you know. Who the hell is this guy anyway?' she asked, turning to Jessica for enlightenment.

'Paul,' she mumbled, wishing he hadn't felt the need to be quite so harsh.

'Really?' squawked Dulcie. 'Him?' Her incredulous expression said it all.

Jessica glared at her, hating herself for caring more about what Paul thought than her oldest friend.

'I'm probably going to book Lisa Wright this week anyway. Her plot lines are pretty huge right now,' said Kerry flatly.

'Lisa who?' said Dulcie, looking downright deflated, but still not having clicked that it was most definitely time to call it a day.

'Wright,' sighed Kerry, who'd noticed Julian looking very doubtful. 'I know it's not ideal, but trust me, I think she'll be OK. Besides, I can always cancel her if someone better comes up last minute.'

'Er, hello?' flapped Dulcie, indicating herself.

'Not you,' Kerry snapped.

Jessica held her head in her hands, like a small child watching *Doctor Who*, who was too frightened to look properly, scared of what she might see. Only when Dulcie had *finally* got the hint and announced she was leaving did she look up again.

'I'll see you out,' she said.

'Make sure you take her right out of the building,' said Paul drily.

'Oh, I will,' said Jessica.

19

Jessica spent the rest of the day dealing with the fallout from Dulcie's impromptu trip to the office while stressing out about what Natasha might be thinking. She had obviously decided there was something suspicious about Jessica, and was scrutinizing everything she did and said. She kept fishing for information about Jessica's life back home, asking question after question, almost in the hope of tripping her up. Still, Jessica robotically stuck to Dulcie's story, while keeping detail to a bare minimum, figuring the less she said, the less she'd have to remember. Still, there was one question she found very hard to deal with, though it wasn't Natasha who asked it.

It was the next day, after work, and the usual suspects had popped to the pub for a quick drink. Jessica was chatting to Luke when suddenly, out of the blue, Paul said, 'How can you bear to be friends with someone like that?'

Despite having half-expected something like this from him, Jessica didn't appreciate being asked in front of everyone. She also thought it was a little ridiculous of him to sound so personally affronted by her friendship with Dulcie.

'She's not that bad,' defended Jessica, 'you just need to get to know her. She's really a sweet person deep down.'

Paul looked mystified. 'Really? Only from where I was sitting, she seemed dreadful. Spoilt and egotistical, and those were the good parts.'

Jessica could sense that Paul's disappointment stemmed from the fact that he thought more highly of her, which was kind of a backhanded compliment, only one that wasn't really wanted. What right did he have to cast judgement on her friend, even if Dulcie had given off a lousy first impression?

The evening after the whole debacle Jessica had returned home to find a remorseful Dulcie waiting for her in Pam's kitchen. Having had a chance to think things through, she was sincerely sorry for what she'd done and Jessica could tell that the lukewarm reception she'd received from her workmates had rather taken the wind out of her sails too. It also seemed to have made Dulcie realize what a brave thing it was that Jessica was doing, plus helped her to finally accept that Jessica wouldn't be taking a day off work. That said, she was still only going to be in town for a week so wanted to see her every evening. What with working so hard, all the after-work activity, plus commuting, Jessica's new 'normal' lifestyle was starting to take its toll and she already felt like she was gaining some insight into how easy she'd always had it.

By Wednesday Jessica was feeling so weary that when Kerry asked her if she wanted to come into Hammersmith at lunchtime for some retail therapy in Primark, she declined the invite. The other girls spoke of 'Primani' so affectionately, but the one time she'd gone with them she'd failed miserably to find anything, which had made her realize that maybe some of her mother's fashion influence *had* rubbed off on her after all.

Alone and deep in thought, she made her way to the canteen. Ten minutes later she was just about to reach the end of the usual slow-moving line.

'Penny for them?' said a voice in her ear.

Jessica jumped and turned round to find Paul regarding her with those incredible eyes of his.

'Oh, hi . . . um, oh – nothing,' said Jessica. 'I was just wondering what you Brits have got against fresh fruit and veg.'

Paul looked at her. There was something about Jessica Bender that intrigued him. An air about her that made him want to tease her mercilessly on the one hand, while on the other, made him want to . . . look after her or something. If he wasn't so into Natasha he'd be tempted to say he was attracted to her and yet there was so much about Jessica that wasn't his type, traits she possessed that normally he would dislike. Yet somehow what irked him in others – her naivety, her all-American, girl-next-door persona, her lack of astuteness about certain things – added up to an appealing package. Jessica Bender puzzled him, he realized in a sudden moment of clarity.

'Look, feel free to say no if you like, but I'm just going to grab a latte and then I need to run through some of my links for tomorrow. Maybe you could listen to a few and give me some feedback?' he said, wondering why he felt so unsure of himself.

'Sure,' said Jessica, looking surprised. 'I'd love to, though I'm not sure how much help I'll be . . .'

'Come on,' said Paul, grinning. 'And forget the latte, I can get an instant in the office.'

'Fine,' said Jessica, happily abandoning her tray again.

Paul started walking back towards the production office and Jessica followed, smiling to herself. She felt ridiculously pleased to have been singled out, but immediately chastised herself. This was judgemental Paul, so who knew how long it would be until he next offended her. Still, they were definitely making progress and there was no getting away from it. Whenever she was around him she felt positively silly with desire. He was sexy, she admitted finally. Sexy as hell.

Once they'd reached the office, Paul went straight to the kettle. 'Coffee?' he asked.

'No, thanks. I've got some water in my bag.'

'I forgot,' replied Paul, giving her a sidelong glance. 'Your body is your temple, isn't it? No pints, no booze, no caffeine. Must be a riot round your house.'

Jessica just shrugged. If he only knew half the things that went on at her house, half the people who passed through, he might just stand corrected.

'Still, nice temple though,' he said, grabbing his mug and heading for Mike's office in the corner.

Wondering if she'd heard him right, Jessica flushed to her roots, hating him for teasing her. Why was he saying flirty things like that? Did he know she liked him? Why did she permanently feel so wrong-footed around him?

Checking no one else was using the room, Paul ushered her into Mike's empty office so that they could get some peace and quiet. Once he'd shut the door behind them, Jessica suddenly felt very aware of the fact that they were alone. She sensed he did too.

'It's great not having Mike around,' he said eventually, dispelling the awkwardness. 'Let's hope he's having such a good time in Tuscany he decides to stay.' He spread his stuff out on Mike's desk, including his feet which he swung up somewhat disrespectfully.

'Why don't you like Mike?' asked Jessica shyly. 'He seems OK to me.'

Paul looked up and Jessica's heart and stomach seemed to flip a beat as he regarded her thoughtfully. He always gave off the impression he had double the average amount of thoughts swirling around in his brain. She wished she knew what they were.

'It's not that I don't like him exactly, I just don't trust him and I can't stand it when people don't tell you the whole truth,' he said eventually.

Jessica gulped. 'Well, what can be so bad about Mike?' she ventured timidly.

'Not what, who,' he answered mysteriously, sitting down and switching on the computer in front of him. 'Now, I'll read you some of these links, but no false laughing. If they're shit, it's better I realize now.'

'OK,' said Jessica, before curiosity got the better of her. 'So is he having an affair or something?'

'Who, Mike? No. Why would you think that?'

'I don't know,' she shrugged. 'I guess I thought maybe . . . Natasha?'

An odd expression flickered across Paul's face. 'No, the only shady thing about Mike, as far as I'm aware of at least, is that his boss, David Bridlington, is his father-in-law.'

'Oh, right,' said Jessica, not looking particularly thunderstruck by this revelation.

'So he probably doesn't have to worry too much about job security, does he?' explained Paul slightly patronizingly, before thankfully changing the subject.

'How does working in London compare with working in LA then?' he asked, tapping his password out. 'You mentioned working at Fox and in an agent's office, but what were you doing exactly?'

By now Jessica had had plenty of practice at answering this type of question, so was able to answer both promptly and convincingly.

'I was an intern at Fox and then I assisted an agent for a while, which is why I guess I don't feel too intimidated by the ones over here.' Then her open and honest nature drove her to add, 'I also worked at a gallery as a receptionist and helped plan charity events for a while.'

Paul looked surprised. 'Sounds like you've squeezed a lot in. Bit of a grafter, are you?'

'Um, something like that,' replied Jessica, inwardly wincing at the compliment she didn't deserve. She could only imagine what Paul would make of the way every job she'd ever had had been handed to her on a plate and how the rest were figments of her imagination. Just then her cell phone rang. It was a withheld number.

'Hello . . . ?'

'Jessica, I'm so glad to have got you,' said an unmistakeably French voice.

Shit, it was her mom. She must have looked surprised because Paul was raising his eyebrows questioningly.

'Oh, hi, um . . . it's not really a good time right now.'

'I'm sorry, it's just I've been trying to get you for ages,' said Angelica. 'I left you lots of messages but when you didn't phone back I worried that I might have upset you. I am so, so sorry we left you in such a hurry at the hotel. I think Graydon was just worried about me. I have to admit it was a shock seeing Pamela again after so many years, but I would love to try and explain to you –'

'Yes, yes,' interrupted Jessica, desperate to get her off the phone. 'Well, thanks for calling, but can we speak later?'

'OK,' said Angelica, sounding hurt. She could tell she was being given the brush-off. 'Well, I'm in LA at the moment but I'll be back next week, so let's get together then. And I'll call you tonight at the hotel.'

'No, don't do that, call me on my cell again, because I'm staying at Pam's,' said Jessica, determined not to sound apologetic for this.

'Oh . . .' said Angelica, 'I see. I will then because there is so much I need to talk to you –'

'OK, speak soon,' replied Jessica brightly before cutting her off. She felt guilty, but her guilt was tinged with anger. Why did her mother's timing always manage to be so spectacularly bad? Admittedly, she should have returned her calls, but when you had no idea what to say, there was never a good time.

'Everything all right?' asked Paul lightly.

'Great,' said Jessica a bit too cheerfully.

'Can you concentrate if we have music on?' said Paul, pulling a CD out of his bag, swinging his legs back down off the desk and reaching over to Mike's stereo.

'I find it easier.'

'Me too,' said Paul, giving her a smile that made her insides lurch in an alarmingly pleasurable way.

'Who's this?' asked Jessica as a tune with a very distinct, unusual sound started.

'Er . . . Elbow?' replied Paul, seemingly flabbergasted she didn't know.

'Don't look like that,' said Jessica, giggling at how unnecessarily appalled the expression on his face was. 'I love music but there's a lot of it out there, so there's no reason why I should know the same stuff as you, is there?'

'I suppose not,' conceded Paul, resting back in Mike's swivel chair, his arms behind his head. Judging by his relaxed pose he seemed more interested in chatting than getting down to any work. 'So, come on then, Miss Bender. Who do you know? What's on your iPod for instance?'

For a very brief second Jessica considered giving a somewhat embellished answer. One that went along the lines of what she always felt people wanted to hear: the Beatles, Mozart, the Stones, followed by loads of cool bands (like Elbow), alongside the allowed amount of necessarily kitsch pop that demonstrated that you weren't too up yourself. She didn't bother though. Other than telling certain necessary fibs, she liked Paul enough to want him to get to know her for herself.

'Well,' she replied, sitting tentatively down in the chair opposite Paul, which only added to the feeling that she was being interviewed, 'I've always loved Motown music but I'd say that the majority of stuff that I spend time listening to is pure, unadulterated pop. Mostly from the eighties and nineties. I like electronic-sounding groups like the Pet Shop Boys and Erasure. Also Madonna, Michael Jackson, Duran Duran, George Michael, Abba, Stevie Wonder, Diana Ross, the Eurythmics. I don't know really . . . anything . . . anything uplifting that puts a smile on my face. I love house music and, ooh . . . Coldplay and the Killers ,' she finished passionately.

Paul tilted his head to one side. As Jessica waited for a response she felt furious with herself for feeling so discomfited. She'd never cared in the past what anybody thought of her taste in music, so why start now? Unable to hold Paul's inscrutable gaze any longer, Jessica found herself staring at her hands.

Paul laughed. 'What?'

Jessica frowned. 'Nothing.'

'OK, it's just that you've gone bright red. Am I really that much of an arsehole that you can't even tell me what music you like?'

'No,' said Jessica, but her cheeks were obviously giving her away so she decided to elaborate. 'It's just that you strike me as one of those people who might judge others based upon what music they like, that's all.'

Paul looked faintly insulted. 'Really? God, I know I can be a bit of a grumpy shit but I'm not that bad, am I? Besides, I don't think you'd be saying that if you met my sister. Now she really has got dubious taste in music. Round my mum's house it's all Take That, Girls Aloud and Katy Perry, and that's on a good day.'

'Sounds like a girl after my own heart.'

'She's fifteen,' added Paul, grinning.

'You see,' said Jessica, no longer embarrassed but indignant. 'You do judge and you've just made out that I'm a — what's the word you guys always use? — oh, yeah, a "twat" for liking what I like.'

'I don't mean to,' Paul said, rocking back on his chair, happy to take the criticism and amused by Jessica's usage of the word 'twat'. 'If it makes you feel any better, I'm quite prone to a bit of Neil Diamond.'

Neil Diamond was a good peace offering and Jessica felt herself puff back down to normal. They both smiled and Jessica suddenly wondered when Paul was going to actually start reading her some of his links, but he still didn't seem in any hurry.

'In all honesty,' he said, resting his arms on the table, 'I far prefer people who are just truthful about what they like and dislike as opposed to saying what they think they should be saying. It just so happens though that I do have great taste.'

'Oh, whatever,' teased Jessica, narrowing her eyes, grateful that she hadn't bothered buying any lunch because right this minute she certainly wouldn't be able to eat a thing. Her eyes were drawn to Paul's arms suddenly. She liked his watch. It was old, scuffed-looking, chunky and silver, and looked great on his wrist, which she liked even more. Jeez, she needed to get a grip.

Paul had swivelled back round to the screen and was screwing his eyes up in concentration as he re-read something he'd written.

'You are right though,' said Jessica. 'Music is definitely one way people reveal themselves as pretentious if they are. In fact, do you want to know what one of my real pet hates is?'

Paul nodded, tapping away on the keypad at the same time.

'When you go to a club and the DJ plays boring track after boring track that no one's ever heard of. No one dances until finally he puts on one familiar tune, something that everyone knows and then the crowd can't get to the dance floor quick enough. Suddenly the DJ's a hero and at that point I realize that I'm not mad to love pop so much. There's a reason it's called "popular" music and if only people weren't so snobby about it then going out would be a lot more fun.'

'Thanks for that, Miss Bender,' said Paul good-humouredly, spinning back round to face her. 'And remind me to take you to Hyde Park soon. I can show you Speaker's Corner and we can take some underground, really serious trance music with us to get you all hot under the collar. Then we'll just let you go and you can expound to your heart's content about the evils of non-popular music.'

Jessica couldn't help but laugh.

Paul retrieved a biro that he'd stuck behind his ear and chewed on it thoughtfully. 'So what was it that made you decide to leave the States and come to England?'

Jessica mulled over what to say, but plumped for the truth. 'I was having a few problems at home and then one day I realized that, apart from a handful of people, there wasn't anything to stay for.'

'No boyfriend then?' enquired Paul casually, suddenly keen to know the answer.

'No boyfriend.'

'What about your dad? He must have been a bit gutted about you coming away?'

'Yes,' answered Jessica honestly, smiling as she thought of her lovely dad, who she'd always adore no matter how much he enraged her. She was already missing him dreadfully. 'He was a bit gutted, but he knows I'll be back . . . at some point.'

'You're close then?'

'Yeah,' said Jessica vaguely, not comfortable with the route the conversation was suddenly taking. 'Anyway, let's not talk about that. I want to know more about this exquisite taste in music that you have. So what would you say is your all-time favourite track?'

As she said this she leaned in across the desk, just as Paul did the same. Suddenly her face was close enough to his for her to really imagine what it might be like to kiss that gorgeous mouth of his. The air between them felt thick with something out of the ordinary, something that had been building up slowly over the last week or so. They were gazing at each other so intensely that when Kerry stuck her head round the door, it took them a while to even register she was there. When they did, however, they both got an enormous fright and sprang back in their chairs.

'Sorry, Jess, I was just wondering where you were,' Kerry said, not missing a thing. 'Are you busy or can I steal you back? I need to sort out some fruit baskets for our guests and was hoping to lumber you with it. I want to show you what I got in Primark too. G-strings for a quid, which as far as I'm concerned is all you should pay for something that's condemned to spend the rest of its life wedged up your bum crack, eh?'

Paul made a big show of grimacing and Jessica giggled. 'Sure,' she said, still laughing. 'Sorry you couldn't find me, we were just –' She stopped. She'd been about to say that they'd been reading links, but they hadn't.

'Actually, I dragged her in here to help me out with some links but I've ended up quizzing her instead about her quite spectacularly horrendous taste in music,' said Paul.

Kerry looked from him back to her assistant and smiled

to herself. It looked like Jessica was the latest victim to fall for the incredibly complicated but utterly lovely Paul, although judging by his dappy expression the feeling was perhaps mutual.

'Jess,' he was saying now, a soppy grin plastered across his face, 'has been very helpful but maybe too honest for her own good. She likes George Michael, but there you go.'

'I'd take George over Elbow any day of the week,' said Jessica, looking away coyly.

'"Jess" is it now?' Kerry teased.

Hearing the insinuation in her voice, Paul instantly reverted back to type. It was like flicking a switch. 'Anyway,' he said, almost grumpily. 'Bugger off now, you two, I need to get on.'

And, just like that, he burst the bubble. Jessica's face fell. What was she thinking anyway? It was a good thing Kerry had come in when she had, she decided. As far as she was concerned, Paul Fletcher could only spell trouble for her in one way or another. Feeling rather foolish, she stood up, but Kerry, who felt bad for teasing, decided to be kind.

'By the way,' she said casually, 'Jess is coming clubbing with us this Saturday, Paul, and I think a few others are coming from the office. You should come. Jessica's even bringing her delightful mate Veruca Salt with her, who she assures us will be on her best behaviour, so don't let that put you off.'

Paul didn't look up, busy now on the previously ignored links, but after a second or so he mumbled distractedly, 'Sounds OK, why not?'

Jessica was already halfway out the door by now but, try

as she might, she couldn't suppress the huge beam that instantly appeared. Kerry grinned, though not in over-sensitive Paul's direction. Paul never, ever went clubbing with them so it looked like her hunch was right after all, which she was genuinely pleased about, although it was also bloody typical. If only she could find what she was searching for under her very nose in this office. Some people really did have it far too easy.

20

Saturday arrived and while Jessica was getting ready Angelica rang yet again.

'Mom, hi,' said Jessica, balancing the phone under her ear while she tried to put on her eyeliner.

'Hello, I'm so glad to finally get hold of you.'

'I know, I'm sorry. I've just been so busy with work and everything. In fact, I hate to do this but I'm kinda busy right now too. I'm going out with people from work tonight and I'm running late so . . .'

'OK, but before you cut me off again,' said Angelica, her tone unusually stern, 'can we at least put something in the diary? I'm free on Monday. Shall we meet then? Maybe go for something to eat? I really want to fit it in because then I have to go away again, probably for some time, maybe even a couple of months for –'

'Great,' said Jessica, more concerned about the fact she'd just jabbed herself in the eye with her mascara wand. 'Let's catch up properly then, OK? Actually, Mom, I have to go – that's the doorbell, which means Dulcie's here. I'll see you next week.'

She rang off, took one last look in the mirror, grabbed her bag and thundered down the stairs, knowing she'd given her mother slightly short shrift. Still, maybe she'd think a bit harder the next time her boyfriend bullied her into doing something she didn't want to do. This thought didn't extinguish her guilt entirely though. She knew she should have found the time to return one of her many recent calls, but these days she was just so busy all the time and preoccupied. Still, maybe now Angelica would know how it felt.

Jessica had arranged to meet Kerry and the others in the Toucan in Soho and she and Dulcie arrived together promptly at eight thirty. Despite Jessica's instructions to dress casual, Dulcie was wearing a most fashion-forward outfit. Determined to make the last night of her trip a good one, she'd chosen a leopard-skin jumpsuit by Alexander Wang, which she actually looked pretty damn sensational in, even if she did stick out like a sore thumb. As they made their way to the bar, Jessica realized that, apart from Kerry, they were the first to arrive.

'Blimey,' Kerry said sarcastically to Dulcie as soon as she saw them approaching. 'You could have made an effort.'

Never having seen Kerry dressed for anything other than the office before, Jessica was amazed by how different her boss looked. She was wearing a very slimming black dress with red cork wedges and her unruly mane had been tamed for the evening.

'You look amazing,' Jessica said. 'I love your dress. You look so different.'

'She's right,' said Dulcie. 'I actually didn't recognize you.'

'Good,' said Kerry, 'that way you won't nag me about coming on the show.'

'Well . . . I . . .' began Dulcie, but she didn't finish what she was going to say. Jessica was giving her such a dirty look she didn't dare. She'd been lectured enough.

'You look great too by the way, Jess,' Kerry added, nodding

to Jessica's purple mini dress, which showed off her toned limbs to perfection. 'Paul's going to love it.'

Despite the fact that this was exactly what Jessica secretly wanted, instead of thanking Kerry for her well-aimed compliment she retaliated with an equally loaded one.

'And I think Luke might be quite pleasantly surprised tonight too.'

'Luke!' Kerry repeated, aghast. 'Are you having me on? As if Luke would ever look twice at me. Come to think of it, as if I would look at him twice either. We're the same bloody height, though I suspect he probably has a smaller waist than me. I'd crush him.'

'Well, I don't think he'd mind being crushed.'

Dulcie stifled a giggle and Kerry was just on the verge of telling Jessica to keep her ridiculous comments to herself when in through the doors came Isy, Vanessa, Natasha, then just behind them Luke and finally Paul. As soon as he appeared, Jessica's heart did a weird somersault in her chest. She sighed as she realized her palms had gone all sweaty and that her mouth was dry as a bone. What a dreadful cliché of someone with a crush she was being. Dulcie poking her in the ribs wasn't helping. Feeling like this wasn't supposed to happen.

The girls from the office bounded over to say hello and Jessica was touched to note that, for her sake, they all greeted Dulcie in a friendly enough manner. Though when Natasha started bombarding her with questions, Jessica did slightly suspect her motives.

In the meantime, she couldn't resist stealing another look in Paul's direction. He was chatting animatedly to Kerry but just at that moment he looked up and caught her eye. Simultaneously they both smiled broadly and Jessica knew she wasn't just imagining things. There was something between them, like a delicious secret they were both aware of. Then he noticed Dulcie and purposefully did a sort of horrified double take. It was so comical that Jessica couldn't help but giggle.

'Are you OK here for a minute?' she said to Dulcie. 'I'm just going to go to the bar.'

'I'm fine, sweetie, just enjoying this very English experience. I've never been somewhere for a drink that's actually carpeted, or that smells of dog. It's unique.'

Leaving Dulcie with Isy, Jessica gulped down the dregs of her vodka and tonic and went to the bar to order another. Even with her back to him, she could feel Paul's eyes on her and found herself flicking her hair and nibbling delicately on a finger in a coquettish manner that would normally have her puking, while hoping he might come over. Suddenly, acting like the antithesis of what women's lib had fought for felt like the only natural way to be. She turned round to sneak another peek and, sure enough, their eyes met.

'Someone's got the hots for you, girl,' said Kerry drily, leaving Paul to come and join Jessica at the bar. 'He's being all nice and I haven't seen him wearing an ironed top since he went out with Natasha,' she added, just as Luke appeared at her elbow. Jessica had no choice other than to swallow this last comment that had cannon-balled through her, triggering questions galore along the way.

'All right,' Luke said nonchalantly, his trilby perched at a rakish angle. 'You've scrubbed up all right tonight, Kezza. Hoping to pull, are you? Or are you meeting one of your Internet sex pests?'

'Shut up, arse face,' retorted Kerry, though slightly less aggressively than she might usually. Try as she might, she couldn't put what Jessica had said earlier out of her head. She knew it was utter rubbish and, as for her fancying Luke, well, it had never even crossed her mind before. It was impossible, however, not to have your interest piqued when somebody told you someone fancied you, she decided. Especially when it had been so long since someone *had* fancied her. Frankly, at this stage, if Colonel Gaddafi was interested she'd be grateful. She glanced at Luke, who grinned back, catching her eye for just a second longer than was necessary. Oh, bugger it. Bugger Jessica and her stupid ideas. Luke was just the office twat who took the piss out of her the entire time, pestering her like a little boy in the playground, pestering the girl with the pigtails, telling her he hated her when in fact he . . .

'What can I get you?' said the barmaid finally, with a world-weary air that Jessica found hilarious. In the States the service industry was that exactly, an industry, and one that took customer satisfaction seriously. In London people serving you often made you feel grateful if you got what you actually asked for, while managing to make you feel bad for asking in the first place.

'What do you want, guys?' she asked Kerry and Luke.

'Put your money away, Bender,' said Luke 'These ones are on me. I'll even buy one for your mate, old Scary Spice, and the lovely Kerry, of course.'

'Gee, thanks, Luke,' said Jessica, deliberately catching Kerry's eye and winking. 'I'll have a vodka and tonic, please.'

'I'll have a pint,' said Kerry and Jessica smiled inwardly.

Luke's expression said it all. A chick who drank pints. She was so obviously the girl of his dreams.

'So, Kerry,' said Jessica, trying and failing to sound casual, 'I was just wondering. When Paul and Natasha went out with each other, did he really like her? Out of interest,' she added hastily, hating herself for being unable to resist asking.

'Yeah, he did,' said Kerry plainly. 'But they weren't right together at all and she made him bloody miserable, so don't sweat it.'

'Yeah, don't,' said Luke, grinning inanely. 'Paul may think he's in with a chance with Natasha again, but it isn't what he wants deep down. Or rather, who he wants,' he added sweetly. 'Your name's been bandied about our flat a lot recently.'

Jessica smiled weakly. She felt reassured by this, but only mildly. God, she was a fool. If Paul still had feelings for Natasha, who frankly was a bit of a goddess, what chance did she stand? And, besides, there was no point getting involved she reminded herself, though this mantra was starting to ring less and less true.

Their drinks arrived and Jessica was just taking a rather huge slurp of hers to steady her nerves when Paul himself sauntered over.

'All right?' he greeted her with a small nod. She could smell his aftershave. It smelled divine. His own unique smell, blended in with cigarette smoke, washing powder and whatever citrusy potion he'd clearly splashed on his face. 'Drink?'

'No, thanks,' Jessica replied primly, taking another large swig. 'Luke's just got me one, thanks.'

'Well, judging by how that one's slipping down it's not going to last long, so why don't I get you another anyway?'

'Fine,' she replied, almost sulkily, battling with the ugly jealousy that had consumed her about Natasha. The amount of vodka she'd already drunk wasn't exactly helping keep her emotions in check either. She'd always been a cheap date, even by LA standards.

Just then Natasha slunk over to join them. 'Did I hear you say something about getting the drinks in? I'll have my *usual* please, Paul,' she said pointedly. She'd chosen her words carefully and looked at Jessica to make sure she'd got the message. She didn't want Paul herself but didn't necessarily want anyone else getting their claws into him either. Still, Paul wasn't stupid and due to how he'd started to feel about Jessica was less blinded when it came to his ex these days.

'You'll have to remind me,' he said, knowing exactly what she was up to. 'What is your usual? I've totally forgotten.'

Natasha looked furious but, not wanting to lose face in front of Jessica, resorted to making Paul look mean instead.

'That's right. I'd forgotten how little you used to like putting your hand in your pocket. Why would you remember?'

'Let me get you a drink,' said Jessica. The last thing she wanted was to make an enemy of Natasha.

'Go on then,' she said, not caring enough to push things any further. 'I'll have a spritzer, with soda, and then I want to get going. DJ Delish is playing the second set and I've heard he's exactly that. Fit, apparently.'

Paul rolled his eyes and shook his head, and then he stopped. How fantastic. For the first time in a long time he realized that what Natasha had just said had had precisely no effect on him whatsoever. DJ Delish was welcome to her. Brilliant.

As Natasha went back to join the other girls at a nearby table, Jessica smiled at Paul, any fears she'd had about Natasha having been put to rest for now. He looked gorgeous tonight and had that look about him that manly men always had when they'd made a real effort with their appearance. As if he'd spent a whole hour in the shower scrubbing himself as clean as it is possible to be. His dark, almost black hair was freshly washed and his clothes smelled noticeably clean. He was wearing a T-shirt with a really nice light sweater. His gorgeous butt was clad in the same kind of jeans as ever and he was wearing his usual battered trainers. A desire to nuzzle into his neck and sniff washed over her, though needless to say she didn't follow it up.

Just then Kerry saved them from self-conscious silence by announcing to the group that it was time to drink up and head for the club. Feeling decidedly tipsy, Jessica slugged back her latest drink.

'So is this club we're going to any good?'

'Never been,' said Paul. 'Though I suspect it'll be my idea of hell. You know it's called "Guilty Pleasures", don't you?'

'Er, sure,' said Jessica, suddenly worried that their evening might entail being whipped, tied up or spanked.

'Which refers to their music policy,' explained Paul. 'They only play tunes that most normal people would deem to be shit. Stuff like Take That, Abba, Spice Girls. Cheese,' he finished nonchalantly. 'You'll feel right at home.'

'No way,' said Jessica happily, having learned by now

not to take him too seriously when he wound her up, chuffed instead that he'd remembered their chat. 'It sounds like, totally awesome,' she giggled, heady from a cocktail of booze and lust.

'Yeah, like totally,' replied Paul, taking the piss.

'Oh, fuck off,' she replied, blushing madly and hitting his arm. 'Anyway, if you hate the music so much, why are you even coming?'

'Why do you think?' he answered straight away, giving her such an extraordinarily sexy look it made her shiver with longing right down to her toes. 'Though I don't know why you had to bring your mate,' he added, slightly ruining the effect.

'Because it's her last night in town and she's my best friend,' said Jessica firmly. 'I know you didn't take to her, and admittedly she didn't show herself in a great light that day, but I promise you, underneath that LA veneer she is a sweet, down-to-earth girl.'

'She looks it,' said Paul, nodding his head in Dulcie's direction and Jessica followed his gaze to see Dulcie wiping her glass with what could only be an antibacterial wipe.

21

The last time Jessica and Dulcie had gone out dancing in LA had been a few months ago. They'd gone to a party in Paris Hilton's legendary basement, which was actually a nightclub, complete with dance floor and pole to swing round. It had been a fun night and everyone had let their hair down to a degree, though never at the expense of their looks. The girls there had been careful to drink only enough to make them feel more uninhibited than usual, but not so much that they lost their handbag or control of their lip gloss coverage. When a tune came on that they liked they'd whooped coquettishly, raising one limp hand in the air, while continuing to dance sexily in their sky-high heels. Heels that were agonizingly painful to dance in, but that elongated their calves.

It seemed like a small thing at first but, as the rather well-oiled group left the pub, Jessica noticed that while the British girls' heels were high, they weren't so high that they wouldn't be able to have a 'bloody good dance'. Somehow she knew this would have been a factor in their decision to choose clumpy wedges over spindly heels and it spoke volumes to her. It seemed symbolic of the difference in attitude between the Brits and their privileged Hollywood counterparts. In short, Kerry and the others cared more about having fun than looking good and Jessica felt something akin to relief to confirm that the weird, image-obsessed microcosm she'd been brought up in wasn't the only way.

They weaved their way through Soho, an experience in itself on a Saturday night, and upon reaching the club found they had to wait in line, despite being on the guest list. When the rope was finally lifted for the group, Dulcie couldn't resist saying, 'I can't believe I'm even doing this. I've never waited in line for anything in my life.'

'First time for everything,' said Paul sharply before walking in.

'Please,' Jessica implored her friend, 'can you at least try to sound a little more down to earth?'

'All right,' said Dulcie, 'but don't go loco on me. You know half the time I only say things for the sake of it.'

By this time they were walking downstairs to the basement club and could hear the first strains of the music inside. Isy, who was just behind them, was the first to figure out what tune was playing. She let out the sort of delighted shriek normally reserved for a hen night in Magaluf and barged past them, so desperate was she to get inside.

'What is it?' said Jessica. 'What are they playing?'

Dulcie was next to work it out, though didn't stop to explain either. Instead she shoved past Jessica and raced Isy to the dance floor, any pretence at being cool having been abandoned. It was 'Girls Just Wanna Have Fun' by Cyndi Lauper. Jessica was soon hot on their heels and it wasn't long before the three girls were swirling around on the dance floor, singing along loudly. At one point, thinking that Isy was doing a funny dance for their benefit, Jessica and Dulcie laughed out loud until they realized that she wasn't and that it was just her unique style. Their faces fell as they worried that they might have hurt Isy's feelings, but they needn't have panicked. Isy was dancing with such passion she remained oblivious to the various odd looks she was getting, and not just from Jessica and Dulcie.

Paul, who for obvious reasons hadn't exactly had the same reaction to the tune, entered the club at a more relaxed pace, but grinned the minute he spotted Jessica and her friends. He was surprised to see Dulcie entering into the spirit of things so enthusiastically but, then again, recently he seemed to be feeling permanently surprised about something . . . or someone. He stood and watched Jessica spinning around, mouthing the words of the song and exuding so much happiness he felt positively uplifted. Jessica Bender definitely put a smile on his face and at this rate he might be in danger of losing his mean and moody reputation. She was gorgeous and she looked so fit in that dress.

Luke signalled across to him. He'd found some seats right next to the dance floor from where they could watch their female colleagues flinging themselves around in comfort.

'Bloody hell,' said Luke. 'What is Isy doing? She looks like she's left her medication at home or something.'

Paul grinned. 'She's like one of those drama students. You know, the ones who express themselves through movement. I am a tree.'

'At least Scary Spice is joining in,' shouted Luke as the DJ mixed the next track in. 'And Bender's not a bad little mover, is she?'

Paul flicked his friend the finger but grinned as he did so. The music was so loud there wasn't much point in talking so they sat back and enjoyed the show, both concentrating on the women they were interested in. Although, unless you were extremely observant, when it came to Luke it was hard to tell who that was.

Luke was used to keeping the way he felt about Kerry hidden, but the fact was he'd been in love with her for as long as he could remember. For as long as he could remember, Kerry had also been very vocal and very clear about her list. Her list of what she did and didn't want in a bloke. Her list that she had shared with the entire office . . . As a result of said list, Luke knew that Kerry *did* want to meet someone who could make her laugh. That part he felt he could manage. She also wanted someone who was solvent, kind and honest and who loved her more than she loved him. Ditto all of the above.

She *didn't* want, however, to be with anyone who didn't like dogs. Luke loved dogs. She also didn't want anyone racist, snobby, pretentious or stuck-up. Fine. Though she definitely did want someone with a good head of hair and her ideal man had to be tall. These particular criteria she'd announced on more than one occasion, to more than one person. Luke was never going to be tall and there was a reason he always wore his beloved hat.

Furthermore, Kerry didn't want to be with anyone who worked in the same industry because she worried they'd never have anything to talk about, and she definitely couldn't be with a mummy's boy. Luke worked in TV and loved his mum a ridiculous amount. In fact, if he had flu he couldn't swear, hand on heart, that he wouldn't want his mum to look after him over and above everyone else. In a nutshell, over the year and a half that Luke had known

Kerry she had said enough to ensure that he didn't feel able to let his feelings be known as she'd made it clear that if he did, for some of the reasons above, she would reject him. So he settled for adoring her from afar, spent a lot of time praying that she wouldn't meet anyone else and, for one very worrying day, considered investing in some Cuban heels.

Meanwhile, Jessica was in a world of her own. This place was her idea of nirvana. The vibe was amazing and so unlike the places she went to in LA. She wasn't the only one to notice.

'Oh my gosh, Jess,' screamed Dulcie, her eyes shining with excitement. 'This is so cool. I'm having . . . fun. I can't even remember the last time I just went for it without worrying about what people would think of me.'

'Good, isn't it?' said Jessica, grinning at her friend, enjoying seeing her so happy and relaxed.

'It's great,' agreed Dulcie. 'I have to admit I can even kinda see why you like it here.'

'I know, the music's brilliant.'

'I didn't mean that. I meant here in London, with these people. They're OK, you know? And you seem happy. In fact, seeing you doing your own thing has made me understand why you needed to get away.' The two girls embraced. 'But, listen, don't think you need to babysit me. I'm cool hanging with your friends if you want to go find lover boy.'

'Don't be silly,' protested Jessica.

'I'm not,' said Dulcie. 'He's a judgemental asshole, but I can tell you like him and he is nice-looking.'

Jessica shook her head. 'I admit there's something about

him . . . maybe, but there's no real point getting to know him better when I don't even know how long I'm going to be here for.'

'Why not?' asked Dulcie, looking genuinely puzzled.

'Because it's not like it could ever work out or anything.'

Just then Isy emerged from the crowd, looking dishevelled. 'Dulcie, my old leopard snake, come and do the wolf dance with me.'

'Coming,' called Dulcie. 'You know what?' she said to Jessica, her dark eyes glittering. 'I think you're so brave for coming here, but when it comes down to it you're too scared to give anything that might actually force you to feel something a go. I don't get it, Jess,' she said, shrugging despondently.

'Come on,' said Isy, dragging Dulcie away.

'I love this girl!' yelled Dulcie over her shoulder. 'She has to come to LA. She's a scream. Paris would love her.'

Jessica briefly put her finger to her mouth, warning her friend to keep quiet about life back in LA. What Dulcie had just said had annoyed her. She did like Paul, it was true, and she was seriously tempted to encourage a fling, but didn't want to end up hurt.

'Hey, you,' said a voice in her ear. She knew who it was without having to turn round.

'Do you want to come and sit down?' Paul asked.

Contradicting everything she'd just been thinking, she nodded, even ignoring the fact that 'Dancing Queen' had just come on, which proved how much she liked him.

They found a free table and she flung herself down next to him. 'Hi,' she said shyly, feelings of self-consciousness returning by the bucketload.

'Having a good time then?' Paul asked her.

'Oh, gosh, yes,' she answered, amazed he couldn't tell. 'This place is awe– oh – you're kidding, right?'

'Yes, Miss Bender, I am kidding,' he said.

They regarded each other for a while and as Jessica stared into his eyes she noticed, not for the first time, that he had the most amazing eyelashes. The funny feeling in her stomach returned. Paul uncrossed his arms, leaned forward and brushed a stray bit of her hair back behind her ear. She gulped. She had never wanted anybody to kiss her quite so much as she wanted Paul Fletcher to kiss her right now. What would be so wrong with having a holiday romance anyway? Typically, however, just when Paul seemed to be thinking the same thing, Kerry barrelled over, hotly pursued by a very drunk-looking Luke. The two of them were clearly on a mission and were carrying trays of potent-looking shots.

'Here you go, you two,' she said. Then, 'Isy, Van, Tash, Scary Spice!' she screeched at an impressive decibel that the girls could hear from the other side of the dance floor.

'Wow,' said Paul. 'Your voice is like . . . a dog whistle – not that I'm calling them dogs or anything,' he added hurriedly as they all came dancing over. Jessica noticed that Dulcie couldn't keep her eyes off Isy. She looked positively star-struck by the younger girl.

'Oh my God,' Isy was screeching breathlessly now. 'I just snogged a Japanese tourist who told me I'm the best dancer he's ever seen in his life.'

'I'd like to see the worst,' said Luke and, as Isy proceeded to do her impression of what the worst might look like, everyone cracked up. One by one, they all went to grab a flaming Sambuca from Kerry's tray and as they did Jessica felt quite overwhelmed by the wonderful feeling of camaraderie amongst these new friends she'd made in England. God, she was drunk. So was Dulcie.

'I'd like to say something to the group,' her friend was saying now, her voice a little slurred.

'Go for it,' said Kerry good-humouredly.

'OK, well, I know we didn't exactly get off to a great start, and that you wouldn't have me on your show in a million years, but I still think you guys are pretty awesome. You're wrong too, obviously, because I'd actually be a brilliant guest, but you're still awesome nonetheless. So thanks for having me tonight and please make sure you look after Jess for me when I'm back in the States.'

'We will,' said Kerry.

'You can count on it,' added Vanessa, her accent more pronounced than ever. Dulcie stared at her blankly, clearly not having understood what she'd said. Jessica giggled. It wasn't just her then.

'I reckon she's doing quite a good job of looking after herself,' piped up Paul with only the slightest edge to his voice.

Dulcie narrowed her eyes. 'Well, it's up to you,' she said, 'but you have no idea what you'd be up against if you messed her around in any way. Oh my God, Mr G gets pissed even if –'

'OK, let's not bore everybody about that, Dulcie,' yelled Jessica, sort of launching herself at her friend.

'Oh, sure,' agreed Dulcie, checking herself.

'I always get this feeling there's something you're not telling us, Jessica,' shouted Natasha across the din.

Jessica was just debating what to say when she was saved

by the DJ's next choice of record. It was 'Baby One More Time' by Britney Spears and as soon as they heard the familiar opening chords, all the girls, including Natasha, decided that dancing was more of a pressing need than interrogating Jessica and rushed back to the dance floor. Jessica's head was left swirling. Should she follow them? Then Paul reached out for her hand. She sat back down. There was no contest really.

'It's my soundalike,' she said loudly. By this point nothing was being said any more, only shouted. 'Didn't you guys decide I sound like Britney?'

Paul grinned. 'We're horrid to you, aren't we?'

'Kinda,' she said, shrugging. 'But, hey, you're all pretty nice underneath.'

'Good,' said Paul. 'So you'll be staying in England for a while then?'

Jessica thought of home, and her dad and about Dulcie leaving tomorrow, and experienced a sharp pang of homesickness, yet knew she was here a while longer.

'Yes. I think I will. I like England,' she replied, the drink making her feel uninhibited. 'Even if it is a weird old place.'

'Can't be weirder than the country that let that idiot Bush run them for all those years,' said Paul unimaginatively. He was drunk too.

'Whatever,' Jessica retorted, laughing, 'and besides, shouldn't you be looking at how many great things there are about my country, and how much of our culture you guys love? What track is the DJ playing right now, for crissakes? And you know we make the best shows, so get over it.'

Paul laughed. 'You are hilarious, Jessica Bender. Not

my cup of tea in so many ways and yet I can tell you're all right really.'

'Oh, really?' she said, displaying her straight, white, orthodontically dealt-with teeth.

'Really,' he replied, flashing his own slightly crooked, home-grown ones.

'Well, that's very good of you to say so,' she said simply and he grinned. The two of them sat in happy silence for a while, laughing now and then at the others' antics on the dance floor. Vanessa was holding on to Isy's ankles and guiding her round the club like a wheelbarrow, until they both collapsed on the floor from laughing so hard. The Japanese tourist was clutching his sides and taking hundreds of photos, clearly enamoured with Isy, who was wearing her quirkiest outfit yet, an original concoction of tartan, lace and Doc Martens.

'You'd never catch any of my friends at home doing that kind of thing.'

Paul shot her a quizzical look, as if a world without people doing wheelbarrows in nightclubs was unimaginable.

'It's true,' said Jessica. 'You Brits are so much more relaxed about stuff. Take people's attitudes to how they look, for instance. I was watching something with my aunt. I think it was called *Coronation Street*? Anyway, I couldn't believe how ordinary the cast looked, which is so cool, because that way you don't end up comparing yourself unfavourably with people the whole time and ... am I making sense?'

'I'm enjoying the speech,' said Paul. 'Carry on.'

Jessica blushed and scrunched up her nose.

'I'm serious,' said Paul, and for once he sounded it. 'I

like hearing you chat about things. Tell me what other conclusions you've come to about our green and pleasant land.'

'Really?'

'Really.'

'OK,' said Jessica, battling against the volume. 'Well, I love how London just reeks of history, cliché I know, and I also love how you guys speak, especially your newsreaders. They sound so regal, which isn't surprising, I guess, considering they're from a country that actually has a royal family. I mean, even the name of your country sounds stately. The United KINGdom. I love that. It just sums England and the English up. It's so classy, so dignified.'

'You sure about that?' asked Paul, his face completely deadpan, at which point Jessica followed his gaze across the room to see Kerry clambering on top of a speaker in a very unladylike manner. Once she'd mounted it, due more to sheer perseverance as opposed to any athletic ability, she proceeded to shout something at the top of her lungs. From where Jessica was sitting it looked like 'Let's be having you.' Then a large bouncer appeared from nowhere and dragged her off. Jessica cringed as the whole club got a glimpse of her knickers.

'Admittedly,' she said, 'that's probably not the best example of British decorum I've ever seen, but then again . . .'

'Oh, shut up will you and come here,' said Paul, and unable to wait a second longer he reached out for her, his hand finding the back of her head, and pulled her gently towards him. He then proceeded to kiss her so unbelievably well, Jessica honestly thought fainting was a distinct possibility. As his tongue explored her mouth she felt a sensation that started in her knickers, worked its way right up through her belly and ended in her brain, little tingles appearing throughout. Kissing him felt utterly right and she would have been quite happy to stay like that for the foreseeable future only just then the sound of Isy whooping on the dance floor carried across the club. It seemed to act like a trigger, for Paul immediately stopped and, as quickly as he'd started, pulled away again.

Jessica was left awash with disappointment and paranoia. Would it be that awful to be seen kissing her? She couldn't say anything because now some of the girls from the office were advancing, one of them being Natasha.

Clearly ruffled, Paul ran a hand through his hair and visibly tried to compose himself, just as Mark Ronson's 'Valerie' came on and a huge cheer went up in the club.

'At last, a tune I actually like,' he said jokily, his voice tellingly hoarse.

At least he was as turned on as she was, Jessica thought ruefully, giving him a perfunctory smile by way of reply, too wrapped up in her own thoughts to do much more. Did Paul not want to be seen kissing her out of embarrassment, or because he cared what Natasha thought, or because he was just being sensible? She wasn't sure and was too drunk to figure it out, though it briefly crossed her mind that come Monday morning she might be more concerned herself about being the subject of office gossip. As it was, she'd been totally carried away in the moment. A sobering thought.

'Wotcher!' yelled Isy, breaking the spell completely but also dispelling some of the tension.

'Hi,' said Jessica, smiling at her.

'OMG, I am so thirsty,' said the younger girl. 'I could lick that sweaty bouncer's forehead I've got such bad dry mouth.'

'No need,' said Natasha, sauntering over with a jug of tap water and some glasses. Suddenly Jessica was horribly aware of how good the other girl looked in her French Connection playsuit and platform sandals.

'Not dancing, Pauly?' enquired Natasha, as Isy grabbed the jug from her and drank directly from it.

'You know I don't dance,' Paul said to his ex.

'I do,' she agreed. 'But I thought you might make an exception for this tune.'

This last comment was loaded with meaning and Jessica felt sick to the stomach. Paul and Natasha had tunes that meant stuff to them. They had history and yet here she was, having known him a mere couple of weeks, getting completely ahead of herself. She was so naive. What was she even thinking?

'Well, I'm going back for more,' said Vanessa, having also downed about a pint of water.

'Me too,' said Isy, leaving the jug on the low table in front of where Jessica and Paul were sitting before heading back to the dance floor with Natasha and Vanessa.

Once they'd gone Paul immediately turned to her, but Jessica avoided his eye, for now it was Dulcie's turn to dance over to them. This time Jessica was pleased of the distraction. She had some serious thinking to do when it came to Paul Fletcher and she suddenly wasn't so sure of the wisdom of leaping feet first into an ill-advised office romance. She certainly didn't want to be treading on Natasha's toes.

She smiled at her friend. Dulcie really did stick out like

a sore thumb, but in a good way, and even Paul couldn't help but crack a grin as she bobbed her way over to them.

'Room for a little one,' she yelled, squeezing between the two of them. 'Don't worry, I'm not staying long, I just wanted a quick word with lover boy here, seeing as I'm off tomorrow.'

Jessica cringed and nudged Dulcie hard in the ribs.

'Ow!' screeched Dulcie, slightly ruining the effect.

'If you're going to issue another warning, you needn't bother. I'll look out for Jess,' said Paul and Jessica's heart nearly popped out of her chest and went for a hopeful little dance by itself. Unfortunately, however, she couldn't ignore for another second how much she needed the toilet.

'I'm going to the bathroom,' she told them, feeling torn. She hated leaving them alone, wary of what might be said, but was completely bursting. Damn that litre of alcohol.

'So,' said Dulcie, once Jessica had scuttled off, 'I can tell you've decided not to like me, but you should know that actually I'm not all bad.'

'I never said you were,' said Paul. 'I don't even know you. We're just . . . different.'

'Well, of course we are,' exclaimed Dulcie. 'We come from totally different places, but that doesn't mean we can't find a way to get on. Besides, if you're going to be getting it on with my BF, we should make the effort. It'll be good for you anyway. You're so closed.'

'Oh, God,' moaned Paul. 'Psychobabble on a Saturday night in a club. My favourite. And who said anything about "getting it on" with Jessica?'

Dulcie answered with a look that spoke volumes about

how ridiculous she found this comment. 'I've got eyes, haven't I? Look, Paul, there's a huge rock of granite on your shoulder but you must have some redeeming features because Jessica has decided you're OK. So I'm willing to give you the benefit of the doubt.'

'You're willing to give *me* the benefit of the doubt?' repeated Paul, dumbfounded but laughing despite himself. 'Look, the feeling's mutual, OK? Jessica obviously cares about you so you must be all right because she's all right, but that doesn't mean we have to be best mates. I'm sure you are a lovely person, underneath all that . . . leopard-skin, but we're never going to have stuff in common like Jess and I do for instance.'

'Oh, yeah?' said Dulcie, getting agitated. 'So in what way are Jess and I so different then?'

'I'm not saying it's your fault,' said Paul earnestly. 'It's just, unlike you, Jessica has always had to work hard. She's had to make something out of nothing, whereas you've been handed it all on a plate. She's on my level. Her dad drives your dad, for Christ's sake.'

'Paul,' sighed Dulcie, shaking her head, 'have you ever stopped to think that maybe you get on with Jessica because she's an amazing person and not because of her background? And let me tell you something else for nothing: if someone does come from money it doesn't necessarily mean their life is one long walk in the park.'

Paul didn't look convinced.

'Besides, how can any of us help who our parents are, or how we're raised?'

Paul regarded her for a while. 'Look, I didn't mean to

upset you and you're right, that stuff *shouldn't* matter,' he said, offering Dulcie a hand. 'But sadly it does, though I'd like to call a truce.'

'A truce,' agreed Dulcie, her even white teeth breaking into a glorious grin.

'I suppose we're all just a product of our upbringings to some degree,' said Paul philosophically. 'Our parents' fuck-ups.'

'You can say that again,' agreed Dulcie, who could tell Jessica was in for a tough time if she pursued this one. Apart from anything else she'd *have* to come clean about who she was eventually and, when she did, she didn't think Paul would be letting her off the hook that easily. God, she'd love to see the look on his face though, if and when she did.

Just then Jessica returned from the bathroom.

'You two OK?'

'Yup,' said Dulcie and Paul at the same time.

'Oh my gosh!' Jessica suddenly yelled.

'What?' said Paul.

'Look!' shouted Jessica, feeling so happy she thought she might burst. Paul looked over to where she was pointing. On the dance floor, Luke had clearly decided (or was just drunk enough, one of the two) that tonight was the night to make his feelings known, whether Kerry bloody well liked it or not. Now he was striding purposefully towards her, a look of serious intent on his face and, having noticed, Jessica had immediately guessed what he might be about to do. By contrast, entirely unaware of her impending suitor, Kerry was still hurling herself around the dance floor to Amy Winehouse's dulcet tones, a bouncer to one side keeping a very close eye on her.

Looking painfully nervous, Luke reached her. His shoulders were so rigid he looked like he had a coat hanger in his jacket and Jessica found herself crossing her fingers. Meanwhile, Paul, who was slowly cottoning on to what was happening, was watching as intently as an England football fan watching a penalty shoot-out at the World Cup. He was just as nervous of the outcome too and when Luke tapped Kerry on the shoulder, boss-eyed with fear, Jessica prayed she wouldn't reject him.

Meanwhile, a still-bouncing Kerry turned round, not particularly surprised to find Luke standing there until he leaned in to say something in her ear. Then, before their very eyes, Kerry's expression changed from carefree to stunned, for before she'd had a chance to react to what Luke had said, he took her in his arms, swept her downwards and proceeded to passionately snog her face off.

'What the hell?' yelled Paul, who could hardly believe what was unfolding. He started to laugh, more out of shock than anything else. 'Way to go, Lukey boy!' he shouted.

'God, I miss Kevin,' said Dulcie wistfully before getting up to go and find Isy.

When Luke finally let go, Kerry looked like her first instinct was to slap him hard around the face, but then it seemed to occur to her that actually she'd quite enjoyed kissing him. Sensing he might be in with a chance, Luke grabbed her again and the two of them began kissing like people who'd been told on good authority the world was about to end. A crowd gathered around them and, thinking on his Adidas-clad feet, DJ Delish whipped off what was playing and replaced it with 'Young Hearts Run Free'. The onlookers cheered with the romance of it all and, when they finally came up for air, for once Kerry was lost for words. Luke, however, having waited a bloody long time for this, punched the air in delight in a way that made Kerry's normally tough façade crumble away altogether. As people started to approach the 'happy couple', shaking their hands and offering their congratulations, she looked completely choked.

Jessica clapped her hands together delightedly. 'That is so awesome,' she squealed.

'Luke and Kerry?' said Paul, still marvelling at what had just taken place. 'What were the chances of that happening?'

'Oh, they were high,' said Jessica sagely, giving him a flirty sidelong glance.

Paul's face grew serious again. 'I was thinking, perhaps after this, if you feel like it, I might invite a few people back to mine and Luke's place. Why don't you come?'

Jessica wondered what to do. It was very, very tempting, though it would be less of an interesting prospect if one of the people going back was Natasha. Still, she was pleased he'd asked. Just then, however, the DJ selected 'Holiday' by Madonna as his next tune and immediately a series of lightning-fast connections took place in Jessica's brain. Holiday . . . why was that ringing such loud alarm bells? And then it hit her. Mike was coming back from his holiday on Sunday afternoon. Sunday, which was, by this point, today. She grabbed Paul's wrist to look at his watch.

'Shit!'

'It's not that much of a terrible idea, is it?' said Paul, looking hurt.

'Mike.'

Paul recoiled. That was the last thing he'd expected to hear.

'No, no, you don't understand,' said Jessica quickly. 'It's two in the morning, which means it's Sunday, which means that Mike gets home today and I haven't watered his garden for a week. Not even once. He's going to kill me.'

Paul opened his mouth to protest. In the grand scheme of things Mike's garden was so far down the list of stuff he was concerned about it was unbelievable. Still, he could sense that the moment had already been lost.

'Well, maybe we could go for a drink or something soon?' he said, trying not to sound too eager.

Jessica took his hand, her eyes full of regret, but focused never the less on leaving. 'Maybe,' she said. 'Though I think you need to figure out how you feel about Natasha. I don't want to tread on anyone's toes.'

At this, Paul was quite taken aback. He conceded her point though, despite being more surprised by what she'd said than anything else.

Jessica, meanwhile, was hit by a huge wave of disappointment. The only reason she'd mentioned the other girl was because she was fishing for a denial that Natasha was an issue in the first place.

'Anyway,' she said, trying to be brave. 'I'm just going to go and find Dulcie to say goodbye and then I'm off. If I leave now I can get a bit of sleep and get to Chiswick before Mike gets back.'

'OK, though let's still have that drink some time,' said Paul, but Jessica didn't answer. Instead she stood up, stopping only to turn and give him a little wave before heading off into the crowd to find Dulcie.

Which was how Mike Connor managed to ruin any chance Paul Fletcher might have had that night of getting Jessica Bender back to his place, something he was starting to realize he really wanted to do.

22

Some hours later, in Malibu, it would be fair to say Edward's Saturday night hadn't gone as well as his daughter's. He peeked at the clock, which read five thirty in the morning. Due to a combination of too much alcohol, food and anxiety, sleep was no longer an option. Like Jessica, he and Betsey had also been out 'dancing' for the evening. Needless to say this hadn't been his idea, but he'd gone with it, knowing his wife hoped an evening of 'fun' might save their marriage.

Ironically, as it turned out, the evening had probably killed their relationship off for good. Edward buried his face further into the pillow as if that might help diminish the embarrassment of the evening somehow. Torturing himself, he relived how one of the paparazzi outside the club had mistaken Betsey for his daughter. At this point he'd turned to look at his wife — fresh-faced in her skimpy black dress and killer heels — and had seen how they might look to other people. Instead of feeling chuffed or proud, however, like some men would, he'd just felt sad and rather pathetic. When had the age gap between them become such a big deal? What was this young woman doing with him? And what the hell was he doing here?

This last thought had coincided with their entry into the club, at which point any more thinking had become a complete impossibility. The music was thunderously loud and as Betsey headed for the dance floor it took Edward a second to realize his hand was attached to hers and that she was dragging him with her.

Too tired to compete with the racket, he'd limply followed, wishing his jeans weren't quite so tight while trying his hardest to remember how to dance. Feeling self-conscious, he'd shuffled about, wondering if he looked like the sort of man that young people laughed at. The sort of man who dyed his hair with Grecian 2000, who refused to mature gracefully and who insisted on driving around in open-top sports cars wearing a baseball cap.

At this point Edward had decided it was time to leave, but realized he'd lost Betsey. Not that it took long to find her. She was right in the middle of the dance floor, grinding into a muscular young man's groin. And as he watched her do what would in other clubs be described as a lap dance, the only thing he could think about was the snack he was going to make when he got in.

Now, as he lay fretting in bed, suffering from mild reflux (he'd gone heavy on the mayo), he realized it was time to set Betsey free while she still had time to create a new life for herself. He did love her in a way, just not the right way. He was *fond* of her, which she would hate, and yet that was it in a nutshell. They were fond of each other, but they shouldn't be together.

Bugger. Now he needed a piss, one of the more annoying signs of advancing age. No matter what time he awoke these days, going to the toilet was always an immediate, pressing need. Anxious not to disturb Betsey, Edward slipped out from between the sheets, padded into the bathroom, took a leak and then grabbed his navy Ralph

Lauren robe from the back of the door before sneaking downstairs.

Edward's study was his sanctuary. His huge desk, which had been carved from the wood of a mango tree, took centre stage. The wall behind it was studded with framed posters and stills taken from the many movies he'd made over the years, the Bond ones taking pride of place, of course. In the one from *The World in Your Hand* Edward was wearing his trademark tuxedo and looking down the barrel of a gun at Angelica (Heavenly Melons), who was perched on top of a giant globe in her infamous black bikini. She looked sultry, captivating, the stuff of any red-blooded male's fantasies.

Down the side of the room were glass sliding doors, which when opened allowed the ocean air to infuse the room with its salty tang. Right now, however, the sun wasn't yet up so the ocean view was grey and steely.

At the far side of the room was Edward's viewing area. A huge home cinema screen dominated the back wall and on either side of the giant screen were floor to ceiling shelves that housed his incredible collection of films. Edward hadn't got into the movies by accident. He'd loved films ever since he was a young boy and had been buying them for as long as he could remember on every format there had ever been.

This morning, he already knew exactly what he wanted to watch and, with Betsey asleep, the coast was clear. As he nipped across to his desk, he felt a dart of pleasurable anticipation. He took a small key from his cigar box, unlocked a drawer on the right-hand side and took from it a brown padded envelope, inside of which was a DVD.

Then, furtively looking towards the door to check no one was coming, he scuttled back across the room, slotted the DVD into the machine and took position in his favourite chair. He pressed a button on the remote and the blackout curtains lurched into action and shut. The room was plunged into total darkness. Here we go, he thought, a shiver running down his spine.

Forty minutes later and Edward Granger was an emotional wreck. He was watching the rushes from Angelica Dupree's latest movie, the one she'd been shooting in Morocco, and had been completely blown away by her performance. The film was in French, Angelica's first language, and although Edward was by no means fluent he understood enough to cope without subtitles, which was fortunate seeing as they wouldn't be added until after the film had been edited. He knew only too well how lucky he was to be seeing anything at this raw stage at all and it was only because he knew the producer so well that he'd managed to twist his arm to run him off a copy.

In this scene, Angelica, trapped in an unhappy, fruitless marriage, was telling the man she really loved she could never see him again and that she was honour bound to stay with her pig of an abusive husband. (The reasons for which weren't exactly clear to Edward as he hadn't seen the preceding scenes.) It was a tribute to her acting ability that even with so little of the plot available to Edward she had still managed to move him so much. She was wonderfully understated, letting her big aquamarine eyes do most of the talking.

Edward rummaged in his pocket for a handkerchief and blew his nose hard. He'd always been easily moved to tears during films. He'd always been easily moved to tears full stop, something Angelica had teased him about mercilessly, though in truth she'd found it endearing. In private she'd often used to call him her 'soppy date', an expression she'd heard his sister Pam use and had adopted as her own, and when they'd watched films together, the minute his handkerchief had appeared from his pocket she'd known he was on his way. That he was about to, or was already, blubbing. While Jessica was growing up, school plays, especially nativities or anything that involved children singing had been a complete no-no and Edward had always tried to avoid watching anything too sentimental in public. After all, it didn't really do for James Bond to get caught on an aeroplane blubbing at *Cheaper by the Dozen* with Steve Martin. He shuddered at that particular memory. That really had been embarrassing. Still, in the privacy of his own cinema he could sob as much as he wanted. And he did.

On screen Angelica was turning away from her lover, years of hurt and frustration etched on her face as she began to race for the door. She was superb, which came as no surprise to Edward for, unlike most people, he had always known what an incredibly talented actress she was.

The only reason hardly anyone else had cottoned on to this fact was because whenever she was on screen people were usually so enraptured, so busy, drinking in her delicious beauty that whether she was acting well or not somehow became irrelevant. As a result, whatever she'd done over the years, no matter how powerful a performance she'd turned in, her looks had always managed to totally overshadow it. Only now, after a couple of decades of aging, was she finally getting to the point where the edge was diminishing from her ridiculous beauty and people could actually start to see past it. After this performance Edward was sure she might finally get the credit she'd always been due. Maybe even a nod at the Oscars? She was spellbinding.

He wondered how she'd react if he phoned and told her. He'd been trying to find an excuse to call her back ever since they'd last spoken, but was terrified of all that was unsaid between them. He could still hardly believe she'd rung and had spent nearly every second of every day since wondering whether she'd spoken to Jessica and, if so, why she hadn't called him back again. He had hoped she'd wanted to make peace, but her silence suggested otherwise. Still, maybe it was for the best. He wasn't sure he'd ever be able to forgive her anyway.

Edward looked at his watch. Betsey would be up soon so he should finish. He was just about to switch off, however, when the next scene flickered on to the screen. The camera panned slowly across a beautifully lit room and Edward realized with a start that Angelica was sitting on a bed completely and utterly, and somewhat surprisingly, naked. Her face was luminous and as she looked over one shoulder he could just make out a glimpse of breast, though her long, luscious hair covered the rest. She was breathtaking, even at forty-eight. Maybe even more so than she'd ever been. As Edward stared he suddenly felt like a voyeur, but his body simply wouldn't comply with his brain, which was telling him to turn it off. Enraptured, he watched as Angelica got up and crossed the room to look out of the window, the camera behind her so her bottom was on full display. Her bottom that Edward hadn't seen for so many years and yet was still so utterly familiar, less pert possibly, but all the more real and gorgeous for it. These Frenchies don't hold back when it comes to nude scenes, he thought ruefully. Still, there was nothing sordid about it. It was exquisitely shot. On screen Angelica turned round, her face registering surprise as someone came into the room.

'Jean Paul,' she gasped as her lover rushed into her arms. Then, to Edward's horror, the bastard started kissing her passionately, his mouth smothering her face, her neck, her hair with kisses, his hand at her still full breast. Edward couldn't help it. He kept on staring, completely mesmerized and engulfed by such a complicated, heady cocktail of emotion he could hardly breathe. Then . . .

'What the hell?'

The overhead light snapped on and Edward spun round only to be confronted by a confused and angry-looking Betsey. Her hair was rumpled and she'd thrown on one of his shirts and a pair of Ugg boots.

'Betsey . . . you're up. I'll switch this off. I was just doing some research for my movie and –'

'Are you watching porn?' squealed Betsey, her face trembling with fury as she took in the scene on the screen. Mortified, but hugely grateful that Betsey was unable to make out who the actress was due to the fact that Angelica had now been shoved up against the wall and was being pawed from behind, Edward found the remote and turned the offending images off. He was horrified to feel himself blushing. Jesus, this was worse than getting caught with his hands below the covers by his mother when he was a teenager.

'Of course not,' he protested. 'I know it looked a bit racy but I can assure you it wasn't porn.'

'Aaaeurgh,' wailed Betsey, pointing an accusing finger in his direction. 'You bastard, Edward. You won't have sex with your own wife and yet the minute my back is turned you've got filthy movies on and your hands down your trousers.'

Edward was insulted. 'Now hang on a minute, Betsey.'

But she wasn't having any of it. 'Hang on? You ask me to hang on, well, maybe I should hang on to that,' and she pointed again, only this time in the direction of Edward's groin.

Wrong-footed, Edward's gaze travelled downwards, where he was possibly even more surprised than Betsey to discover he was the proud owner of the biggest trouser tent he'd had in years. Watching Angelica had given him a massive erection and what he made of that he wasn't sure. Betsey, however, was very clear where she stood on the subject. As she switched off the light and slammed the door behind her, Edward was plunged into darkness.

'Damn it!' he shouted. This was going to be a hard one to explain. Literally.

23

As Monday morning dawned over London, Mike Connor was enjoying being back in his own bed in Chiswick. He'd never felt so happy to be home after a holiday in his life, nor so excited to be returning to work, which by comparison would be just the rest he needed. What a disaster the whole experience had been from beginning to end and how lovely it had been last night to climb between familiar sheets. To know that if they ran out of nappies he wouldn't have to drive five kilometres down a mountain to buy them.

He vowed not to go away again with the kids until they were at least twelve. If Diane insisted then he *might* contemplate going to one of those Mark Warner-type places, where they had kids' clubs, babysitters galore and fish fingers and chips on the menu. All things he'd previously abhorred, but which now sounded like a thoroughly sensible idea. The reality of a villa in Tuscany had been quite a different kettle of fish from the blissful idyll they'd imagined.

Carefully, he turned over, desperate not to wake Diane and incur her wrath. He'd had enough of that over the last fortnight. The whole trip seemed to have passed in an unhappy blur of preventing Grace from drowning and arguing with each other, to the point where he wasn't sure who'd done the most crying, baby Ava or Diane. Without his usual excuse of work to fall back on, he'd also been obliged to do the odd three in the morning feed, though he didn't know why he'd bothered. Diane's boobs were so sore, she'd always ended up getting out of bed anyway, seemingly reproachful that he couldn't produce milk from his own intact, non-cracked nipples.

Last night he hadn't exactly had the deep sleep he'd anticipated either. He'd been woken up by a bloody fox rummaging around in the dustbins at some ungodly hour and had been staring at the ceiling ever since, his eyes adjusting slowly to the ever-decreasing gloom. Diane, lying next to him, was seemingly so done in by their 'holiday' that she remained oblivious to the racket the mangy animal was making. She'd even started snoring at one point, something she vehemently denied she did whenever he brought it up, which always antagonized him because how could she actually know one way or another? God, when had life become so deeply unsexy?

He sighed. If before he'd been worried about Diane, then the holiday had only seemed to prove that his concern wasn't unfounded. He'd barely recognized the neurotic, stressed-out version of the woman he'd married and, rather than provide the pick-me-up their relationship so needed, the trip had only served to highlight how difficult Diane was finding Motherhood this time round. He resented how little she desired him these days too. At times it felt like she'd rather do anything than have sex with him. Grout some tiles, bleach the toilet, do a tax return – anything so long as it didn't involve having to make physical contact with him.

He looked at the digital clock on his bedside table. 05.45. The girls would be awake soon. Maybe he should shower now. That way he'd hear them when they woke up and Diane could have a bit longer in bed. A treat before he left her to it . . .

A few hours later, the sun had fully risen in the sky and, over in Hampstead, Jessica was in danger of running late for work for the first time ever. She'd had no trouble waking up on time and had even managed to fit in her usual run; it was just choosing what to wear that was delaying her, which was ridiculous given that she'd seen Paul at work every day for a couple of weeks now. Yet since their kiss everything felt different, as if all the cards had been thrown into the air. What to wear suddenly seemed crucial and butterflies weren't just fluttering in her belly, they were positively flapping their wings furiously, and the wings felt the size of Dumbo's ears. Eurgh, what an image, she thought, grimacing as she pulled a comb through her hair. Think about something else. Think about the kiss again, that amazingly wonderful kiss that was causing her so much turmoil as she wondered what, if anything, it had meant to Paul.

OK, now she was delaying herself even further. Right, denim skirt, Havaianas flip-flops and her blue and white top. Done.

Meanwhile, not far away in Tufnell Park, Paul and Luke were embarking on their usual commute, only today they had a very special guest in tow. In the end, Kerry was the only person to have been asked back to their place in the early hours of Sunday morning. Not that Paul had seen much of her or Luke. They'd been holed up in his room the entire time, emerging only to use the bathroom, make cups of tea and once to pay for an Indian takeaway. Paul was pleased for them, really pleased, yet Kerry's presence in the flat only highlighted the fact that he was alone. As a result, he'd spent most of Sunday wondering if he'd offended Jessica when he'd pulled away from her in the club. He hoped not because, apart from anything else, he didn't really care what anyone thought about him liking her. After all, even a box set of *The Wire* couldn't distract him from thinking about Jessica Bender for very long.

Now the motley bunch were headed for the tube, Luke sporting a smile so wide it looked painful and Kerry wearing the same dress she'd worn to go clubbing, only with one of Luke's T-shirts over it, stretched across her ample bosom. Paul was slightly alarmed by how his two friends seemed to have transformed overnight into Liza Minnelli and David Gest circa their wedding. Watching someone's tongue entering and waggling around in another person's mouth is never a particularly pleasant sight. What might feel nice to the people partaking always looked revolting to those watching. Funnily enough, he'd never have had either of them down as the touchy-feely type and yet now they were seemingly glued together and were being hideously tactile. Still, hopefully they'd settle down a bit eventually. In the meantime he was just looking forward to getting into work and seeing Jessica again. He wanted to set things straight in her mind and to let her know that his relationship with Natasha was a thing of the past, something he'd realized once and for all.

Back in Chiswick, once Mike had left for work, Diane Connor's day got underway. The holiday she'd been counting on to solve all her problems was over. Not only was it over but it had been worse than useless in terms of sorting out her head. If anything, she felt more wretched than she had before. She probably would have felt better if she'd stayed at home and drunk an extra cup of tea, she mused.

She gazed down at her baby daughter and tried to adjust the position of her mouth at her breast, but little Ava was having none of it. The sheer power of her suck was incredible, like when you try to vacuum the sofa and you think the whole cover's going to come off. Still, once she'd found her stride the sensation that hot needles were passing through nipples started to subside. Then the doorbell rang.

'Buggeration,' swore Diane, trying to manoeuvre herself up without disturbing the baby's feed. By walking carefully she managed to make it all the way to the front door without Ava losing her latch. So pleased was she by this that she failed to take into account the fact that whomever was at the door was about to get an eyeful of her veiny udders.

'Er . . . flowers for Mrs Connor . . .?' said the stunned-looking delivery boy.

'Oh, fantastic, thanks,' said Diane, realizing too late the offence she was causing and quickly trying to shield herself behind the door. Even Ava couldn't hold on at this point and released her grip. As she did so, milk spurted out from Diane's breast in a jubilant arc. Lovely.

With the arm that wasn't holding Ava, Diane grabbed the flowers, signed for them as best she could (her signature not actually comprising of any letters), muttered her thanks and quickly shut the door again as the delivery boy legged it as fast he could back down the path.

Ava, who wasn't impressed by the interruption to her

feed, started to scream, so Diane concentrated on wrangling her bosom back into her mouth before shuffling back through to the kitchen. A wry smile spread across her face as she recalled the look on the delivery boy's face. Exposing herself to him had probably been rather undignified but it was all a matter of perspective. Having recently given birth, someone seeing her boob felt like small fry compared to a medical student watching her moo like a cow while naked on all fours.

Minutes later, Ava had finally drunk her fill and was nuzzling nicely into her mother's shoulder. Diane closed her eyes and was just drifting off into a nice sleep-deprived stupor when the phone rang. She jumped out of her skin. Her nerves really were shot to pieces at the moment and with Grace napping upstairs, still tired from the day of travel they'd endured yesterday, she prayed the ringing wouldn't wake her. Wondering if she was destined to be kept awake for the rest of her life, Diane snatched the receiver up, desperate to stop the incessant noise.

'Hello?' she said impatiently.

'It's me,' said Mike.

Diane gulped. She didn't want another row but was already struggling to contain the rage that had sprung up inside. 'I told you not to ring on the landline during the day,' she said, trying and failing to sound offhand.

'Oh, shit, sorry, were you sleeping? Did you go back to bed?' asked Mike.

'No, but if I had done then you would have just woken me anyway.'

'Right, well, thanks for the earache and I'm sorry. I was only phoning to see if you got my flowers.'

Diane was immediately filled with shame. 'I did. They're lovely, thank you.'

'Did you read the note?'

'Yes,' lied Diane. 'It was really . . . sweet.' She resisted the urge to say that the thought of having to unwrap them from their cellophane, cut their stems and find a vase felt like far more hassle than they were worth.

Mike paused. 'Look, I know things are tough at the moment but you're doing a great job.'

Diane blinked back tears before replying incredulously, 'Really? Doesn't feel like I am. I'm so bloody tired all the time and feel like I'm going mad sometimes.'

Mike took a deep breath. Why did she have to be so flipping dramatic about everything? 'OK, well, I'm going for a quick early evening pint after work but I'll be back in time for stories.'

Diane opened her mouth to protest but no words came out. The thought of being able to be so spontaneous was too much. She was overwhelmed by the unfairness of the situation.

'Mummy . . .' A small voice floated over the baby monitor.

'I've got to go,' said Diane, putting down the phone.

'Mummy,' came the voice again, only more insistent this time.

'Muuummmy!' yelled an indignant Grace, who by now was out of bed and standing at the top of the stairs, furious that the safety gate was shut.

'I'm coming,' called Diane numbly, only she didn't notice one of Grace's plastic Dora figures on the floor and her right foot skidded on it.

'Aah,' she gasped as she lurched about, concentrating

hard on not dropping Ava. 'Bugger Dora the fucking Explorer,' she cursed as pain seared through her still-sensitive nether regions.

'Mummy?' said an outraged voice from upstairs. 'Don't say that naughty word.'

'What word, darling?' called Diane hesitantly, mortified that she'd been heard.

'Buggen. Buggen's a naughty word, Mummy.'

Diane slumped down at the foot of the stairs, anxiety spreading its spidery way around her system and at that precise moment it occurred to her that maybe she wasn't one hundred per cent. Normally what Grace had just said would have made her giggle, or at the very least have raised a smile. She'd have made a mental note to tell Mike the latest gem to come from his daughter's mouth (playing down how much she'd sworn). Today, however, it seemed entirely possible that she might never find anything funny again. She plodded upstairs.

What she wouldn't do to have today off. She was so exhausted and the thought of getting through the day alone with two demanding despots for company made her want to weep. So she did. She sat down on the middle stair and cried silently, big, fat, salty tears falling on to Ava's face. Drunk on milk, the tiny baby opened one lilac eye to give her weeping mother a curious look, which seemed to say 'Oi, you, what's your problem?'

24

When Kerry swaggered into the office that morning, looking very eighties in a man-size T-shirt which she'd tied in a knot at the waist, Jessica gestured to Mike's shut door.

'He's back.'

'Have you seen him?' asked Kerry, putting her clutch bag down on the desk.

'No,' said Jessica, eyeing her friend suspiciously. 'Hey, hang on a minute. Is that the bag you had with you on Saturday night? And is that the same dress you were wearing underneath?'

Kerry couldn't pretend a second longer. She simply had to share or she would burst.

'Oh my God, Jess, we were going to be discreet but actually there's no point because Paul knows anyway, plus I'm not sure I've physically got it in me. I've spent the whole weekend at Luke's.'

'No way! Where is he?'

'Gone to get coffees with Paul. But, Jess, listen to this. I have had the best sex of my entire life, and not just because I was gagging for it, which obviously I was, but because actually he's just so lovely,' she gabbled, looking ridiculously happy.

Jessica felt truly delighted for her friend, who had just sunk into her chair, a dreamy expression plastered across her face.

'Who'd have thought it, eh?' said Vanessa drolly, coming over to say hello.

'And, oh my God, some of the things he said to me in bed,' replied Kerry, her eyes wide.

'Oh, it's so romantic,' said Jessica.

'I know,' squealed Kerry in agreement. 'My knickers are twitching just thinking about him.'

'Less romantic,' said Vanessa, and Jessica laughed, just as the cause of Kerry's 'twitching knickers' walked into the office. Bringing up the rear was Paul. Jessica immediately stopped laughing and felt herself turn to jelly. Then her cell phone started to ring. It was Angelica. Damn, she kept forgetting to call her back, but now certainly wasn't the right time to talk (again), so she switched her phone off.

'Good morning, everyone,' announced Luke to the entire room. A statement, not a greeting.

'Bloody hell,' said Julian. 'Is this what it's going to be like around here from now on? Like a frigging episode of *Friends*.'

'Told them all, then?' said Luke, rolling his eyes in mock frustration, when actually you could see he was only too happy to shout about his conquest from the rooftops. He kissed Kerry tenderly on the forehead before delivering their coffees on to the desk.

Meanwhile, Paul strolled casually over to Jessica, hoping to get away unobserved while people concentrated on the Luke and Kerry sideshow.

'Morning, you,' he said softly.

'Hello,' Jessica said shyly, looking up.

'How's Mike's garden?'

'Watered,' she smiled back.

'Lucky it,' said Paul. 'So I hope you know you left me high and dry, playing gooseberry for the whole weekend with love's young dream over there?'

Jessica giggled as she followed his gaze. Luke had draped himself across Kerry's desk and was giving her shoulders a massage. They were both laughing about something and Kerry's expression was positively euphoric. Just then, Natasha arrived through the door. She looked flustered about being late, but not so flustered that she couldn't stop next to the loved-up couple and pretend to stick her fingers down her throat.

'Well, I'm sure you managed,' Jessica said flatly to Paul. The sight of his ex was a timely reminder not to get carried away flirting.

'Did Dulcie get off all right?' enquired Paul, who'd spotted how Jessica's face had fallen as soon as she'd seen Natasha. He'd realized in the club that someone must have filled Jessica in on his dating history, and this had confirmed it. He just hoped (for his ego's sake) that she didn't know all the details about how it had ended.

Jessica nodded. 'Yeah, she got away fine.'

'Look,' said Paul, keen to get things back on track, 'just say if you think I'm being forward, but I would really like to get to know you better and, while I don't give a shit what the rest of the office think about that, it's probably best not to give them stuff to gossip about at such an early stage . . . so . . .'

'So,' echoed Jessica.

'What I'm trying to say is that I think we should go out. I mean, I'd like to take you out.'

'And you don't care what *anyone* here would think about

that, but want to keep it secret?' asked Jessica, feeling as confused as she sounded. Should she be worried about Natasha or not, because she didn't fancy taking her on as a rival for Paul's affections.

'Yes,' stated Paul, who was trying not to laugh now. 'Look, I'll spell it out. Just in case you think I do – and I could be way off here – I don't care what Natasha in particular thinks, OK? I thought in the club that might be what you were thinking, but I really don't. However, I do think it would be better for both of us to see how things pan out without putting extra pressure on ourselves by having everybody talk about us.'

'I see,' said Jessica, blushing at the mere sound of the word 'us'. 'Of course, I mean, I totally agree,' she said coyly, her heart starting to race again as she stared into Paul's eyes.

'So when can I take you out?' he asked, shifting his weight from one foot to the other.

He was nervous, realized Jessica. Adorable.

'Well . . .' she said, playing for time, knowing she should play it cool. Should tell him that she was busy tonight and tomorrow for that matter. That he could take her out on Wednesday or even wait until the weekend. 'How about tonight?'

Paul grinned. 'Tonight sounds perfect. Shall we go straight from here or would you prefer me to pick you up from home later?'

Jessica considered the two options. 'Why don't you pick me up?' she said. 'If that's cool with you.'

'It is indeed,' he said. 'And then I can see where you live.'

'Yeah, though don't get too excited. Like I said the other day, my aunt's house is cute but nothing special.'

'O-K,' said Paul, sounding bemused.

Meanwhile, from the inner sanctum of his office, Mike was enjoying the playful hubbub of conversation from his team outside. It was a comforting sound, he realized. The sound of normality, of people who were relaxed in each other's company . . . and happy. His phone rang.

'Mike Connor,' he answered in an incredibly eighties fashion.

'Mike, David.'

'David,' said Mike, forcing his head back into work mode.

'Good holiday?'

'Not bad, thanks, not bad,' he replied. 'Not particularly great either, to be honest, but not bad.'

'Diane coping, is she?'

'Errrmm,' replied Mike doubtfully.

'I see. Well, Wendy and I have been talking and we think she needs some help. A nanny or whatever it is you call them these days. Acting like a martyr isn't helping anyone, is it?'

'W-e-ell . . .'

'Anyway, I'll leave you to sort that one out. In the meantime, I'm sending you a memo about a one-off special I want organized for the autumn schedule.'

'Great,' said Mike. 'Sounds interesting, I'll get right on to it. But about the other thing – I'm just not sure that . . .'

'Nonsense,' said David firmly, batting away any possibility of a discussion.

'Right then,' said Mike weakly, but David had already put the phone down.

Bossy old bastard, thought Mike. God, it was a nightmare having your father-in-law for a boss sometimes. Diane wasn't going back to work so she didn't want a nanny. He had suggested getting some help, but she'd said she saw it as an admission of failure, or something like that. Still, David had a point. Something had to be done and – judging by the latest phone call with his wife – sooner rather than later. He picked up the phone again.

'Love, you wouldn't happen to know anyone who does babysitting, would you?' he asked his secretary. His secretary, who was in fact a PA, loathed the fact that Mike always referred to her as his secretary, and hated being called 'love' even more. She also had no idea why on earth Mike should think that she should know anyone who babysat. If he was hinting at her, he could think again.

'No,' she replied. 'But I can ask around. Is it for anything special?'

'It's my wife's birthday in a couple of days, that's all. Thought I might take her out for dinner,' said Mike smoothly, feeling like a bit of a Casanova. A new man.

'That's nice,' said Jane, unimpressed. 'Don't you have anyone you usually use then?' she added. She didn't really give a shit but thought she'd ask.

'We did have, but she's gone and moved back to Brazil. Selfish cow, eh?' Mike finished jovially. But Jane didn't laugh, so what he'd said didn't sound funny, just churlish. 'Well, let me know if you have any thoughts,' he said, putting the phone down. Just then, someone stuck their head round the door. 'Kerry, how are you? How's it been going? I'm just about to watch last week's show, which I've heard was fantastic.'

'It was all right,' said Kerry 'Never a minute to bask in the glory though, eh? On to the next one.'

'Yes, remind me again?'

'Marisa Tomei, Michael McIntyre and Jonny Lee Miller.'

'Bloody great,' said Mike, impressed by the starry line-up. 'Jonny's a new booking, isn't he?'

'He is,' said Kerry, trying not to grin at Mike's use of first name only. 'Anyway, I need you to sign off on some receipts please?'

'Sure,' said Mike, taking the papers from her. 'By the way, how's the new girl working out?'

'Bloody brilliantly actually, Mike,' said Kerry whole-heartedly. 'Bloody brilliantly.'

'Good. Ask her to come in, will you, I want to thank her for watering my garden.'

'Lost the use of your legs?'

'Y-e-e-s,' Mike replied, not at all sure how to take that. Kerry had always slightly scared him.

Thirty seconds later and it was Jessica's turn to knock on his door.

'Hi, Mike,' she said cheerfully. 'Welcome home, it's great to see you back.'

'Thanks,' said Mike, wondering what had caused her to look quite so happy with life. 'I just wanted to thank you for –' His mobile rang. 'Hang on, I'll just be a sec, it's my wife . . . Hello, darling? . . . Are you OK? What's wrong now?' he said, looking stressed.

Jessica pointed at the door, wondering if she should come back later and let him have some privacy, but Mike shook his head and raised one hand, indicating that she should stay. So then Jessica had no choice but to listen to what was clearly a very private conversation, while staring about the uninspiring room. There was nothing to focus on so she found herself staring intently at the ceiling, like a builder trying to assess what needed doing.

'Just tell me what the matter is,' implored Mike. 'All right... look, calm down. I won't go to the pub then if it's such a big deal... OK... let's talk when I get home... All right then, love. Yes... yes, I'll see you later. No, I haven't forgotten to buy Calpol.'

Mike put the phone down. His whole face was etched with strain; even his tan couldn't disguise it.

'Um, are you OK?' enquired Jessica politely.

'Yes,' he said distractedly. 'It's just my wife. She's finding things a bit tough at the moment, that's all.'

'Oh, I see,' said Jessica, who didn't really. As far as she could recall, the woman she'd seen in the photographs at Mike's looked like she had every reason to be pretty happy with her lot.

'She's determined to do it all herself, you see,' said Mike, who for some reason felt compelled to try and explain. To make some kind of sense of what was happening to his wife. For his own benefit, more than anything. 'I think she just needs a break but every time I say anything she says she's too tired to think about it. Still, I want to find a babysitter for Wednesday so we can at least go out for her birthday, but –'

Mike stopped, realizing that he was pouring his heart out to someone he barely knew, who had recently given up her free time to water his garden. 'Anyway, you didn't come into work to listen to my boring woes. Besides, the reason

I asked to see you was so I could thank you for watering the garden while we were away. I hope you didn't trek over too many times.'

'Oh, no, no,' said Jessica airily, thinking guiltily of the scorching week during which the garden had lain parched, gasping for a drink.

'I'm just so pleased everything's still alive,' she said.

'Oh, it's not. The pots are all dead, but that's OK,' said Mike vaguely. Jessica gulped, waiting to be reprimanded. However, it quickly became apparent that he wasn't planning on saying anything more about it. He was obviously distracted, concerned for his wife. Jessica's heart went out to him.

'Maybe I could babysit?' she offered hesitantly.

Mike looked up. 'Sorry?'

'Maybe I could babysit for you and your wife? That is, if you trust me enough to stay with your children. I mean, I don't have much proper experience with kids, but I guess if you're going out in the evening they'd be asleep anyway?'

'Yes,' said Mike, giving Jessica his full attention. 'Yes, they would. But, gosh, no, I can't expect you to leap from one favour to another. Not, of course, that it would be a favour. I'd pay you. Pay you whatever you wanted, in fact. Five pounds an hour? No, not enough – six, seven maybe? I don't know what nannies get these days really. My wife usually sorts things like that out, but I'd certainly pay you properly anyway.'

'Oh, well, don't worry about that,' said Jessica, embarrassed.

Mike chewed the corner of his thumb nail, thinking rapidly.

'Look, to be honest, it would be bloody brilliant if you did because at the moment we just don't have anyone. My parents are ancient, hers are bloody useless and she refuses to even consider anyone who doesn't come recommended,' he said as if his wife's reluctance to leave their children with any old freak was tiresome and wholly unreasonable. 'But I don't want you to think I was hinting before, because I wasn't,' he added, getting disproportionately excited. 'Though obviously I'd still have to check with my wife, convince her you're not a kiddie fiddler or anything, but if you're honestly serious then it would be terrific.'

'Right,' said Jessica doubtfully, wondering what she'd got herself into.

'Just a thought though. Probably best not to mention it to anyone else in the office? It's just that it blurs the boundaries a bit. Besides, I'm sure you know by now what terrible gossips they all are.'

'Fine,' said Jessica, only too happy to keep things quiet considering the reaction she'd got the last time she'd offered to help.

'OK, well, I'll call Diane back now then.'

'Wonderful,' said Jessica, turning to leave.

'And, Jessica?'

'Yes, Mike?'

'Thank you,' he said, scrunching up his face to emphasize how much he meant it, which actually made him seem more insincere.

'You're so welcome,' she said, privately thinking that he and his wife seemed to be the very definition of people who really did need to 'get out more'.

A happier man, Mike turned his attentions back to his

in-box. Ah, there was the promised one from David about the autumn special. He read through it quickly. It sounded great, actually. A very good idea indeed. Fantastic, now he would have something substantial to talk about at the meeting tomorrow morning too. Things were on the up. Good old Miss Bender.

25

That evening, at eight o clock on the dot, Pam's doorbell rang.

'He's here, love,' Pam hollered up the stairs. Seeing her niece giddy with the freshness of this new romance had taken Pam right back to the early days of her and Bernard's courtship. In fact, over the last couple of days she'd allowed herself to wallow in memories and romantic nostalgia for a change. Recalling the past didn't seem to frighten her quite so much these days, which she put down to having Jessica around. Her niece had reminded her that life was for living and Jess's happiness and growing confidence was wonderful to witness. On Sunday, when Jessica had managed to mention Paul three times in the space of forty minutes, Pam had even started getting carried away, dreaming of a big white wedding.

As the doorbell rang again, Pam chuckled to herself.

'Listen to me getting completely ahead of myself,' she said to her own reflection in the hall mirror.

Jessica came racing down the stairs, jittery and worried she might look overdone for dinner on a Monday night. Knowing Paul, he was probably taking her to the pub. Still, she'd come home to freshen up so that was what she'd done. The fact that she was wearing a cream vintage Chloe dress her mom had bought her would probably escape him anyway.

'Do I look OK?' she asked her aunt urgently.

'Beautiful,' replied Pam, her hand to her throat. 'He's a lucky man. I'll leave you to it.'

Jessica gave her a grateful squeeze as she passed her in the hallway then stopped to take one last deep breath before opening the door. When she did, however, she was in for a bit of a shock.

'Shit, what are you doing here?' she spluttered, horrified to see her mother standing on the doorstep, looking like the huge Hollywood star she was.

'You're wearing the dress I bought, the cut is really lovely on you,' said Angelica, looking pleased.

Finally computing that what she was seeing was real and not a hologram, the realization that she had vaguely (very vaguely) made plans to meet her mother that night seeped through Jessica's consciousness like icy water. Instantly she realized some serious damage limitation was required and yet her more immediate concern was the fact that any second now Paul would be arriving, and that it would be very difficult to explain why Heavenly Melons was standing on her front step.

'Mom, please?' she pleaded. 'I'm so sorry but I have a date tonight.'

'A date? Tonight? Oh, Jessica, I'm so happy for you. Is he OK about coming with us to dinner?'

'Get in,' said Jessica, realizing the subtle approach wasn't going to work.

'I don't know if Pamela would want me to —' But Angelica didn't get to finish what she was saying because, having quickly scanned the street both ways, Jessica had grabbed her mother and bundled her into the hallway, just as Pamela was emerging from the front room to see what was going on.

'What are you doing here?' the older lady squawked indignantly. She had her hands on her hips and was wearing such a menacing expression she looked quite formidable. Jessica understood for the first time why her mother might feel a little wary of her.

'I'm here to see my daughter,' said Angelica, straightening herself up.

Jessica suddenly felt truly terrible. This was all her fault.

'Look, Mom, I'm so sorry. I should have called, but I wasn't joking. I do have a date tonight and it's one that really means a lot to me.'

'That is so wonderful,' said Angelica, beaming soppily at her. 'I'm so pleased for you, darling, I really am.'

Oh, jeez, thought Jessica. She'd spent years wanting this kind of focus from her mom but right now she just wished she'd get the hint and go away.

'Look,' she said eventually, having realized she had no other option than to spell things out, 'I can't see you tonight. I made a mistake and double-booked and I don't want him to see you. He doesn't know who my parents are and, to be honest, it's really important it stays that way. For once I'm living my own life, and not living in your shadow has been a breath of fresh air. Surely you get that? It's why I'm here, after all!'

Angelica looked unbelievably hurt and seemed to shrink inside her clothes, like a balloon that had been pricked with a pin.

'I see,' she said.

Shamefaced and bursting with frustration, Jessica

blushed. 'I didn't mean it to come out like that . . . it's just . . .'

Angelica gazed at the floor in silence. She was so tired of trying to make peace with her daughter and never getting anywhere. 'I know that things between us aren't as they should be, Jessica, and I'm sorry, but there are only so many times someone can apologize without receiving forgiveness, you know.'

Jessica looked at her mother, stunned. She'd never heard her say anything like that before. Not that her words had quite the same effect on Pam.

'Well, that's a bit rich,' she blustered. 'Surely you haven't apologized enough? Not to her or Teddy. Years he waited to hear from you, desperate to know why you did what you did.'

'But that's not true, I –'

The doorbell rang.

'Shit,' Jessica flapped.

'Oh, well, that's gone and done it,' said Pam as threateningly as she could, given that she was whispering. 'Now, you listen to me, Ange. If you want to get anywhere with your daughter, then do not blow this for her, do you hear me? This chap means a lot to her and she needs to have this date on her own terms.'

'Fine,' said Angelica, looking panicked. 'But what am I supposed to do? My driver's only turning the car round. He'll be here in a minute.'

Meanwhile, outside, Paul was starting to think he might have got the wrong house. He rang the bell again. At exactly the same time Angelica's cell phone started vibrating in her bag.

'That'll be my driver,' she whispered, looking stricken, 'which means he'll be pulling in any second.'

'Hello?' Paul's voice drifted through the letterbox.

Spotting his eyes peering through, Pam panicked. 'Get in,' she ordered, before jostling a stunned Angelica towards the coat cupboard.

Having realized what was happening, Angelica – who hated confined spaces – tried to protest but Pam wasn't listening. Shoving her in, she slammed the door shut, at which point Angelica's pleas became muffled. Just to make sure, however, Pam banged on the door. 'Shut it, missy. We'll get you out of there as soon as we can.'

Defeated, Angelica did as she was told. The cupboard fell silent. By this point Jessica's jaw was practically scraping along the ground and she'd lost any remaining wherewithal. Fortunately, Pam's was still intact and, having realized her niece was rooted to the spot with panic, she went to open the door herself.

'Hello,' she said like a bad television presenter reading autocue, 'you must be Paul. Do come in.'

'Thanks,' he said, and as Jessica came forward to greet him it was hard to say who looked the most freaked out, her or Pam.

'So,' Paul said hesitantly, wondering why everyone was looking so odd, 'you must be Pam. Jessica's told me lots about you.'

'Ooh,' squawked Pam, more loudly than this really warranted. 'All good, I hope?'

'Oh, all very good,' he confirmed.

Just then the sound of a mobile phone ringing could be heard. It was coming from the cupboard.

Jessica and Pam both grinned maniacally at Paul, trying to pretend they couldn't hear it. Meanwhile, inside the cupboard, a claustrophobic Angelica was doing her best to get at her phone so that she could switch it off, which helped matters even less because now the whole cupboard was shaking.

'Is there someone in your cupboard?' asked Paul.

'Sorry?' said Jessica dumbly.

'Your cupboard,' said Paul. 'There's someone in it.'

'Um . . .'

'Don't be so daft. Why would there be anyone in the cupboard?' bellowed Pam, far too loudly. The effect was rather ruined, however, for just at that moment the door to the cupboard creaked open and Angelica, who simply couldn't bear to be in such a small space for a second longer, eased herself out – though in a bid to remain undetected, stood behind the cupboard door.

'Apart from that person obviously,' said Pam, shooting a livid glare in Angelica's direction. 'Oh, we like a laugh in this house, don't we, Jess. Eh? Ooh, look at your face, Paul. It's a picture. Got you good and proper, didn't we?'

Paul looked terribly unsure.

'So,' said Jessica faintly, who knew an explanation would now be required as to why Angelica Dupree had just emerged from her coat cupboard. It was time to fess up. Apart from anything else, she felt terribly sad that the game was up. She didn't feel anywhere near ready to revert back to being Jessica Granger, but she had been left no choice. She turned round to introduce her mother but, as she did, realized that Angelica, who was lurking behind her, had covered her head with one of Pam's silk headscarves and put on a rain mac, both of which she must have got from the cupboard.

Jessica appreciated the effort, except that now, instead of looking like a movie star, she looked like a movie star who didn't want to be recognized. Still, Paul didn't seem to have spotted who she was. Hope flooded her system. Was it possible she might get away with this?

'So, Paul, this is . . . one of my dad's old chauffeuring friends . . . and in fact . . . here's her car now.'

A bemused-looking Paul turned round just in time to see a huge Bentley with blacked-out windows drawing up outside the house.

'Blimey, what an amazing car. But – if she's the driver, then who's driving? And why were you in the cupboard?' he enquired reasonably enough as, seizing her opportunity, Angelica scuttled past him. He didn't get an answer.

'Bye bye,' she called out as incoherently as she could in order to disguise her French accent. As she dashed past Paul, down the front steps and across to the car there followed a long silence during which Pam and Jessica both stared at Paul with frozen grins, until Jessica realized they were being weird.

'Right,' she said, clapping her hands together like a Redcoat. 'Shall we go?'

'Um, yes,' said Paul, looking nervous. 'But I still don't get why there's another driver getting out to –'

'So you'll bring her back safe then, won't you?' yelled Pam, as if saying everything loudly would help somehow.

'Oh, I will,' answered Paul, hoping his eardrum hadn't perforated. He wasn't being entirely honest either. He did hope to bring her back safe (he wasn't a deranged psycho or anything), but if he had his way it would be back to his place.

'Well, be good and if you can't be good be careful,' Pam couldn't resist adding cheekily, so relieved was she to see the huge Bentley finally reversing out of the drive.

'Pam!' admonished Jessica, but as she walked down the steps she breathed a huge sigh of relief too. That had been a very close shave and one she could have prevented. Her mom was making so much more effort than usual and she really needed to reciprocate it. It was just hard when she had so much on her plate, but she vowed to address the situation.

'That was all a bit weird,' said Paul now as they started off down the street. 'And I see you've been having me on.'

'Sorry?' replied Jessica, her heart picking up the pace once more. Had he seen Angelica's face after all?

'Your aunt's house? You said it was nothing special,' he prompted, upon seeing her flummoxed expression. They crossed to the other side of the road.

Jessica smiled back hesitantly, unsure of what to say, getting the distinct impression that she should probably stay quiet till she'd figured out what he was on about.

'Why did you keep going on about how "cute" and normal her house was when she lives in a whacking great Victorian villa on top of one of the most expensive hills in London?' he exclaimed. 'Were you trying to make a point or something? Or do you think I'm as much of an inverted snob as Dulcie does?'

'Er, yeah . . . no,' replied Jessica, at a total loss. She'd told her colleagues that her aunt lived in a nice enough house, that was simple and kinda cute, and genuinely thought this to be a pretty accurate description, yet Paul clearly had other ideas.

'I mean, if you honestly think that a gaff that would fetch well over a million quid isn't special, then I'm not sure I'll be taking you back to mine any time soon,' he continued.

'Oh,' said Jessica.

'I'm joking,' said Paul quickly, 'you can come back to mine any time you like, only no more bullshit, all right?'

'Oh, no, absolutely not,' said Jessica, her mind racing. How could she have got that one so wrong? Could her aunt's place really be worth so much money? Thinking about it, her home in LA was so off the scale size-wise (they relied on the internal phone system to know when meals were ready), it might be possible that she didn't have the most realistic perspective. She felt compelled to try and justify herself. 'The only reason I made out that my aunt's place was anything other than amazing was because I was –'

'I'm not having a go,' said Paul, stopping and turning Jessica to face him. 'It's just a bit odd that you purposefully played it down like that. We wouldn't have judged you if you'd told us that your aunt was loaded . . . It's not like it changes the fact that you and your dad haven't exactly had things easy. Otherwise you wouldn't be working your arse off as Kerry's assistant, would you, and he wouldn't be driving Vincent Malone?'

Jessica opened her mouth to bluster a defence but Paul continued, 'Now what do you want to do tonight? Do you fancy some dinner or would you prefer to get a drink first?'

Jessica gazed at him properly for the first time that evening. He was wearing his usual T-shirt and jeans but had that washed look about him again. His hair was combed off his face and he looked gorgeous. Jessica had a sudden urge to get her hands on what lay beneath his clothes.

'Let's start with a drink and take it from there,' suggested Jessica and, as they strolled up the road, the nerves she was experiencing slowly started to disappear. Who cared where they lived or who they 'were'; she felt so at home with Paul. An effect that was only tempered by the fact that, from time to time, she was almost knocked sideways by the strong ripples of lust she experienced whenever she stopped to think about how good he looked. How could she ever have found him so intimidating?

Later, in a pub they'd found a few streets away, Jessica toyed with the idea of owning up. Maybe she should just get it out of the way and tell him who her parents were now, before anything had really happened between them. Yet she was so terrified of opening up the can of worms which always seemed to spoil everything that she decided against it. Paul seemed so impressed that she was in England by herself, working away, and for now she didn't want anything to ruin that. It would seem like such a lesser achievement if he were to know what kind of back-up she had. Besides, she didn't really want to spend her first proper date with Paul talking about her parents. Why should Edward muscle his way in like he usually did, or Angelica steal her thunder? This one was just for her, for a change. There was plenty of time for the truth to come out.

'You know what?' said Jessica eventually, having prattled on about nothing of much real consequence for ages. 'I don't know anything about you. You're very good at asking questions, but not so great at answering them and I want to know everything.'

'OK,' said Paul, leaning over to put his glass down. His arm brushed Jessica's thigh and she shivered with anticipation. 'I was born in Staines, which is about as inspiring a place as the name suggests. I'll leave you to imagine what the kids in my area called it when we were growing up.'

Jessica grimaced. She could imagine only too easily. Desire subsided for a second.

'I went to school there, but didn't take it at all seriously. Or, at least, I didn't until my dad left, at which point something sort of changed. I suppose I realized if I wasn't careful that I'd probably end up with the kind of uninspiring jobs my mum's always had. By then, though, it was a bit late to salvage much from school so I started working. I did some pretty boring jobs for a while but still managed to have a bit of a laugh and in the meantime tried to broaden my horizons as much as I could. Tried to educate myself a bit, I suppose. Basically, my life's been fine, but deeply average. Or, to put it another way, I'm not sure my life so far would make for a particularly interesting biography.'

'Jeez,' said Jessica, employing some of the sarcasm Paul usually used on her. 'Are we drowning our sorrows here or what?'

Paul laughed. 'I'm not feeling sorry for myself, it's just that I truly believe – truly hope – the best bits are still to come,' he said, in a way that made Jessica's insides melt. It felt like there was an elevator in her tummy, plunging down five storeys at a time. 'Although admittedly things have been pretty good for the last five years or so, ever since I got my break in TV,' he added.

'Are you close to your mom?' asked Jessica.

'Very,' said Paul simply. 'She's the best.'

'So does she still live in Staines? And, by the way, that is the most awful name for a place known to man.'

'Tell me about it, Miss Bender,' he replied pointedly, earning himself a sharp nudge in the ribs. 'Ow, and yes, to answer your question, my mum and my sister still live in the only house I've ever called home. I went to school in Staines, had my first Saturday job in Staines, went to college in Staines and still end up back there most weekends to visit.'

'What was your first job?' enquired Jessica, who was hanging on every word that came out of his mouth.

'Mmm, really sexy it was,' mused Paul. 'Stacked shelves in Safeways until I was eighteen, at which point I graduated on to the tills. My second job was a million times better though. I worked in Our Price for about six months so you can imagine how much I loved that. Spent all my wages on music. It was a bloody disaster.'

Jessica smiled at him shyly while praying he wouldn't ask the question he inevitably did.

'So what was your first job then?'

Jessica swallowed. Truth or a lie? To lie or speak the truth? Would it give too much away, provoke too many other questions, if she admitted that she hadn't even had a job until she was twenty-two? That when she'd finally felt moved to do something other than loll about in Malibu she'd only had to ask? That she'd instantly been made an assistant on the film set of her dad's last hit movie, which in truth hadn't felt much like a job at all? Everyone had been nauseatingly nice to her the entire time and it was this wholly unrealistic experience that had prompted Jessica to start trying to do things her way. To look beyond the movie industry in order to properly experience a bit of life's rich tapestry.

'I worked for – in – a shop too,' she said, chickening out once again from having to explain anything.

'Yeah, what kind of shop?'

'It was a . . .' Jessica's mind went completely blank. She'd never been a natural liar. There was a reason she hadn't had the same calling as her parents. Acting essentially meant lying for a living. 'Do you know, I can't remember,' she said feebly, after rejecting the strange, outlandish and utterly useless suggestions her brain was providing her with. A bike shop? A scuba-diving shop? A watch shop? (A watch shop???)

'You can't remember your first job?' said Paul, amazed. 'My God, I thought they were supposed to scar you so much that you never forgot them. Although, from the little I've gleaned about you so far, it sounds like you've done so many different things that maybe they all blend into one. So forget that then. Tell me more about your dad. Does he like driving Vincent Malone?'

'Yeah,' said Jessica, in real danger of giggling. The thought of her dad with a peaked cap on, driving his best mate around, was too much of a stretch.

'And what's he like as a person?'

Like James Bond . . .

Jessica looked at Paul. He deserved a few straight answers, she thought, as she took in his intent expression and his lovely, masculine, strong-looking hands, which were only inches away from her own. 'My dad is my favourite person in the world,' she stated, the truth suddenly making her feel shy. 'I totally adore him and over the years it's just been me and him really, so he's more than a dad, he's a mom too. A manly looking one with hairy legs, but a mom nonetheless. He's the one who put me to bed when I was little – well, him or a nanny when he was working. He's the one who organized my birthday parties and made sure I had the cake that I wanted. He's the one who had to put up with all my friends coming over for sleepovers and the one who yelled at me when I misbehaved or, more recently, crashed his car.'

Paul looked quite surprised by this admission, almost as if he couldn't imagine it.

'He's kind, funny and incredibly soppy. If I were to tell you that he cried at the movie *Cheaper by the Dozen* . . .?'

Paul looked amazed, then laughed.

'Honestly, and I had to order him not to watch *Marley and Me* when that came out because he simply wouldn't have coped. But on the flipside,' Jessica said, 'he doesn't always listen to what I'm trying to tell him. He interferes too much in my life and at times that can be quite suffocating. Sometimes I feel as though our roles are reversed. As though I'm the one looking after him in a way, which is fine, but I just think . . .'

'What?' encouraged Paul.

'Oh, I don't know . . . it's just, you know, he's married and I guess his wife should probably be the one looking after him now.'

'What's your stepmum like?'

'Honestly?'

'No, I want you to make something up,' he ribbed.

'OK, well, picture Pamela Anderson or . . . Heather Locklear is another one she gets likened to. Only once the excitement of that has worn off, picture a lovely girl who has pretty much no idea what she wants out of life and who means no harm, but who has a voice that could melt tarmac.'

'Really?' said Paul. 'I wasn't expecting that. She sounds hilarious . . . and quite fit.'

Jessica rapped his hand. 'That's my stepmom you're talking about. Though, to be fair, I wouldn't blame you for fancying her. She's not *that* much older than us.'

Now Paul looked really intrigued. 'Blimey, don't tell Luke,' he said, looking at Jessica thoughtfully. Not for the first time, he felt like he had more in common with her than he could ever have realized when they'd first met. She wasn't the only one who felt responsible for a parent sometimes. Maybe they'd both had to grow up a bit quicker than other people.

'If you don't mind me asking, do you ever see your mum?'

'Yeah,' said Jessica steadily. 'From time to time, you know. She's often away, but she comes to see me maybe three or four times a year? Sometimes more, sometimes less.'

Paul noted a flash of something that was hard to translate in Jessica's expression and decided not to pursue that one further.

'Your turn now. Tell me about your mom, what's she like?'

Just like Jessica, Paul felt compelled to speak truthfully. What was happening between them, whatever 'it' was, seemed to warrant total honesty, a purging of things he never usually felt moved to discuss.

'My mum's a star. She works all the hours that God sends in a pub, where she's worked for years just to keep a roof over our heads. She's always put me and my sister first, and she's a wonderful woman who has had a pretty shitty life. There haven't been many treats or holidays to break up the monotony of her dull work, but I've never heard her complain. My sister's great too. She's fifteen so I go home most weekends to hang out with her because, although she's old enough to look after herself, when Mum has to work it can get pretty lonely for Lucy. My dad did a bunk when we were tiny and has never paid a penny towards our upbringing. He's a shit of the highest order and I fucking hate him,' he said matter-of-factly, his tone not changing one iota. 'He cleaned out their bank accounts before he left, shacked up with some old lush he'd met in a pub and drank everything away. He died last year. The drinking finally fucked his liver up. He pickled himself.'

Jessica blinked as she tried to imagine an existence so different from her own, feeling racked with guilt for ever having felt sorry for herself about anything. She also knew she may have done Angelica – whose maternal advances she constantly rejected – a bit of a disservice. 'I'm really sorry,' she said eventually.

'Don't be,' said Paul. 'It's just life, isn't it? Besides, having to grow up a bit quicker has made me more ambitious. More determined to get to the point where I can tell Mum to stop working for good. I pay her mortgage, which is great, and now I'm saving up so that there's a bit of money put aside for Lucy so she can go to college. Mum's saving every penny she earns too.'

Jessica didn't know what to say. Life was so ridiculously unbalanced, so unfair, and when she thought about some of the rich, spoiled brats she knew in LA, it made her wonder what it was all about. She herself had always been savvy enough to suspect, to know even, that there was more to life than the Hollywood bubble she existed within, but most of her friends didn't. In fact, she could think of at least a dozen people who would hugely benefit from a spell in the real world, a spell of meeting 'normal' people. Not that she considered Paul to be normal. He was amazing. The first guy she'd ever wanted to get involved with whom she actually admired. And she *did* want to get involved. There was simply no running away from that fact any more.

'Look at us getting all maudlin,' said Paul, grinning. 'Jesus, things aren't that bad, are they? I'm going to get us another drink. Or do you want to go and eat?'

'Another drink would be great.'

While he went to the bar, Jessica thought about everything she'd just learned. The more she got to know Paul, the more she liked and respected him. Oddly enough, she knew her dad would adore him too. The whole issue of her identity was starting to trouble her though. At what point was she going to tell him the truth? If she got too deeply embroiled, then lying to Paul would just become more difficult and undoubtedly start to feel like more of a deception. *She* knew she was only keeping quiet in order to protect herself, and so that she could get as much as possible out of this trip, but she knew Paul would see things differently. At the same time, however, it was so amazingly refreshing not having to put up with other people's preconceptions that she wanted to enjoy the freedom a while longer.

Paul arrived back with more drinks and a couple of

packets of crisps. 'Sorry if I got a bit heavy before,' he shrugged, wrenching open the packets. He'd given more of himself away than he had to anyone in years and now wasn't feeling quite brave enough to look Jessica in the eye.

'Don't be silly,' she said, waving her hand around dismissively before letting it dive into the chips or 'crisps'. 'I'm sorry too for sounding a bit "woe is me". I feel bad actually. My mom does try and – well, deep down I'm pretty fond of her, you know? I mean, she has her faults but . . . at least I know she loves me, I guess.'

'Good,' said Paul. 'So no more depressing chat about our dysfunctional families, although at least now you know why I can't stand people who aren't straight up. My dad has a lot to answer for.'

'Er, yeah,' said Jessica, trying to swallow away a rather large lump of doubt that seemed to have lodged in her throat.

A couple of drinks later, they left the pub and strolled through the leafy streets, eventually reaching Primrose Hill. It was dark by now and the twinkly lights of the city winked at them through the darkness. Paul stopped and put his arms around her.

'It's so beautiful,' said Jessica.

'So are you,' said Paul, drawing her towards him and kissing her right there and then.

It was an amazing kiss and the force of feeling behind it quite overwhelming. Jessica kissed him back and her hands travelled up his back to his hair, which she stroked, gently pulling his face further into hers.

'Oh my gosh,' Jessica gasped when they finally came up for air a while later. 'That was –'

But Paul hadn't finished. He kissed her again, gently

scraping her bottom lip with his teeth and sprinkling little fairy kisses around her mouth before sliding his tongue back in again. Jessica was now, without a shadow of a doubt, in kissing heaven and she found herself pressing up against him, wanting more. She honestly couldn't imagine anywhere she'd rather be in the world and any last remaining doubts she may have had about getting involved disappeared altogether. Not that she had much choice. Her mouth couldn't get enough of him. His lips were the perfect combination of firm yet soft. When they did eventually pull away Jessica couldn't get rid of the huge beam that had taken up residence on her face.

Meanwhile, Paul, who was equally saturated with both desire and happiness, was dying to be at home in his bedroom with her so much, it was taking all his restraint not to just flag down a cab and bundle her in without asking. Still, that could be translated as kidnapping, so instead he whispered for the second time in a week, 'Come home with me, Jess?'

And ignoring all her instincts, Jessica found herself replying, 'Not yet.'

'Really?' said Paul, looking unbelievably disappointed before leaning in to gently kiss her again.

Jessica sighed. The combination of the almost full moon and the streetlight meant that she could see just how much he wanted her in those intense, beautiful eyes of his. She could feel it too, thanks to something she'd just noticed pressing against her. She was only grateful that females didn't have to deal with giveaway erections, for if they did, hers would have probably catapulted Paul down the hill by now. There was no question that she wanted them to be in bed together as much as he did, but something (something annoying) was making her want to wait a little longer. Probably the fact that, deep down, she wanted this to be more meaningful than some holiday fling, wanted to be able to look back one day and be able to say she'd waited. Yet until now she'd convinced herself that the only thing that could happen between them *was* a holiday romance, in which case why bother waiting? Besides, if he liked her anywhere near as much as she liked him then why would he think less of her? Had she just been programmed to think that you only 'put out' after at least three dates? God, who even gave a shit? She was out of breath with longing, dizzy with desire and desperate to be naked in bed with him. She knew it would be mind-blowing, so what the hell?

Jessica pressed into him again, inviting him with her pelvis to persuade her to change her mind. However, to her bitter disappointment, now Paul was the one pulling away.

'As much as I don't mind admitting that I am dying to get you back to my place, you're right,' he said reluctantly.

'I am?' said Jessica, gulping, determined to disguise how gutted she was. Why had she said no? What an idiot. Disappointment and frustration practically engulfed her and yet she was comforted by the fact that she knew they both wanted it to happen one day.

Having admitted defeat, and knowing full well that there was one thing guaranteed to dilute the atmosphere, she added, 'Oh, well, I guess we do need to be on top form for tomorrow's production meeting.'

She was right. The merest allusion to Mike was enough to kill the moment and put things back on to a friendly footing. Paul had to laugh before saying, 'I'll try not to feel too insulted that you're turning me down for the sake of being fresh for one of Mike's production meetings. Although I like to think I could have shown you a slightly more interesting time,' he added hopefully, bending his head down to give her one last lingering snog.

As Jessica kissed him back, she nodded. Of course he would have done, which was why – unbeknown to him – she had been on the very brink of saying, just as Kerry would have done in her shoes, 'Fuck it.'

They'd better sort out their next date quickly though, she thought ruefully, as she wasn't sure how much more waiting she could cope with.

26

'Right, you 'orrible lot,' joked Mike, delighted to be back at the helm of yet another Tuesday production meeting. He was in good spirits today. Last night he'd managed to persuade a sceptical Diane to meet with Jessica tonight so she could decide whether she was good babysitting material. He was purposefully wearing a white shirt that showed off his tan and had already clocked a few appreciative looks. He'd definitely got one from Natasha and was pretty sure that Vanessa had given him the once-over too. The lion was back in his lair.

'Firstly, I want to say well done for coping so well while I was away.' Paul snorted loudly at this but Mike continued unabashed. 'Secondly, I want you all to listen up because I've got big news. Huge, in fact.'

People visibly perked up a little. Isy even went as far as lifting her head up off the desk.

'I've finally persuaded David Bridlington that it's time we reinvented the wheel a little,' announced Mike, being slightly economical with the truth. 'It took some doing, as you can probably imagine, but I think I've brought him round to my way of thinking. As a result, I'm pleased to announce that in September we are going to be doing a two-hour special which has been designed especially to coincide with a huge event in the showbiz calendar.' He paused and started pacing the floor behind his chair. 'Now, we're going to be navigating uncharted waters here. It'll be our first ever themed show and we need it to feel fresh, yet slick, because if it goes well then "t'powers that be",' he said in a mock northern accent, instantly managing to offend about a quarter of the people present, 'might look at us doing some more specials. So any guesses as to what the theme of the show is going to be?'

Twenty faces stared back, some baleful, others curious, though in the main, vacant was the key expression. Maureen's eyes appeared to be closed. Mike frowned.

'Maureen!' he yelled at the costume supervisor, causing her to jump three feet in the air.

'What?' she said, gathering her wits about her. 'Um, so Bradley's going to be in royal blue this Thursday and I've also received a twenty per cent discount card for River Island should anyone want to borrow it.' This warranted a ripple of applause.

Mike sighed. 'Come on now, guys. Has anyone who's not half asleep got any ideas about what our show's theme might be?'

Jessica, who was sitting directly behind Paul, stared longingly at the back of his neck, wishing she could kiss it and reliving last night's date scene by scene. She loved how dark his hair was, and longed to run her hands through it. Then she jumped as Paul twisted round in his seat. 'I wonder if he's ever considered just telling us a bit of information without turning it into a drama?'

She stifled a giggle, torn between seeing Paul's point while actually feeling quite sorry for Mike, whom she knew was just desperate to evoke a bit of interest from the team. She'd agreed to go and meet his wife and kids after work later, though they'd both promised not to tell anyone. Her only reservation was that if she passed inspection, she wouldn't be able to see Paul tomorrow night either as she'd be babysitting. Then it would be show day on Thursday . . . God, how frustrating.

'It's not fashion week, is it?' guessed Natasha, earning herself a grateful smile from the boss who'd been patiently waiting for an answer.

'No, but thanks. Anyone else?'

Some shrugged, some made comedy faces to show they were at least trying to think. Others continued to look blank.

'OK,' said Mike. 'I'll give you a clue. What film is due to come out in the autumn? A film that is part of a brand in itself?'

Suddenly there was one person in the room who knew what the answer might be.

'Jessica?' said Mike, who had noticed her flinch. 'Any ideas?'

She didn't trust herself to speak, so she just shook her head vigorously and flushed red.

'Ooh, hang on a minute,' piped up Luke, looking enthusiastic about something other than pawing Kerry's leg under the table for the first time that morning. 'It's not Bond, is it? Isn't the next Daniel Craig movie coming out around that time? It would be fucking wicked if it was Bond.'

'At last,' declared Mike triumphantly. 'Somebody is bloody listening,' he said, pretending to put an imaginary noose around his neck and pull it. 'We have lift off!' he declared, having finished pretending to hang himself.

'Bond!' he shouted, really getting into his stride and startling Jessica, whose nerves had already managed to fray themselves. 'Double-oh seven! Everyone's favourite spy. The latest Daniel Craig is out on twenty-seventh September and we are going to do a whole special dedicated to it. So, Kerry and Jessica, while I appreciate that we only have about seven weeks to book guests, I'd like to brainstorm with everyone now about who, in an ideal world, we would love to have on. Of course, we absolutely need at least one Bond to make it a goer, a Bond girl –' he paused to give a laddish leer – 'and a villain would be good. So, any ideas please?'

Jessica had an idea. Her idea was to get up, leave and throw herself from the top of the building. She tried desperately to think of an excuse that she could use to extricate herself from the room, but her mind was blank. The only thing in it was panic, which was racing up and down like a headless chicken . . .

'Well, initial thoughts are that I'll be starting with Daniel Craig and working my way back from there,' said Kerry. 'I'd say there's a pretty good chance he'll do it. After all, he's already guaranteed to be in town for the première anyway and they won't get a better chance to promote the movie than this.'

'Oh, can't we get Edward Granger?' whined Natasha.

'Edward Granger, eh?' said Mike, his hands on his hips in a way that made him look ever so slightly effeminate.

'Ooh, yeah,' she replied, flirting outrageously. 'He's the best. Everyone pretends it's all about Daniel Craig but deep down what they really want is Edward . . . or Pierce. I wouldn't mind a look at his lethal weapon either.'

'Naughty girl,' said Mike, pretending to look shocked but loving every minute of it.

'My mum met Edward Granger once,' piped up Paul, causing Jessica to stare at him as if he'd just announced an intention to blow up the building. 'It was years ago,' he continued, blissfully unaware of the palpitations he was causing Jessica. 'She won a competition to go to one of his premières and he was there with Angelica Dupree. Mum still raves on about how "dishy" Edward Granger was. Apparently old Heavenly Melons went into labour that very same evening too.'

'At which point they became Milky Melons,' quipped Luke.

'Wow,' said Natasha. 'That's so cool.'

'Well, I'll definitely put a call in,' said Kerry. 'Let's face it, I'll put a call in to all the Bonds. More the merrier, I reckon.'

'Or Roger Moore the merrier,' interjected Mike, looking truly delighted by his play on words.

'But I can tell you now,' continued Kerry, ignoring Mike but wondering vaguely why Jessica was looking so odd, 'Edward Granger's agent, Jill Cunningham, is one of the toughest in Hollywood and given that he doesn't have anything he needs to promote at the moment it's not like he needs the publicity. I bet she'd make a stink about him sharing the limelight with other guests.'

Jessica sank a little lower in her seat, as low as she was able without slipping off altogether. She felt sick and her heart thumped loudly in her chest. This was literally the worst thing that could have happened and she'd have to quit, surely? There was no way she could endure having to listen to people talking about her dad . . . and quite possibly her mom too . . . oh, God.

'Shame,' added Vanessa on cue. 'I bloody love Edward Granger too. He's frigging gorgeous and that scene where he escaped from that mad African despot and then scaled that tower to save Heavenly Melons was hot. The way he flung her on to the bed for a quick one before saving her always got me going.'

For once Jessica was glad she couldn't understand much of what her colleague had said. She wanted to put her fingers in her ears and sing. Blood thumped round her head.

Julian piped up. 'I don't know how you girls can be sitting here talking about the cheesy housewife favourite Bonds while missing out the original and the best. I'm sorry, but without a shadow of a doubt the best possible guest we could get other than Craig would be Sean Connery. And, quite frankly, to say otherwise is akin to Bond heresy.'

A few people muttered their agreement. Mike put his hands in his pockets and chewed his lip as he mulled this over, loving the debate that had ensued.

'Actually,' said Paul, 'while I agree with Julian that Connery is undoubtedly the best Bond ever by far –' Julian gave him a satisfied thumbs-up – 'thinking about it now, if you could get Daniel Craig, who – let's face it – is vying for the top spot with Connery and has to be the guest we most need, then if you could get Heavenly Melons on as our Bond girl, I think we'd have a ratings winner. I don't know one man alive who didn't fall in love with her in *The World in Your Hand*, for two very obvious reasons. In fact, other than possibly Ursula Andress or maybe Halle Berry, she is unquestionably the sexiest Bond girl of all time. Quite apart from that, I bet she'd be really interesting to talk to too. I mean, she wasn't just in a Bond film, she married one, didn't she?'

'Yeah, she wasn't just in a Bond. Bond was in her,' added Luke crudely, causing ripples of mirth.

Jessica was beyond dismayed. Her parents were always going to be part of any Bond discussion but she would have hoped they wouldn't have entered it quite so promptly. Plus, this was the first time in her life she'd ever had to hear anything other than blatant sycophancy about them and she'd certainly never had to hear a boyfriend of hers admit to fancying her mother, even if she always suspected that they probably did. Unable to listen to any more, she leapt to her feet, knowing there was a strong chance she might be about to throw up.

'Excuse me,' she said, stopping only to grab her bag before she raced out of the room, her hand to her mouth.

'Jesus,' said Mike, looking astonished as the office door swung despondently in Jessica's wake. 'What is it with the girls in this office running out of my meetings? Shit, I hope she's not ill,' he added, suddenly less worried about what might be wrong with Jessica and more about his potential dinner plans.

He wasn't the only worried person in the room though and Kerry and Paul both scrambled to their feet, determined to find Jessica and to see if she was all right.

27

'Are you OK, babe?' said Kerry, hammering on the door.

'I'm fine,' croaked Jessica, who was in fact slumped on the toilet, silent tears coursing down her face.

'Are you ill or something? What's wrong?' persisted Kerry. It was unsettling to see Jessica anything other than cheery. To a large extent they all took her lovely, happy nature for granted.

'I'm fine. Honestly, I just felt a bit sick, that's all,' cried Jessica mournfully, desperately trying to stave off her tears.

'Paul hasn't upset you, has he?'

Paul. Jessica smiled a small, sad smile. 'No, Paul hasn't upset me.'

It wasn't his fault that, like the rest of the world's population, he wanted to sleep with her mother. It also wasn't his fault that Mike had decided to do a stupid Bond special, meaning it was highly likely she was going to be found out and her adventure would be over, along with any hope she might have had of getting it together with Paul. Even if she came clean now, her lies would inevitably seem like a bigger deal. She may have been in England for a month and a half now but was still only in her third week of employment and things had come crashing down already. It was so unfair.

'Good,' said Kerry. 'Because he's hanging around outside

these lavs like George Michael, so I need to tell him you're OK. He's really worried about you,' she added gently.

Jessica took a deep breath and adjusted her gaze heavenwards in order to stem the flow. She didn't want Paul to be worried but couldn't face him just yet. Plus she couldn't believe his mom had actually met her parents. Christ, his mom had nearly met *her* by the sound of it. What were the chances?

'Tell him I feel a bit sick, but I'm fine and I'll be out in a while, yeah?'

'All right,' said Kerry. Although concerned, she felt satisfied that Jessica wasn't going to do anything silly. Like drown herself in the toilet bowl.

The sound of Kerry's footsteps diminished and the door creaked back into place. Jessica exhaled. Left with the empty silence, she was overcome with a huge and sudden urge to speak to her dad. Whenever she felt unhappy, it was always him who helped her gain perspective on things, his calm, reassuring voice that restored balance again. She'd been so preoccupied with Paul recently that she'd grown very slack about ringing him, but now she longed to see him and yearned for one of his big old bear hugs, which always made everything seem OK. Ironic, considering that, as ever, he was at the root of all her problems. She didn't even have the option of talking to her other parent. Having finally psyched herself up to call Angelica, she'd been dismayed to discover she was off on a promotional tour of Europe and wouldn't be in London again for weeks. Angelica had sounded really fed up about it but there was nothing she could do, so instead they'd promised to get together as soon as she was back in town. A rendezvous that was bound to be fairly awkward. Jessica sighed. She needed to get a grip and extricate herself from this toilet cubicle before Paul sent in a search party.

She unlocked the door and approached the mirror with caution. She'd been right to do so. Her blue eyes were red, puffy and watery. Her fair complexion was blotchy and red. An attractive combination.

When she finally emerged, a stressed-looking Paul was still keeping vigil outside. 'Hey, you,' he said, his face wreathed with concern. 'What's up? Kerry said you don't feel well.'

'I'm OK, probably just coming down with a cold or something,' she said lamely.

'Are you sure? Only for a second I was worried I might have offended you . . .' he said hesitantly, his voice trailing off. 'One minute I was wittering on about Heavenly Melons and the next you'd bolted. I hope you weren't –'

Jessica raised a hand, albeit weakly, to stop him from saying any more. Bless him, but she wasn't that pathetic. Had he chosen Honor Blackman or Jane Seymour to wax lyrical about, it wouldn't have bothered her in the slightest. But he hadn't, and the inappropriate utterance about her mother would be etched in her memory forever. How could she ever explain that, far from suffering from some form of jealous hissy fit, what she'd had to cope with felt like incest of the weirdest kind?

'Just feeling a bit under the weather. If I go home then I'll be fine by tomorrow, I'm sure,' she mumbled.

Paul didn't look convinced and his concern was making her feel horribly guilty and utterly confused. It was all too much to compute.

'OK,' he said, still looking worried. 'You get yourself better though, won't you? I'm holding you to that date, so if this is all an elaborate ploy to get out of seeing me then . . .'

Jessica managed a weak smile. 'Silly,' she said tentatively, swinging her hand out to take one of his. 'It's not.'

'OK,' said Paul, slowly looking less freaked out. 'I was just checking, you know.'

Jessica swallowed. Damn this horrid, awkward turn of events. All she wanted was to be with Paul and for things to unfold between them as they had been doing so beautifully, up until now. Until this.

'Right,' she said calmly, gathering herself together. 'Would you mind telling Mike that I've gone and that I'll be in tomorrow?' She wasn't entirely sure this was true. She had a lot of thinking to do.

'Of course,' said Paul, who couldn't shake the uneasy feeling that Jessica wasn't telling him everything. 'Let me walk you out of the building and put you in a cab though. If you're ill you shouldn't get the tube.'

'I'm fine,' protested Jessica, on the verge of sorrowful tears once more. She needed to get away as soon as possible. 'I will get a cab but you really don't need to see me out.'

Paul regarded her, trying to work out how much he could protest before he just started to be annoying. He wanted to see her out. That was the thing.

'I'll see you tomorrow,' she said firmly, sensing his doubt. And with that she scurried as quickly as she could away to the elevators, leaving Paul thoroughly discomfited. If there was one thing he wasn't, it was stupid.

Ten minutes later, Jessica was safely ensconced in the back of a taxi when her cell phone went. It was Mike.

'Jessica,' he said. 'Are you all right?'

'I'm fine,' she said for what felt like the thousandth time that day before remembering that she was supposed to be meeting his wife later. 'Oh, gosh, Mike, I'm so sorry, I left without seeing you. It was just that –'

'No, no, don't worry. If you're ill, you're ill,' he answered, trying to disguise how disappointed he was. 'You must go home and get better and – not that it's important at all – but I'm assuming you won't be coming round tonight?'

Jessica thought about it. She didn't want to let him down if she didn't have to. It clearly meant so much to him, but then again she needed him to think she was ill in order to have some much-needed thinking time . . . 'Well, I'm not really that ill. I mean, I don't think it's contagious,' she began tentatively, testing the waters.

'Really?' said Mike, leaping on this titbit of information. 'Well . . . gosh, I don't want you feeling you have to drag yourself over if you don't feel up to it . . . I suppose I could always ask Isy, though I'd probably spend the night worrying in case she set the house on fire or something.'

'It's fine,' said Jessica, almost laughing by now at the ridiculousness of the whole situation. 'If I rest up this afternoon then I'm sure I'll be fine to come by yours, if that's OK? I don't want you to think like I'm cutting class or anything. I do feel awful, but I'm just as sure that I can shrug it off, and I'd love to meet your little girls,' she added, finishing before she tied herself in a complete knot.

'Right, brilliant,' said Mike. 'So just go home and rest and then come over when you're ready.'

'OK,' sniffed Jessica, 'I'll see you later then. You said earlyish so that they're still up. Is six OK?'

'That would be wonderful. I'll try to leave as early as I can too so that I can see you.'

Mike put the phone down and sat back feeling relieved but also mildly guilty in case he'd just put pressure on an ill person to come and do something she didn't really want to do. What he didn't notice was Natasha, who had slipped unseen into his office for a chat about something and who was now looking at him with a blatantly suspicious expression on her face.

A little before six, Jessica was on her way to Chiswick when her phone went. She was surprised, but not in a good way, to discover Graydon on the line.

'I'm glad to have caught you,' he said ominously.

'Right . . .' she said, sounding as unsure as she felt.

'Because we're going away for quite some time, though I'm sure you've heard all about it from your mother.'

'Yes, I have,' said Jessica, feeling defensive. She may not have asked Angelica that much about her forthcoming trip but then her going away was hardly a big deal. She was permanently away.

'Right, well, I wanted to have a word on her behalf before we left,' he said smoothly, 'because I believe you saw her the other day, only didn't honour the arrangement.'

Honour the arrangement? What the hell was he talking about?

'It was a misunderstanding,' said Jessica. 'I got my wires a bit crossed but –'

'Right,' said Graydon. 'Only it's affected her quite badly and, your mother's mental health being what it is, I worry about you doing it again.'

'What do you mean, my mother's mental health? What are you getting at?'

'Look,' said Graydon as if he was talking to someone a bit slow, 'your mother is of a very sensitive and delicate disposition so it is up to me to protect her and make sure she doesn't have to face situations she's not equipped to deal with. You rejecting her the other day was a kick in the teeth and I simply can't allow it to happen again.'

Had she been having the best day ever, Jessica would have still reacted badly to the poisonous dross that was coming out of his mouth. As it was, she was in no mood to endure it for even a moment longer.

'With all due respect, Graydon,' she protested, 'what goes on between my mother and me is none of your goddamn business.'

'Well, that's where you're wrong,' he said. 'It's very much my business and if I have my way that will become official before too long.'

Feeling sick to the stomach, Jessica replied, 'Well, I'm pretty sure Mom would be fairly unimpressed to find out you've been threatening me, Graydon, so if I were you I'd back off.'

'Now don't overreact. I'm merely expressing concern about the way you treat your mother. That's all,' he said lightly. 'Besides, I'm not so sure you do have the upper hand. It's not like the two of you are really bonded, is it?'

Jessica felt like she'd been punched in the solar plexus. The bastard. 'I don't care what you think,' she said, trying hard not to cry. 'Just stay out of my business.' Fuming, she cut him off. The cheek of the guy. What an idiot and how dare he get involved. He had no idea of the years of complicated history she and her mother shared and, frankly, if Angelica was running back to the hairy ape, moaning about how Jessica was 'treating' her, they could both fuck off.

By now she was approaching Mike's house so, banishing the last unpleasant five minutes from her mind, Jessica pulled herself together and rang the bell to number twenty-six. She'd been through so much today already she wasn't really feeling nervous about this latest situation she found herself in and at least she knew what to expect. She remembered from the photographs she'd seen in the kitchen that Diane was attractive with long dark brown hair. She had a curvaceous, fairly voluptuous figure and a pretty, pleasant face. Which was why Jessica was somewhat thrown when a Neanderthal in a stained T-shirt and dressing gown opened the door, with skin the colour of putty and greasy, dishevelled hair.

'Er, hi,' Jessica said, looking behind this scary creature, expecting Diane to appear any second now and explain why there was a cave woman standing in her hallway.

'Is Diane in?'

'I'm Diane. You must be Jessica?'

'Yes,' said Jessica over-loudly, trying desperately to rectify her mistake. 'Pleased to meet you and I hope I'm not too early. It's just Mike said to come when the babies were still up.'

'No, no, it's fine,' said Diane quietly. 'Come in. It's very kind of you to come. It's bath time so it's a bit chaotic, but do come on up.'

Jessica could hear shrill laughter coming from the first floor and felt quite excited. There had been a distinct lack of small people in her life so far, but when she did come across children she usually got on with them pretty well. Diane stomped wearily up the stairs and, still not over the shock of how dowdy and unkempt she looked, Jessica studied her from behind. Her bottom was very large but then in LA women probably got any leftover pregnancy fat scooped out of them surgically, she mused.

'So,' said Diane wearily once they'd reached the landing, as if simply speaking to another person was a monumental effort and one that she didn't have any spare energy for, 'this is Grace. Grace darling, come here and say hello. This is Jessica from Daddy's work.'

A small whirlwind, dressed only in pants and a vest, with a shock of tangled curls, sped out of one of the bedrooms and Jessica couldn't help but smile. She was so sweet. She had an impish little face, a button nose and a high forehead. Her bright, inquisitive eyes checked Jessica over and then the questions started.

'Who your name?'

'What's your name,' corrected Diane, reaching forward to pull her daughter's vest up over her head. 'Come here you, your bath's ready.'

'My name's Jessica and you're Grace, aren't you?' said Jessica, kneeling down on the landing to talk to her.

'When we went on holiday,' said the little girl, 'we went out at night for our supper.'

'Did you?' said Jessica, genuinely fascinated by the random turn the conversation had taken. 'And what did you eat?'

'Um.'

Grace thought this one over while her mum pulled off her pants, lifted her up, carried her into the bathroom and plonked her in the water.

'Pizza and ps-getthi,' she lisped.

'Spaghetti, darling,' said Diane, seemingly on autopilot as she started pulling plastic toys out of a box and dropping them into the bath. Suddenly she turned questioningly to Jessica. 'I know you've only just got here, but are you OK to watch Grace for a second, Jessica? Just while I get Ava. I've left her in the cot looking at her mobile but she'll be grizzling for a feed in a minute.'

Right on cue, the sound of a mewing cry drifted through from the baby's nearby bedroom.

'Sure,' said Jessica. 'Of course.'

'Thanks,' muttered Diane.

As her mother left the room, Grace rolled her eyes conspiratorially at Jessica in a way that was so clearly copied from grown-ups it made Jessica giggle.

'Mummy says rude words,' she whispered mischievously, her face breaking out into a joyous grin.

'Grace,' warned Diane as she appeared back in the bathroom, carrying a small, grunting, babygro'd bundle.

'Oh my gosh,' exclaimed Jessica, who was blown away by the tiny dimensions of the person in Diane's arms. 'She is so cute.'

Diane sat down on the toilet and regarded little Ava as if she hadn't stopped to consider this before now. 'Yes, I suppose she is, isn't she?' she said, though by the tone of her voice Jessica got the impression she wasn't entirely sure. She could certainly see why Mike was worried about his wife. She looked absolutely exhausted. Like the most tired person in the world, and as if she could happily curl up now on the bathroom floor and drop off. She also seemed rather detached, which didn't make Jessica feel at all uncomfortable but did make her feel as though she should be doing something to help.

Grace started singing to herself in the bath. Jessica was amused to note it was 'The Winner Takes It All' the three-year-old was strangling, as opposed to a nursery rhyme.

'She loves *Mamma Mia*,' said Diane by way of explanation.

'Don't we all,' said Jessica to Grace, wishing she could offer signed photographs from Pierce Brosnan, which would only be a phone call away.

'Thanks so much for coming round,' added Diane, the first really direct thing she'd said to her since she'd arrived. Jessica was about to say that it was a pleasure when she was distracted by the sight of Diane rummaging around with one hand underneath her T-shirt. Having achieved whatever it was she was trying to do, she shoved it up, revealing folds of soft skin on her belly. Then, one large, pendulous, milk-filled breast flopped out. As quickly as it appeared some of it disappeared again as it was stuffed into Ava's rooting mouth, which was feverishly trying to find it. Jessica's jaw briefly fell to the ground.

She'd never seen anyone breastfeed before in her life and didn't know where to look. Wherever she did decide upon, however, it seemed there was no escaping the sight of Diane's enormous brown nipple. Or rather, not her nipple exactly, because that was stuffed firmly into the baby's plunger-like jaws, but the area around the nipple that was hanging out of one of the strangest bra-like contraptions Jessica had ever seen. It looked like a chocolate digestive.

'You don't mind, do you?' said Diane with a start, as if it had only just occurred that social convention probably required her to at least enquire, given that there was a relative stranger in her bathroom.

'Gosh, no,' said Jessica, trying to be terribly European and cool. She remembered Angelica telling her once that, generally speaking, Americans' attitude towards feeding had always enraged her. It was an unexpected memory which evoked an unusual pang of tenderness in Jessica towards her decidedly continental mother, followed by a deeply resentful one as she remembered what Graydon had said earlier.

'Sorry,' said Diane. 'Sometimes I forget that not everyone is existing in a strange insular bubble that revolves around feeding and wiping and not sleeping.'

Jessica smiled reassuringly at her and when Diane smiled back she spotted for the first time a glimpse of the woman from the pictures downstairs.

'I want some more toys,' demanded Grace suddenly and stridently. She'd obviously grown tired of singing and of submerging her frog under the water.

Diane, who had just settled into a vaguely comfortable position, rolled her eyes as if the timing of Grace's request was completely typical. She looked done in, defeated, but started nevertheless to move to get some more toys. The minute she did, however, Ava – livid to have been interrupted from her feed – started screaming. Jessica was quite taken aback that such a screech could emerge from such a small body. At the same time, Grace started to kick off too, whining that she wanted more toys NOW, until the cacophony of wailing became quite extraordinary. As Diane shuffled around, like the Hunchback of Notre-Dame in a dressing gown, Jessica leapt to her feet.

'No, no, please let me. You just carry on feeding that little one,' she said over the din, unable to watch Diane struggling any longer. 'Right,' she said to Grace, 'what are you after? There's a boat in here, you've got a digger, some fish.'

'I don't want those. They're boring,' whined Grace, barely audible against Ava's screaming. The toddler was going a funny shade of puce, her bottom lip trembling dangerously.

'Grace,' snapped Diane, who had finally got Ava positioned back on her boob. 'Don't start, OK? That's what we've got, so just don't start. Mummy's very tired and it's been a long day. And you say please when you ask for things, or you don't get them.'

'Hey? Your mom's right, you know,' agreed Jessica calmly, but with a friendly smile on her face. 'Still, how about I see if there's something in your room that we could play with?' she suggested, keen to help diffuse the situation.

'In my room?' repeated Grace, looking stunned by what she obviously thought was a very left-field suggestion, tantrum seemingly forgotten, though Jessica sensed it was only one wrong move away from returning.

'Sure,' said Jessica, popping out of the bathroom and into the little girl's bedroom. She hoped Diane wouldn't mind her using her initiative but Jessica suspected that Diane would prefer her just to help without asking tons of polite questions.

Seconds later, Jessica returned to the bathroom with a plastic tea set. It was an instant hit and harmony was restored.

'Thank you,' said Diane gratefully a bit later as she watched Grace and Jessica making each other cups of tea.

'Pleasure,' said Jessica. 'Actually, I hope you don't mind me suggesting this, but seeing as I'm here, why don't you go feed Ava somewhere a little more comfortable? I could give Grace a wash and play with her a little.'

'Oh, that's OK,' said Diane, looking unsure from where she was perched uncomfortably on the toilet. In order for her to ensure that Ava didn't fall down, her leg had to be raised, crossed over the other in a pose that would surely lead to years spent at the osteopath. 'You only came about babysitting. I'm sure you don't really want to do her bath and stuff.'

'If you're not sure then I totally understand,' replied Jessica, 'but I'd love to, actually. It would be a real pleasure.'

'Er, well, OK then,' said Diane. 'Maybe I will. If you're sure you're all right?'

'Go away, Mummy. I want Jessica to do my bath,' demanded Grace, bored of the polite pussyfooting around.

'Don't be rude,' said Diane, looking defeated but shuffling nevertheless towards the comfort of her bedroom, Ava sucking away contentedly.

Ten minutes later, Ava, having had her fill, stopped chomping and released her mother's boob from her jaws. Diane got herself even more comfortable on the bed; Ava nestled into her shoulder so she could wind her. As she rubbed her youngest daughter's back she listened to the sound of Grace next door having the best fun bath she'd had in ages. Then she heard Jessica suggesting that maybe they should wash her hair and cringed, hoping she hadn't sniffed it. A hair wash was rather overdue. Still, she was impressed that Jessica had taken matters into her own hands. Mike was right. She seemed like a lovely girl and her instinct was that she would be a caring and responsible person to leave her precious girls with. She'd probably be better than her at looking after them, she thought sadly.

A bit later and Ava was starting to fall asleep so Diane got up and went to settle her into her cot. At the same time, Jessica was heaving a well-scrubbed Grace out of the bath and wrapping her in a towel.

'Where are her nightclothes?' Jessica asked.

'On the bed in my room,' said Diane, amazed by how Jessica was managing to blend seamlessly into their routine. How her presence was making everything so much easier. 'I usually dress her in there so that she can watch CBeebies before we do stories.'

'Oh, right, OK,' said Jessica, who wasn't going to intrude further by entering her boss's bedroom. It didn't seem appropriate. However, sensing that her mummy was about to take over again, Grace piped up.

'But I want Jessica to put me in my 'jamas.'

'Ssh, darling, Mummy can do it,' protested Diane firmly but quietly as she shut Ava's door behind her.

'No,' whined Grace and it was immediately obvious that another scene from the tired-out toddler was on the cards. Hoping to nip it in the bud, Jessica interjected.

'I don't mind if you don't.'

Diane exhaled as she weighed up the alternative, a screaming match with Grace.

'Well, if you really don't mind, please feel free to come

in our bedroom,' said Diane, hoping that between herself and Grace they weren't putting Jessica off altogether.

On the contrary, the only thing Jessica was worried about was treading on Diane's toes. Then again, she figured, a woman who wasn't bothered about being seen in such a revolting T-shirt, and who lopped her boob out within the first five minutes of meeting her, probably wouldn't mind her seeing the state of her rather messy bedroom. When Diane bent down to retrieve a pair of knickers off the floor she still extended the courtesy, however, of pretending she hadn't seen.

A happy Grace let Jessica dry and dress her with none of the usual fuss, and Diane sank into the armchair in the corner of the room, too tired even to move a heap of washing that had been waiting there for days to be put away. Grace let Jessica comb out her wet hair, at which point Diane almost checked to see it *was* still her daughter in the room. It was amazing how instantly Grace had taken to this complete stranger, though she wasn't entirely surprised. After all, Jessica was young, pretty, sweet, smiley and fun, and as the two of them chatted away to one another Diane relished the unusual scene of domestic bliss. Usually at this time of the day it was tantrums and squealing all the way, and that was just from her. As it occurred to Diane how little fun she'd been recently, she felt the familiar acute sadness wash over her once more.

Mike was right. She did need some help. If not for her sake then for Grace's, who simply didn't deserve to be around someone who was so . . . depressed. Oh . . . was that what this was all about, she wondered, in a moment of clarity? Realization made her gasp. If it was, she simply had to find her way back to herself and fast, because she didn't recognize anything about herself any more and it couldn't go on.

28

The next day, Jessica was in a very odd mood. At work all anyone seemed able to talk about was Bond. It was hideous.

'Daniel Craig is brilliant though,' Luke was saying. 'The way they reinvented him as this dispassionate killer, but on the flipside, one that falls in love with the girl. The whole revenge thing in *The Quantum of Solace* was brilliant too. I love a bit of back story.'

'Bet you do,' said Kerry, sounding very *Carry On*.

'I still don't understand why none of you think George Lazenby was the best,' said Isy, looking mystified.

'Well, I miss the days of the little jokes and catchphrases,' said Julian, ignoring her completely. 'Naming a character "Pussy Galore", "Heavenly Melons" or "Honey Ryder" would never get past the PC police these days, which is kind of sad.'

'Sad?' questioned an increasingly indignant Isy. Sometimes she felt like no one was on her wavelength (probably because they weren't). 'Why is it sad that women aren't demeaned any more? You don't get male characters called Willy Cannon or . . . Hugh Bulge, do you?'

'Or Dick Fudgenudger?' encouraged Kerry.

'You're right, Isy,' agreed Vanessa. 'Though they did occasionally get humiliated by the fashion department. Do you remember the banana-yellow ski suit Roger Moore wore?'

'Fuck, yeah,' agreed Luke. 'In *The Spy Who Loved Me*, which had probably the best opening to a Bond film ever. The eerie silence, the Union Jack parachute – amazing.'

'No way,' shouted Natasha. 'I mean, you're right, it was brilliant, but what about Edward Granger's opening in *The World in Your Hand*? That was pure genius. Do you not remember that chase through the Arabian bazaar? Then, at the end, Angelica Dupree rolling out of a Persian rug and landing at his feet, all boobs and teeth?'

'That was marvellous,' agreed Hassan emphatically. He didn't usually contribute much in the way of office banter, but felt moved to do so on this occasion.

Jessica sighed.

'I rewound that bit over and over again as a boy. That bit, and the black bikini scene obviously.'

'Obviously,' concurred Luke lasciviously, earning himself a jealous evil from his girlfriend.

'Well, I think the sexiest Bond moment of all time was Daniel Craig coming out of the sea in *Casino Royale*,' Kerry declared, determined to steer the subject away from Angelica Dupree's breasts. 'And, what's more, it looks like he's going to come on the show. His agent's going to confirm later but it's looking good,' she grinned. 'Though I'd still love to get one more Bond. Connery and Moore have both said no, so you might be in luck, Natasha, because next on my list to approach is Granger.'

'Wicked. If we get Granger, can we swap jobs, Jess? I reckon I might be his type, you know. Have you seen pictures of his wife? She's a right dolly bird. Big fake bangers and everything.'

'He won't do it,' Jessica said between gritted teeth and then flushed red as she realized what she'd said.

'How do you know he won't?' demanded Kerry. 'I told you I wanted to call Jill Cunningham. You haven't gone and done it, have you?'

'No,' said Jessica quickly, feeling a bit like she might be about to throw up . . . again. Her mind scrambled into action, searching for an explanation. 'I just – I googled Edward Granger and the show is happening just before his birthday, so he'll probably be . . . celebrating that . . .'

It was a feeble and strange reply. Kerry gave her a weird look. 'Right, well, it's still worth a call, on the off-chance his agent might play ball, I reckon. Brosnan's busy filming so can't be persuaded and does anyone really want to see Dalton or Lazenby? Apart from Isy, I mean. No, Granger's the only other Bond worth having, I reckon.'

Kerry smiled at Jessica but her assistant just sat rooted to the spot, looking as though someone had told her that her skirt had been tucked into her knickers for the last month. Then she stood up. 'I'm going to the canteen,' she said, leaving the office without so much as a backward glance.

Paul, one of the few people trying to do some actual work while all this was going on, watched her go. From the minute he'd set eyes on her this morning he'd known that whatever was up hadn't resolved itself, and had been desperate to get her on her own ever since. So despite the fact he was in the middle of writing a speech for Bradley that was needed for an awards ceremony later in the week, he abandoned it and went to find her.

'Jess!' he shouted, having spotted her blonde head down the corridor. She'd obviously taken off at quite a speed and appeared not to have heard. Or had she? If anything, she'd picked up the pace even more. He sprinted after her, frantically trying to catch up as Jessica tore ahead. Things must be worse than he'd suspected for her to be acting like this. What the hell was going on? Finally he reached her and when he did he forced her to turn round and face him.

'What is it?'

'It's nothing,' she said, tears rolling down her face.

'Please tell me,' Paul implored, now terrified about what on earth it could be. 'For God's sake, Jess, what is it? What's happened? Is it me? I know you're not ill so don't tell me that again.'

'It's nothing,' repeated Jessica lamely.

'I don't believe you. We had such a great time on Monday night but two days later and you can hardly look me in the eye, so what's changed between now and then?'

Jessica stared at her toes, unable to look him in the eye.

'See me tonight?' Paul persisted. 'I don't know what's wrong but I hate seeing you so miserable and I just hope . . .'

Jessica looked up.

'I just hope it's nothing I've done,' ventured Paul, looking as vulnerable as he felt.

Jessica blinked hard as she considered for the hundredth time coming clean about her situation, but couldn't find the words. 'I can't see you tonight,' she said eventually.

'Right,' said Paul, who felt like he'd been punched. 'Why? What are you up to?'

Jessica sighed. She didn't want to break Mike's trust by telling Paul she was babysitting. Of course, ordinarily she would have loved nothing better than to be seeing Paul, but given what was going on at work now, hanging out with Grace and Ava felt like a far preferable choice anyway. They certainly wouldn't be asking any complicated questions. Plus, yesterday, once the babies were in bed, Diane had ended up pouring her heart out to her about a few things and she was keen to make sure she was OK.

'I'm . . . I'm . . . just doing something with Pam,' said Jessica, feeling exhausted. Having to lie all the time was draining.

'What are you doing with Pam?' Paul enquired gently, breaking Jessica's heart as he did so.

'I just said that I would see her tonight, that's all,' said Jessica, her eyes pleading with him to understand.

'Fine,' said Paul, looking hurt.

'How about tomorrow though?' she suggested hopefully, not wanting to extinguish what had been started altogether. 'I know it would be late but maybe we could have a drink after the show or something?'

Paul's face instantly changed. He grinned with relief. 'Of course I'm free, but on one condition.'

'What?' sniffed Jessica, wondering how bad she must look right now. She wasn't a pretty crier. She was more from the 'blotchy red patches on the chest' school of weeping.

'That tomorrow you tell me what's wrong and why you're so upset. Whatever it is I'll understand. Trust me,' he insisted.

Jessica considered this for a second, her face grave. 'OK,' she said finally and she meant it. Tomorrow she would tell him everything. Not about babysitting for Mike and Diane. That was different. Diane had confided in her last night and she wasn't going to betray her trust by telling

Paul. However, she would tell Paul who her mom and dad were, which would instantly explain why this whole Bond special was such a pisser to be around. That much she owed him and she'd just have to pray he'd understand.

'Thursday it is then,' he said, his face serious. He hated seeing Jessica look so sad and realized in that moment just how much he was starting to like her.

Tentatively he stepped towards her and, once he'd gleaned that a cuddle would be welcome, he gave her a hug. It was just the hug she needed and was also the first time that physical contact between the two of them had been anything but sexual. As Jessica buried her face into his chest she felt so safe she could have quite happily stayed there all day. Of course, seconds later, what had started out as comforting and friendly began to creep into the realms of sexual and arousing as it occurred to her how broad his chest was and how strong his arms felt around her. Meanwhile, he was aware of the feel of her breasts pressed up against him and was starting to imagine for the zillionth time what it would be like to be in bed with her naked.

Just at that moment Jeremy Paxman marched past, his presence providing a necessary reminder that they were in a corridor in the middle of the BBC and that feeling turned on was wholly inappropriate.

Paul pulled away. 'We'd better get back,' he said reluctantly, and an emotionally drained and confused Jessica allowed him to lead her back to the production office.

Later, Mike asked Jessica for a word.

'Hi, there,' he said, once she was in his room and the door was shut. 'All set for tonight?'

'Yes,' said Jessica, 'don't worry, I haven't forgotten.'

'No, no, of course not,' said Mike, looking faintly sheepish. 'OK, I'm just going to come out and say it. Is there any chance you could leave work a bit early today? It's just that, as you know, Diane hasn't been feeling all that great recently and I popped home earlier so she could go to the doctor's. Turns out she might be suffering from a rather severe case of the baby blues, maybe even post-natal depression.'

'I'm so sorry.'

'It's fine,' said Mike. 'Well, actually, it's not fine, it's completely terrifying, but at least now we know. In fact, thank you for suggesting that she go. I think chatting to you yesterday really helped and I know how useful she found it having an extra pair of hands at bath time, which is why it would be great if you could pop along today. I'd go myself, but having snuck out once already . . .'

'Of course I'll go,' said Jessica, pleased there was something she could do to help. Poor Diane.

Mike looked really sad for a second. 'I should have known,' he said quietly. 'She hasn't been happy for such a long time, but I kept putting it down to tiredness. Still, we'll just have to do what it takes to get her well again.'

Jessica felt rather fond of Mike at that moment. She'd always thought Paul's disdain towards him was a little uncalled for. She could tell he really loved his wife.

'I'm pleased to help in any way I can,' she said. 'Besides, I'd love to give Grace her bath again.' She wasn't lying. She'd enjoyed her brief foray into domestic chaos.

'Fab,' said Mike. 'You're a star, and please don't tell anyone else on the team, will you? I want this to remain private.'

'Of course,' nodded Jessica fervently.

'I'll make something up about why you're leaving. Why don't you get to mine for about six?'

'Sure, or even five?' she suggested, spotting an opportunity to wangle another hour off from having to hear anything to do with James Bond. 'That way I could help feed Grace her tea. Diane mentioned that it's always a bit of a logistical nightmare at that time of day.'

'Really? God, you're marvellous. I'll have to start calling you Jessica Poppins,' Mike teased.

'Right,' she agreed faintly, her heart too heavy to feign enthusiasm for crap jokes.

In the end, Jessica escaped the Bond-obsessed office even earlier, much to Natasha and Kerry's annoyance. Still, if they hadn't started playing 'cliff, marry, shag' and included her father in their sordid fun, she might have stuck around a bit longer.

'But why would Mike arrange for *you* to go to a showcase and not me?' said Kerry, who Jessica had been appalled to discover would rather shag Piers Morgan over her dad. She didn't know whether to be pleased or insulted.

'If this new comedian's any good, why isn't Mike sending me? No offence.'

'None taken,' said Jessica dolefully. She hated the fact things had to be so secretive but would have said anything by now if it meant being able to make a getaway to Chiswick.

'Maybe Mike thinks she needs cheering up?' suggested Luke, giving Jessica a reassuring squeeze on the arm.

'Or maybe he thinks you're far too busy sorting out

tomorrow and wouldn't want to leave me in charge,' improvised Jessica, which Kerry seemed to buy more.

'I hope I don't sound like a bitch,' she said now. 'I know you're a bit down at the moment.'

'Unbelievably sexy bitch,' said Luke, approaching his girlfriend for a tongue sandwich. Jessica turned away.

'Get a fucking room, would you?' complained Natasha. Then, turning to Jessica, she said in a low voice, 'Hope there isn't any other reason why Mike and you have been having so many private conversations.'

Jessica didn't have the strength to deal with her accusatory tone so she pretended that she hadn't heard, grabbed her bag and made to leave, knowing full well that from across the office Paul was watching her go.

29

That evening, looking after Grace and Ava went unbelievably well. The children were gorgeous and Jessica found their innocence and simplicity a wonderful antidote to everything that was going on at the moment. The basic practicality required in order to tend to their needs appealed to her too. She enjoyed helping make Grace's tea, making sure it was cool enough to eat, that she didn't spill her juice and that she ate her vegetables. After much encouragement from Jessica, she even managed an 'empty plate', which pleased Diane so much she allowed the little girl to have ice cream for pudding. Jessica watched, fascinated, as she ate it. She'd never seen anyone concentrate so hard on eating anything before and it seemed to Jessica, at that moment, that children had it right. They lived completely in the present, not having the capacity to do anything else, of course, but were so able to enjoy small things as a result. Sitting at the kitchen table with Grace, Jessica experienced a rare stillness. At five thirty, while the rest of the modern world raced around, battling to make a living, coping with the strains and stresses of everyday life, Grace was oblivious to everything but her ice cream. Whereas Ava's only concern was how much of her little fist she could cram into her mouth.

'She was up half the night. I think she's teething,' Diane explained, looking even more tired than she had done the previous day. Still, she was also ludicrously excited to be going out and when Jessica had arrived early, saying that she wanted to give Grace her tea, she'd burst into grateful tears, which was a little alarming but understandable given that she'd just been diagnosed with depression.

Bedtime was chaotic. Grace was horribly over-excited by the unusual activity in the house and Ava was screaming, but as soon as the baby was in her cot Mike and Diane left, leaving Jessica to deal with their eldest. With her parents out of the way, Grace immediately calmed down and Jessica read her four stories before tucking her up in bed.

Jessica was just creeping downstairs when her cell phone vibrated in her pocket. Predictably, it was a worried Diane checking on how things were going.

'They're fast asleep,' whispered Jessica, as she went to switch on the baby monitor in the living room. 'I was just about to text you.'

'And Grace went to bed OK?'

'Good as gold.'

'You're an angel. Thanks so much and remember, if you need me, please ring, and you've got the number of the restaurant in case there's no reception, haven't you?'

'Yes,' reassured Jessica. 'Now go and have a lovely evening and try not to worry. They're fine and I promise I'll call if I need you.'

Finally able to relax, Diane did as she was told and for the first time in a long time started to wind down and to talk to her husband properly and openly about how she had been feeling. By the time they were on dessert she already felt like she had more perspective on things than she had since Ava was born.

'You see,' she said, 'I don't actually think I am depressed. Not properly anyway. I mean, I don't want to harm myself or anything . . .'

'Jesus, Diane,' exclaimed Mike.

'What? Look, I'm sorry if you don't like hearing about it, but I've been on the Internet and, believe me, that does happen to some women. But, the fact is, I'm saying I'm *not* that ill,' she continued. 'I probably just have a major case of the baby blues, stemming from being so knackered all the time. Do you remember how much blood I lost during the birth? Well, today the doctor told me that being anaemic can contribute towards post-natal depression.'

'It's the fact that you've felt like this but battled on without saying anything that I have a problem with,' said Mike, determinedly not hearing the last bit of what she'd said. He was terribly squeamish and at the time had been convinced that childbirth was every bit as traumatic for him as it was for Diane. Still, having voiced this out loud once, he knew if he valued his testicles not to do so ever again.

Meanwhile, Diane was wondering how Mike could have been so dense as to have not realized how low she was. Surely the signs had been obvious? The daily tears, the inability to cope, the lethargy, the permanent bad hair days. Tonight was the first time her bronzer had come out in months, medicine in itself.

Still, Mike knew his wife well enough to suspect what might be going through her mind. 'I'm sorry, Di,' he said sadly. 'I'll do more to help, I promise. Just tell me what to do and I'll do it.'

'Oh, it's not your fault,' admonished Diane, trying not to cry. 'And I know I'm a nightmare to live with at the moment, but maybe having one proper night's sleep a week would help? That and the pills. I think I need to think about going back to work when Ava's a bit bigger too. I know I said I wasn't going to, but I'm not sure I'm cut out to be a housewife.'

'Well, whatever you decide you've got my support, and tonight you're going up to the spare room. I can give Ava a bottle in the night,' he said, a few weeks too late, reaching for his wife's hand.

'OK,' said Diane, feeling choked. 'Gosh, I can't believe how much just having a tiny bit of a break has helped already. It's pathetic really. In fact, I know Jessica works for you, but maybe she could come one day a week or something? Or even a couple of afternoons, till I've got myself sorted out.'

'Why don't we just call an agency tomorrow? There must be loads of great people out there,' offered Mike, delighted that Diane was finally ready to accept some help, which in turn could only mean that life was going to get better for him. For them all.

'I don't know,' said Diane hesitantly. She knew it was churlish, but she wanted Jessica. 'It's just, I like Jessica so much and they won't all be like her. Maybe I'll just carry on as we are? I'm sure Jessica will babysit again, so at least we can have another evening out. This has been nice.'

'It has,' agreed Mike, who knew what his wife was really getting at. But how could he entice Jessica away from her job without being sued for professional misconduct? 'Now, coffee?'

'Oh, yes, something to keep me awake all night, just what I fancy,' replied Diane sarcastically. 'No, I'll leave that to the babies, thanks. Now, we should get back –' Just then her phone bleeped, signalling a text. When she saw that it was from Jessica she almost leapt three feet out of her seat. 'Shit,' she said, panic making her look instantly deranged. Then, 'Oh . . .' Her expression changed to beatific in an instant. Her hand went to her chest. 'Oh, she is amazing. Look, Mike.'

Mike took her phone and read:

> All well here. Ava woke 4 a
> min so changed nappy and
> rocked back 2 sleep. V happy 2
> give her bottle at 11 if you
> like? Didn't give 2 her now as
> didn't want 2 ruin routine.
> Enjoy and don't worry. Both
> sleeping like . . . babies!

Mike looked at Diane's face and could tell his wife was smitten. Not with him, but with one super, child-friendly, capable Jessica Bender.

30

As it turned out, Paul and Jessica never did get round to having their drink that week, for the next day Paul's mum rang to tell him that his sister Lucy had contracted the glandular fever virus. Fortunately she'd finished her GCSEs, but Anita was still incredibly worried as it could spell many weeks of illness for Lucy, which in turn would mean a lot of time spent on her own while Anita had to work. Hardly the carefree summer Lucy had been planning.

One side effect of Paul's worry about the situation was that finding out about Jessica's problems got sidelined. Not that Jessica minded one bit. She was only sorry to see Paul looking so troubled and wished there was something she could do to help. Of course, there was no way he could escape home during a show day, so he had no choice but to try and forget about it for the moment and throw himself into work instead. Later, however, once the studio had been wrapped, he came to find Jessica and, as she'd suspected he might, asked if she wouldn't mind postponing their date.

'I'm just a bit stressed out,' he said, running one hand through his hair. 'So I hope you don't mind, but I want to be on good form when we see each other. Not fretting like I am now.'

'Of course,' Jessica replied, hating to see him look so anxious. 'I totally understand.'

'Thanks, Jess, I knew you would. Being from a single parent family and everything, you know what it's like when you have to shoulder some of the responsibility.'

'Sure,' she answered, wishing she did, for then maybe she wouldn't feel like quite such an inadequate human being at this precise second. 'And, hey, it's not like I'm going anywhere,' she added softly.

Which was a good thing because glandular fever lingers in the system for ages, meaning that over the coming weeks Paul found himself spending a lot of time to-ing and fro-ing from Staines. Partly to keep his listless, bedridden sister company, and partly to alleviate his mum's workload a little by helping out with the household chores Lucy would usually have done herself. As a result, for the time being anyway, his and Jessica's fledgling romance was on hold.

Not that their feelings for one another were. On the contrary. In fact, at times it was borderline torturous being in such close proximity to one another at work, while trying to keep a lid on things for the benefit of their colleagues. Though in some ways (and she felt guilty for even admitting it) Jessica felt like she'd been given a reprieve, a bit of breathing space, during which she managed to calm herself down about the whole 'Bond' situation and get things in perspective. No one had suddenly found out who she was just because of the special, which made the whole thing start to feel like less of a problem. She was even growing immune to the constant references to her parents, which had eased off a little, though not entirely.

With Paul so distracted by what was going on at home and the two of them being so busy at work, the next few weeks slipped by before Jessica even had time to really register them. Typically, on the rare nights when Paul *was* free and up for doing something, she'd invariably have arranged to be at Diane's babysitting. Still, they did at least manage to snatch a few lunches in the canteen together, and a few less intimate after-work drinks with everyone. On the whole, Jessica kept her head down, knowing that Paul was going through a tricky time and not wishing to add to his burden by nagging him about when they were going to go out.

Despite seeing him every day she missed him terribly, which was a strange conundrum, but in the meantime she was genuinely enjoying babysitting for Mike and Diane so said 'yes' whenever they asked. Slowly she was discovering she had a real way with children and Diane seemed to love having her around too. Not only because she appreciated the help but because she seemed to feel able to confide in her about all sorts of things. She'd even hinted heavily that she'd love Jessica to spend more time working for her, an idea which appealed, but not one she took particularly seriously given that she was currently employed by Diane's husband.

Before Jessica knew it, July had been and gone, along with the variable weather. Suddenly it was August, London was in the middle of a heat wave and, unbeknown to Jessica, things were finally about to step up a gear on a few other fronts too.

On the first Thursday in August, Mike was prowling the studio looking for Jessica. Diane's incessant nagging about Jessica had recently turned into a full-on campaign, which had finally paid off. Mike had been broken down and knew when he was beaten so had decided to address the situation. It didn't take him long to find the object of his wife's affections. Jessica was in the studio by the trestle table where the large urn was set up, making tea for Davina McCall, one of today's guests. Kerry had assigned herself the task of greeting Will Smith and his entourage as they arrived. The whole studio was incredibly excited about his appearance.

'Thanks so much again for babysitting the other night,' Mike whispered, making sure no one else could overhear their conversation.

'Such a pleasure,' Jessica replied, wondering how to broach the subject she'd been mulling over all day. How to get time off to go to her dad's party. She was growing increasingly worried about the fact she hadn't yet sorted this out and suddenly the Bond show was looming scarily close on the horizon, as were Edward's birthday celebrations.

Last night she'd phoned Edward for the first time in ages. It had been lovely to speak to him, though all he'd talked about was how excited he was about seeing her at the party. Not going wasn't an option, but suddenly it was a mere month away. If it came to it, she'd have to quit her job. He'd also asked if she'd spoken to her mother recently and had sounded almost disappointed when she'd said she hadn't, which was a bit strange.

'Look, I'm going to come straight to the point,' Mike said, looking around cautiously. 'How would you feel about helping Diane out with the children some afternoons? Obviously I'd have to wangle it with Kerry somehow and, of course, there's always the chance you might hate the idea of hanging out with my nutcase children and slightly depressed wife . . .'

Jessica raised an eyebrow in surprise.

'Joking,' said Mike airily, wondering why he always found himself saying the wrong thing. 'Anyway, say if I'm being out of order, but you're such a natural and Grace has really taken to you.'

'Has she?' asked Jessica, delighted.

'Oh, yes. So has Diane. In fact, she's been nagging me for weeks now to ask you, but I was just a bit worried about making you feel as if you were being coerced into something you didn't want to do. I mean, Christ, you know what Diane's like – if she had her way, I think she'd have me move out and you move in . . .'

Jessica deposited her used tea bag in the big black bin, smiling at the way Mike always talked himself into knots. Then she stifled a giggle as she remembered the picture of him in his too-tight swimming trunks. It made her giggle every time she was at the house.

'I'd really like to . . .' she answered truthfully. Any excuse to get away from the office was fine by her. Frankly, she preferred being with the little ones. Last night she'd remembered the chat she'd had with Pam when she'd first arrived all those many weeks ago, about wanting to do something with a point to it. Helping Mike's family might not be most people's idea of fun, but it was hers. She was obviously good at it too. She could tell by how desperate Mike was for her to say yes. This was the moment Jessica realized she should perhaps be bargaining harder.

'I need a week off in September though,' she blurted out. 'I know it's bad timing but I need to go back to the States after the special. If you let me go, I'll definitely help you out.' Jessica flushed red. If playing hard ball was the only way she could get home for her dad's party then needs must. 'But you'd need to think of something to tell the office.'

One more lie couldn't hurt. She was already living in a web of pure deceit anyway.

'Done,' said Mike immediately.

'Really?' said Jessica, delighted that her first-ever attempt at blackmail had gone so smoothly. If she'd known it was going to be so effective she would have resorted to it far earlier. 'Are you sure?'

'Positive,' nodded Mike. 'Since you're helping me out so much, I can make an exception. Go whenever you like, just promise you'll come back. As for the other thing –' he lowered his voice, having spotted Natasha ambling towards them – 'I might tell Kerry that on Wednesday and Friday afternoons, say, I need you to do some research for another show.'

'Whatever you think,' said Jessica, 'but I'd better go now. Davina's tea is getting cold.'

The good thing about it being studio day was that nobody had time to sit around debating anything to do with James Bond, which made a nice change. The fact that Hollywood royalty was in the building was a good distraction too. Will Smith had arrived and seemed every bit as nice as his reputation. As Jessica ran an errand for one of his entourage, she couldn't resist a grin. Her dad often played golf with Will and she could only imagine her colleagues expressions if she were to introduce herself to him as Jessica Granger.

The day sped by and Jessica only got a few tantalizing

glimpses of Paul before the day was out, once at supper break and once when she bumped into him dashing on to set to discuss something with Bradley. As soon as the crew and team had been wrapped, however, he instantly appeared at her side.

'Hey, you.'

'Hi,' Jessica replied. Never in her life had she known anyone who had such a huge effect on her physically. The minute she was in his vicinity she became a mess of swirling emotions. 'How are you? How's your sister? I feel like I've barely seen you this week.'

'I know,' said Paul apologetically. 'The whole situation's starting to take its toll on Mum a bit so I upped my visits this week. Still, Lucy's finally feeling a bit stronger, thank God, so hopefully life might start getting back to normal.'

'And how are you? Are you OK? You must be exhausted trying to juggle everything.'

'I'm fine,' he said, smiling at her in such a way that made his eyes crinkle up at the sides. In that instant he looked so devastatingly attractive that Jessica felt a huge pang of longing. 'I'm just so sorry I haven't had any time to take you out, or even just see you for a drink on our own. You've probably given up on me altogether by now.'

'No,' replied Jessica, blushing.

'Really? Well, that's good because you always seeing Pam when I *do* happen to be free is starting to make me think you've gone off me.'

'Look,' she said, not wishing to dwell on her lies for too long, 'you might not be in the mood, but how about doing something now? I mean, I know it's late but –'

'Sure,' interrupted Paul, looking surprised but really

pleased. 'Brilliant. Definitely. So what do you want to do? It's probably a bit late to go and eat now, unless you want to, that is?'

'Oh, no, I'm fine. It's ten thirty already and I had that pizza and stuff earlier, but a glass of wine would be good.'

'Great,' said Paul. 'Shall we go ... somewhere near me?'

'Yes,' muttered Jessica, trying to look casual. *Somewhere near me.* Was it possible, Jessica wondered, that after all this time tonight was finally going to be the night?

They flagged down a black cab outside on Wood Lane and the minute she'd slumped into the black leather seat, Jessica realized just how exhausted she was. Studio days consisted largely of running around and her feet and legs were aching, crying out for a warm bath.

'Paul?'

'Yes?'

'Do you think maybe we could just get a bottle of wine and go to your place instead? It's just I'm so tired I don't think I could handle a noisy bar right now, and I haven't seen you for so long. It would be nice just to talk and catch up, somewhere we can actually hear each other,' she added, having decided that tonight might be a good time to finally come clean about everything. A confession was long overdue after all, plus she hadn't forgotten the promise she'd made to him all those weeks ago to tell him what was wrong.

Paul kissed her lightly on the nose. 'Talking's not all we need to do,' he said, and Jessica felt a strong twinge of desire.

'And by the way, I'm really sorry that I've been so self-absorbed recently,' he added, putting an arm around her. 'It's been impossible to get you on your own and I realized you never even got to tell me what you were so upset about that day. Is everything OK now?'

'Um . . .' she said, enjoying the feeling of his arm around her. It felt nice and comforting. Reassuring. Then he stroked her face, which also felt nice. Really nice. 'I mean, there have been a few things going on but nothing really important . . . I suppose . . .' She trailed off. For as long as he was touching her like that she wasn't going to be capable of anything more coherent, but didn't want him to stop.

Now Paul's other hand started to stroke her leg, which felt amazing and was even more distracting. In fact, before she'd had time to think about what was happening, Jessica found herself turning towards him and, seconds later, he was leaning in to kiss her. At this point all her worries vanished, and telling him anything suddenly seemed incredibly unimportant and almost absurdly irrelevant. Now the cab couldn't get them back quick enough and, as they arrived at Paul's, all the tension and covert flirtation which had been building up between them over the last couple of months finally spilled over. As soon as they'd paid the cab driver, they were kissing and pawing one another so frantically that Jessica was only vaguely aware of a black front door, of somehow climbing two flights of stairs and of Paul fumbling for his keys to open yet another door. Miraculously she was suddenly no longer tired at all. Instead she felt alive, like she was firing on all cylinders and, as they fell through the door, Jessica didn't even have time to register much about the small hallway before Paul was kissing her passionately in the direction of his living room.

'Luke and Kerry,' Jessica gasped at one point.

'What about them?' Paul said breathlessly, kissing her on the neck while one hand ventured up the front of her top.

'Are they coming back tonight?'

'No,' said Paul. He'd already checked. Luke and Kerry were planning on staying at Kerry's place. Not that he was bothered either way at this precise moment. In fact, he probably wouldn't have cared if they'd walked in right that second.

As Paul kissed her face, her neck, her mouth, Jessica finally stopped thinking and allowed herself to dissolve with longing. They tumbled down on to the sofa and he pulled her round so that she was on top of him. As his hands found her bra strap, however, she pulled away again.

'What?' said Paul, concerned in case he was going too fast. 'Do you want me to stop?'

She looked away, hating herself for having to ask but knowing she would burst with curiosity if she didn't. She simply had to clear one thing up before they went any further.

'I know you told me ages ago that you weren't . . . you know . . . bothered about Natasha, but I really don't want to upset anyone so I have to ask. Would *she* mind if she knew that we were, you know . . . seeing a bit of each other?'

'Which bit?' said Paul, being deliberately obtuse.

Jessica blushed and rolled her eyes, feeling stupid.

'Sorry,' he said, smiling affectionately. 'And to answer your question, no, I don't think she would, and if she *did*, she wouldn't have any right to whatsoever given that she dumped me.'

'Did she?' replied Jessica, amazed that anyone would do such a thing.

'Yeah,' admitted Paul, looking slightly sheepish, 'which probably makes you wonder what's wrong with me, but the truth is we just weren't right for each other.'

'Oh, right,' said Jessica.

'Anyway, do you mind if we don't talk about her any more?'

Jessica just nodded her head, desire having rendered her silent. Then slowly she turned to find his mouth again, but this time controlled the pace of the kiss. Paul gave up unsuccessfully fiddling with her bra, mortified to have failed that mission, and moved his hands slowly round the front of her body instead. He stroked her breasts and she gasped as he did so.

'I was supposed to be talking to you tonight,' she panted, breaking away yet again, terrified by the feelings he was unleashing inside her. She'd never been so turned on in her entire life.

Paul stopped. 'OK,' he said, as he removed his hands from her top and sat up, straightening his T-shirt as he did so. 'If you want to talk, let's talk. Tell me what's been going on with you. I do really want to know and sorry if I got a bit carried away. It's just being around you all day every day in the office does funny things to me. In fact, there've been times over the last few weeks I've almost needed a cold shower and . . .'

But Jessica was only half listening. She couldn't believe she'd just stopped things yet again, and something inside her was screaming at her to take the leap of faith, to stop analysing and to live. Telling him her stupid secret now might ruin things completely and did she really want to take that chance?

'Forget it,' she said decisively, sliding back on to him and starting to undo his belt. Scrabbling around, Paul willingly helped her out and seconds later he was in his boxers. Now Jessica could really see just how much he wanted her. She gulped.

Meanwhile Paul was absorbing every bit of Jessica, trying to imprint into his mind every single detail of this amazing girl who seemed hell-bent on turning his whole world upside down. He swallowed and for a few seconds they stared into each other's eyes as if they could hardly believe the other existed.

'Jess,' he said, and his voice was slightly croaky.

'Don't,' she said, and to his dismay her eyes filled with tears. 'Shit, I'm sorry,' she said, laughing at herself. 'It's just that I –'

'It's OK,' he said, seeming to understand that, like him, she was overwhelmed by what she was feeling. He placed one finger on her mouth, stroking the outline of her face before pulling her towards him again. They kissed and kissed and it felt so unbelievably right that they both would have been quite happy to stay like that forever, kissing, exploring each other's mouths with their tongues, gently and then more passionately. Kissing had never felt like this before. He stroked her face, which by now was wet with the tears she was unable to keep at bay any longer.

'Are you OK?' he whispered in her ear.

'Yeah,' Jessica sniffed and they both laughed as her voice came out strangled with emotion. She was just so unbelievably happy she was finally here with him like this.

Paul twisted round underneath her and got up from the sofa, before bending down to take her hand, indicating that they should go to his bedroom. She followed him in, her eyes briefly taking in how many hundreds of books and DVDs littered his shelves, before he was kissing her again.

After that, all thought was banished, for Paul started touching her in a way that made her shiver with longing. Clumsily, he edged her towards the bed. Then, in a tangle of elbows, kissing, embarrassment and banged knees, they somehow managed to sit down at the same time.

'Not quite like in the movies,' he said breathlessly, grinning at her, her favourite stray lock of dark hair falling into his eyes. 'Lie down,' he whispered.

Jessica lowered herself back on the bed, feeling like a self-conscious teenager. They soon got into a comfortable position though and the kissing began again. Then Paul undressed her and before long both of them were naked. For the first time in her life, Jessica felt beautiful.

Afterwards, they lay in bed for hours, talking, listening to music and kissing indulgently. Then they had sex again, only this time it was slower and less frenzied, but just as mind-blowing. After, as Paul lay on top of her, still inside her, panting but reluctant to move, she laughed.

'You look happy,' he said, looking at her.

'I am.'

'Earlier, you said you wanted to talk to me? Was there something in particular?'

She shook her head. It wasn't the right time and, a typical man, Paul wasn't going to protest at missing out on a heavy conversation. He kissed her nose. 'I'm so happy you're here. I've missed you. I think you're really great.'

Jessica grinned. Paul always had just the right words at his disposal until, it seemed, he really needed them, and yet a simple 'you're great' meant so much more to her than all the over-the-top platitudes insincere boyfriends had heaped on her in the past.

'What?' enquired Paul suspiciously.

'Nothing,' she replied innocently.

Paul narrowed his eyes at her and she giggled. 'Cow,' he said, which made her laugh even more, just at the same time as a rousing guitar introduction was making itself known to the room. It appeared Paul had put together a playlist which included some of her favourite songs, a modern day mixed tape, made with her in mind.

'If it's any consolation, I happen to think you're pretty great too,' she said, burying her face into his neck.

'Sure?' he asked, holding her tight.

'Oh, yes,' she said.

'Good, because I think you're amazing, Jess. Seriously, the way you've come to England, to get away from a difficult life and start again. It's inspiring really.'

'Oh, I wouldn't say that,' said Jessica, dismayed. 'I mean, I really wouldn't say my life is difficult.'

'You're modest too,' Paul added, smiling at her. 'You wear your heart on your sleeve, and there's no bullshit with you. You're intriguing and yet I know you won't muck me around. Modest, gorgeous, honest, funny, and you've got a great arse. What more could a bloke ask for?'

Jessica was feeling a bit panicky and wasn't sure what to say, so was grateful when Paul answered that one for her . . .

'Apart from an appreciation of the Smiths.'

31

It didn't take long for the rest of the office to work out that Jessica and Paul had finally got together. Firstly, Luke found one of Jessica's bangles down the back of the sofa and, secondly, their feelings had simply become glaringly obvious. As a result, Paul and Jessica quickly decided it wouldn't do any harm to let people know they were an item and, apart from one or two bitchy remarks from Natasha, everyone seemed really pleased for them.

Jessica was so happy she made a conscious decision to cut herself some slack, deciding it would be best to keep the secret of her identity to herself a while longer. That way she could really enjoy these early days as Paul's girlfriend without overcomplicating matters. Besides, working two jobs, nurturing a new relationship and making time for her aunty Pam was keeping Jessica busy enough without having to throw an upending bombshell into the equation.

To a certain degree Jessica was sticking her head in the sand, of course, for what she was choosing not to examine, but knew deep down, was that the second she'd cemented her relationship with Paul, the tissue of lies she was embedded in had begun to feel traitorous in a way they never had before. Not surprising considering how many new fibs there were to remember. There was still 'who she was', plus now the fairytale of an excuse that Mike had concocted for Kerry so she could look after his children.

Then, in September, she planned on flying home for a party she couldn't be honest about, plus she was still coping with Bond jokes and comments about her parents. 'Being Jessica Bender' had become a veritable minefield and continued to be so for the entire month of August. However, her dogged determination to let things lie coupled with her hectic schedule meant that, as the weeks whizzed by, the lies started to become her reality and felt normal to the point where she almost stopped questioning them.

Mike had ended up telling Kerry that he needed to pull Jessica off the show for a couple of afternoons a week, because the BBC needed market research on what young Americans thought of their programming. Kerry had fallen for it, but probably only because she was so distracted by Luke. Still, this excuse had meant that on top of everything else Jessica also had to contend with jealous remarks from her workmates about getting paid to watch TV and accusations of slacking.

Still, things with Paul continued to go from strength to strength and by the beginning of September their relationship had blossomed to the point where it felt entirely natural calling him her boyfriend. To some degree they were both still trying to keep things on a fairly light basis because they knew that inevitably one day Jessica would go home. But they weren't really kidding anyone except themselves. They couldn't keep their hands off each other and any time apart felt like time wasted. The truth was, they were crazy about each other.

However, on the rare occasion Jessica stopped to consider all the things Paul didn't know about her, her head started to spin. Keen to avoid a scene like the one from

The Exorcist, she decided something had to be done. And so it was that one day in early September, when the Bond show and her trip home were both fast approaching, Jessica decided to at least tell Paul about her moonlighting. Like a little light entrée of truth before she served up the rather more meaty main course. Sneaking off to work for Diane had become her favourite part of her working week and Jessica was sure that by now, as long as she ran it by her first, Diane would trust her enough to let her tell Paul what was going on. The other 'Bond' stuff would have to wait though. Every time it seemed like the right time to tell him she simply couldn't find the appropriate words.

So, as yet another week on *The Bradley Mackintosh Show* drew to a close, Jessica found herself heading to Diane and Mike's. It was one of those glorious September evenings that manages to be hot but also to have that first tinge of autumn light to it, making the day feel like the last bit of summer is being rinsed out of the skies. Jessica was booked in to put the babies to bed and babysit and had promised herself she would talk to Diane about telling Paul, whom thankfully she wasn't missing out on seeing. He'd already arranged to go home to see his mum and his sister for a couple of nights. Lucy was much, much better and had even started college, but he had a script that needed finishing for another show and knew he'd be better off writing at home, away from the distraction of his girlfriend. They'd planned to see each other on Sunday, which would be the last chance they'd have to relax before the Bond special, after which she'd be leaving for the States. When she got back, they'd talked about him taking her to Staines to meet his family.

'Hello,' Jessica called as she let herself into Diane's.

'We're in the utility room,' yelled Diane. 'I've been elbow deep in poo and wee all day.'

'Nice,' replied Jessica, smiling to herself. Diane always launched into a rant as soon as she arrived. Apparently it was the release of having another adult to converse with.

'I've had a pig of a day which began at five thirty a.m. when Grace decided it was time for me to find her Buzz Lightyear stickers. Anyway, because Grace had got up so stupidly early, she was grumpy as anything so ended up having a tantrum because there wasn't any Alpen, which made us horribly late. Though how I can be late getting her to nursery for nine thirty when I've been up since five thirty I shall never know. Then I was in Waitrose and Ava shat herself so badly the poo leaked down the side of her babygro, which was unbelievably revolting and that's coming from her mother. They let me use the staff toilets but there was a distinct lack of loo roll. I'd just realized that I hadn't brought any wipes with me either when I got a call from nursery saying that Grace had wet herself, they couldn't find her change of clothes and she was currently wearing nothing but a pair of wellies and a backless apron.'

'Sounds like great fun,' said Jessica, who had been rewarded with a heavenly, gummy smile from Ava as soon as she'd walked into the kitchen.

'Jessica!' yelped Grace, launching herself at her.

'Hi, angel, I hear you wore a backless apron at school today?' she said, giving her a big squeeze.

'She looked like she was going in for an operation when I got there,' said Diane. 'Still, she didn't seem to mind too much.'

'I showed them my bum,' said Grace solemnly.

'I'm sorry you've had such a stressy day and I can't believe Madam was up so early again,' she said to Diane. 'Hey, Grace, you know what I was thinking we should do after tea?'

'What?'

'Painting.'

'Yessss,' Grace lisped, punching the air. 'Can I do play-dough too?'

'They should send her into the Middle East. She'd make a marvellous negotiator,' said Diane drily, retrieving some apple puree from the fridge to warm up for Ava.

'Only if it's OK with your mom,' said Jessica.

'I suppose so,' said Diane. 'Just don't let her take it out of this room.'

'Yay,' said Grace.

'No worries,' said Jessica, rooting around in the cupboards so she could start preparing Grace's tea.

'What would I do without you?' Diane said suddenly, looking quite moved and utterly shattered, though overall she'd been looking a lot healthier recently. The other day she'd even joked that it was nice not to be looking like a crack addict any more and Jessica had seen how she and Mike must click in terms of humour. Over the weeks she'd found it immensely satisfying to witness Diane's gradual transformation back into something resembling a human. Obviously there was a way to go. She was still exhausted and probably would be until Ava started sleeping through the night, but getting a bit more rest, a bit of help, a bit of breathing space, oh, and antidepressants, seemed to be helping enormously.

'I need to talk to you actually, Jess,' she said, shovelling puree into Ava's mouth, though most of it seemed to ooze back down her chin.

'Oh, really?' replied Jessica. 'Grace, don't bash the cupboard with the guitar, please.'

'Yes, I've decided to go back to work, on a part-time basis. I've missed it, to be honest, and compared to being at home it'll probably feel easy.'

'OK,' said Jessica neutrally, while chopping some carrots. 'Grace, please don't open that drawer, you'll trap your fingers. In fact, come and sit up here,' she said, lifting the little girl up and sitting her on the work surface.

'I know being a stay-at-home mum is a privilege some women would kill for,' Diane added, for she could sense Jessica didn't wholly approve and wanted to justify herself. 'But these early years can be tough and . . . lonely at times. No one tells you if you're doing a good job and the pay's shocking,' she said jokily. 'You know I love my kids more than anything in the entire world, don't you? I hope you don't think I'm a bad person.'

Jessica shook her head and quietly continued preparing Grace's tea. She knew she should be saying something encouraging but bought herself some time by handing Grace some carrot to chew on. She'd always had rather strong ideas about motherhood and child-rearing, undoubtedly based on her own upbringing and the fact that her mother had essentially abandoned her. Unsurprisingly, she'd always vowed that if she were to have children of her own one day then she would spend every second with them. That she would sacrifice anything for them and that her own needs would be unimportant by comparison.

However, Diane was starting to help her understand that maybe the subject wasn't quite as clear cut as she'd once thought. She could see now that children didn't need a martyr for a mother but one that loved them, one that gave them consistency and security and one that was happy in herself. She thought of Angelica and felt more confused and sad than ever about how she could have left her all those years ago, because as much as Diane might find motherhood tough, there was never any question that she'd be anything but there for her children, even if she did go back to work. Still, Jessica also realized that her anger and resentment meant she'd never stopped to ask any questions about why her mother had left. All she'd ever done was apportion blame.

'Diane, you don't have to justify anything to me,' she said eventually. 'I can see how much you love your kids. You're a great mom.'

'The thing is though, Jess,' said Diane, looking anxious. 'I just can't see any of it working without you in the equation. As much as I'm convinced going back is the right thing to do, it doesn't mean it doesn't terrify the life out of me. So what I'm really trying to say is would you consider leaving the show and being my nanny for four full days a week when I start back?'

Jessica, who was just carrying Grace's food over to the table, put it down, lifted Grace into her seat and looked at Diane, a huge grin threatening to engulf her face. 'I can't think of anything I'd like more,' she replied, realizing as she said it that this was unquestionably true.

'Really?' squealed Diane.

'Really,' said Jessica, and she meant it. Compared to

nannying, Jessica's 'proper' job now seemed insignificant. She adored looking after the children and on the days she did she felt like she was 'escaping' the office. Over the last couple of weeks she'd really felt the inklings of some kind of vocation starting to emerge.

As Kerry's assistant, she'd proved she was capable of ingratiating herself with a team, that she could be useful on the phone and pro-active in terms of helping around the studio, but what had she actually learned? She wasn't a creative person like Paul and for obvious reasons had never been interested in the celebrity world, so the job didn't challenge her particularly, didn't excite her. By contrast, what some considered dull, mundane work, gave her more satisfaction than anything ever had before. She was developing a dangerously soft spot for Grace, who could be a handful at times but responded beautifully to Jessica's firm but fair manner. Little Ava was adorable too, a placid, greedy baby, with downy, soft little feet and cheeks that were filling out by the day. And she liked Diane. She might not necessarily make the same decisions if she was in her position, but that didn't mean she couldn't respect them. Only one thing was clear. Whatever choice a mother made, it was never going to be clear cut, easy or without its drawbacks.

That evening, once Diane and Mike had left, Jessica found herself grinning down at Grace as she tucked her into bed. They'd had rather a battle about what she could and couldn't take to bed with her, but Jessica had won. Sort of. After much negotiation Grace had eventually agreed to relinquish the empty bottle of Evian and her scooter helmet, but wouldn't budge when it came to the plastic farm. Her small arm was wrapped proprietorially around it, though Jessica intended to extract it from her grasp once she was deeply asleep.

Damn. Just then Jessica remembered that yet again she'd forgotten to talk to Diane about telling Paul she was her nanny. What was wrong with her? The trouble was, she decided, that she was always so busy here, and when she wasn't here she was either at work or it was too late to ring in case she woke the babies. She was halfway out of Grace's bedroom door, wondering if it would be too late to broach the subject when they got back later, when her phone began to ring.

'Hello?' she whispered.

'Jessica,' said a silky French voice. 'It's me.'

'Mom, are you back in London?'

'Yes, I want to see you. When are you free?'

As she thought about the answer Jessica realized this was *another* thing she'd have to lie to Paul about and yet after her horrid conversation with Graydon there was no way she was missing this opportunity to get things straight. Besides, there were more than a few questions she needed to know the answer to.

The next evening Jessica found herself on her way to Claridge's where Angelica was staying. When she'd spoken to Paul earlier, he'd been so absorbed in his writing he hadn't even thought to ask what she was up to, so for once she hadn't had to make anything up . . .

As Jessica entered the vast, beautiful reception of the hotel it struck her how completely at home she felt in such opulent and glamorous surroundings. Although she hadn't missed luxury per se, she would have been lying if she'd said it wasn't nice to have a taste of it once more. Or maybe she only noticed the luxury so keenly precisely because she hadn't had it for a while?

The receptionist called up to Angelica's room and seconds later Jessica was travelling upwards in the lift. An excited Angelica, dressed in an elegant cream Stella McCartney skirt suit and beautiful Louboutin boots was waiting for her as the doors slid open.

'Jessica,' she exclaimed delightedly, rushing forward to kiss her daughter warmly on both cheeks.

'Hi, Mom,' said Jessica, noting how – as ever – her mother looked immaculate and gorgeous. 'How are you?'

'I'm well, my darling, come.' Angelica went to link arms with her and Jessica let herself be led in this manner down the corridor and in through the open door of her suite.

'Hi,' Jessica said shyly to her mother's assistant, who was sitting at a coffee table busily typing something up on his Mac.

'Daniel, please can you find the room service menu so that Jessica and I can order some dinner?' asked Angelica politely. 'So,' she said, turning her attentions back to Jessica. 'How are you?'

'I'm fine,' Jessica replied. 'And I'm so sorry about last time I saw you. It was really stupid of me to forget our arrangement. I hope you weren't too upset.'

'It's fine,' said Angelica bravely, 'completely forgotten as far as I'm concerned and it's just nice to see you now.'

'Really? Because that's not what Graydon said.'

'What do you mean?' said Angelica, looking confused.

'Before you went away he rang to tell me how much he

disapproved of how I'd been to you. He also told me what a state you were in and how unable to "handle" it all you were. In fact, to be honest, I'm surprised he didn't try and stop you from seeing me altogether.'

Angelica flushed red and her expression was instantly shifty.

'Oh my God,' exclaimed Jessica. 'He did try and stop you from seeing me. Didn't he? Mom, how can you be with a man who tries to stop you from seeing your own daughter?'

'Don't be silly,' said Angelica. 'Nobody could, or would, ever stop me from seeing you.'

'But he tried, didn't he?' Jessica persisted. It was so frustrating. How could she not see what a controlling bully he was?

'Graydon just gets very over-protective, Jessica, but the truth is I know the two of you just need a bit of time to get to know each other properly. I can also assure you that he is starting to realize that I am not quite as delicate as he likes to think I am. Anyway, enough about him. I want to know what you've been up to and all about this new chap of yours.'

Jessica slid down on to a ludicrously comfortable sofa while Angelica poured them both a glass of water. Maybe the change of subject was for the best. Otherwise she'd end up losing her temper. Besides, it sounded like Angelica had told him what for anyway. Good.

'Actually, I've been working pretty hard.'

'Yes, tell me all about what you're doing.'

'I work on *The Bradley Mackintosh Show* as an assistant to the celeb booker.'

'No!' exclaimed Angelica, one hand at her chest. 'Ah, *merci*, Daniel,' she added as he appeared with two menus. She handed one to Jessica. 'I don't believe it. That is so funny. My agent told me only the other day about that show because they want me as a guest. Was that your idea?' she asked, looking flattered. 'Because you know I don't do things like that, but maybe if you wanted me to go on then . . . ?'

'Not my idea,' Jessica said, shaking her head. 'In fact, I was quite enjoying the job until they decided to do a "Bond" special. Now all I hear about is Bond this and Bond that, plus I hear stuff being said about you and Dad all the time, which is awful. It's typical that the one thing I've been trying to escape has tracked me down . . . sorry,' she added as she realized how mean that sounded. It wasn't her mom's fault. 'Anyway . . . it's lovely to see you,' Jessica added, feeling rather unnerved. It was almost like she was programmed to give her mom a hard time, a difficult habit to unpick.

Angelica regarded her with an expression which said that as much as she wanted to believe her apology, she didn't. Jessica shrugged. 'So you wanted to know about my boyfriend?'

'What is his name?'

'Paul,' replied Jessica, smiling at the mere thought of him. 'Paul Fletcher and he's amazing. He's intelligent, really sweet and handsome.'

'*Mon Dieu*,' said Angelica. 'You are in love.'

She didn't deny it.

'Well, congratulations. I am happy for you and I just hope I can meet him one day.'

Strangely, the idea wasn't that repellent, though sadly it was also impossible, unless things changed.

'I hope so too,' replied Jessica, hoping that this response would go some way to making up for what had been said earlier.

'If you married him, you'd be like Angela Lansbury in *Murder She Wrote*,' noted Angelica. 'Jessica Fletcher.'

Jessica frowned, then realizing her mother was absolutely right, burst out laughing. 'Oh my gosh! That's so funny. Not that I am ever getting married in a million years, but I must tell Pam – she'll find that hilarious.'

'Oh, yes,' said Angelica, her beautiful face creasing up with mirth. 'Pamela Anderson, that always made your father and me laugh so, so much.'

Jessica picked up her water. 'Actually, it turns out – and this is a bit weird really – but it turns out that Paul's mom met you and Dad when you were together at one of his premières. She said you were about to have me, so it must have been the night you went into labour.'

'Gosh,' said Angelica, struck by the coincidence. 'How bizarre.'

'It is,' agreed Jessica. 'Do you remember meeting anyone called Anita Fletcher that night?'

'Er ... *non*, I don't think so ... maybe ... it's just we always met so many people, you know?'

Jessica nodded, feeling mildly disappointed somehow.

'Terrifying, isn't it?' said Angelica a few seconds later.

'What?'

'Being in love,' she stated simply.

Jessica was surprised. Her mother was clearly speaking from experience. How odd, she suddenly thought. It was always weird to think about your parents as people who made mistakes, who had feelings and weaknesses of their own. Being Mom and Dad was what usually defined them.

'What do you want to eat?' asked Angelica.

'Soup and a chicken sandwich, please?'

'*Mais oui*. Daniel, please order one soup, one chicken sandwich and for me the ricotta and spinach tortellini? A small portion.'

Angelica had always subscribed to the French way of keeping slim. Eat whatever you want, even if it's covered in cream, only in small amounts, little and often.

'I've also been doing some work as a nanny,' began Jessica, as Daniel went to place their order in the other room. 'I've been working for my boss's wife, Diane. She's a really nice lady but has been quite depressed since having her second baby.'

'Oh, really, what are the children like? How old are they?'

'Five months and three and a half,' said Jessica, her face unable to hide the affection she felt for them. 'They're so cute. Grace can be quite demanding sometimes and very cheeky but only because she's so bright and, actually, with me she's really good.'

'And the mother?' asked Angelica softly.

'Diane's cool. You can tell she adores her kids but she's not been herself since she had the second one. She's exhausted and has had trouble coming to terms with being a stay-at-home mother and not working any more. Anyway, she's been depressed but she's on tablets, which seem to be working. Plus her husband's helping out more and she's figuring out what she wants to do in terms of work and stuff . . .'

Jessica trailed off because her mother was looking at her in a way that had made the hairs on her neck stand on end. 'What is it?' she asked, experiencing an odd sense of foreboding.

'Nothing,' said Angelica in a strange, tight voice. 'It's just that she can't be that depressed if she's feeling better already . . . but I think it's wonderful that you're helping her. I can imagine you being very good, very patient with children, in fact.'

Jessica gulped. A horrible, quite unimaginable thought had just occurred to her. Or, at least, she thought it had only just occurred to her, until on closer inspection she realized it had probably been lurking in the shadows ever since she'd started working for Diane. Suddenly she knew her relationship with her mother would never stand a chance until she got some sort of explanation as to why she had left. She was owed one, surely? They'd always skirted around the issue before because truthfully, until now, Jessica hadn't known if she could handle the answer. But now she had to know.

'Mom, why did you leave? Were you depressed?'

The silence that greeted this unavoidable direct question seemed to stretch indefinitely. Then, after the most suspense-filled seconds of Jessica's life, a sad-looking Angelica finally plucked up enough courage to confront what she'd been trying to bring up herself for weeks.

'Yes, I was depressed. I was very, very ill, Jessica, only I just didn't know it at the time. I thought . . . I thought it was me . . .'

Angelica sat rigid, wringing her hands together in her lap as she tried to keep a lid on her feelings. Unlike Edward, she wasn't particularly given to outpourings of emotion but years and years of hurt and undiscussed grief were bubbling dangerously close to the surface. Jessica had always wished her mother would display some regret about what she'd done, hoping that she'd offer some explanation, but now she was doing so there was no satisfaction to be taken from it.

'Why didn't you tell me?' asked Jessica. She was so confused by the revelation that her mother had been suffering from depression that it only seemed to lead to hundreds more questions. She felt drenched in guilt for all the years she'd spent hating her mother, hating her for what she had always thought was utter selfishness. She had assumed so much about everything and yet it wasn't her fault she'd been kept in the dark. 'Why didn't you stay and get help? Why didn't you ever tell me you were ill? Why didn't Dad tell me?'

'Oh, Jessica,' said Angelica, dabbing at her eyes. 'I don't know where to begin.'

Jessica rolled her eyes in frustration.

'OK. I will tell you,' Angelica placated, knowing that this was it. There was no going back. She took a deep breath and prepared to launch into the tale she'd always wondered if she would ever tell. 'When I found out I was pregnant with you, Jessica, I was delighted. Delighted but very scared. Terrified, in fact. I was so young, you see, even younger than you are now and much more immature, I think. At the same time I was being touted as the next big thing in Hollywood and all I'd ever wanted was to act, so I was very worried for my career. Though I need you to know, and this is important –'

Jessica met her mother's gaze and was startled by the intensity in her eyes.

'I never, ever considered not having you. I was deeply in love with your father and being his wife meant everything to me. I already loved this person in my belly that we had created, but I was so naive,' recalled Angelica, her face sad as she remembered the maelstrom of feelings from that time. 'I was totally unaware of what having a baby really meant, and thought it would all just fall into place. I honestly believed that being so in love was enough to make everything OK.'

She turned her head away, as if it were easier to remember and confront certain more unpalatable truths without looking at her daughter, and for the millionth time Jessica wondered how her mother had ever come to be so beautiful. She was almost other-worldly, although now Jessica could see how she was softening with age. How lines were making her more human and her beauty less threatening. Strangely, she felt rather proud of her suddenly.

'When you arrived you were a very beautiful baby, Jessica, I remember that. I remember looking at you in the hospital and hardly being able to believe that I had a daughter, a beautiful daughter who needed me. Though after that, truthfully, I don't remember much.'

Jessica tried not to look hurt.

'Please don't take anything I say personally,' said Angelica. 'It's just that if I'm going to tell you how things were it has to be the total truth. *Oui?*'

Jessica nodded.

'Anyway, with hindsight I know now that I was ill from the minute you were born. The birth was traumatic though

I don't even know if that had anything to do with it. All I know is that suddenly everything was black, literally. There are hundreds of euphemisms for depression. People talk about black dogs, black clouds, black cloaks of depression, and they're all true. Jessica, I had never experienced sadness like it before and hope I never do again. I was desperately unhappy and felt so worthless. I had some quite manic episodes too. I didn't have the kind of depression where you can't get out of bed. *Au contraire*, I was up and about, trying to pretend that nothing had changed, when of course the truth was everything had changed. I was terrified of losing Edward and the studio were putting pressure on me, but I just couldn't accept that I wasn't in control of anything any more. You see, when you have a baby, the whole deck of cards gets thrown up in the air and, of course, this should be a wondrous experience. Yet for me, having no idea where those cards were going to fall was something I struggled to cope with. It felt like a bomb had gone off in the middle of my life.'

As her mother paused to light her second cigarette of the evening, Jessica hardly dared to breathe, feeling like, if she did, Angelica might clam up again.

'I honestly believed you would be better off without me. We had nannies, of course, and because they were there from day one they just took over, which I think only enhanced the problem. Then, by contrast, your father was so wonderful with you. A natural from the word go, the bond between you unbreakable,' she added ruefully.

'Excuse the pun,' quipped Jessica bitterly, hating herself for the uncharitable thought that it couldn't have been *that* hard, given all the help and money she'd had at her disposal. Angelica continued to smoke quietly, staring fixedly somewhere into the middle distance with glassy eyes.

'Look, Mom, I understand that you were ill,' Jessica said eventually, 'but you're my mother, didn't you love me? Diane would never leave her children in a million years.'

Angelica looked stung. 'Jessica, from the sound of it I was much, much more ill than Diane,' she said plainly. 'And I don't want to upset you but there were moments when I really felt suicidal. I detested myself and had no sense of self-worth whatsoever. In the end, I think I left precisely because I did love you so much. You see,' she added more gently, having noticed how rattled Jessica was, 'in those days there wasn't so much knowledge about post-natal depression. It wasn't something that people looked out for like they do now. Edward honestly had no idea how bad things were because I hid it from him. He was worried, of course. I was losing weight, I was anxious and not myself, but he just thought I wasn't coping, so his answer was to provide round-the-clock care for you and to do more himself, which only added to my feelings of self-loathing. Everything worked beautifully without me and I didn't know what to do to make things right. I didn't think I'd ever know how to love you properly or be able to be the mother you deserved. So I left, and I will never stop punishing myself for that mistake.'

As Angelica started weeping, tears also streamed down Jessica's face. Tears of sadness for herself and for her mom, tears of regret for so many wasted years and, above all, tears of relief.

'I thought you left because you didn't love me enough,' she sobbed and Angelica rushed over to the sofa to embrace her daughter, distraught and guilty for the hurt she'd caused.

'I have always loved you so much I cannot even begin to tell you. Maybe I couldn't feel it at first but it came and when it did I knew that it had always been there. I'm so, so sorry, Jessica. Truly, not a day goes by when I don't question what I did. How could I have left my baby? But I have to believe that it wasn't really me doing it. I was very sick.'

'When did you get better?' wailed Jessica. 'Why didn't you come back then? Why didn't you tell Dad all of this? I know he pined after you for years, and he didn't meet anyone else for ages. You could have come back. I could have had a proper family.'

Angelica stopped stroking Jessica's hair and looked sadly at the floor. 'I'm not so sure about that,' she answered diplomatically, deciding that enough was enough for one day. Her daughter had plenty of information to digest already. 'And, besides, I didn't get better for years, Jessica. Depression became a part of my life eventually. Without diagnosis I had no treatment, so I just assumed that the wretched way I felt was some sort of fitting punishment for being such a terrible mother. So I worked. I threw myself into my acting because being somebody else felt so much better than being me. It was only one day when the depression started to lift a little, maybe ten years later or so, when I began to question everything. Finally I got some help and slowly learned how to stop blaming myself and to accept that I'd been ill. But I want you to know,' she said, cupping her daughter's tear-stained face in her hands, 'that I never stopped loving you.'

'And what about Dad?' sobbed Jessica. 'Did you stop loving him?'

Angelica looked taken aback. Then, still stroking her daughter's hair, she looked away slightly, eyes brimming with tears, before answering quietly, 'Yes.'

And in that instance, Jessica knew beyond all doubt that for the first time that day her mother wasn't telling her the whole truth.

32

On Sunday Jessica met up with Paul as planned but almost wished she hadn't. Her mind was so busy trying to make sense of everything her mother had told her that she only felt half present. She was dying to speak to Edward too. She knew she'd have to tread carefully but wanted to try and figure out how much of Angelica's illness he'd been aware of. If he was as in the dark as she was, wouldn't finding out change the entire way he'd perceive what had happened?

By now she felt completely weighed down by the strain of all her secrets and was desperate to come clean to Paul. However, she decided it would be wiser to wait until after the show. With the show imminent, everybody was suffering from a renewed dose of Bond mania, so telling him about her parents now would be like rubbing salt into a paper cut, along with a bit of lemon, vinegar and some nail-varnish remover. 'Four more sleeps', as Grace would say, and it would all be over. It had finally got to the point where telling him was something she was almost looking forward to getting over and done with.

Monday and Tuesday were difficult days in the office so by the time Wednesday came around Jessica was delighted to sneak off early to Diane's as usual, much to Kerry's annoyance for she was frantically making last-minute arrangements for the Bond special.

Within five minutes of walking in the door at Chiswick

Jessica *finally* got round to having a much-needed heart to heart with Diane about everything. Being a reasonable woman, Diane understood Jessica's concerns about their deceit and agreed things couldn't continue as they were, especially since she planned on poaching Jessica as soon as the Bond show had been filmed.

'Look, say no if you want,' Diane suggested, 'but I was thinking, after this wretched show's out the way and you're back from the States, why don't you and Paul come for dinner? I might invite Kerry and Luke too. Maybe even Natasha? That way, you can tell everyone about me and, if they're cross, I can help explain things to them over dinner. Give you a bit of support.'

'That's so sweet,' said Jessica. 'But you don't have to do that.'

'I know, but I'd like to. Anyway, it'll give me a chance to meet some of the people Mike works with. Between you and me, I think he thinks *they* think he's a prick.'

Startled, Jessica did her best not to show that Mike was spot on and left that evening feeling calmer and relieved to have some kind of a plan.

The line-up for the show was finalized and looking good. It consisted of Daniel Craig (even Jessica was excited), Christopher Walken, who played the baddie Max Zorin in *A View to a Kill*, Dame Judi Dench (the legend), John Cleese and the young Russian starlet Nadia Vladinokova, the latest Bond girl to join the history books. It promised to be a cracking show. Though when Thursday finally arrived, as Kerry was about to find out, all the preparation in the world couldn't avoid certain fiascos.

At eleven thirty Kerry was in make-up, briefing Robbie: 'So Daniel Craig has said he's definitely happy for you to do him, as is Dame Judi.'

'Oh my God!' squealed Robbie. 'I just hope I can keep my hands from shaking.'

'Anyway, Bradley can't be hanging out in here today like he usually does. He's going to have to use his dressing room because we'll need to give them their space. Oh, and by the way, proving the theory that the biggest stars aren't always the ones with the biggest egos, the only person bringing any kind of an entourage is Ms Vladinokova. She's also insisting we stump up for her own make-up artist, hairdresser, a stylist and a masseuse, which is just fucking weird if you ask me.'

'Silly mare,' agreed Robbie.

Just then Kerry's phone rang for the hundredth time that day. As she answered it, she leaned forward to dump all the folders of information she was clutching on the side. Robbie watched in concern as her face slowly drained of all its colour.

'You are joking?' she was saying. 'Because, with all due respect, I don't care how ill she is, you'll have to dose her up and bring her in –'

Just then Jessica barged in, clutching bottles of mineral water to leave out for the guests. She immediately noticed how harassed the usually unflappable Kerry was and mouthed, 'What is it?' to Robbie, who just shrugged non-committally.

'Look, this is completely unprofessional,' Kerry spluttered, 'and I shall have to talk to my producer because in the contract – now there's no need for that. This has been arranged for ages and – right, well, call me back.' As Kerry rang off she sank, defeated, into a chair and placed her head in her hands before dismally peering through her fingers into the light-bulb-framed mirror. 'Fuck, fuck, fuck it,' she raged.

'What is it? It's not Dame Judi, is it?' enquired Jessica.

'Find Mike,' Kerry said, looking wild-eyed with anxiety. 'Tell him we need to talk, now.'

Knowing better than to question further, Jessica took off.

Two minutes later, she was still racing around searching for their boss when she bumped into Paul, who was strolling down the corridor, deep in conversation with Bradley.

'No running in the corridors, you,' said Bradley. 'Wouldn't want to land on that nice bottom of yours. Or, as you might say, your peachy ass.'

Behind Bradley's back, Paul made a gesture to demonstrate that he concurred with this description of her bottom, but Jessica was too intent on finding Mike to be amused or flattered, or to accuse him of sexism.

'Where's Mike?' she urged.

'In the gallery, talking to Julian,' said Paul. 'But I wouldn't interrupt if I were –'

But Jessica had already sped off again. Mike initially looked quite irritated to have his chat with Julian interrupted, until he realized there was a potential problem with one of the guests.

'Please don't let it be Daniel Craig,' Mike muttered, leaping up and racing off towards make-up with Jessica on his tail.

At this point, despite sympathizing deeply with Kerry, Jessica couldn't help but marvel once again at how film and television people made problems appear so life-threatening. Show business-related hysteria was something she'd struggled to care about her entire life. Sure, a guest dropping out was a bummer, annoying and unprofessional, but in the grand scheme of things did it really warrant quite so much drama? Leaving to work for Diane was definitely for the best. Fun though this world was, she didn't think she'd ever care quite enough about it. Still, as she dashed after Mike she made sure her face was displaying the required grave expression. Now was not the time to get the giggles, she told herself, especially since Kerry was the one who'd be under fire from all the people who *did* view this show as a matter of life and death.

In make-up, Kerry was having a full-blown argument on the phone. 'That's totally unreasonable,' she was saying forcibly. 'You know how important this show is for us . . .'

Jessica and Mike could hear whoever was on the other end getting louder, like the voices in cartoons on the end of phones.

'Look,' said Kerry, trying to stay in control, 'our make-up artist, Robbie Baines, is one of the best in the business and I know he could sort this out –' But whatever she meant, her pleas were falling on deaf ears. She rang off. 'Shit,' she said, turning to Mike.

'Nadia?' he said.

'Yes, frigging Nadia Vladinokova. Her management tried telling me she was ill but I double-bluffed Cherie, her London agent's assistant, and she told me that the silly bitch has only got a cold sore. She's not ill at all, just run down from all the frigging partying she's been doing since arriving in town.'

'Let me speak to them,' said Mike. 'Jessica, run and get the contract for Nadia, please?'

'Sure,' she said, turning on her heel at once.

'No need,' said Kerry. 'I've got it here.'

'Right,' said Mike. 'Where's Bradley?' he enquired, as an afterthought.

'With Paul, though I'm not sure where they're going,' said Jessica.

By now they were all talking like army officers.

'OK, well, shut the door and wave at me if he appears, OK?' instructed Mike.

Jessica was impressed by how calm he was remaining. Kerry looked grateful too. That was the thing with producers. Half the time it looked like they were just milling around, picking their noses, but when the shit hit the fan they were there to step up to the plate, which was exactly what Mike was doing now.

Mike spoke to Nadia's 'people' for twenty minutes. He cajoled, pleaded, even threatened, but they weren't budging. As far as they were concerned, being seen with crusty, oozing facial herpes was career suicide for an actress who was about to make her debut as a Bond girl. Everyone in the room knew they had a point.

'I'm so sorry, Mike,' said a distraught Kerry. She was so diligent she couldn't help but see the cancellation as a reflection on herself.

'It's not your fault,' said Mike, already anticipating the bollocking from his father-in-law and picturing the look of sour disappointment on his face.

'It's still a great line-up,' offered Jessica tentatively. 'It would have been much worse if Daniel Craig had cancelled.'

'I know, but the show will be missing the female sex factor, that's the thing,' stated Mike wearily. 'Right, Kerry, I know you've probably exhausted all the possibilities, but think. Which other Bond girls could get here in a few hours and might be tempted by a huge financial carrot?'

Kerry shook her head. 'None. Well, maybe one, but not a well-known one and one who doesn't want publicity. Oh, God, this is a nightmare, Bradley's going to freak.'

'I'll deal with him,' said Mike dolefully, and the two of them sounded so fed up, looked so beaten, that Jessica's heart went out to them.

Unnoticed, she slunk out of the room, checking first that her cell phone was still in her pocket. Then she walked calmly down the corridor towards the lifts and, finally, out of the building completely.

Before she made her call, she asked herself if she really wanted to do this. Her hands were clammy with nerves, but in the pit of her stomach she knew she did. She wanted to help – mainly Kerry, who frankly she owed, but Mike as well, who despite other people's reservations had always been good to her. Also, she'd had an idea, albeit one she hadn't had time to examine properly. A ridiculous one that probably proved she was a deluded screw-up with serious issues, but one she couldn't resist anyway. There was a risk her secret might be prematurely revealed, but it was a risk she'd have to take. Besides, there was no guarantee she'd say yes anyway. She made the call.

'Mom, it's me. I have a huge favour to ask.'

33

'But how did you do it?' Kerry asked Jessica for the third time in a row.

'We-ll . . . I just think you've made a really good impression with her people whenever you've spoken to them in the past,' improvised Jessica, wishing Kerry would just accept that Angelica had agreed to come on the show and be pleased.

'And she really doesn't want paying?' repeated Mike. 'Because that I just don't get. Her manager must have known they had us over a barrel.'

'I know, plus I'm amazed you even knew she was back in the UK again,' spluttered Kerry. Angelica Dupree was the best possible replacement guest and how Jessica had swung it with one phone call was a mystery. It would be a world exclusive.

'Look,' said Jessica, who was starting to regret helping them out, 'it was a long shot, I know, but she's coming and it wasn't a big deal. Like I said, I think Kerry had already done the groundwork and I just happened to call at a good time.'

The expressions she was met with were all fairly dubious.

'Anyway, shouldn't we be getting on? Telling people and stuff? She . . . her manager wants us to organize a car to pick her up from Claridge's as soon as possible, if that's OK?'

'Is that OK?' exclaimed Mike. 'I should bloody say so. Jesus, if she wants I'll go there myself and give her a piggyback.'

Jessica stared at the ground and tried to suppress a grin. The thought of her elegant mother spreadeagled across Mike's back was too much.

'Paul and Natasha,' Kerry exclaimed, as shock subsided and professionalism kicked in. 'They'll need to start thinking about links and questions. Mike, would you mind telling Bradley and then Paul, and I can brief him as soon as we've worked things out?'

After that it was full steam ahead. Everybody sprang into action, including Jessica, her mind spinning as she busied herself attending to the other guests while trying to figure out how best to use this situation to her advantage. Half an hour later, she found herself scuttling surreptitiously towards Bradley's dressing room, a half-formed plan dancing on the edges of her brain. As wound-up as a sprung coil, she tapped on the door.

'Come in.'

'Um, hello,' said Jessica nervously, sticking her head round the door.

'Hello,' said Bradley, who was dressed immaculately from the waist up, but had yet to put his trousers on to prevent them from creasing. Though, thankfully, he did have his pants on. 'What can I do you for, young lady?'

'Um, well, I'm sure you've heard about the change to the guest line-up,' she began timidly.

'Yes, funnily enough they did think it worth letting me know.'

'Of course,' said Jessica, still not entirely sure what she

was doing. 'Only I wondered if I might be able to suggest a couple of questions for –' She stopped mid-sentence. Kerry and Paul were coming down the corridor, clearly on their way to see Bradley.

'Spit it out,' said Bradley, looking puzzled. 'Questions for whom? Old Heavenly Jugs?'

'Er . . . no, don't worry,' said Jessica, aghast. She gaped gormlessly at Bradley who was looking vaguely nervous, probably wondering if she was a threat to security. 'Um, I'll leave you to it,' Jessica said, before darting back down the corridor in the opposite direction to her boyfriend and her boss.

Paul had seen her though, and called out, 'Everything all right, Jess?'

'Fantastic,' she yelled back, trying not to sound too deranged before scurrying away, her face hot with embarrassment. Damn it. Oh, well. That was that then and maybe it was for the best. She felt angry for having got carried away in the first place.

Ever since she'd seen Angelica at Claridge's she'd been harbouring the crazy notion that her mother still had feelings for Edward and today she'd let that thought get the better of her. Before she knew it she'd found herself wondering what would happen if Angelica was confronted with the subject of Edward on TV. Under pressure, would she reveal how Jessica suspected she really felt? If she did admit to having feelings for him, surely there was no way Edward would be able to ignore what she'd said? Then they'd have to speak. Or was the whole notion that her parents needed the past reconciled all in her head?

Forcing her mother's hand in such a public way was

probably an ill-conceived idea and, if she really thought about it, her motivation was probably highly dodgy. It was just that she'd always yearned to have a proper family, which in her mind involved two parents who loved, or at least liked each other, but it was too late. She was twenty-six years old, for goodness' sake. Far too old to be lusting after a game of happy families. Plus there was the small matter of Betsey. Her stepmother might be annoying (and far too young for her dad), but she was harmless enough, Jessica admitted guiltily. Certainly more bearable than Graydon at any rate.

As she wandered round the circumference of the busy studio, Jessica sighed resignedly. It looked like she'd be spending a lot more time with Monkey Fingers in the future so she'd just have to learn to live with it and accept that she couldn't change the past. Forcing herself to breathe deeply, Jessica decided to ignore everything she should be doing and headed for the relative peace of the production office.

The only person in there was Natasha, who was busy typing out Bradley's new questions.

'All right, Jess. How did you swing this one then? Kerry can't believe it and if you want my opinion I reckon you've pulled a few strings somewhere. Reckon you've got more than one friend in a high place, if you know what I mean?'

Jessica played dumb. Being around Natasha always made her faintly nervous, but if she slipped off again now it would only make things worse. Ignoring what she'd said, Jessica sat at her desk to check her emails.

Natasha stopped typing and flexed her fingers. 'I hate doing things so last minute. What do you reckon to these questions then? I thought first Bradley should ask why she hasn't been on a chat show for so many years. Then talk about her new movie. Then ask about the differences between the American, British and European film industries and which she prefers. What her favourite Bond film of all time is, obviously, and what she remembers of her time as a Bond girl? I can ask Kerry to ask her if she's got any interesting anecdotes.'

'They sound great,' said Jessica neutrally.

'I know they're not very spicy, but Kerry said she doesn't want any personal questions. Miserable old bitch.'

'Not wanting to talk about her personal life doesn't automatically make her miserable or a bitch,' remarked Jessica icily.

'All right, keep your wig on,' replied Natasha, unperturbed. 'Right, that'll have to do. Knowing Bradley, he'll probably make it up as he goes along anyway, or spend half an hour banging on about her tits.'

'He should ask how she feels about Edward Granger these days. Maybe ask if they're in touch at all and, if not, why not?' said Jessica on impulse. Maybe she hadn't quite given up on her hare-brained idea after all.

'Are you deaf, Bender?' replied Natasha, looking at her like she was some kind of moron. 'I just said she doesn't want to talk about personal stuff.'

'Well, that's not what she said when I was . . . talking to her agent,' challenged Jessica.

'Tell me what it is,' said Natasha, narrowing her eyes.

'What what is?'

'Whatever it is you're not telling us,' she said suspiciously. 'I see you having little powwows with Mike all the time and I also seem to be the only person round here who thought it was a bit strange when you pulled a celebrity mate out of the bag. And now you want to risk your job by getting Bradley to ask probing questions. So what's the story?'

'There isn't one,' said Jessica defiantly, though her stricken face said otherwise.

Natasha wasn't convinced. 'Mmm, maybe I should start doing a bit of digging. Or ask Paul why you're so bothered about what Bradley asks Angelica Dupree who, by the way, I'm pretty sure knows Vincent Malone, doesn't she? Yes, of course she does,' she said almost to herself as she started to tentatively put two and two together. 'So there's a link somewhere.'

Not for the first time that day, Jessica's mind started to run away without consulting her properly beforehand. Moments later, she found herself resorting to blackmail for the second time. 'Look, Natasha, there isn't anything going on at all. I swear there isn't, but if you promise to butt out then you can have this. Look,' she said, rummaging frantically in her bag and finally producing the bit of card that had been languishing in there for weeks. It was the invite for a shopping experience at Jimmy Choo's.

Natasha made a grab for it. 'Oh my God,' she said, handling it like it was the Holy Grail itself. 'Is this for real?'

'Yes,' Jessica said firmly.

Natasha's eyes grew wild and huge. 'You'd better not be mucking me around, Bender,' she said, sounding vaguely threatening. Obtaining some Jimmy Choos was quite clearly a matter of life and death for her. 'I mean, where did you even get this?'

Jessica swallowed. 'From . . . Dulcie,' she improvised.

'Mmm,' said Natasha thoughtfully. 'Well, thanks, though you know it makes me wonder even more about you. I mean, why would Dulcie give you this? She looks like a girl who likes her shoes, if you ask me.'

Jessica shrugged. 'She's got plenty of money to buy them.'

Finally Natasha stopped speculating long enough to have a quick think about which side her sartorial bread was buttered. 'Well, frankly, if you're giving this to me then I don't care if you're a drug-dealing, pre-op alien who's harbouring a known criminal in your house while having an affair with the boss and living here with no passport.'

'Ri-ght . . .' said Jessica uncertainly. 'Well, I'm not – and I have a passport, thank you.'

'Great,' said Natasha, still sounding vaguely uncertain. She was simply too cynical to accept the fact that thousands of pounds' worth of shoes might just have fallen into her lap. 'Look, I need to go and check something with Kerry about one of the other guests. Are you cool to print the questions out for me and stick them on to cards?'

'Not a problem, leave it with me,' Jessica called after her departing back. The door slammed shut, leaving the office feeling eerily calm. Jessica sat fretting about what she'd just done. She would have to call Jimmy Choo's PR girl to make sure she knew Natasha had been given the invite from her or they wouldn't let her use it. Though buying Natasha's silence with Jimmy Choos was probably the equivalent of putting a plaster on a wound that needed stitches. It was a very short-term solution, she knew, but right now she didn't have much other choice. Besides, everyone was going to have to know the truth about everything sooner rather than later anyway, and as long as Paul was the first to know it didn't really matter any more. As soon as the show was over and she'd got back from her dad's party she was telling Paul . . . everything.

This last thought pootled slowly away like a Sunday driver only to be replaced by a boy racer of an idea that screeched into her head with a handbrake turn. Jessica leapt to her feet. The questions. It must be fate, but still briefly she procrastinated. If she stopped to consider her mom's feelings she knew she probably shouldn't be meddling. Angelica was an intensely private person, hence the lack of publicity all these years, and she wasn't sure if her mother could cope with being bombarded by insensitive questions from Bradley of all people. Then she thought of her dad and of all the wasted years the three of them had spent wondering about what might have been. Surely they had nothing to lose by facing up to a few truths, and everything to gain?

Ten minutes later and Jessica had added a couple of choice questions of her own to Natasha's, before mounting them on to cards. Then she dashed back downstairs to studio one and personally delivered them to Bradley in his dressing room. On her way out she bumped into Natasha.

'What are you doing?' Natasha demanded to know. 'I've been looking for you. I only asked you to print the questions out. I was going to give them to Bradley. That's my job.'

'Sorry,' said Jessica, praying Natasha wouldn't insist on going in to check them. 'Bradley's very happy with them anyway,' she said, 'but he asked for five minutes' peace before he has to go on set . . . by the way, you do know that Jimmy Choo make incredible bags as well as shoes, don't you?'

Natasha narrowed her eyes. 'If I find out this is bogus I'm definitely telling people there's something dodgy about you.'

'Well, you won't have to,' called Jessica, who by this time was running backwards down the corridor. 'Why don't you go to the store on Saturday?'

'Right,' called Natasha, looking sceptical, but Jessica didn't have time to worry about her any more. Racing through the studio, she charged up to the gallery where Ross, the technician, was busy loading all the clips and VTs that would be played out during the show.

'Ross,' said Jessica, looking vaguely demented, 'is there any chance you could run off an extra DVD of today's recording for me?'

'Shouldn't really,' he replied, 'but seeing as it's you, why not? What do you want it for?'

'Oh, just as a memento of all you guys,' Jessica ad libbed airily. Ross seemed satisfied by her answer, however, and after giving her a thumbs-up got back to reading the *Sun* and scratching his nuts. Secret mission completed, Jessica returned to the studio at a more civilized pace. She was halfway there when she realized she should probably start breathing again.

Meanwhile on set, word was out that Angelica Dupree was going to be giving her first proper interview in years and a small crowd had gathered around Kerry to congratulate her on saving the day. She was refusing to take the credit though.

'Ah, there you are,' she said, having spotted Jessica. 'I've been trying to tell this lot that getting Heavenly Melons on the show is all down to you, not me.'

By this point Jessica was starting to feel terribly uncomfortable. Phoning your own mother was hardly much of a stretch and when Paul, who she hadn't initially noticed was in the group, proudly picked her up and twirled her round, breaking his back wasn't the only thing she was worried about.

Half an hour later and Angelica Dupree herself was in the building. By now Jessica had decided to hide out of the way completely. She knew she could depend on her mom not to give away the fact they were related, but wasn't so sure she could rely on her own rather more dubious acting skills to continue the pretence. She was also on tenterhooks about how Angelica would handle Bradley's questions and how she herself would cope when people realized the questions had been meddled with.

In the meantime, Kerry had assigned herself the task of looking after Angelica. Daniel Craig was already ensconced on set, so Jessica got on with making sure everyone else was happy. Once the show got underway, however, everyone was so focused on Daniel Craig's interview that Jessica finally felt able to poke her head round Angelica's dressing-room door.

'Pssst! Mom,' she whispered.

'Darling,' replied Angelica. Sitting alone at the big dressing table, she looked rather vulnerable, but delighted to see her daughter. 'Everything OK?'

'Fine,' said Jessica, 'but I can't stay. I just wanted to say thank you. You've helped save Kerry's neck and I appreciate it.'

'*Pas de problème*,' replied Angelica, genuinely pleased to be of help, even if she was dreading going on. 'By the way,' she added, 'I met Paul.'

Jessica raised her eyebrows questioningly, dying to know what she thought.

'He seemed *très*, *très* nice,' said Angelica sincerely. 'He was extremely professional and charming, and I got the impression he is very bright. Handsome too.'

Jessica nodded, delighted by her mother's seal of approval. Then she remembered tampering with Bradley's questions and her grin vanished like a cardigan slipping off the back of a chair. 'So anyway, good luck, Mom,' she said, backing nervously out of the door. 'I'll be watching, but I should go now before anyone sees me.'

With that, she gave Angelica a grateful but slightly guilty smile and a wave, before slipping back into the corridor. Checking first that no one was around, she shut the door behind her.

The show was fantastic. Daniel Craig was the perfect guest, entertaining, witty and fabulous-looking. For once Bradley stuck to the script, probably in part because he was so star-struck himself, and the programme got off to a sizzling start.

After Daniel Craig it was Christopher Walken's turn, then Dame Judi and John Cleese. Bradley would be talking to Angelica last. As the show slowly progressed, stopping and starting for cameras, sound and on several occasions for Bradley, Jessica's nerves mounted. When she thought of how her mother's kindness was going to be repaid with a grilling from Bradley, she felt horribly guilty. After all, if ever she'd needed a sign that her publicity-shy mom truly loved her, agreeing to appear on the show was it, the ultimate gesture.

Across the walkie-talkie Jessica could hear through the crackles that Kerry was being instructed to fetch Angelica from make-up. At this point her nerves gave way completely and she decided that she couldn't bear to watch from the sidelines where she was presently standing. Nor did she wish to be watching on a monitor anywhere near other people. Then she had a brainwave. She snuck out of the studio and down the corridor until she reached Bradley's empty dressing room. No one would find her in here. She darted in. Her disappearance would probably annoy Kerry, but she was prepared to take that risk.

Gingerly, Jessica sat down on Bradley's armchair, first moving what looked suspiciously like a panty girdle, which she placed on the table before turning her attention to what was happening on the monitor.

'Next up, ladies and gentlemen, we have a world exclusive for you,' Bradley was announcing to lots of accompanying 'oohs' from the audience. 'For my next guest,' he read from the hastily written autocue, 'is one we're incredibly grateful and thrilled to have on the show. She's the Bond girl of whom I personally have extremely fond memories . . . as does my right hand –'

'Cut!' yelled Julian down everybody's earpieces. 'For fuck's sake, Bradley. Too much, mate. Stick to the autocue, please? OK. Standby everyone, running up and . . . turnover.'

Jessica frowned. Bradley could be such a dick.

On screen the presenter cleared his throat, still determined to embellish what he thought was a rather mundane intro. Adjusting his tie, he started again. 'She's the Bond girl who shall forever be linked with the words "black bikini". Ladies and gentlemen, I'm slightly aroused to introduce to you Ms Angelica Dupree.'

The audience went mad. A huge cheer went up as they clapped and whooped enthusiastically and finally a clearly very nervous but dazzlingly beautiful Angelica walked on set. Jessica's heart lurched. The crowd's warm reaction to her mother made Jessica feel quite moved, overwhelmed by a sense of proud affection.

Angelica had dressed for the occasion in top-to-toe Armani. She was wearing a silk dress with a pair of matching, oyster-coloured, satin heels and looked beyond stunning and incredibly elegant.

'Welcome to the show,' said Bradley, trying not to dribble.

'Thank you for having me,' said Angelica, looking terrified.

It was then that the enormity of what she'd done hit Jessica. Just how much of a trial would this be for her mother? What had she done?

'So firstly may I just say, Ms Dupree, that – like a fine wine – you've aged fabulously well. Don't you think, everybody?'

The audience duly responded with more 'oohing' and 'aahing' and a smattering of applause. Angelica smiled politely in their direction.

'And am I right in saying that this is your first appearance on a chat show, either here or in the States, for well over twenty years?'

'That is correct.'

'So what made you decide to come on now, after all this time?'

Angelica paused, as she considered what to say. Fortunately for Jessica, she didn't settle on the truth. 'Well, Bradley, I don't usually do much promotion but recently I've made a film I feel very proud of. One that, I hope, has given me the opportunity to show I can really act.'

'Fantastic,' said Bradley. 'And we'll come to your new film in a minute but firstly – and I apologize because I know you're probably bored of talking about it – but where's the infamous black bikini these days? Tell me you still put it on from time to time?'

Jessica was busy cringing when the door to Bradley's dressing room creaked open. She jumped out of her skin. It was Paul.

'I've been looking for you. Why are you in here?' he asked curiously. 'Doesn't Kerry need you?'

'I – er . . . came to see if Bradley needed anything and then got side-tracked watching the – er . . .' She trailed off, but Paul just motioned to her to budge up. There wasn't room for both their bottoms on the leather armchair though so she ended up sitting on his lap.

'How's it going so far?' he enquired.

'OK,' mumbled Jessica vaguely. She didn't want to miss a word but now felt obliged to make sure her thighs were the ones taking her full body weight as opposed to Paul's. As a result, said thighs were starting to tremble. She hated sitting on men's laps.

On screen Angelica was saying, 'I'm not one hundred per cent sure but I think the bikini is in a Hard Rock Café somewhere, though I forget which one, so no, I don't ever put it on, though I doubt I'd be able to anyway. I was a young girl in *The World in Your Hand*. I also had a baby not long after, plus of course I'm fast approaching fifty now.'

'Wow,' said Bradley. 'An actress who doesn't mind talking about her age! That's a first, but I think we all agree that you haven't lost your figure at all, Angelica. You look amazing, doesn't she, ladies and gentlemen?'

Angelica looked visibly irritated by yet another reference to her beauty, but smiled politely. Apart from anything else, Angelica found talking about her looks incredibly boring.

'So what are your secrets then?' said Bradley flirtatiously. 'Do you work out a lot? Are you permanently dieting? Because I read a fascinating article about you recently claiming that unlike most actresses of your age you haven't ever had Botox. Would that be correct?'

'Oh, gosh,' replied Angelica a little testily. 'That's certainly not my idea of fascinating. I mean, does anyone even care? I didn't notice you asking Daniel Craig about how he keeps in such good shape or making comments to Christopher or John about their looks.'

'Yes, but in the eighties not every single man in the country wanted to make the beast with two backs with them, did they?' shot back Bradley smugly, earning himself a furious yell in the ear from both Julian and Mike up in the gallery, which culminated in cameras being instructed to 'CUT!'

'Oh, God,' said Jessica faintly, unable to bear it any longer. 'If he keeps saying things like that, she's going to freak.'

Paul looked puzzled and Jessica immediately tried to look like someone who didn't know that for sure. Meanwhile up in the gallery, Julian was busy lecturing Bradley and instructing the studio on what to do next. While this was going on Jessica saw Kerry appear on set to placate and reassure the by now rather flustered Angelica Dupree. Robbie dashed in to powder them both then the cameras turned over again. For the sake of the edit, Bradley was told to briefly revisit his banal enquiry about his guest's face, on the understanding that afterwards he would move on to more substantial questions. The questions he'd been given. On 'action' he asked her again.

'It is correct, yes,' replied Angelica wearily. 'I have not had Botox and I don't ever intend to either. How can I act if I am devoid of all expression?' she said, gesticulating wildly. Bradley may not have realized it yet but he was skating on very thin ice.

'Fair point,' he said cheerily. 'Now, you mentioned earlier that you had a baby so I'm sure you won't mind me bringing this up, but there was quite a scandal when your marriage to Edward Granger broke up, wasn't there? Rather unusually, wasn't it him, if I recall correctly, who retained custody of your child?'

Angelica's hands gripped the side of her chair, her knuckles completely white. In the gallery they went ballistic.

'What the hell is he thinking?' yelled Julian. 'Someone get Natasha and find out if she knew he was going to ask that – but keep rolling,' he added, in case anyone wasn't sure.

'So why was that?' pried Bradley, oblivious to the commotion upstairs. As far as he was concerned, at this point he was only doing as he'd been told.

Angelica froze and, for an awful second, looked like she might be about to burst into tears. Just as quickly, however, she seemed to recover and, summoning up as much dignity as she could, prepared to answer. The studio fell silent. Audience members didn't dare even crunch on a sweet in case they made a sound. Backstage everyone was equally gripped and by now Jessica could only watch through her fingers. She was so tense. Part of her felt like swinging on set like Tarzan and scooping Angelica up and away; the other wanted to grab her by the shoulders and give her a good shake while yelling, '*Answer the question, I beseech you!*' loudly in her ear.

Paul, although similarly spellbound by this rare insight into such an enigmatic star's life, had a rather more pressing concern – how to get Jessica off his lap without offending her. She'd stopped caring about trying not to squash him a while ago, so he'd been taking her full weight for some time now. As a result his legs had gone numb and he had terrible pins and needles in his right foot. He gave her a little squeeze but she was so engrossed she didn't even seem to notice. In fact, she was so absorbed by the show she looked like she wouldn't mind trying to climb into the screen. In the end he sort of tipped her to the side and slid out of the chair from beneath her.

'Shhhh,' said Jessica, which he thought was a little harsh given that he'd temporarily lost the use of his legs.

'If you don't mind,' said Angelica, who was so stunned it hadn't even occurred to her to throw a diva hissy fit and stop recording, 'I would prefer not to talk about that. It was a long time ago and it's a very private matter.'

In the gallery Julian looked at Mike to see if he should stop recording but Mike shook his head. Bradley's handling of the guest might not be ideal, and he'd have to have a serious word with Natasha, but this was TV gold.

'What I will say is that I'm only human,' Angelica continued bravely. 'I've made mistakes over the years but some things need to be kept between myself, Edward and my daughter.'

'Spoilsport,' remarked Paul, shaking his leg about vigorously to get rid of the last remnants of pins and needles. Jessica stared at him blankly, not really registering what he was saying.

'Oh,' said Bradley. 'Well, I apologize if I've upset you in any way, I just presumed that with your break-up having happened such a long time ago you wouldn't mind talking about it. However, I can tell I've touched a nerve so let's move on and –'

'You haven't upset me,' said Angelica defensively. 'Not at all. My marriage is in the past. I just prefer not to discuss it.'

'I understand,' said Bradley.

Upstairs, Julian pressed the button to speak into his ear. 'Move it on now, we've got the clip of her movie ready. Ask about her film please, before she loses it.'

'One last quick thing on the subject,' Bradley said, glancing at his cards, 'and then we'll move on. Are you and Edward friends nowadays? I only ask because those of us old enough to remember you as a couple saw the two of you as a genuine love story, the romance of the decade. When the marriage ended, the news came as a genuine shock to your legions of fans, which is why it would be so lovely for us now to know that you still hold one another in some form of high regard or affection.'

Jessica squirmed as she watched her mother in the spotlight, trapped like an insect under a magnifying glass. This was awful, especially since it was all her doing. Equally, she longed to hear her answer.

'Bradley,' Angelica said calmly. Too calmly. 'I have so much to talk about. I have worked on some amazing films in my time, been to *incroyable* places, met some very talented and interesting people. *Enfin*, I could sit here and converse with you about so many things. So why would I want to talk about personal stuff from my past that I barely understand myself?'

'Right,' said Bradley. 'So it's complicated?'

'Yes, it's complicated,' raged Angelica, her composure disappearing rapidly. 'Of course it is. Edward is the love of my life, but that was then and this is now. I have another man in my life now so this really is not appropriate.'

'Is the love of your life?'

'*Pardon?*'

'Is . . . you said *is* . . .'

'I did not.'

'You did,' insisted Bradley. 'Not that I want to argue with you, of course, but you did say "is the love of my life".'

'If I did, it was a slip of the tongue,' said Angelica, looking ruffled. 'Look, if you insist, I will tell you. Edward and I did not stay in touch after we broke up. I tried but . . . anyway, the point is, I will always love the father of my child because he is the father of my child. He was a huge part of my life, you can't just switch that off, and yet, if someone doesn't want to know, you have to move on.'

'But I thought you left him?' said Bradley, sensing a scoop.

'Yes, I left 'im,' said Angelica, her French accent growing more pronounced by the second.

'She sounds like René from *'Allo 'Allo*,' remarked Paul, earning himself a furious glare from Jessica, who apart from anything else had never heard of the hit show from the eighties.

'Sorry I spoke,' Paul added. He was starting to get a bit irritated by his girlfriend's complete absorption in the show.

'But it wasn't as straightforward as it might have seemed at the time,' Angelica was saying. She was starting to look really upset now. 'I did write,' she said quietly. 'I wrote every week for a long, long time. I tried to work things out, but I think he was hurt and so . . .' By this point Angelica's huge aquamarine eyes were looking dangerously watery. Then it suddenly seemed to occur to her that millions of people (including Graydon) would be watching this interview when it went out. 'Anyway,' she said more brightly, visibly pulling herself together, 'none of that matters any more because actually I have some wonderful news.'

'Really?' said Bradley, who couldn't have written it better himself.

'Yes, and I had planned on telling my daughter first, but since I know she will be watching anyway, I am pleased to announce that I am engaged to be married.'

'Fantastic,' gushed Bradley, who knew this was the interview of the year and was already visualizing the Bafta in his downstairs loo. 'Who's the lucky man?'

'Graydon Matthews.'

Jessica's heart sank to her boots.

'And when's the big day?'

'Well, obviously I can't tell you that,' replied Angelica, 'but let's just say it's imminent. After all, when you reach my stage in life, once you've made up your mind there's no point waiting around.'

Jessica could almost hear Graydon saying precisely this, desperate to get the deed done before Angelica had the chance to see the error of her ways.

'OK,' said Bradley, sensing that he'd pushed his guest enough. 'Now let's see a clip from your new movie, which the critics are hailing as a strong contender for the Oscars...'

'Blimey,' said Paul, as Bradley segued into the clip. 'What a booking. Clips of that are going to be shown for the next fifty years. She was amazing. Incredibly cagey and prickly in one way and yet at the same time more... God, what's the right word, more... open than celebrities usually are.'

Jessica nodded dumbly. Astonishment had rendered her mute and she was completely choked by everything her mother had just said. What letters could she possibly have been talking about and how could her mother even think about marrying hairy-ape features? And why had her dad never said anything about any letters?

She sprang to her feet, keen firstly to find her mother so she could ask what the hell she thought she was playing at, and secondly to retrieve the tape of the show from Ross. As she sprinted off (to Paul's surprise), the word her boyfriend had probably been searching for suddenly occurred to her. Her mom hadn't been open, she'd been honest. Something she was starting to think she probably should have been herself from the beginning.

34

The next day, Edward Granger was in the middle of a meeting about his upcoming party with, amongst others, party planner Pierre.

'So,' continued Pierre, who was as camp as Christmas, 'I'm thinking arum lilies, in three different shades of red, intertwined in giant glass domes and mounted on top of gold columns. What do you think?'

Edward thought nothing. He literally had no opinion on the matter. In fact, the only thing that had occurred to him was that when Pierre had used the word 'mounted', it had sounded faintly sexual. But maybe that was an awfully homophobic response, an antiquated hang-up from his youth? He proceeded to answer, with as much enthusiasm as he could muster (so not much), 'I don't know really, though if you say those ar– those . . . lilies would be great, I'm sure they would.' Maintaining the peace was the only reason he hadn't told Pierre to stick his lilies up his ar–

'Arum, darling, arum,' said Pierre in an unbelievably patronizing tone.

Edward sighed. He couldn't concentrate. All he wanted to do was watch the DVD Jessica had FedExed to him again, so that he could search Angelica's face for more clues. He'd only received it three hours ago, but had already watched it eight times. When Jessica had phoned, insisting he watch Angelica being interviewed as a matter of urgency, she'd said a lot of strange things and now he didn't know whether he was coming or going. His head felt like it was about to spontaneously combust. She was getting married. He couldn't bear it. Not only that but it seemed Angelica *had* finally talked to Jessica about why she'd left, just as he'd asked her to. According to Jessica she'd come up with some pretty solid reasons too and now there was all this talk of letters. None of which made any sense. His eyes felt suspiciously moist. Tears were trying for an invasion, which wasn't surprising. Having spent nearly a third of his life mourning and grieving the fact he was no longer with Angelica, if he were to find out that things could have been different he wasn't entirely sure he could cope.

Suddenly Edward noticed Betsey glaring at him, which brought him back to the here and now. 'Er, where were we?' he said hastily. 'Ah yes, flowers.'

Things were rather delicate between himself and Betsey at the moment. Finally having accepted that their marriage had run its course, they'd taken the decision to end it, at which point the level of sadness which had swamped them both had surprised them. When Betsey had insisted upon leaving the marriage with only the minimum amount of alimony, Edward had even felt a pang of quite tangible regret, despite knowing deep down that it was the right thing to do. In order to gain some much-needed breathing space they'd agreed to put off the announcement until after his party.

As Pierre prattled on about chandeliers and lighting, Edward found himself wondering if there was anyone left in the world, apart from his estranged first wife and his sister, who remembered, or cared for that matter, that prior to becoming a rich, famous Hollywood movie star he'd simply been Teddy Bender from Pinner. That he'd grown up in a modest bungalow and that as a young man his idea of high-octane glamour had been a splash of Brut aftershave, dinner at a Bernie Steakhouse and going to a party where no one got into a fight. Angelica was the one person who had managed to both unearth and accept all the different layers and facets to him. She had understood how his less sophisticated roots occasionally made him feel like an alien in his own home, yet hadn't seen anything wrong in how easily he'd adapted to his new luxurious lifestyle. She hadn't judged him for erasing some of his old identity, like his name and his accent, and used to laugh with him about the more frilly and ridiculous aspects of being famous. God, he missed that. It had pained him so much to hear Jessica pleading with him to come to England to try and persuade Angelica not to get married. Like she'd listen to him! Even if she did listen to him, according to his panicked daughter the wedding was taking place tomorrow. Angelica had decided to have a small, private ceremony and apparently didn't see the point in waiting, which surely meant she must be desperate to marry Teenwolf's cousin. And it wasn't as if she'd phoned him back after having spoken with Jessica as agreed. At least he thought they'd agreed . . . hadn't they?

'Edward, Pierre needs a decision on the lighting,' said Clare, interrupting his reverie.

'Let me show you,' minced Pierre, waving his hands excitedly about in the air. 'Let's consult my mood board.'

'Mood board?' whispered Edward morosely to Clare

while Pierre started barking instructions to his minions. 'What will that say? Exuberant? Annoying? Faintly ridiculous?'

'Here,' said Pierre, as his beleaguered assistant set down an easel. He flung a huge sheet of A3 back. 'What do you think?' he asked, stabbing a heavily ornamented finger towards a picture of a room bathed in red and gold light.

Sensing that Edward was stumped again, Pierre turned to Betsey, who seemed a more willing conspirator.

'I think it's amazing,' she said. 'Isn't it, Edward?'

'What? Yes, I suppose so,' he replied distractedly. 'Though, in all truthfulness, I'm more concerned about the right people being here to share it with me.'

'Like who?' asked Betsey, narrowing her eyes.

'Well, my daughter for one,' said Edward plainly. 'I mean, without the people you care about, does it matter what flowers you have? What music, what caterer, or invitations? Of course it doesn't, because nothing else matters,' he said, teetering on the verge of self-pitying tears. Quickly, he stuffed a fist in his mouth to prevent this potentially career-threatening debacle from occurring.

Pierre's minions had stopped in their tracks, their faces a picture of surprise. Was James Bond crying about his party?

Edward steeled himself, gulped hard and recovered. Then, in a manner far more associated with a leading man, spoke up in a deep, composed voice. 'Betsey, why don't you take over the decision-making for a minute? Jill, may I have a word?'

'Really?' beamed Betsey, spotting a once-in-a-lifetime opportunity to finally express herself in this house before she left it. 'Oh, Pierre, we are going to have so much fun.'

Betsey may have been dignified about the divorce but she didn't see why she shouldn't enjoy this opportunity to give Edward's credit card a bit of a work-out. Pierre, who had quickly deduced that this meeting had most definitely ended up working in his favour, clapped his hands together.

Edward led Jill out of the study and towards the kitchen.

'I'm going to London,' he declared.

'What? Not this again,' sighed Jill. 'I told you, Jessica is going to be home in a matter of days, so there's no point.'

'I'm not going there to see her. I need to see Angelica, and right away,' he stated.

Jill's jaw practically hit the ground. 'Are you out of your mind, Edward? Why?'

'Because we're unfinished business. Always have been, always will be, and there are things I have to know or I will go to my grave a madman. She says she wrote me letters, Jill. Every week. Why would she say that?'

'Because she's ill,' said Jill at once. 'Don't forget who you're dealing with here, Edward. This is the woman who left you high and dry. The woman who nearly cost you your career.'

'But what if there was a reason? What if she did explain why she left and I just didn't get the letters?'

'Why would you not have? She's a liar, Edward, and as your agent of the last thirty years I strongly urge you not to do this, please. What's got into you? This is madness.'

But Edward had made up his mind. 'It's too late, I'm going. Now where's Clare? I need a flight.'

35

Jessica couldn't believe her hastily thought of plan was actually coming together, albeit in a rather hectic, haphazard and reckless fashion.

She was at Heathrow Terminal One waiting for her father to appear. Special services were taking care of him, meaning he would be taken through passport control in a private room, but then he should be coming through Arrivals just like everybody else. The anticipation was excruciating. It was now or never for Edward and Angelica, and Jessica wished she could separate her own feelings from the situation, wished she could know for sure that her motives weren't blurred by a deep-rooted desire simply to see her parents back together. Still, when she recalled Angelica trying to tell her that she didn't care about Edward, the real answer was written all over her face, and her father was even easier to read. All her life Jessica had sensed how much it pained him to hear her mother's name, and had always suspected that he carried a torch. Edward hadn't had one girlfriend who wasn't jealous of Angelica at one point or another, despite the fact they never even saw each other. So what did that tell you? As far as Jessica was concerned, Graydon was just a complication that needed addressing. There was no way her mother could seriously want to spend her life with someone so odious. And if she was right and her parents really were in love, then shouldn't they be together for their sake and not just her own? At that moment she spotted Edward and the determined look on his face immediately told her she hadn't been imagining things. Here was a man who had not got over his wife. A man who was on a mission.

'Jessica!' he yelled.

As her over-excited father bounded towards her like a happy Labrador, a tired-looking Clare bringing up the rear, any doubts Jessica had been experiencing were positively slung to one side for a second, chucked over her shoulder. Seeing him after all this time had the same effect as a triple espresso.

'Daddy!' Jessica called, forgetting herself entirely and propelling herself forward into his outstretched arms. After that it was chaos. First one photographer, then another, and then another, all of whom happened to be waiting for Victoria Beckham to arrive, spotted this gift of a photo opportunity at the same time, at which point all hell broke loose. Jessica was mortified. There was no way she wanted her face splashed all over the tabloids for all her office (and Paul) to see. Thinking quickly, she pulled her jacket up over her head, gripped on to Edward's hand and hoped for the best.

Eventually airport security had to be called upon to break up the scrum, at which point Clare bundled Edward and Jessica towards their waiting taxi. Once they were safely inside and the crowd had been dispersed, Jessica laughed as Clare's eyeballs almost took a running jump, so disapprovingly did she roll them at Edward. 'I told you not to draw attention to yourself.'

'Hee hee,' laughed Edward gleefully. 'Ah dear, bit of

chaos now and again never harmed anyone, eh? Oh, stop looking so disapproving, Clare,' he said dismissively as she frowned at him via the rear-view mirror. 'You'll give yourself wrinkles. And as for you,' he said, turning his attentions to Jessica who was sitting next to him in the back, 'give your old dad a hug.' He enveloped her in his strong, familiar arms. 'I've missed you so much.'

'Me too, Dad,' said Jessica, only now realizing quite how much. 'Shit, I hope no one did get a picture of me.'

'They didn't,' reassured Clare. 'You were too quick for them, though they'll probably have you labelled as a mystery girlfriend.'

'Gross,' laughed Jessica.

'Creepy,' agreed Edward.

Once they'd pulled away and got going it didn't take long for Edward to hit his daughter with a torrent of questions.

'Now, you horror, I want to know everything. What have you been up to? Why do you think your mother's going to speak to me? Did she say anything about the letters to you? Who's this Paul character you keep mentioning? Would I approve and when are you coming home for good? What?' he finished innocently as Jessica shook her head resignedly.

'Oh, don't look at me like that,' he admonished. 'Do you have any idea what you've put your old pa through these last few months? I've barely bloody slept. I hate you being away and I hate not knowing what's going on.'

'Tell me about it,' said Jessica. 'Look, all I know is that Mom can't marry Graydon. She doesn't love him. That much I know for sure. But right now we don't have much time. It's so annoying you couldn't get an earlier flight. The wedding's at three and we've got to get all the way to Chelsea. Mom's already called me four times this morning and I had to make up some story about why I couldn't get there before.'

'OK,' said Edward immediately, looking horribly nervous. 'Oh, Christ, I'm still not sure. *How* do you know she's not happy?'

'Dad, the man's an idiot. He can't even take a crap without taking his clothes off and you saw the show, what does your instinct tell you?'

'What do you mean, he can't take a crap without —'

'And Mom told me that he doesn't make her laugh.'

'Really?' said Edward, his voice suddenly hopeful.

Traffic was excruciatingly slow but with all the pleasure of catching up it was a while before either of them noticed quite what terrible progress they were making. Eventually, however, it became rather obvious.

'Oh my God, I'm not sure we're going to make it,' said Jessica, looking alarmed as they encountered yet another set of roadworks. It was twenty to three and they were still only at the beginning of the King's Road.

Edward had ants in his pants. He hadn't flown all this way for nothing. He simply had to see Angelica and ask her about the letters. Jessica was right, she couldn't marry Graydon if there was even the smallest chance she was doing the wrong thing. He subtly adjusted his trousers. The thought of seeing her in the flesh after all these years was doing funny things to his insides and the blood kept rushing towards his groin. It was quite extraordinary. Ever since he'd spoken to Angelica on the phone it was as if parts of him had decided to come out of hibernation. As the lights turned red again, he couldn't take it any longer.

'I think I should get out,' he said agitatedly.

'And do what?' asked Jessica, bewildered.

'Run if I have to,' said Edward.

The driver was unable to resist turning round. 'Gosh, sir, never thought I'd hear James Bond saying something like that in my cab.'

'Are you sure?' interjected Clare. 'You might get spotted and mobbed by fans and you're wearing loafers.'

Edward was jet-lagged and the plane meal was repeating on him but he was also an actor with an ego that was still vaguely intact. The driver was right. He was James Bond for goodness' sake, and since when would 007 sit in a taxi and allow the traffic to stop him from claiming back the love of his life? Graydon 'hasn't got a sense of humour, lavatorial issues' Matthews wasn't going to marry Angelica simply because he'd managed to be late. Yes, he was wearing loafers, but would James Bond let his footwear determine whether or not he could run?

'Right,' said Edward, trying to convince himself that tearing up the pavement was the right thing to do. Admittedly it would be tricky sprinting when the street was so densely packed with pedestrians. Worn out after his journey, he felt like running about as much as he felt like gouging his eyes out with a rusty nail, but needs must. Jessica and Clare watched anxiously as, having made up his mind, Edward decisively opened the door and dodged the oncoming traffic to make it on to the pavement.

'Dad!' Jessica called out of the window, not at all sure he was doing the right thing.

'Will you pay our driver, Jess, or do you need me to do it?' he said, having broken into a trot by now. The lights had turned green, so in effect he was running alongside the taxi, which was still crawling along slowly. Now Edward felt really torn. Maybe he should get back in the car? It would be bloody sod's law if the traffic cleared and the cab ended up going faster than him. As he picked up the pace a little he belched softly and wished he'd thought to chew on a Rennie. A small fart also escaped due to the exertion. Then another and another, like a machine gun that was loaded with wind. 'Maybe I should get back in?' he yelled at Jessica.

'No, just go,' she yelled back, having noticed that up ahead the traffic was grinding to a halt again.

Right, thought Edward, ignoring the looks he was getting from a few people who had clearly recognized him. Ten to three. Time to get serious. Just then a bus whizzed down the empty bus lane before stopping at the bus stop, which was one hundred metres or so away. It was a number 14 and if Edward's memory served him correctly it would be heading straight down the road and ultimately past the town hall. 'Wait for me!' called Edward, breaking into a sprint. The last passenger was just getting on.

'W-a-a-a-a-a-i-t!' he yelled, but to no avail. Just as he was drawing up to it, the bus started to pull away.

'Bugger it,' Edward cursed, his chest heaving with exertion, but he wasn't giving up. Instead, summoning all his strength, he gave chase. The bus hadn't got far, as it was still easing itself into the flow of traffic. With an almighty effort Edward came within a hair's breadth of the white pole at the back of the old fashioned Routemaster, but then it was off again. If he could ... just ... reach ... Stretching out his fingertips, he nearly made it. He was so close, so nearly there. With one last supreme effort Edward finally managed to make contact with and grasp the pole, yet just as he was wrapping his fist firmly round it, to his horror, the bus accelerated. Instead of managing to swing himself up and on to the bus, he ended up being dragged along by it, his side scraping on the road.

'Aaaeeeeeuehgh!' he yelled in pain, to the alarm of passengers who were taking their ride in a more traditional manner. That is to say, they were sitting on the bus, as opposed to being dragged by it.

Meanwhile, Jessica, who was only a few metres behind in the taxi, could see everything that was unfolding and was horrified. Her poor dad. How ... embarrassing. By now their taxi was only fractionally behind the bus and fast catching up, so the whole thing was unnecessary too. Clare, it seemed, had gone into shock so it was left to Jessica to scream out of the window, 'Somebody stop that bus! My dad, my dad!'

No one could hear but, thankfully, an old lady had the wherewithal to finally alert the driver to the fact he was essentially pulling a man up the bus lane. The horrified driver slammed on the brakes, at which point a bruised and battered Edward skidded to a halt – at such a pace that he swung right underneath the bus. Jessica, Clare, their driver, the passengers on the bus and hundreds of passers-by held their breath, some covering their faces in horror with their hands as they waited to see if the poor man would emerge.

'Oh my God, Dad,' whispered Jessica. Her driver pulled

over in the bus lane and Jessica leapt out of the car. As she ran towards the bus, Clare hot on her heels, she prayed harder than she ever had before and thankfully someone answered. When she was about thirty feet away, suddenly from underneath the bus she could see Edward's familiar hands appearing, somehow managing to pull himself back out from under the bus. Staggering slightly, he got to his feet and a large cheer went up. Ever the pro, Edward nodded and played to the crowd, holding his grazed hands up as if to say 'it was nothing'. At this point people started to recognize who they were staring at and inevitably a jolt of something like electricity darted through the crowd.

Meanwhile, the entire right-hand side of Edward's body was covered in dirt, his shirt was torn and his torso was horribly grazed. He felt like he'd backed into a bacon slicer, but more alarming than the pain was the slow realization that he might be out of time to halt the wedding.

'Are you all right, mate?' asked the concerned bus driver, who had clambered down and come round the bus to investigate, terrified that he might be sued.

'I'm fine,' lied Edward, brushing himself down, wincing in pain as he did so.

'Bloody hell, it's Pierce Brosnan! What are you doing trying to get the bus anyway? Nice to meet you, mate. Can I have your autograph?'

'I'm afraid I don't have a pen on me and besides I'm not . . . I mean, great to meet you too,' Edward corrected himself. Pierce could take this one for him. 'Now, if you don't mind, I have some business to attend to.'

'All right then, well good luck and you know we're all right behind you.'

A cheer went up from the rest of the bus. People were squashed against the windows, filming events on their phones. As Clare finally caught up with her, Jessica heard her groan heavily and she knew why. It would be all over YouTube by the afternoon. Meanwhile, Edward had more pressing things on his mind so – mustering up what little dignity he had left – he limped across the pavement and up the stairs of the town hall. (The only upside of the whole debacle was that rather conveniently his 'journey' had come to a stop right outside their destination.) Could he really see Angelica for the first time in twenty years in this state? Still, there was no time to be thinking about that now.

Jessica buttoned her jacket up over her head once more and, leaving Clare to deal with the chaos, made a run for it.

'Probably should have stayed in the car then. Are you OK?' she panted, her face wreathed in concern (not that anyone could see it).

'Truthfully?' said Edward. 'No, I'm in more pain than I've ever been in my life and I'm not entirely sure my ribs aren't broken. Worse still, I think our efforts may have been in vain. Look at the time.'

Peeping over the top of her jacket, Jessica followed his gaze to his Rolex watch that was sporting a large scratch across the face.

It was ten past three. A large, very curious crowd was gathering so an unbelievably disappointed Jessica opened the door to the building and they both darted in.

'What now?' gulped Jessica, pulling her jacket back down, trying not to cry as they stood just inside the entrance, having shut the door on the chaos they'd left in their wake.

'Well, you should probably go and offer the happy couple your congratulations, and I shall wait till things have calmed down outside then get Clare to find the nearest chemist and buy some Savlon,' said Edward bravely, though his desolate face told the real story. Just then, however, a groom appeared through a door to their right. It was Graydon, decked out in full wedding attire, complete with hairy knuckles. There was no sign of the bride.

'What the hell are you doing here?' asked Graydon, looking almost as fed up as Edward, only much, much smarter.

'I was just . . . passing?' tried Edward. Despite her disappointment, Jessica couldn't help it, she had to giggle at this ludicrous answer.

Edward frowned.

'Sorry, Dad.'

'Where's Angelica?' asked Edward. 'I wanted to . . . congratulate you both.'

'Like fuck you did,' seethed Graydon. 'Don't you dare try and make a fool of me.'

'Seriously, where is Mom?' interrupted Jessica, suddenly genuinely concerned for her mother's welfare. Graydon's usually smooth composure seemed to have slipped and he looked vaguely unhinged.

'Claridge's,' he snarled, looking hatefully at the pair of them.

'What do you mean?' asked Jessica.

'She's ditched me, and don't try to pretend you don't know why,' he spat petulantly.

'Actually, I'm not pretending,' said Edward. 'So why don't you spill the beans because I'd love to get your insight . . .'

'Well, Jessica not bothering to turn up certainly didn't

help but I suspect your daughter's also been putting ideas into her head, confusing her,' he added, making it sound as though Angelica was vaguely senile.

Jessica interrupted. 'Look, I'm not being funny, Graydon, but you know as well as I do that you bullied Mom into this wedding so I can't say I'm sorry that it hasn't worked out.'

'I don't really care what you think,' he replied stonily.

'Oh, cheer up,' said Jessica, who'd had enough and had also just realized that with the wedding off there was no real reason left to be polite. 'It's not like the person you love most in the world has jilted you. You're still here, aren't you? You should marry yourself.'

'Jessica,' reprimanded Edward. He liked what she was saying but paternal habits die hard and he didn't feel able to condone such rudeness. Still, Jessica was past caring, as was Graydon.

'You little shit,' he blustered, rather revealing his true colours.

'No, you shit,' retorted Jessica. 'Only apparently with some difficulty and never with your clothes on.'

'How dare you? You bitch,' spat Graydon, practically convulsing with rage.

'Don't speak to my daughter like that, you prick,' said Edward.

'Fuck you,' retorted Graydon.

'No, fuck you,' said Edward, before punching him squarely on the nose.

36

Ten minutes later, having beaten a hasty retreat from Graydon and his bloody nose, Jessica, Edward and Clare found themselves back in the car again, heading optimistically for Claridge's.

'Mom, it's me,' panted Jessica into her cell phone. 'Are you OK? Oh, gosh, don't cry,' she soothed. 'I know . . . yes, I saw him. Oh, don't worry, you've definitely done the right thing . . .'

Edward sat rigid, unable to cope with the tension of not knowing whether she'd agree to see him. It was obvious from the way Jessica was talking that Angelica was deeply upset and it pained him to think of her so unhappy.

'I know,' Jessica was saying, 'but listen, I'm going to come there now. Yes . . . but just listen a second. I'm with Dad and I think you guys should talk . . .'

There was a pause. Edward cringed and not just because his scraped side was stinging.

'OK,' said Jessica, putting down her phone.

'Well,' said Edward, 'what did she say? Tell me, for Christ's sake.'

'She said OK,' said Jessica.

'She did?'

'She did.'

*

Half an hour later, Edward Granger was standing in the corridor outside the door to Angelica's penthouse suite. This was the moment he'd dreamt of for over two decades and he could hardly believe it was happening. He was completely terrified. His mouth had gone dry, his heart was pounding and, worst of all, he was feeling incredibly paranoid about how he looked. Last time he'd seen Angelica he'd been a man in his prime, blond with the merest suggestion of grey, twenty pounds lighter and . . . vital. He also hadn't looked like he'd been dragged down the road by a bus. His hand was poised to knock but, bottling it yet again, he lowered it once more. 'I'm just not sure, what if –?' he said, turning to Jessica who was standing behind him.

'Oh, for God's sake,' said Jessica impatiently just as a maid came down the corridor. Stopping outside Angelica's door, she looked uncertainly at the furtive pair who were clearly loitering with intent.

'Edward Granger,' said Jessica, as if that explained and excused everything.

'Oh, yes,' the maid replied excitedly. 'Are you waiting to go in?'

'He is,' said Jessica. 'But we really want to surprise Angelica. Could we borrow your key?'

'Well, I'm not sure,' she prevaricated, 'but . . . I suppose it's OK.'

Edward gave her his best movie-star beam, at which point the nervous maid seemed to accept that, despite the fact he looked like he'd been in a fight and was covered in tarmac, the famous occupant of the suite would be happy to see him. Fame got you everywhere, thought Edward, as she handed over her key card.

'Go on,' said Jessica impatiently. 'I'll wait for you out here.'

At last, taking a deep breath, Edward inserted the key and quietly let himself in.

'Hello,' he said.

Angelica, who had her back to him, spun round from where she was standing in front of a full-length mirror.

In that instant Edward realized she'd been scrutinizing her own appearance and, as it dawned upon him that she was as nervous as he was, his jitters miraculously disappeared.

'Edward, you startled me. I was just . . .' She blushed.

Edward's heart pounded as he absorbed his first proper sight of her in over two decades. My God, she was beautiful. It was so good to see her and she was as exquisite as ever.

'Don't be embarrassed. If it makes you feel any better, it took me ages to select which shirt to wear today, and then I ruined it all by getting dragged under a bus,' he said ruefully.

Angelica felt her entire body relax. Looking up demurely, she smiled at her ex-husband in a way that made him shiver with nostalgia. She had no idea what he was talking about but he hadn't lost the knack of putting her at ease. A wonderful quality she'd always admired him for.

'How bizarre,' she said shyly in her accented voice. 'I haven't seen you for so many years but somehow now it only feels like yesterday.'

'I know what you mean,' said Edward. 'Can I come in, by the way?'

'You are – in,' she said rather lamely.

An awkward silence ensued. Often the way, when there is so very much to be said. Eventually Angelica broke it, however, by saying, 'You're bleeding.'

'Am I?' said Edward jumpily. 'So I am,' he concurred,

having noticed the drops that were falling at a fairly rapid rate on to the pale carpet. 'It's nothing really, just a surface wound,' he added, though in reality the only thing keeping him apart from accident and emergency was adrenaline.

'Right,' said Angelica, looking unsure. 'Well, maybe you should at least take that ripped shirt off. There is gravel on it. Were you serious about the bus thing?'

'Yup,' said Edward, blushing to his roots and suddenly horribly body conscious. There was no way in hell he was getting his man boobs out.

Angelica picked up the phone to call housekeeping. 'Hello, please could you find a gentleman's shirt for me and bring it up right away? Collar size thirty.'

'Thirty-six, actually,' interjected Edward, mortified by how much chin he'd gained in recent years.

'Oh – thirty-six. *Merci.*' She put down the phone. 'In the meantime, would you like to borrow a robe from the bathroom?'

'A robe,' said Edward, leaping upon the idea. 'Yes, there's one in the bathroom, is there? I'll just grab it,' he said, scuttling across the room to the bathroom and re-emerging a few moments later ensconced in a fluffy piece of robe heaven.

'I've imagined this moment many times but somehow I never pictured myself wearing a lady's robe,' he said drily.

Angelica stifled a giggle.

'It's good to see you, Ange,' Edward said, his face suddenly serious.

'Why didn't you reply to my letters?' she said, cutting to the chase by asking the question she'd been wondering the answer to for much of her life.

Edward shook his head. 'I never got a letter.'

'Not *a* letter,' said Angelica, trembling with emotion. 'Letters, Edward. I wrote you hundreds of letters, hundreds. And in them I explained everything and begged for your forgiveness.'

'Swear on Jessica's life you wrote them.'

Angelica's eyes flashed with anger. 'How dare you insult me? Is it not enough that I have lived with your silence all these years, knowing that I hurt you so badly that you couldn't forgive me? Knowing that I made a mess of the one thing that mattered to me? Of course I swear on Jessica's life and my own.'

'Didn't you hear me? I didn't get them,' Edward replied. 'And as it happens, Ange, you aren't the only one who's been hurt. You just upped and left. One minute you were there, my whole world. The next you were gone, only you didn't think to talk to me first. Jessica said you were ill. Is that true, because if it is then I don't understand why you didn't just tell me?'

'I did,' replied Angelica, all pretence at self-control having deserted her. 'Or at least I did try, but you kept telling me it would be fine, not to worry, that I should have more help and to cheer up. Only it wasn't the kind of help I needed, Edward. Truth be told, I was seriously mentally ill so "cheering up" wasn't something I was capable of.'

'OK,' said Edward, a lone tear already coursing down his face. 'I get that, but how could you have left our baby? She was three, Ange, and for years I had to figure out how to be her mother and her father all on my own, while the one person I would normally turn to when things got tough had buggered off. You weren't the only one feeling down, let me tell you. I missed you so much it hurt. Really bloody hurt.'

Angelica hung her head in shame. All the fight seemed to have left her body and she collapsed on to the bed in a defeated heap. 'I'm sorry,' she said in a voice so faint Edward could only just make out what she'd said.

'And why didn't you ring?' he demanded to know.

'Because you made it very clear you wouldn't talk to me unless it was through Jill, so I gave up.'

'No, not then. I mean now, recently? I thought you were going to ring me after you'd spoken to Jessica, but you didn't.'

'I didn't realize you wanted me to,' said Angelica. 'You made that pretty clear.'

Edward just shook his head in frustration. How had they made such a hash of everything?

'So, these letters,' he said eventually, sounding desolate. 'Why do you think they never reached me?'

Angelica shrugged, but having spent years pondering exactly this conundrum the temptation to share her theory was too much. 'I think Pam . . . maybe?'

'Pamela?' repeated Edward. 'But why would she –?'

'She never really liked me,' said Angelica, 'and when I was ill she just couldn't grasp why I was struggling when I had everything I could possibly need. Plus she wanted a baby so badly but couldn't have one . . .'

Edward shook his head, unable even to contemplate what she was saying. 'No, I just don't think Pam would do anything that underhand.'

'Well, can you come up with a better idea?' Angelica asked and she raised her face to stare Edward intently in the eye.

'I don't know, but it wasn't Pam. She saw how devastated I was and she would never hurt me like that.'

Angelica gave the smallest of shrugs. If he wasn't prepared to even consider what she was saying there was no hope.

Meanwhile, Edward just stared at her, drinking in everything about her. God, she was devastating in every sense of the word.

'What?'

'Nothing,' said Edward. 'It's just so weird seeing you after all these years. It almost makes me feel young again.'

'Don't start getting all maudlin about your age now,' said Angelica, smiling despite herself. 'My God, at least you're a man. Getting older has got to be easier for you than it is for us women.'

But Edward wasn't fooled. 'Oh, bollocks, Ange. I've seen your recent movies and you look happier in your skin now than you ever did, and still as beautiful.'

Angelica shivered. Hearing him call her Ange was such a thrill and one that evoked so much nostalgia. Equally thrilling was hearing him admit that he'd watched her movies. She'd always imagined he'd cut her off in every way, as if she had never even existed, but apparently not. She gave him a cautious smile.

'Although, hang on, we don't say that, do we?' he said now. 'Let me correct myself. You are still as wonderfully intelligent and engaging to converse with.'

Now Angelica flung her head back and let out a real belly laugh as she recognized the reference to what had been a private joke between them for years.

At one Hollywood party, not long after they'd got

together, Edward had decided to count how many times people complimented his stunning girlfriend on her appearance. During that one evening alone it turned out she was told a staggering fifty-nine times that she looked 'beautiful', 'breathtaking', 'gorgeous', 'stunning'. No wonder then that such platitudes had never resonated with her particularly. Later that night, as they'd talked in bed, Angelica had admitted that she'd initially fallen for Edward because one day on set he'd complimented her on how funny she was. Later, in private, she'd almost cried with gratitude.

'Don't you see?' she'd said, snuggled tightly into Edward's arms. 'When you're beautiful, all you want is for someone to tell you that you're clever, or funny, or anything positive at all that refers to your personality. In fact, it takes a truly intelligent man to understand that in order to bed a beautiful woman he would do well to tell her that she's clever. Whereas the plain girl, who has got by in life by making herself the funniest, the wittiest, the most profound person possible, really just wants to hear that she's beautiful and desired. It's that simple.'

Since that day Edward had taken great care not to hark on about how beautiful he found Angelica and to concentrate on all the other wonderful things about her that made her the woman she was. The woman he adored. Clearly, he still remembered.

Laughing, Angelica said, 'The sad thing is, I know my looks are fading because these days I'll take any compliments I can get.'

Edward laughed too. 'I know the feeling.'

Angelica looked at him and, as their eyes met, their

faces grew serious and a powerful frisson passed between them. Without thinking, Angelica stood up and reached for his hand. 'You have no need to worry, Edward; you are still the most beautiful man I have ever known.'

Her touch was like an electric shock and Edward's nerve endings instantly stood on end while impulses fired though his body, making him feel like the king of the world. Even while wearing a woman's robe . . .

Emotions he hadn't let himself feel for years flooded every part of him, though they were tinged with a huge sadness for all that they had lost. He was also experiencing a sudden, if not entirely unexpected, stirring in his loins. Gazing into Angelica's almond-shaped green eyes he fought an almost uncontrollable urge to reach out and stroke her cheek, to trace the contours of those incredible cheekbones with his finger. To kiss her.

He gulped and, before he could get any more carried away, pulled his hand back. Angelica also removed her hand at exactly the same time, breaking the moment as quickly as she had created it.

'Why didn't you marry him?' asked Edward.

'I don't love him,' replied Angelica plainly. Having lived with years of unanswered questions, she wasn't going to waste more time with anything less than the complete truth. 'I haven't truly loved anyone since you,' she admitted and Edward's stomach lurched alarmingly as again he was swamped by a desire to pull her into his arms. There was nothing he wanted more.

'Whereas you clearly haven't had that problem,' she added slightly bitterly.

'My marriage is over actually,' interrupted Edward. 'Betsey and I have split up. We just haven't made the announcement yet.'

'Oh,' said Angelica, her green eyes stunned. 'Right,' she said briskly, furious with herself for feeling what she was feeling. 'Maybe she was too young for you?' she suggested for want of something better to say. 'Sorry, none of my business.'

'No, it's not,' said Edward, experiencing a stab of loyalty towards Betsey. Angelica looked mortified and terribly hurt, so he added quickly, 'You're probably right though. She is very young, though not as young as the women they're trying to cast me against these days. I had a fucking awful meeting the other day with an utter prick of a producer and you wouldn't believe who he cast as my love interest.'

'Who?' asked Angelica, curious to know.

'Juliana Sabatini,' said Edward.

'No!' exclaimed Angelica. 'She's a baby.'

'Tell me about it,' said Edward, ecstatic that finally someone was on his wavelength. 'That's what I said. Stupid bastard said it was perfect casting.' Edward rolled his eyes at the memory. 'I'd like to wriggle out of it, but Jill's insisting I do it.'

'Have you expressed your concerns?'

'Oh, yes,' said Edward wryly. 'The other day we met again and the producer said "Juliana's gorgeous, you should be grateful." Well, you can imagine how that comment went down. I ended up raging at him, shouting, "Grateful? What, like an old lech at a Christmas party? Like a big, fat sex tourist who picks up young prostitutes while kidding himself that they like being humped by someone old enough to be their father?"'

Shocked, Angelica covered her mouth with her hand.

'Anyway, there you have it.'

'There you have it,' agreed Angelica, stifling a giggle. Silence descended once more.

'Anyway,' said Edward.

'Anyway,' repeated Angelica.

'Come to my party,' Edward said on impulse.

Angelica looked very unsure.

'Look,' said Edward, his face gravely serious, 'I'm not saying things between us are by any means sorted out or resolved, but our daughter has put up with years of us playing silly buggers and not talking, which I've only realized recently has affected her a great deal. Don't you think that for her sake we should attempt to be at best friends, at worst civil? So come to the party. It's on Thursday night, at the house, and you'd be very welcome.'

Angelica paused. This was a huge decision. The thought of seeing people like Vincent and Jill after all these years was terrifying, but how could she say no? She owed it to her daughter.

'I'll be there,' she said simply.

37

The next morning, Jessica hugged Paul. 'I can't believe I'm leaving you,' she said, despairing at the mere thought. 'I'll call you every day.'

'As much as that would be wonderful, I don't want you getting a phone bill you can't afford,' replied Paul, kissing her cheek tenderly.

She'd have to be on the phone to Australia for months before she couldn't afford the bill, but there wasn't much she could say to that. Damn him for being so practical.

'I can't believe Pam's coming with me. My dad will be so excited,' she said, giddy at the thought of everything that had changed recently. She still couldn't believe her scheming had paid off. Her mom was actually coming to Edward's party. She realized now her notion about them maybe being more than friends had been totally far-fetched, but if they could at least handle being in the same room as one another, she'd be happy. It would be a start and would make life so much easier, happier and pleasant.

'How did Pam get over her fear of flying?' asked Paul.

'Well,' said Jessica, suddenly coy, 'she said it was all tied up with the fear of doing anything without Bernard, but that since I've been on the scene she's felt a lot stronger for some reason and has gained a new lease of life, which is amazing.'

'It is and I sort of know how she feels. I'm going to

miss you,' said Paul gruffly, desperately trying to stick to his plan of not getting completely attached. After all, this was like a dress rehearsal for the day when he'd have to say goodbye for good.

'Me too,' said Jessica with feeling.

It was only when Jessica took her seat on the plane that she realized quite how exhausted she was. It was as if all the tension of the past couple of weeks had finally caught up with her and she and Pam both slept the entire flight, though Pam's drowsiness was less to do with tiredness and more to do with the knockout Valium she'd swallowed earlier. The two of them walked through Arrivals still trying to shed the inevitable post-sleep shroud of groggy confusion, but as soon as they got into the waiting limo that Edward had sent for them, excitement perked them up.

'Ooh,' squealed Pam as they turned on to the freeway, the sunshine practically blinding them, the blue sky stretching endlessly into the smog-filled horizon. 'I'm glad I didn't pack my vest.'

Jessica grinned. It was good to be home.

The next few days zipped by. Edward was so excited to see his sister on his home turf he wept with happiness when she arrived (not that this came as a great shock to anybody) and deemed her presence to be the best present he'd ever had. However, as soon as Pam had had time to settle in, he took her to one side and asked her directly if she knew anything about any letters from Angelica. He simply had to know.

Pam, who had been filled in on a lot of things by Jessica,

was livid that he could ever think she'd do such a thing and said as much. 'I might not have liked what she did to you, Teddy,' she raged, 'but I would never keep something as personal as a letter from anybody and I'm furious you think I would. Besides, I've been feeling a bit bad about Angelica if you must know. I didn't realize she'd been so ill.'

Edward raised an enquiring eyebrow.

'Jessica told me.'

Still clueless about the missing letters and not entirely convinced they'd ever even existed, Edward decided to try and forget about them. If Angelica was lying to him, it was probably because she felt so ashamed. Unfortunately such a lie made it impossible for him to totally forgive her, but seeing her again had been so wonderful that he wanted being friends to still be an option. They'd had two long conversations on the phone since Claridge's, raking up what had happened all those years ago, which had been painful and at times tense, and yet finally having an explanation to hold on to was like healing balm for the emotional wounds he'd suffered from for so long.

Over the next couple of days Edward charged around the house, feeling more energized than he had in years, making last-minute arrangements and trying not to get wound up by the campest party planner Jessica had ever met (and that was saying something). It was hard not to be infected by Edward's exuberance and, after everything Jessica had recently gone through, being back in sunny Malibu was like taking medicine. She felt carefree for the first time in a long time, even with Edward nagging her about when she was coming home for good.

'I don't know, Dad,' she replied one lunchtime for the nineteenth time. Edward had given Consuela the day off and had fired up the barbecue. 'It depends what happens with Diane and stuff, and Paul.'

'Ah,' said Edward, poking a piece of chicken rather viciously with his tongs. 'The famous Paul who doesn't even know I exist. Do you know how hurtful that is?'

'Don't take it personally,' answered Jessica, trying not to laugh at Edward's churlish expression. 'I'm going to tell him soon and if it were possible I'd love you to meet him, though the reality is we'll probably have to split up at some point, I guess. Long-distance relationships are usually doomed to failure.' She shuddered as she said this, refusing to confront the possibility this might actually be true. 'Still, if you do meet him, I just hope you like him as much as I do.'

'Even if I were into "man love", I'm not sure that would be possible,' suggested Edward wearily. 'I just thought you might be bored of this whole "being normal" thing by now.'

'Do you want to know the truth?' said Jessica. 'There are things I am sick of. The climate is pretty unpredictable in London and I am so over getting the tube every day, to the point where I can't believe there was ever a time I actually enjoyed it. I feel unhealthier than I have in years and I've never needed a break from working like I do now. I've put on eight pounds, I'm utterly exhausted and yet, you know what? I also feel fulfilled for the first time in my life and *needing* a holiday is probably how it should be, isn't it?'

'Well, I suppose . . .' ventured Edward.

'Seriously, Dad, this trip is the best thing I ever did. I feel like I have a purpose. Just having a job that I need to be at gives life meaning. Yes, it can be tough out there and I realize I still don't really know what it means to have it hard, but at least I've proved that there's more to me than being your daughter. I also truly appreciate for the first time just how hard you must have had to work to achieve all this.'

'Chicken kebab?' offered a rather choked Edward, who was suddenly feeling terribly proud.

The next day Jessica spent the entire day with Dulcie. Having kept in regular contact by phone and email, they were already up to speed on what one another had been up to. It was wonderful to speak face to face, however, and as with all true friends, it was as if they'd only seen each other yesterday, especially since Jessica was launched straight into bridesmaid duties once more.

'It's as if I've never been away,' Jessica teased happily while waiting patiently for her friend to emerge from the changing rooms in the bridal department of Saks Fifth Avenue in Beverly Hills.

'Oh, I don't know about that,' joked back Dulcie from behind the curtain. 'I've never heard you talk about a guy so much. Paul this, Paul that. It's like you're obsessed.'

Jessica felt quite indignant at this. Just then, however, Dulcie stuck her head out, winked and said, 'Only joking, honey. You talk away; let's face it, I kinda owe you.'

Placated, Jessica flashed her a grin, though it soon faded when the shop assistant finally flung the curtain back and Dulcie made her entrance. A vision in Reem Acra lace and silk. Jessica clapped her hand to her mouth, gasped and burst into soppy tears.

'Oh my God, I'm such a cliché but, Dulcie, you look absolutely beautiful,' she cried, genuinely choked.

'Do I?' her friend asked shyly.

'Hell, yeah, I mean I don't even believe in marriage, but if it meant wearing a dress like that I could almost be tempted. You look like a princess. Your mom would be so proud.'

Which was exactly what Dulcie had been hoping to hear.

There was so much going on around her that it took Jessica, to her shame, an entire two days to realize she wasn't the only one who'd been busy making some life changes. She had noticed Betsey's absence, but had assumed her stepmother must be at one of her yoga retreats or something.

'We've split up,' Edward explained after Consuela had let the cat out of the bag, prompting Jessica to finally ask the question.

'Oh my God,' Jessica exclaimed, genuinely shocked.

'It's fine,' said Edward calmly. He was in the study, taking a break from Pierre's histrionics, watching *Bridge Over the River Kwai*. 'To be honest, it was on the cards for a while and actually now we've split up we're getting on much better. I think the end came as a relief to both of us. You'll see her at the party anyway. She's still coming because we've agreed not to tell anyone until after.'

'Was there someone else?'

'No,' said Edward hastily, blushing red, and Jessica didn't enquire further but hoped her dad's ego hadn't taken too much of a battering. She'd always worried that Betsey would dump her dad for some young beefcake one day, but took no pleasure in having been proved right.

Jessica had forgotten how easy life in LA was, hanging out by the pool in the sunshine, not having to think about anything at all mundane, so it was a testament to her feelings for Paul that she still missed him desperately. He was the one missing ingredient that prevented the trip from being perfect and she'd done a ridiculous amount of texting since she'd arrived. She longed for him to be there, sharing it all with her, and her heart ached as she wondered how on earth she would cope when one day they had to say goodbye. She loved him and hoped he felt the same, though neither of them had said it yet, both too unsure of what the future held for their relationship. It was simply easier and more sensible to drift along, enjoying the ride while they could.

On Thursday, as Jessica climbed into the new Phillip Lim dress she'd bought earlier that morning on Rodeo Drive, she grinned at her reflection, wondering what Paul would make of her looking so 'done'. Her hair had been blown out, her nails were painted pink and on her feet were a kick-ass pair of Manolos. She wasn't the only thing that had been transformed either. An army of caterers, florists, musicians, waiting staff, barmen and security had all descended upon the house to do their jobs and it was pretty clear that the party was going to be one to remember.

It was due to start at eight and at seven thirty Betsey turned up early in order to pretend she was still living there. Jessica had to smother a shocked grin when she saw the inappropriateness of her outfit.

'Hey, Betsey. Wow! That's some dress.'

'Thanks,' Betsey replied, wondering for the first time if maybe her dress was too much. Or too little? What she was wearing was more a scrap of material than a dress. It was white, halter neck, backless and very, very short. If she wasn't with someone already, she clearly didn't intend to stay single for long, thought Jessica. Though what type of guy did she think she was going to attract? What kind of guy wouldn't she attract, more like? Thank God she didn't have to introduce her to Paul any time soon.

Just then Edward made his entrance down the staircase, dressed in a pale pink shirt, linen trousers and Tods. A Ralph Lauren jersey was knotted round his neck.

'Hey, Granddad, I see you've reverted to type fashion-wise,' drawled Betsey. Shocked, Jessica looked at Edward to gauge his reaction to this insult but he didn't look even remotely put out.

'Ah, hello, Betsey. I was going to ask you if you wanted to dance later but I can see the only thing you'll be dancing with is a pole,' he said good-humouredly before making his way over to her, kissing her on both cheeks and ruffling her hair. 'How are things at the Sunset? Are you still happy there, because if not, you know you're welcome to stay here until my realtor finds something?'

'I'm fine,' said Betsey. 'In fact, I'm kinda hoping the perfect place doesn't turn up anytime soon. I'm having a fabulous time and meeting some great people. At the moment every night is cocktail night.'

Jessica couldn't believe what she was hearing, but seeing as Edward was so cool with things she could hardly begrudge Betsey having a good time. As she watched the two of them gossiping away amicably she realized he really hadn't been lying. Whatever had happened between them had obviously ended cordially and when Betsey cracked a gag about trying to pull another movie star that night, only a younger model, Edward didn't even bat an eyelid. He just roared with laughter. How modern, thought Jessica, who was left feeling faintly perplexed, a feeling which turned to amusement when Pierre the party planner raced by in an emergency state of neuroses about something. He was almost foaming at the mouth.

Pretty soon the first of the guests started trickling in and amongst them was Angelica, arriving uncharacteristically punctually, beautiful in peach chiffon, diamonds and silver Jimmy Choos.

'Hi, Mom,' said Jessica, greeting her with a warm hug. 'I can't believe you're actually here and thanks so much again for coming on the show last week.'

'Yes,' said Angelica wryly. 'You had me well and truly duped, but I don't mind. It's good that your father and I are on speaking terms again.'

'And, Mom, I'm so pleased you didn't marry Graydon.'

'Me too, Jessica, though not as pleased as my waxer is now she's back to only doing me,' she said, giving her daughter a cheeky wink. 'Now, where is Edward? I should say hello.'

'Through there,' said Jessica, laughing as she pointed in the direction of the loudest room in the house where she'd last spotted Edward running in with Vincent, like schoolboys who were planning trouble.

The party went with a swing. It wasn't your average sixty-fifth birthday party and at one point Dulcie and Jessica had to laugh as they watched their fathers jiving away as if their lives depended on it, sandwiched between breasts all younger than their owners. Later, Vincent and Will Smith performed the most brilliant live duet together and afterwards, when Edward proudly introduced Jessica to Will, a flicker of recognition passed across his handsome face as he tried to recall where he might have met her before. Heady on champagne, Jessica giggled, but didn't help him out. Instead she headed for the gardens in search of fresh air and her friends, only to find Angelica and Pam having the most almighty row, at which point she wished she hadn't bothered.

'Why would I waste my time keeping your wretched letters? Yes, you're right, I did think you were a lousy mother,' Pam was shouting, 'but that doesn't mean I would resort to anything so low.'

'Mom, Pam,' said Jessica, rushing over to stand between the two women. 'Stop this. Now!'

Angelica's eyes were blazing and Jessica had never seen her so riled. She was so caught up in what she was saying to Pam that she hardly even registered Jessica's presence.

'I knew you had a problem with me. You were so protective of your little brother, you couldn't even bear the fact that he might actually care about a woman properly for once in his life. You couldn't boss him around quite as much any more and I know you resented me because of it –'

'Utter tripe. I don't know what you're talking about and another thing . . .'

Jessica looked from one woman to the other. They looked like two animals who were about to pounce, and she realized she needed back-up. Leaving the two of them screaming at each other, she ran back to the house to fetch her dad.

Minutes later, the troops had gathered and Edward,

Vincent, Jill and Jessica were all trying to make themselves heard over the din of Angelica and Pam's argument.

'Quiet,' said Edward, but to no avail. By now the two women's insults had reached fever pitch.

'You come in here, thinking you can wipe the slate clean after twenty-odd years –' screamed Pam.

'Stop it!' hollered Jessica.

'If Bernard could hear you now he would be ashamed,' yelled Angelica, at which point Pam lost control and slapped her round the face.

'Don't you dare bring my Bernard's name into it,' said Pam, her eyes flinty and her entire body shaking with anger.

'Pam, Mom, stop it NOW!' screamed Jessica. 'That's enough.'

Trembling, Angelica clutched her face then began to weep quietly. Pam still shook with fury.

'Listen to me,' said Jessica. 'All of you. I won't have this any more. Until a short time ago I thought my mom had walked out on me because she didn't care, but it wasn't true. Mom was really ill, seriously ill, so give her a break because it's incredibly brave of her to come here today.'

Everybody shifted on their feet nervously. Pam looked faintly ashamed.

'I shouldn't have hit you. That was unforgiveable,' she muttered.

'And Mom, I know Pam wouldn't have hidden the letters that you wrote. She's one of the kindest people I've ever met and far too honest, so if she had, she would have told you by now anyway. So stop obsessing.'

'OK,' sobbed Angelica. 'But I wish I knew who did because they may have changed the course of our lives.'

'Well, I don't think we're ever going to find out,' said Jessica. 'So we just have to get on with concentrating on the here and now.'

Just then, Consuela, who had been given the night off and was there as a guest, emerged from the house. Spotting the group, she waved and politely called over, 'Hi, Mr G, this is a wonderful party.'

'Good, glad you're having a good time. You deserve it,' called back Edward.

Consuela gave him a little wave and staggered back in the direction of the house, clearly a little the worse for wear.

'Her,' said Pam, staring after Consuela, her face a picture of astonishment. 'That's it. Who would have daily access to Edward's mail? Not me, by the way, which rather puts a spanner in your theory,' she added, shooting Angelica a filthy look. 'The answer is staring us in the face. It must have been Consuela and I always thought she was a bit in love with you, Teddy.'

'Oh, for God's sake, Pam,' said Jill in frustration. 'Will you all stop with these ridiculous theories?'

'Why?' said Angelica 'I think she may have a point.'

'She does have a soft spot for you, Ed,' piped up Vincent, who was swaying slightly.

'Oh, for Christ's sake,' said Edward. 'She would never do anything so awful. Would she . . . ?' He thought about it for a fraction of a second and then yelled in his best booming baritone, 'Consuela? Could you come over here for a second?'

Jessica swallowed. She loved Consuela. It would break her heart to find out she wasn't quite as trustworthy as they'd always thought she was. This didn't feel right somehow.

Up ahead, Consuela turned round and weaved her way back to the group. 'What is it, Mr G?'

'We were just wondering. When Angelica left all those years ago, did you ever see any letters arrive from her? It's just that we can't figure out where they might have got to.'

'No, Mr G, if I had I would have put them to one side, but anyway, Jill usually takes care of the post because only a small bit of it comes here. The rest goes to the office.'

'Oh, right,' said Edward calmly. 'Of course.'

For a second, silence descended while everyone tried to accept the fact they would probably never know the truth behind the letters. Moments later, however, their alcohol-soaked brains seemed to catch up and all raced to the next possibility.

'Hang on a minute,' said Edward, spinning round to face his manager. 'I thought only fan mail went to the office.'

'It does,' said Jill, flapping her hands around. 'You're all starting to confuse one another here. Look, for crying out loud, let's get back inside and enjoy this party of yours, Edward. Come on.'

'Wait a minute,' said Jessica. 'Thinking about it, Jill, we never got much post here. Usually you bring it with you. Why is that?'

'Yes, why is that?' repeated Angelica, looking ashen and confused.

'Why do I do half the stuff I do for your father?' said Jill. 'Christ, if I didn't do half the things I did he'd still be waiting tables,' she added.

'I'm sorry?' said Edward.

'Jill,' said Jessica calmly, 'if you had anything to do with this then it's time to own up and just tell us. If you care one iota for this family then you have to, because living with not knowing is tearing us apart.'

'I didn't do anything with any . . .' Jill trailed off. The game was up. 'OK,' she said, going for another tactic. 'I did shield Edward from the letters,' she conceded, 'but it was for the good of his career and his well being. I spent a long time coercing him out of the slump you'd left him in,' she spat at Angelica. 'So when you started writing every five minutes I didn't want him going backwards. He'd found his feet again but if he'd heard from you he would have taken you back in a heartbeat, which would have ruined his reputation. How can a leading man go back to the woman who left him? Don't you see? It would have been the end of his career.'

'Don't you think that was my dilemma to work out?' asked Edward icily.

'Not really,' said Jill defiantly. 'As your manager it's up to me to look out for you, to protect you and make sure you do what's right for your image.'

'I'm going to get a drink and get back to the party,' said Vincent, who looked horrified by what he was hearing. 'Edward, I think you should do the same. We've heard enough.'

'I'll be there in a second,' he said stonily, not moving his glare from Jill who was looking more unsure by the second.

'How could you?' said Jessica, echoing what the rest of the party all wanted to know.

'It was easy,' said Jill. 'And I still believe to this day that I did the right thing.'

'Then you're fired,' said Edward.

'Over this?' asked Jill incredulously.

'Oh, yes, and you can tell that producer Brendan to stick his picture up his arse because I won't be doing it whether they sue me or not. After that I don't want anything to do with you ever again.'

Jill shot him the filthiest look she could summon but, knowing she was beaten, stalked back to the house, bristling with resentment and furious to have been caught out.

'I'm so sorry, Pam,' said Angelica suddenly.

'It's all right, love,' soothed Pam, looking deeply sad but like she meant it. 'We've all been through enough. It's time to put the past to bed.'

Now Edward turned to Angelica. 'I'm sorry, Ange.'

'For what?'

'For doubting you and for all those years we missed.'

There wasn't much Angelica could say to that so Jessica went up and wrapped her arms around her mother, enveloping her in a hug she'd never needed so much in all her life.

38

Later, as the party started to wind down – early by British standards, late by LA ones – Jessica found herself sitting on a step in her huge hallway, watching Dulcie slow dance with her husband to be. Having finally taken some time to properly get to know Kevin, Jessica had to admit he was an absolute sweetie. He was a wannabe, there was no getting away from that. He was also a little naive and a bit star-struck, but he clearly adored Dulcie for all the right reasons. The two of them were besotted.

'Hey, you.'

Jessica turned to find Betsey approaching. Her ex-stepmom sat down next to her, and as she did so her skirt rode up until it looked like she wasn't wearing one.

'Hey,' Jessica said, vaguely wondering what Betsey wanted. It was unlike her to seek her out. Still, they sat in perfectly comfortable silence until Jessica said, 'You OK?'

'Yeah, fine. Better than I thought I would be, actually.'

Jessica swallowed. Maybe assuming that Betsey and her dad were totally cool about breaking up had been presumptuous.

'So I'm assuming you've met someone else,' said Jessica.

Betsey turned and looked Jessica square in the eye, an odd expression on her face. 'You should never assume anything, but you should talk to Edward about it,' she said eventually. 'You guys are so close, after all. I thought you shared everything.'

Jessica was just wondering how to respond to such a defensive, ambiguous answer when Betsey spoke up again.

'Look, I know you don't like me much, Jessica, but I want you to know that I married your father for all the right reasons, and in the end we let each other go for all the right reasons too. You know, everyone deserves to be adored, right?'

Jessica nodded. Her dad certainly did. 'I guess so,' she said quietly, experiencing another pang for the person *she* adored. It felt like a lifetime since she'd seen Paul. 'Betsey?' she ventured.

'Yeah?'

'I don't . . . not like you.'

'Good. I don't not like you either, and hey, you never know, maybe now Edward and I aren't together it might be easier for us to be friends?'

Jessica nodded but didn't say anything. It might have been easier if she hadn't dumped her father. As it was, her loyalties lay firmly with him.

'Anyway, I'll see you around, Jess,' said Betsey, giving her a slightly awkward hug before slinking off back into the last remnants of the party, her buttocks undulating in her ridiculously short skirt, reminding Jessica of a racehorse.

Suddenly she felt tired. Tired to the marrow in her bones. She glanced at her phone again, checking for messages from Paul. She missed him so acutely it was almost painful. It was time to find somewhere quiet to escape to. Maybe even go to bed.

Her shoes were starting to hurt so she took them off and padded towards the kitchen where the staff were clearing up all the food debris and hundreds of used glasses. She got herself a glass of water, said goodnight to everyone and headed for the main staircase. As she reached the landing, however, she heard a sound coming from Edward's bedroom. Yuk, she thought primly, wrinkling her nose as it dawned upon her that someone was making out in her dad's bedroom. Gross.

She wondered what to do, but in the end took a detour down the corridor to investigate. It would be better if she found the culprits as opposed to her dad, who would not be impressed and might well punch their lights out. Edging closer to the door, she felt quite offended as a woman squealed and then groaned, obviously in fits of passion. How dare they come up here? The upstairs part of the house was supposed to be off limits. It was downright rude. Standing there on the landing, she was on the verge of ignoring it when the groaning and panting started to pick up the pace again. At that point she swiftly reached a self-righteous, champagne-fuelled decision. She was going to sling the perpetrators out of her dad's room. Apart from anything else, she didn't think she'd be able to sleep with this racket going on only metres down the corridor from her room.

Determinedly she flung the door open, only to be met with the deeply inappropriate sight of her father in bed with someone (presumably that sneaky nymphomaniac Betsey). Caught in the act, Edward sat up guiltily, but she just yelped and buried down into the sheets, covering herself up.

'Jessica!' exclaimed Edward, his face on fire.

'I'm sorry,' Jessica mumbled, turning to go. Turning to run. Preferably out of the house and into the ocean.

'It's not what you think,' tried Edward.

'Oh, I don't think,' countered Jessica. 'Believe me, I don't want to give this a minute's thought ever again.' She felt a bit sick. Seeing one of your parents 'at it' was repellent. No matter what age you were, it was preferable to imagine that you had actually been delivered by a stork and that your own conception had been immaculate. Parents didn't, *shouldn't* have sex.

Then embarrassment and revulsion slowly gave way to hot rage. What the hell were they even playing at? Making out like a couple of teenagers when the party hadn't even finished and guests were waiting downstairs to say goodbye. It was so rude. And why had Betsey given her all that crap about being friends? If that was what she really wanted then leading her dad on wasn't the best way to go about it. And what a jerk he was, falling for that pathetic cry for attention that she was wearing. Freaking assholes.

'We'll talk about this in the morning, Jessica,' said Edward authoritatively.

'Fine, I'm going to bed so keep the noise down if you wouldn't mind, Betsey,' she said in disgust before turning on her heel.

'Oh, for goodness' sake, didn't we agree? No more secrets, Edward,' a familiar voice spluttered from under the sheets. A familiar voice with a French accent.

'Mom?'

'Jessica,' said Angelica, timidly pulling back the sheets. She sat up, pulling the covers tightly around her as she did so. Her hair was wild and all over the place but at least she had the good grace to look mortified with embarrassment.

'I'm so sorry you had to find out like this. We have obviously had too much champagne, but I think if you're going to discover your parents having hanky-panky, better that it is with each other, *non*?'

Jessica, who was dying to escape to her room where she planned on smothering her head with a pillow, wasn't so sure she agreed. Then she started to see the funny side.

'Well,' she ventured grudgingly, feeling slightly more forgiving now she knew who her father had been seeing to, 'at least now I can say something I've been dying to say for years.'

'What's that?' asked Edward.

"Night, Mom, 'night, Dad.'

'Goodnight, Jessica,' her parents chorused.

She shut the door.

39

Jessica flew back to England on the Friday night wondering how the next few days were going to pan out. She was glad she had the whole weekend to hang out with Paul and recover from her jet lag, but knew it was to be punctuated by a few confessions to her workmates, her resignation and a dinner party at Mike and Diane's, all of which she could probably have done without. On the plane she reflected upon everything that had happened, wondering where she could even start when it came to telling Paul about her trip. Her parents were officially back together and, though she fervently regretted finding out in the way she had (*la la la la la*), she was pleased. She was scared too, of course, and worried about what might happen if it didn't work out, what it might do to them all, but also ecstatic that they were giving it a go.

In one way she was quite sad to be leaving already. She hadn't seen everyone she'd wanted to see and could have done with a couple more days with her parents. Her *parents* – using the word in the sense of a couple was so alien. In another way she was proud that, after only a matter of months of living in another country, she had so much to get back for. Her time in England wasn't over yet, but she knew now for sure that one day she'd be coming home. It was just a question of when. Once or twice she'd indulged in fantasizing about Paul coming with her, but knew he'd probably never leave his family, so when it came to that particular issue she preferred to stick her head back in the sand.

It was weird, Jessica mused, one eye on the movie; now she knew it was Edward who had fallen for somebody else, the person she was left feeling sorry for was Betsey. Throughout her marriage to Edward she must have sensed she was competing with something unbeatable, which probably explained much of her demanding behaviour, maybe even her quest for a baby. Her mind flitted back to Paul. Even if there was the slightest chance she could still be with him years down the line, would they be strong enough to weather all the strange, terrible and wonderful things that life would inevitably throw at them? After all, her parents were the perfect example that love alone wasn't always enough to bind people together once life had shoved one if its spanners in the works.

The minute she landed at Heathrow in the early hours of Saturday morning, all Jessica could think about was reaching Paul, which was why, one long tube ride later, when she finally arrived at his flat, she was puzzled and a little disappointed by his lukewarm greeting.

'Hey, you,' she said, flinging herself towards him as he opened the door.

'Hi,' he said, scooping her up. They kissed and she felt exquisitely happy until a sixth sense made her pull away.

'What is it? Are you OK?' she questioned, noting apprehension in his expression.

'Yeah, I'm fine. Let's get you and that big bag in.'

But Jessica had travelled too far and been through too much to let anything lie, even for a second.

'Wait,' she said, feeling panicky, and remaining rooted to the spot in the hallway. 'Seriously, what's up? I can tell there's something and I don't want to spend the whole day wondering what it might be so just tell me. Please?'

Paul looked terribly uncertain and Jessica knew then for sure that something was causing him inner turmoil. One of the things she'd always found so attractive about him was his underlying vulnerability, which right now was paddling worryingly close to the surface.

'Please tell me,' repeated Jessica shakily.

Paul sighed. 'It's nothing, Jess. It's just . . . while you were gone, Natasha made a few weird comments about stuff. Stupid things that I'm sure she's probably bullshitting about anyway.'

'Like what?' she demanded to know, cold dread worming its way round her belly.

'Just silly stuff,' dismissed Paul, regarding Jessica thoughtfully for a second before admitting defeat. Finding out the truth had to be preferable to being eaten up by suspicion. 'OK, Natasha said that you gave her this thing which enables you to get free designer shoes or something. Anyway, she went to the shop and they wouldn't let her take anything because it was registered to someone else's name. She was really peeved about it and then said that before you went away you and Mike kept having chats about stuff in his office.'

Jessica opened her mouth to explain but Paul continued.

'She looked in his diary and there was a note which said "ask Jessica if she's free on 14th October" . . . or something like that,' he said casually, trying not to look as though he'd remembered it verbatim, which he had. 'Anyway, I'm sure there's some explanation. Or maybe he just knows another Jessica?' he suggested hopefully. 'Because obviously there would never be anything going on between you and Mike, would there?'

'What the hell was Natasha doing looking through his diary?' blustered Jessica, furious to have been put in this position, and hating the fact that Paul had been given cause to feel suspicious, something she knew would have tormented him terribly. How could she have been so stupid as not to have rung Jimmy Choo to warn them Natasha would be coming instead of her? She needed to get to Natasha before she wreaked any more damage.

'Hardly the thing I'm most worried about right now,' Paul snapped, frustrated and annoyed suddenly. He'd been waiting to be reassured for nearly a week now and his patience had just run out.

'OK,' said Jessica, wishing she didn't have to do this now. She felt grimy and horrid from travelling but knew it couldn't wait. 'Firstly, there is an explanation and, secondly, when I tell you what it is, you'll understand why I couldn't say anything before.'

'Go on,' said Paul. Now that she'd admitted there was 'something' to explain, his voice had taken on a cold edge.

'I've been babysitting Mike's kids,' she said quickly.

Paul couldn't have looked more surprised if she'd told him she was an Elvis impersonator in her spare time.

'He and Diane, his wife, were in a real fix, so a while back I offered to help out. Anyway, it turned out – and if you repeat this to anyone, I'll be so upset. Promise you won't?' she said.

'Promise,' said Paul dumbly.

'It turned out that Diane wasn't very well. Since having their second baby, Ava, she's been rather depressed, so I've been helping out on a regular basis, afternoons here and there and a bit of babysitting, you know? Anyway, I really like the kids and I've enjoyed it actually,' she said defensively. 'I'm sorry I didn't tell you, it's just I promised Diane and Mike that I wouldn't tell anyone. They didn't want the whole office gossiping about them.'

'I see,' said Paul, astonished and a little irked about how much had been kept from him. 'And you really felt you couldn't tell me any of this? I mean, fair enough if Diane's been ill. I can see why she wouldn't want everybody knowing about that, but why didn't you just tell me you were doing babysitting for them?'

Jessica swallowed.

'Oh, I get it. So all that market research stuff is bollocks then?' he said, starting to figure things out aloud. 'And you must have lied to me some evenings too.'

Now Paul was looking pretty unimpressed and Jessica found herself struggling to come up with a decent defence. Maybe she'd got so used to being secretive in England that all her lies had meshed into one. She probably had lost a bit of perspective. What harm would it have done to have given Paul a bit of a heads up? She knew she could trust him implicitly.

'Mike didn't want anyone to know, but I *was* going to tell you anyway. I just wanted to check with Diane first,' she said truthfully. 'Which I finally got round to the other day, just before I went away. I've been meaning to for ages, but every time I go round there, it gets so busy with the little ones I end up getting side-tracked.'

Paul shrugged his shoulders, almost giving himself a bit of a shake, as if to rid himself of the air of unease that had been surrounding him. Jessica was right. She hadn't done anything wrong. In fact, she'd been helping people and it just hadn't been the right time to tell him. He walked towards her.

'Look, let's just forget about it, shall we?' he said firmly. 'I don't want to spend any more time worrying about bloody Mike. Not when we've got dinner at his house to get through tonight and not when we've got serious catching up to do.'

'Me neither,' giggled Jessica. She could see she'd been let off the hook and felt swamped with relief. Happily she let him pull her towards him and kiss her gently, then more hungrily as their feelings took over.

'As long as you haven't got any more deep, dark secrets hidden away,' laughed Paul, leading her towards the bedroom.

Jessica didn't reply. After all, how could she?

Still, telling Paul about her sideline in childcare had come as a huge relief and the time had come to fill Kerry in too. Now that the Bond show was over, she was ready to give in her notice and officially become Diane's nanny.

40

'All quiet on the western front?' asked Mike as Diane crept into the kitchen, having just put the girls to bed.

'Think so. Had to promise Grace we'd save her some pudding though.'

'No worries there,' grinned Mike. He'd gone rather overboard on food, so excited was he about entertaining his younger colleagues tonight. He wanted them to have a really nice time. He also wanted to show them that he wasn't such a bad guy and that he wasn't so different to them either. Of course, being Mike, he hadn't stopped to think that a 'spag bol' and a few beers might, in that case, have been more appropriate. As it was, his guests were going to be treated to a three-course meal, which included stuffed sirloin of beef, home-made chocolate mousse and some very expensive wine. He'd be offering them champagne on arrival and had put olives, crisps and cheese straws out for people to nibble on.

This was the first dinner party Mike and Diane had given since they'd had Ava and tidying the house, laying the table, preparing the food, getting two children fed, washed and into bed had been an enormous challenge, but one they'd risen to rather well as a couple, he thought. He was inordinately proud of his wife. She'd raced around just as frantically as him all day and as long as no one looked in any of the cupboards (where they'd stuffed most of the children's plastic crap), no one would ever know what a feat it had been to get it all done in time.

'Well, if you're under control in here then I might just go and put some lippy on quickly,' said Diane.

'Yes, do, darling, I'm fine. Though I'm wondering which wine glasses we should use. The normal ones or our wedding crystal?'

'Oh, normal I think, definitely,' said Diane. 'It's not Christmas. You don't want to look like you're trying too hard.'

Mike considered this for a second. The crystal probably would be a flourish too far, he thought, as he went to retrieve some freshly baked ciabatta from the oven. 'Right as ever,' he conceded. Then, 'Come here, you. You look lovely in that top. Makes your boobs look great.'

'Thanks,' said Diane, going to give her husband a hug. There was no need to tell him she'd hiked them up with a Wonderbra. Two children later, what had once been her pride and joy looked a bit like deflated balloons these days. Spaniel's ears.

'I have to say, I feel all right too,' she said. 'I'm actually looking forward to this evening, whereas a few months ago I couldn't have even contemplated it.'

'Mmm,' said Mike, suddenly feeling a bit fruity. Diane had finished breast-feeding and, while he knew it wasn't very 'new mannish' of him to admit it, he was happy to reclaim what were rightfully his once more. 'Well, if you play your cards right,' he said suggestively, 'maybe later we could do something else we haven't done in months?'

Diane giggled. 'Maybe,' she replied just as the doorbell rang. 'They're here,' she squealed, beyond excited about seeing Jessica. She had a delicious secret to share with her, one she'd been hugging to herself all day.

Forty minutes later, Kerry, Luke, Natasha, Paul and Jessica were seated around the Connors' dining table. Conversation, which had been stilted at first while they'd all taken in their surroundings and got used to the fact that Mike was wearing an apron, was now flowing. They'd all devoured Mike's tasty avocado and crab salad starter and he was serving up delicious-smelling beef, potato dauphinoise and vegetables. Meanwhile, Diane had decided that now was as good a time as any to bring up the elephant in the room. Having spoken to Jessica on the phone earlier, she knew everyone was now aware of what had been going on, in terms of her looking after the children. She also knew that Kerry hadn't taken the news that well.

'Kerry, I honestly don't know what I'd have done without Jessica over these last couple of months,' piped up Diane, 'but I want you to know that I never deliberately set out to poach her. Did I, Mike?'

'Er, no,' her husband answered doubtfully.

'And Jessica only kept it secret because I asked her to,' added Diane bravely. 'You see, I wasn't in a particularly good place. I was suffering from post-natal depression, to be completely frank. Not a very severe case, but bad enough, so she was helping me out in more ways than one . . .'

Jessica glanced nervously at Kerry to gauge her reaction. She wasn't exactly cracking open the party poppers, but she did give Jessica a small smile. Bless Diane for speaking up like that.

Having phoned everybody earlier to tell them about her moonlighting, and to tell Kerry that she planned on leaving once she'd helped her find a new assistant, Jessica had decided that one secret at a time was enough to cope with. The revelation that she'd been working for Mike as opposed to anything more suspect seemed to have silenced Natasha too, for now. So instead of telling Paul her life story she'd kept quiet, figuring one more day couldn't possibly make any difference. As a result, the two of them had spent a lovely day, happily lazing around in bed, watching DVDs, making love and sleeping. She planned on having the 'other chat' with him on Sunday. Tomorrow.

'Kerry,' said Jessica, 'you've been an awesome boss and I've enjoyed working for you so much, but I bet your next assistant will be better than me. I'm not sure I'm entirely cut out for showbiz really, whereas I love being around children. In fact, for the first time ever I'm starting to work out what I should do with my life. And, besides, you've got me for two more weeks so I'll help set up all the interviews.'

Kerry shrugged, not convinced. 'Well, I thought you were great at the job myself. I doubt whoever I get next would be able to salvage a disaster like you did the other week when Nadia Vladinokova dropped us in it.'

Jessica blushed and was about to reply when, to her surprise, Diane winked at her.

'So what have you decided you want to do?' asked Paul, picking up on what she'd said before. 'You never told me that part.'

'Well, I'd rather not say yet,' Jessica said coyly. 'Not till I've looked into it a bit more and stuff.'

'Oh, hang on now,' said Diane. 'You can't keep us in suspense like that. At least give us a clue?'

'Yeah, go on,' encouraged Luke.

'O-K,' said Jessica hesitantly. 'Well, I was thinking that while I'm working for Diane I might also look into doing a course in child psychology. I think I'd like to be some kind of child therapist one day.'

'You'd be amazing at that,' enthused Diane. 'You've got such a great way with children, so it follows that you'd be brilliant at understanding how their minds work.'

'I agree. I mean, I haven't seen you with the kids but you've said yourself you're not that fussed about working in TV so I think it's brilliant that you're finding out what it is you really want to do,' said Paul supportively.

Natasha rolled her eyes. She was growing heartily bored of this 'Jessica appreciation' evening. 'Well, I'm just relieved there won't be any more cloak and dagger behaviour in the office,' she interjected. 'I mean, at one point I thought you and Mike were having an affair.'

Diane swivelled round to glare at Natasha, her expression thunderous.

'I mean . . . not an affair obviously . . . that was a joke . . . just something fishy . . . Anyway, where did you two meet?' Natasha improvised hastily, scrabbling out of the hole she'd created.

'You tell them,' grinned Mike, reaching over to squeeze Diane's hand affectionately.

'At a rave,' said Diane, still glaring at Natasha.

Paul couldn't help himself. 'Come again? You met *Mike* at a *rave*? As in a rave in a club?'

'Yes,' said Mike. 'Well, it was more of a warehouse than a club really, wasn't it, darling?'

'Yes,' said Diane, a wistful smile playing on her lips. 'I'll never forget you writing your phone number on my tummy.'

Paul looked so stunned that Jessica had to giggle. Luke was similarly flabbergasted. Kerry and Natasha had both stopped eating, even though their mouths were full of food.

'I always had you down as more of a James Blunt kind of guy,' said Luke eventually.

'Oh, I am,' said Mike. 'I love James Blunt. Don't you?'

Luke didn't reply. He was too busy struggling with an image of Mike, Mike who played golf and talked about property all the time, wearing white gloves and dancing on speakers to drum 'n' bass. It was turning out to be quite an evening, although he was still mortified about his earlier faux pas. Mike had offered him a glass of 'poo' as soon as he'd walked in and not ever having heard this middle-class shortening of the word champagne before, he'd assumed Mike was making some kind of juvenile, lavatorial joke. As a result he'd replied, to Mike's alarm, 'No thanks, but I'll have a glass of piss, please.'

Mike had looked totally baffled until a highly amused Kerry had pointed out his mistake. And now all his assumptions about Mike were being challenged. Maybe his boss hadn't segued from school uniform straight into chinos and dinner parties after all?

'Blimey,' said Paul, impressed as the world of the Connors seemed to turn on its head.

'Oh, everyone has a past, you know,' said Mike, looking at Paul. 'And it's not always what you think.'

Jessica chuckled to herself, loving the revelations and

proud of Mike and Diane for managing to silence some of the most outspoken people she knew.

'In fact,' said Mike, getting up, 'let's put a few old house tracks on now, shall we?'

Bounding eagerly over to where his iPod was, he switched off the carefully constructed dinner party playlist that was currently emanating from it and scrolled through his tunes till he found a Utah Saints track.

'It's true,' shouted Diane, struggling to compete with the thudding bass line that was suddenly booming around her kitchen. 'People are never what they seem on the surface.'

As she said this, once again Jessica was alarmed to note that Diane was staring right at her, a disconcertingly knowing expression on her face.

The evening continued apace, everyone having to shout to be heard over the hardcore house music that Mike was now insisting on playing. For the first time ever he'd sensed some grudging respect from his workmates and as a result was determined to go with his new image of a raver. An image that was rather ruined when, as he doled out dessert, Diane suddenly started flapping at him to turn the music off. When he did, the sound of Grace screaming for her mother could be heard through the monitor.

'Switch that bloody racket off,' snapped Diane. 'It's woken Grace.'

'Shit,' said Mike sheepishly, dashing over to turn the volume down.

'I can't wait to see her,' said Jessica longingly. 'I've really missed her.'

'Then let's both go,' insisted Diane. 'Come on.'

Grace was delighted when both her mother and Jessica

appeared in her room, but was so sleepy that she didn't take too long to settle back down.

'Switch my light on,' she instructed, her eyes already drooping shut. 'Stroke my hair.'

'Yes, madame,' whispered Diane affectionately, nodding at Jessica to go. Jessica started creeping out of the room but Grace immediately opened one eye again and whined, 'I want Jessica to stay too, Mummy.'

'OK, darling, Jess will stay. We both will,' Diane said, stroking her little girl's hair, soothing her back to sleep. Jessica crept over to the chair in the corner of the room and sat down. A couple of minutes later when it looked like Grace had finally dropped off, Diane turned to Jessica. 'Are you OK?'

'Yeah, I'm having a great time, thanks,' Jessica whispered back. 'The food's delicious. Mike's a great cook.'

'Listen, before we go back down I have to tell you something,' said Diane, grinning madly.

'OK...'

'I think I know.'

'Know what?' said Jessica, at a loss.

'That you're Edward Granger and Angelica Dupree's daughter, aren't you?'

Jessica gaped at Diane, who was staring at her expectantly. It was such a shock to hear that said out loud. Her secret had been so well kept in England, she honestly couldn't believe she'd been found out.

'You are, aren't you? Go on, you can tell me.'

'How do you know?' managed Jessica eventually, realizing there was nothing to be gained from a denial. This clearly wasn't a random guess.

'Well, I was having a quick flick through *Hello*,' said Diane, looking thoroughly pleased with herself. 'And there was this huge picture of Edward Granger at an airport, with a girl who clearly didn't want her picture taken because she had a jacket wrapped round her head. Anyway, for some strange reason the girl's legs caught my eye and, you're going to think this is mad, but I sort of recognized them. Anyway, the more I stared, the more this person reminded me of you, because I could have sworn you had the same jacket too. Anyway, at first I thought it must be coincidence, so I was just staring and thinking, well, if it was Jess, what the hell would be she doing with Edward Granger? So then I got on the Internet, looked up Edward Granger and eventually a picture of you cropped up, taken a while back I think, with your friend – Dulcie, isn't it? At some fundraiser.'

Jessica nodded mutely and Diane clapped her hands together, delighted by the gossip. 'I just can't believe you didn't tell me.'

'I haven't told anyone,' said Jessica quickly, suddenly on her feet, her body having gone into fight or flight mode. 'Not even Paul.'

Diane's hand flew to her mouth. 'You're joking? Why not?'

'It's a long story,' replied Jessica vaguely, feeling nervous. She didn't like not being in control of the situation any more. It was the end of an era, she thought sadly. The end of quiet anonymity.

'Well, I'm sure you had your reasons, but I want you to know I'm a huge fan of your dad's. He's my absolute favourite Bond – well, maybe apart from the divine Pierce

Brosnan – and of course it explains how you managed to get Angelica Dupree on the show the other day. You look a lot like your dad, don't you? As soon as I knew I saw the resemblance straight away.'

This was exactly why Jessica hadn't told anyone . . .

'Diane, please don't mention this to anyone yet, will you?' pleaded Jessica. 'I really need to tell Paul and I don't want him finding out from anyone else.'

'Well, mum's the word then,' said Diane, smiling at Jessica and signalling to her that they should probably leave the room. Grace was fast asleep and it was time to rejoin the party.

'And can I just say,' said Diane, whispering at the top of the stairs, 'that although it's fantastic goss, I really couldn't care less who your parents are. You're the star as far as I'm concerned.'

It was just what Jessica needed to hear and she was so touched by the heartfelt compliment that she felt an urge to give Diane a hug. So, feeling much more reassured, she did so before following Diane back down the stairs. 'Grace asleep?' enquired Mike in an over-cheerful voice.

'Like a lamb,' said Diane. 'Now, how's the mousse? Any more for any more?'

'No thanks,' said Mike, and only then did Jessica realize that something was seriously wrong. Everyone was staring at her, there was a deathly hush and Paul was looking at her with an expression of utter contempt and something else that was harder to read. He'd also gone rather pale.

'You OK?' she said tentatively, slipping back into her seat.

'Great,' he said in a voice that suggested otherwise. 'It's amazing what you can find out through modern technology these days,' he added sarcastically, his voice unrecognizably hard and dripping with disdain.

Jessica had no idea what he was talking about. Diane looked like she did, however. Her heart racing with nervous anticipation, Jessica followed Diane's gaze until her eyes came to rest on the baby monitor that was sitting innocently in the corner.

FUCK!

'I can explain,' began Jessica.

'But I don't want you to,' retorted Paul coldly. 'In fact, I want you to fuck off and leave me alone. Or rather, I'll fuck off. Mike, Diane, thanks for dinner but I'm going now. I couldn't stomach another thing, I'm afraid.'

And with that he pushed his chair out and went off in search of his jacket.

Jessica stared helplessly around the room, searching for some support, but no one could look her in the eye. Natasha looked like she was trying not to laugh, but in the kind of way one did at a funeral or something. Nervously. 'Can't believe I didn't spot it myself,' she said now. 'Still, Edward Granger's daughter. I knew there was something special about you, Jess.'

Jess? This was transparent even by Natasha's standards.

'I'm sure you had your reasons for keeping it quiet,' offered Kerry, who wasn't enjoying seeing Jessica look so distressed. She knew how much she loved Paul. There again, she wasn't particularly happy about how hurt Paul was either and this was just the sort of thing guaranteed to wind him up. It was so frustrating. Why hadn't Jessica just told them? And what the hell was all that crap about getting her mother on the show?

'So,' attempted Luke, 'did you know Mike before? Was it part of the deal of doing the Bond show or something?'

'No,' said Jessica weakly.

Mike shook his head and was about to speak when Paul reappeared with his jacket on, looking furious still. 'Well, thanks for a great night,' he said to Mike.

'Er, pleasure,' said Mike bemusedly. He was dumbfounded by what they'd all just learned via the monitor, but was more impressed than cross. Daughter of Bond had been in their midst no less. Extraordinary really and not, as far as he could make out, any reason for Paul to get his knickers in such a twist.

'Please don't do this,' implored Jessica, but her voice came out as barely a whisper and Paul refused to even look at her.

'I won't ask if anyone knew about Jessica's little scam,' said Paul from the doorway, looking directly at Mike. 'I'll take it as a given, seeing as some of you have no problem with nepotism.'

Mike flushed red then sighed, top teeth resting on his lip. 'Do you know what, Paul? I'm glad you said that, because it just confirms what I've always suspected you really think of me. Though perhaps you'd think differently if you knew what working for my father-in-law is actually like?'

'I don't want to know,' muttered Paul, turning to leave. 'Wouldn't have minded knowing what was going on in my girlfriend's devious mind, but unlike her you don't owe me an explanation about anything.'

'Look, hold on a minute,' replied Mike, who was quite drunk. 'For a start, I didn't know anything about Jessica being related to Edward Granger, though why you're so fed up about it I shall never know. Secondly, I'm not stupid. I know you think I'm just a puppet, kow-towing to David and getting a helping hand whenever I need it, but in truth it's not really like that. Well, not completely. Anyway, to be honest, I bloody hate it. It adds enormous pressure and if ever I want to disagree with him about anything it's a nightmare because there's always a chance we're having lunch with him on Sunday.'

Paul felt ashamed suddenly. He'd only alluded to the David thing to make a dig at Jessica, but it was probably churlish of him. It wasn't Mike's fault Jessica had lied to him.

'I'm sure it must have its disadvantages,' he conceded doubtfully. 'Anyway, it's none of my business and I'm sorry if I was out of line. Thanks for dinner again, Diane. Luke, Kerry, I'll see you later.'

'Don't do this,' urged Jessica again, starting to cry. She pushed back her seat, no longer bothered about salvaging any dignity from the situation. She followed Paul out into the hallway. 'Please, Paul,' she begged. 'I care about you so much and I was going to tell you.'

'Oh, really?' said Paul, his eyes glistening with what looked suspiciously like hot tears, his expression one of disgust and disappointment. Jessica knew she needed to provide him with a proper, decent explanation but couldn't. She felt exhausted, spun out from jet lag, a bit drunk and now devastated. A combination that made finding the right words a challenge to say the least.

'I was . . . going to . . . tell you . . . tomorrow,' she just about managed.

'Well, that's easy for you to say, isn't it?'

'I was and I wanted to tell you before, but there was never a right time,' Jessica wailed, tears coursing down her face now, her nose filling up with snot. 'If I'd known I was going to meet you I never would have –'

'Save your bullshit, Jessica,' Paul replied angrily. 'You know how much honesty means to me and now I don't know if anything about us was actually real. I mean, when I think of some of the crap you've fed me,' he ran his hands through his hair frustratedly, 'when I think that we sat watching your own mother on TV together, for fuck's sake, and not once did you think to say anything. Not once. And *Cheaper by the Dozen*,' he yelled suddenly.

Jessica jumped.

'You even told me that your dad cried at *Cheaper by the Dozen*. I mean, what kind of a sick fucking laugh were you having with me then? As if Edward Granger, one of Hollywood's hardest actors of all time, would ever do that in a million years? Oh, how you must have been laughing.'

'No,' said Jessica, tears streaming down her face. 'That was true.' She couldn't stand seeing Paul like this. Couldn't believe she was the one who had caused him so much pain, when he was the last person in the world she wanted to be unhappy. How could she have let this happen?

Paul's mouth opened and for a minute it looked as though he was going to counter what she'd just said, but then he seemed to think again and a look of such awful pain flickered across his face that Jessica shuddered. Clearly not able to be around her any more, Paul zipped up his jacket and finally left, slamming the door in her face before heading off up the street as quickly as he could. There was no way he was going to give Jessica the satisfaction of seeing how upset he was. He'd opened up to her in a way he'd never felt able to with girlfriends in the past and now it turned out she was nothing but a liar and a fraud.

Still, Jessica had no such qualms about letting anyone see her cry. She stood sobbing in the hallway for a full five minutes before realizing she should probably return to the kitchen and face everyone and their questions. She was a sorry sight by now and, though it was hard to tell through her mist of tears, the faces looking back at her were, in the main, sympathetic.

'Ah, there you are,' said Mike, trying to sound as if he hadn't just heard her breaking up with her boyfriend. 'I was just going to put the kettle on. Who's for peppermint?'

41

After Jessica and Paul's row, the dinner party spluttered to a rather desultory standstill.

As everyone sat around staring mournfully at one another, Mike was first to break the silence. 'By the way,' he said, pointedly staring first at the baby monitor and then at Diane, 'the *divine* Pierce Brosnan, eh? Didn't realize you had such a crush.'

'Oh, shut up,' his wife snapped, putting him firmly in his place.

Embarrassed and unsure what to do next, Mike turned from one displacement activity – making tea – to another – washing up. Deep down, all he really wanted to do was ask Jessica loads of questions about her dad but suspected it might not be quite the right moment.

By contrast, Diane was feeling too utterly wretched to help or do anything. She was in absolute turmoil about having unwittingly wrecked things for Jessica, and wished she could turn back the clock. She also wished she could offer some comfort to Jessica but doubted the poor thing would want her anywhere near her. Still, she couldn't just stand around watching her cry her eyes out, so in the end she decided to risk being told to piss off and went to hug her better.

'I'm so sorry,' Diane kept saying once her hug had been

accepted, stroking Jessica's hair in much the same way as she had Grace's earlier.

'No, I'm the one that's sorry,' Jessica sniffed. 'I've messed up everyone's night and I should have just told you all before, but I . . .' she trailed off, too upset to continue.

'Yeah . . . I think I'm going to call some cabs,' said Natasha, wondering why on earth everyone was feeling so sorry for Jessica. They'd just found out she must be minted. Were they thick? Her dad was Edward Granger, which meant the problem was what exactly? She felt quite chuffed with herself too. She'd always known there was *something* about her. Her only regret was not having been more friendly to her . . .

A painfully long forty-five minutes later, Luke and Kerry's cab finally arrived. Typically, Natasha's had arrived in seconds, leaving Luke and Kerry to make polite conversation with the Connors, which due to the fact that they were all a bit pissed and tired, and that Jessica was sat in the corner quietly sobbing, was a fairly stressful experience.

'Thanks for a . . . really great evening,' Kerry said, darting to her feet as soon as they heard a rap on the door.

'Yeah, thanks, it was really nice and don't worry about her,' yelled Luke over-brightly, trying desperately to compensate for Jessica's misery. 'She'll be fine in the morning, I'm sure,' he said, hoping to mollify Diane who was still wringing her hands, feeling riddled with guilt about the whole situation.

'Christ, you can't half cry, Jess,' said Kerry as they spilled on to the street, Kerry and Luke dragging Jessica between them. Kerry had never been so happy to see a cab in all her life.

'My head hurts,' mumbled Jessica.

'I'm not surprised,' said Kerry, shoving her into the back seat. 'Here, I think I might have some Nurofen in my bag. Do you want one?'

'No,' replied Jessica, her voice shuddering with misery. The pounding headache she'd managed to give herself was deserved, she thought weakly, so she would suffer it like a monk in a hair shirt. Even if there was a chance that without tablets it might transform into a vomit-inducing migraine.

Kerry and Luke climbed in and when the driver enquired 'where to?' almost had their first proper row as they tried to decide what to do with the wreck that was Jessica Bender, née Granger, who had broken into a fresh round of tears.

'We can't take her back to yours,' Kerry hissed, who by now had had enough of Jessica's histrionics, had had enough of Jessica in fact and of the whole wretched shambles of an evening. 'It's not fair on Paul. She's the last person he wants to see right now.'

'She can sleep on the couch,' argued Luke. 'It's not like we have much other choice. I'm not paying to take her to Hampstead first and we can't leave her here.'

'Well, let her have this cab and we'll get another one,' said Kerry in exasperation.

'Oh, yeah, because going back into Mike's for another scintillating hour of slurred, hideously self-conscious conversation is just what I fancy now.'

'Just leave me here,' snorted Jessica suddenly, clutching wildly for the door handle. She looked dreadful. Her skin was blotchy and smeared with snot. Her eyes were surrounded by black where she'd rubbed her mascara into her face. 'I don't care where I go. I just want to be on my own.'

'See?' said Luke, folding his arms and giving Kerry a look as if to say 'Point proved. She's a suicidal maniac.'

'Fine,' said Kerry huffily. 'Yours it is then.'

'Thank God for that,' said the driver. 'So Tufnell Park, yeah? And you're sure she's not going to be sick?' he added, pointing at Jessica who was trying to get herself into something resembling the foetal position. No mean feat with three of them squashed in the back.

As it turned out, Kerry needn't have worried. When they finally got back to the flat just after midnight, Paul wasn't in, though Jessica would only accept this fact after she'd checked under his bed and poked around in his wardrobe. Relief that he wasn't going to see her in such a state mingled with disappointment and outright fear she might never see him again. Being in his room where they'd shared all their most intimate moments was too much and she sank on to his bed, sniffing his duvet for signs of his smell, wanting to be close to him in some way.

'Jesus,' said Luke, sounding nervous, as he stood observing in the doorway with Kerry. 'At least we know she really cares about him. She wasn't making that bit up, was she?'

'No,' said Kerry, shutting the door on Jessica so that she could be mad and hysterical in peace. 'All a bit bloody weird though, isn't it? I keep thinking of things we may have said about her dad at work and stuff. I don't know how she managed to keep quiet all this time.'

'I know,' said Luke, flopping exhausted on to the sofa in the sitting room and pulling Kerry down next to him. He pulled her close for a hug.

'Sorry about before. I didn't mean to get shirty with you.'

'That's OK.'

'Kerry?'

'Yeah?'

'James Bond's daughter is in my flat.'

'I know,' laughed Kerry suddenly as the absurdity of it all got the better of her. 'And not just that. James Bond's daughter is in your flat, sniffing Paul Fletcher's bed linen.'

'Well, he has got a licence to thrill,' quipped Luke.

'Though tonight he was more shaken than stirred,' added Kerry, giggling.

'Judging by the look on his face when he left we should probably rename him *Thunderballs*.'

'That was crap,' laughed Kerry out loud. 'Still, maybe he wants to knock *The Living Daylights* out of her?'

'Ah, Miss Moneypenny, I like it, apart from the fact that you've just made my best mate sound like a wife beater.'

'Actually,' said Kerry, 'I can understand in a way why she might not have wanted any of us to know.' Slightly sobered by this thought, she snuggled into Luke before saying, 'Anyway, where the hell is Paul do you reckon?'

'His mum's, I suppose,' came the reply.

42

By the next morning, Jessica had come to pretty much the same conclusion as Luke. Paul must be at his mum's. Now he'd found out who she was, in such a dreadful way, she needed desperately to find him, to try and explain how this whole thing had happened, even if she barely knew herself.

When she first opened her eyes after a fitful night's sleep, for a lovely few seconds it was like nothing had happened, probably due to the fact she was in Paul's bed. And then she remembered. Everything had happened and it was all disastrous.

Her head ached, her body ached, but most of all her heart ached with sadness. Still, lying around in Paul's bedroom certainly wasn't going to get her anywhere, so after a shower she headed dolefully back to Pam's, having decided that Paul probably needed a day or so to cool off. He certainly wasn't answering his phone at any rate. She'd see him at work tomorrow.

However, upon arriving at work the next day, to Jessica's dismay he wasn't there. He'd phoned in sick, which Mike had sensibly decided not to dispute. Having psyched herself up for a showdown, Jessica felt herself deflate back into her previous pitiful state. The day was endless, she couldn't concentrate on anything and she was convinced everyone in the office was talking about her (they were), so it wasn't long before she was online, researching into tickets home. She never got as far as booking one though. Apart from the fact she'd made a commitment to Diane, she also knew deep down there was no way she was going anywhere till things were reconciled with Paul.

At one point, keen to escape curious eyes, she left the office under false pretences and headed for the canteen where she rang Dulcie, who wasn't as sympathetic as she'd hoped she might be.

'Listen, Jess, you knew what kind of guy Paul was when you first hooked up with him. He's principled and totally unimpressed by celebrity, for some strange reason. You should have known he was going to freak out about this. However, for whatever reason, you like him, so don't just sit around feeling sorry for yourself. Get out there and sort it out.'

'Really?'

'Really,' said her friend.

The next day Paul came into work, knowing that Mike would only tolerate one day of skiving before it became an issue. He looked dreadful. Tired, drained and utterly fed up.

'Hi,' Jessica said, having nervously approached his desk. The relief at simply seeing him again was immense but he barely even looked up.

'I'm busy,' he muttered. 'Need to catch up from yesterday.'

'Right,' she said, sloping away, feeling about as big as a gnat and wondering what on earth she could do to make things better again.

The day crawled by, punctuated by the usual production meeting and people sidling up to her desk asking her questions about her parents. She didn't want to be rude but also didn't see what business any of it was of theirs, and couldn't bear the judgemental scowls Paul kept sending in her direction. When it was finally time to leave, Jessica followed him down the corridor. 'Paul!' she called but he didn't even turn round.

Feeling utterly bereft and beaten, Jessica shuffled despondently back to the office where only a handful of people remained and slumped on to her desk.

'Still not talking to you?' asked Kerry, who was about to leave for the day with Luke.

Jessica shook her head. 'He's so *angry*.'

'Well, what did you expect?' said Luke, reasonably enough. 'You know what he's like. Paul is the man people like me aspire to be. He's solid, a properly decent bloke, and he's never been able to understand when people are anything but straightforward.'

'But I didn't mean to hurt him,' wailed Jessica. 'I just messed up, but not because I'm a bad person. I've just been stupid. Really stupid and selfish, I guess, because I just wanted to be me, without any of the fuss that surrounds my family.'

'Well, I don't know why you're telling us all of this. It's him you should be telling,' said Kerry frankly.

Jessica looked up. 'You're right,' she said, a determined look in her eye. 'Where's Paul going now?'

'His mum's,' said Luke, earning himself a sharp nudge from Kerry who wasn't convinced Paul wanted her to know.

Ten minutes later, Jessica Bender, née Granger, was headed for the land they call Staines, albeit after an argument with

Luke and Kerry about giving her the address. (Paul had made a point of telling Kerry not to let Jessica have it.)

Setting off to do something about fixing the mess she'd created felt like the first sensible thing she'd done in ages, although the wisdom of her plan felt rather flimsy when the journey took hours. Literally. First she had to wait ages for a tube. Then the train she got on at Waterloo spent centuries sitting on the tracks in between stations for no apparent reason. Still, it all felt like penance to Jessica and also put off the moment of truth. The moment she'd find out if Paul could forgive her.

What felt like years later, she finally arrived in the fairly non-descript place that is Staines. She asked a succession of passers-by for help with directions, some of whom were quite helpful, others of whom were either thick or deliberately trying to sabotage her finding Paul. She was exhausted by the time she did eventually find the right place but not exhausted enough to miss the fact that Paul's mum's house would have fitted into Pam's three times over. It looked pleasant enough. It was small, red brick and semi-detached but with no discerning features. Just a red-brick box with a well-cared-for front garden. No wonder he hated her. She hated herself, she thought sorrowfully.

She rang the bell.

A sixteen-year-old girl who Jessica knew must be Lucy answered.

'Hi,' said Jessica quietly, nervous as hell, a wan smile on her face.

'Hi,' said Lucy.

'Nice to meet you,' said Jessica. 'I'm Jessica.'

'I figured as much,' said Lucy. 'You look upset,' she added when Jessica looked at her questioningly. 'And Paul's been in a foul mood so . . .' She trailed off, unsure what to say. She loved her brother and it was with him that her loyalties lay. Still, like Mike, when Paul had told her what had happened she'd failed to see what real crime Jessica had committed just by being the daughter of someone famous. Besides, Lucy was desperate for them to make up so she could find out loads of gossip and possibly meet James Bond one day.

'Is Paul in?'

'Er . . . no?' replied Lucy, nodding her head at the same time.

'Oh . . . right,' said Jessica, at a loss to know what to do next.

'Sod it,' said Lucy after a moment's consideration as she stood back to let Jessica through. 'Life's too short . . .' she said, pointing through to what must be the lounge.

Jessica took a deep breath and tried to gather her strength. 'Thanks,' she muttered, walking past Lucy down the tiny hallway. Right, here goes. Terrified, she pushed open the door to her right, only to find a very dejected-looking Paul slumped on the sofa watching football.

'Hi,' she said cautiously.

'What are you doing here?' he said dispassionately, not taking his eyes off the game. 'I thought I'd made my feelings clear.'

'You have,' mumbled Jessica, 'but I really want to explain. You see –'

'No,' said Paul. 'I don't see and I don't want to either. In fact, I'm not interested in anything you've got to say.'

'But —'

'How could you?' he interrupted, slightly contradicting what he'd just said. 'Was there really not one moment when you thought it might be a good idea to tell me the truth?' he asked incredulously.

'It wasn't like that,' began Jessica, but Paul obviously wasn't in the mood for listening.

'And now you come to my house, which by the way I'm sure you probably think is a squalid little shit-hole. I mean, even your aunt's house is only small and "kinda cute" by your standards, isn't it?' he said, cruelly mocking her accent.

'Now hang on a minute —' tried Jessica, whose patience was fast running out.

'No,' said Paul, turning to look at her for the first time since she'd arrived. 'You don't get to tell me anything any more. You see, you might be used to snapping your fingers and getting your way, but that won't work with me.'

At that point something in Jessica did indeed snap but it wasn't her fingers. Defeated, disappointed and unbelievably furious at his reaction, especially when she'd made this pilgrimage across London just so that she could explain things, she gave up. She'd had enough, so she turned on her heel and left the room, past Lucy who was sitting on the stairs, not even bothering to pretend she wasn't listening.

'Oh, don't give up on him,' Lucy called after her.

'Why shouldn't I?' asked Jessica, who to her dismay felt like she was on the brink of tears again.

'I know he's being a twat, but he definitely loves you. He's been so happy since he met you.'

'Well, I'm not so sure, Lucy. You know he's so busy

feeling sorry for himself that he hasn't even stopped to think for a second how weird this whole thing has been for me, from beginning to end.'

'He's had a lot to get his head round,' stated Lucy, 'and I'm sure there's a big part of him that's terrified that you won't want to be with him. That you'll swan off back to Hollywood once the novelty of being with someone normal has worn off.'

In the sitting room, perfectly able to hear everything that was being said, Paul sighed, an internal debate going on furiously in his head. His pride was screaming at him to turn the volume up on the telly, and to forget that Jessica Be— whatever her bloody real name was, had ever existed. His heart, however, and interestingly enough his head, were saying the opposite. They were telling him to at least hear what she had to say. They were telling him that forgetting about her would be an impossible task and that all he wanted was for things to be right between them again.

It was two against one. Decisively he got up and came into the hallway, just in time to see Jessica walking out of the door.

'Fine,' he called after her. 'If you want to explain, go ahead. Though I doubt there's much you can say.'

Jessica, who was halfway up the front path by now, turned round, her eyes blazing with outrage.

'Please?' said Paul, coming out of the house and finally sounding something other than aggressive.

'All right,' she said in a low, angry voice. 'I will.'

'Good.'

'Good,' she repeated. 'So . . . firstly, when I come to think of it, you're probably right.'

'About what?'

'Well, you are a novelty in some ways.'

Paul looked furious and was about to protest but Jessica cut him off.

'You are a novelty because, if you must know, you're the first boyfriend I've ever had who actually seems to like me for me and not just because you want to date someone rich, or work in movies, or meet my mom and dad.'

Paul looked away, at a loss to know what to say, so Jessica continued, taking advantage of his silence.

'You're also a novelty because I've never felt like this before, about anybody. And while I know there are certain things I didn't tell you,' she said in a wobbly voice, 'I have never lied to you.'

'Oh, bollocks,' Paul muttered despairingly, his eyes turning skywards.

'Just hear me out,' snapped Jessica angrily, which took Paul quite by surprise. He nodded at her to continue.

'I came to England to find myself,' she began. 'I know that sounds clichéd but it's true. Despite the fact that I have had an incredibly pampered life in many ways, being the daughter of two living legends hasn't always been easy. Before I came here I was completely lost. I didn't lie to you about that. My dad has always interfered in everything I've ever done and I *was* beginning to feel suffocated by him and by people's reactions to me. I wanted a clean slate here and I find it sad that you don't seem able to understand even a little why I might have felt like that.'

Paul said nothing, but at least he was listening.

'All my life it's been the same thing. The minute people find out who I am they change towards me. Sometimes they feel sorry for me for not being anywhere near as beautiful as my mother. Then, once they've got over that one, they generally tend to assume one of two things. Either that I'm someone special, who must want to do extraordinary things with my life. Or that I have no brain, which is probably the more common assumption, actually. That's the one that labels me an airhead just because my parents are rich and famous, which if you want to know the truth is actually kind of boring. It's frustrating too and ironic because I've seen firsthand how unhappy my mom has been, and she's the most beautiful woman in the world, which leaves me wondering why people would ever think I'd like to be lumbered with that particular cross to bear. Secondly, I don't want to be — nor have I ever wanted to be — famous. In fact, I don't see what's wrong with being mediocre because, as far as I can make out, being mediocre probably makes for a less pressured, happier existence. That being said,' continued Jessica, raising her hand to warn Paul not to interrupt when it looked like he might be about to do so, 'I am not an airhead. I do want to work hard and I do want to do something that fulfils me, though if it wasn't for this trip I still wouldn't have a clue what that might be. So if you're asking me if I've regretted coming here, if I regret having had a break from people's preconceptions about me, then the answer would have to be no. Do I regret you being hurt and not telling you everything sooner? Then the answer is yes, of course. But, Paul, I didn't set out for this to happen. I didn't know I was going to meet you. Though, actually, I'm kind of glad I did meet you as Jessica Bender and not as the daughter of a film star, because if I had you never would have given me the time of day anyway.'

'That's not true,' retorted Paul, amazed to be the one being accused of anything.

'Yes, it is,' replied Jessica plainly.

They stood looking at one another for a second, both struggling with what they were feeling.

'Well, I don't think it is,' said Paul feebly.

'Paul, I came to England to be me,' said Jessica eventually. 'I wanted to be somewhere where I could walk into a room before my identity, just for once. Does that really make me such a bad person?'

Paul wasn't sure. Having heard everything she'd had to say he could probably understand her motivation for staying quiet about who she was, but was hurt that she thought he was so judgemental. However, he was also intelligent enough to realize that if there was no truth in what she'd said then he wouldn't be feeling quite so hurt, but would be cross instead. The truth does indeed hurt. He still felt like he'd been taken for a fool though and said as much.

'I don't appreciate people laughing at me behind my back,' he said defensively, nodding politely as they both stood back to make way for a lady who was trying to pass by with a buggy.

'Who's laughing?' asked Jessica, bewildered.

'You must have been,' said Paul. 'Pretending to me that you didn't have any money. That thing about your dad being soppy and crying at everything. Choosing the name Bender, for Christ's sake. Why would anyone do that unless they were having a laugh?'

'Maybe I was unaware of certain English colloquialisms?' Jessica suggested huffily.

Paul shrugged.

'My dad's real name is Teddy Bender,' she said quietly. 'And if you tell anyone that he'll kill me. He's originally from Pinner, where he went to the local comprehensive. He had elocution lessons in order to sound like he does.'

Paul frowned in disbelief but the frown soon faded as it dawned on him that Jessica really wasn't lying. She couldn't be. She looked so grave and, besides, why would she make that up? Teddy Bender! Priceless.

'And,' continued Jessica, reluctantly deciding that in order to regain Paul's trust she was going to have to trust him an awful lot, 'I didn't lie about the other thing . . . the crying thing . . .'

Paul thought about this, digesting the repercussions of what that actually meant. Once he had, he had to force away the smirk that was fighting to appear across his face. He mustn't laugh. To do so would show that he'd forgiven Jessica and he couldn't do that yet, not until he knew she wasn't going to dump him and bugger off to her real, far more glamorous world.

'Fair enough,' he said. 'But obviously I won't be able to compete with the kind of guys you must have after you in Hollywood. They can't all be gold-digging arseholes, so while I forgive you for lying, I would rather just break up now before I get more involved. Seeing as it's inevitable, I don't see the point in drawing things out. I'm not stupid. I know you can do better than someone with an average life and a less than average bank account.'

He stopped, hoping against hope that the next thing he heard would be reassuring, comforting, absolving any insecurities he might have. He was to be sorely disappointed.

'Have you even heard yourself? God, you can be such an asshole,' cried Jessica, taking him by surprise. 'I just can't freaking believe you sometimes. Paul, you're an amazing person, but after everything I've just said to you, for that to be your reaction then you must have some pretty major issues. My relationship with you is one of the best things that's ever happened to me, if you must know, so why would I be prepared to throw that all away? I actually hate the thought of this only being a holiday romance and if you'd actually met any of the jerks I've gone out with, maybe you'd realize why. And how can you still think I'm so shallow?' she asked, frustrated beyond belief. 'Or, rather, how can *you* be so shallow? Why can't you judge me on what you've seen, on how I've been to you? Who my parents are is something I have no control over. Nobody does.'

'Yeah, I do know that, Einstein,' Paul said, slightly shamefacedly.

'Well, then, maybe you should try showing it,' said Jessica indignantly. 'You know, we all get dealt a different hand of cards to play with in life, but the only thing that matters is what we choose to do with them. Making the best of our "cards" is all any of us *can* do. Jeez,' she suddenly added, frustrated beyond belief.

'Yeah, but it's not like . . .' attempted Paul, but Jessica wasn't listening. She was on a roll.

'Is life fair? Of course it isn't. Is it fair that I don't have to worry about money? No. Is it fair that home for me is a mansion in Malibu? No. But it's also not my fault and I am so –' she swallowed hard but it was no good, the tears were making a comeback – 'I am so . . . tired of having to apologize for who I am.'

'Well . . . you shouldn't have to,' ventured Paul.

'I know,' said Jessica. 'I know I shouldn't have to but I'm not sure I'll ever be able to help myself because I am so aware of what people like you think of people like me.'

'I don't –'

'You have such a huge chip on your shoulder, Paul,' Jessica rushed on, 'which you have to get rid of. I mean, I know my life's pretty perfect, but if I really wanted to then I'm sure I could find a few shit parts to dwell on. I could blame my insecurities on my mom leaving me when I was a little girl. Or my lack of direction on the fact that when I was four I'd spent so much time with my nanny that Spanish was my first language. It's been pretty weird living with my dad and a stepmom who's not much older than myself. And did I really want to catch my dad humping my mom at his birthday party? No, I did not,' she said with feeling.

Paul's jaw dropped to the pavement and a woman who was walking by crossed the road.

'Shit,' said Jessica, who had got rather carried away. Purging herself of so many truths was rather like having a detox. 'Forget I even said that. Anyway, the point is that in life, nine times out of ten, you only have yourself to blame.'

'What point about me are you trying to make exactly?' said Paul, feeling defensive yet choked.

Jessica sighed. 'You won't believe this, I'm sure, but in

some ways I feel envious of you. I don't even know them yet, but just hearing you talk about Lucy and your mom, you sound like such a close unit. A close family is all I've ever wanted and just because you're from Staines and I'm from LA, just because your dad was a lousy father and mine happened to hit the jackpot, how the hell does that have any bearing on us?'

Paul blinked and swallowed hard. He knew she was right. She had uncannily managed to know exactly what demons he was battling with before he knew himself. He did have a habit of blaming everything on his dad and of weighing up people's circumstances before he'd given them a chance to show him who they were.

'I'm sorry,' he said sadly. 'You're right. I've been a twat and I know I can be a bit . . . down on myself sometimes.'

'Well, it's better than being arrogant, I guess,' said Jessica quietly.

Paul stepped towards her tentatively. 'I think maybe I'm just a bit, you know, scared about losing you,' he admitted finally.

Jessica sniffed and gave him a watery smile. 'Well, you're not going to.'

Paul looked away, his hands stuffed firmly in his pockets. 'I know you think I'm a berk . . .'

Jessica laughed. 'I don't, although if that's the best that one of London's top comedy writers can come up with then . . .'

At this, Paul grinned. 'At least I'm not going out with a Bender any more,' he said.

Jessica punched him on the arm.

'Ow,' he said, rubbing his arm, before finally giving her a very welcome grin. He took her hands and, as he stared at her, his face grew serious once more.

'I love you, Jessica.'

Jessica gasped and looked upwards as her eyes brimmed with tears. She'd waited a long time to hear those words and for a minute there had thought she may have blown her chance of ever hearing them.

'I love you too,' she replied, 'so, so much.'

'Thank you for finding me,' said Paul, pulling her in for a hug.

'You're very welcome,' said Jessica, burying her head into his shoulder briefly before pulling away again to gaze into his eyes. 'Hey, are you . . . crying?'

'No,' said Paul immediately, though in truth he was on the verge. 'Fuck it,' he said. 'I do not do crying. What have you done to me?'

'Oh, don't worry about it and don't bother holding it in either,' laughed Jessica, so happy she thought she might explode and squeezing him tight. 'Just go with it, let it all out, because when it comes to men crying, I promise you I'm used to it.'

Epilogue

Seven Months Later

'Are you OK?' asked Jessica.

'No,' replied Paul truthfully. 'I'm bloody bricking it.'

'Well, I don't know why you watched *Meet the Parents* on the plane. That can't have helped,' Jessica chastised, her own nerves getting the better of her.

'It's one of my favourite films,' Paul protested. 'One of the best pieces of comedy writing of all time. Besides, you don't think it's going to be like that, do you?'

But Jessica didn't have time to answer because at that moment Consuela opened the door, revealing the most palatial hallway Paul had ever seen.

'Jessica,' Consuela shrieked. 'It's so good to see you, sweetheart.'

'You too, I've missed you,' replied Jessica, embracing her warmly before drawing away to include her boyfriend in the proceedings. 'Now, I want you to meet Paul.'

'Ah, Paul, I've heard so much about you. Come in, come in and welcome.'

'Thanks,' said Paul shyly, entering the house just in time to see the man who had made many a Boxing Day bearable appear through a set of double doors. He gulped. Despite all the pep talks he'd given himself over the last few weeks, any good intentions he'd had about viewing Edward

Granger purely as Jessica's dad had flown out of the six-foot windows. It was James Bond and while he'd expected him to look handsome, dashing, tall and pleased to see his beloved daughter, what he hadn't expected was for the world famous actor to break into a trot, pick Jessica up and swirl her about the place like she was twelve years old.

'It's good to see you, kitten,' he said fervently, his eyes looking suspiciously misty. 'I've missed you so much, my pumpkin.'

'Me too, Dad, me too,' replied Jessica happily, wriggling out of his vice-like grip. 'Now, Dad, I'd like to introduce you to Paul Fletcher.'

'Aha, so you're the famous Paul we've been hearing about for months,' he said smoothly, sounding much more like Bond than when he'd been throwing words like pumpkin and kitten around. 'It's wonderful to meet you at last.' He extended a hand.

'Great to meet you too, sir,' said Paul, shaking it in a slightly stiff manner. Nerves were making him sweat profusely and he was suddenly rather worried about marks on his T-shirt. Jessica grinned goofily at the pair of them, her heart pounding in her chest with a mixture of pride and nervous anticipation.

Half an hour later, cold drinks in hand, the three of them were sitting in the shade at the huge outside eating area. Paul surveyed his surroundings, trying to look as if it were perfectly commonplace to be sitting outside a Malibu mansion with an A-list superstar.

'So the course is going well?' Edward was saying as he caught up with his daughter's news.

'Really well,' replied Jessica happily. 'I love it and I can't tell you how good it feels to finally find something I'm actually good at. It'll take years to achieve being a therapist but I'm learning so much, so I know it'll be worth it. And in the meantime I'm still really enjoying working for Diane. Although she's so much better now, I know she'll be OK when I move on too.'

'It just seems so extraordinary that you had to go all the way to England to discover this vocation,' teased Edward. 'Don't you think, Paul? I mean, it's not like there are any therapists out here in LA or anything.'

Paul and Jessica laughed. He had a point.

'Ah, here's Ange,' said Edward suddenly, shading his eyes with his hand. 'Over here, darling,' he yelled across the garden. 'Did it go well?'

'Yes, yes,' said Angelica, picking her way delicately across the lawn as fast as she could in her heels. She'd been at an important meeting with Universal Studios, but had spent most of it fretting about the fact she was missing her daughter's arrival.

In fact, so impatient was she to reach her that now she abandoned her heels altogether and started to run. Equally excited, Jessica flew to meet her halfway. 'It's so good to see you, *ma chérie*,' Angelica squealed as they hugged. 'And Paul, how marvellous to see you too,' she added as he approached somewhat nervously. She was determined to make him feel as comfortable as possible. 'I'm so sorry I was not here to greet you both when you arrived.'

Paul went to shake her hand but Angelica flapped it away, kissing him warmly on both cheeks instead. 'It is so nice to meet you properly and tonight we will have a lovely dinner together, unless you already have plans with Dulcie? Do you?'

'No,' Jessica replied. 'We're keeping out of her way, aren't we, Paul? With only two days to go till the wedding she's like a headless chicken, so we're going to wait and see her at the rehearsal dinner.'

Having greeted everyone else, Angelica strolled over to Edward and planted a kiss on his lips. Lazily, he reached an arm out and extended it round her waist, pulling her down so she was sitting on his lap.

'Hello, my darling,' he said lovingly.

'Hello, my sweet,' she purred.

'So, Dad,' said Jessica, rolling her eyes. The two of them were worse than her and Paul. 'Paul and I are picking our friends up from the airport tomorrow and I wondered if it would be OK if they came here for the afternoon? I know they'd love to meet you guys and then we could hang out by the pool.'

'Of course they can,' said Edward. 'I'd be cross if they didn't. Who's coming again?'

'Well, Isy, or as Dulcie likes to call her, "the little wolverine". Seriously, those two are as odd as each other. Anyway, Isy's a bridesmaid, along with me. Then Dulcie's also invited Kerry, her boyfriend Luke, and Vanessa. In fact, Natasha's the only one who didn't make the list. Much to her disgust.'

'Well, I'm glad,' said Angelica, getting up from Edward's lap to give her daughter another hug. 'I didn't like the sound of her very much.'

Paul glanced across at Edward. He was blinking hard as he took in the happy scene, clearly choked about seeing mother and daughter so comfortable in each other's company, which was understandable. Given their previous history, it *was* touching. Still, Paul found himself respectfully trying to smother a grin as he realized Jessica really hadn't been exaggerating Edward's sentimental streak.

'So,' said Edward, clearing his throat as the two women launched into what was obviously going to be a long and detailed wedding natter. 'I believe your mother and my sister are having a great time together.'

'Yes, watch out Vegas,' said Paul.

'Quite,' agreed Edward. 'Well, this new friendship Pam's struck up with your mother seems to have done her the world of good.'

Paul nodded. It had done *both* women the world of good. Over the last few months his mother and Pam had become inseparable and when Edward had insisted on treating Pam to a well-deserved holiday, she'd immediately invited Anita to come with her.

'When they picked up their car at the airport to go to Vegas it was like the Saga version of *Thelma and Louise*,' joked Paul.

Edward roared with laughter. 'That's very funny,' he chuckled. 'I can see why you're such a good comedy writer.'

Delighted by the compliment, Paul tried to look modest.

'So what have you got planned while you're over here?' asked Edward.

'Well, I'm primarily here for the wedding and to meet Jessica's family, of course, but I've also set up a couple of work meetings, just on the off-chance. I know Jessica wants to move back here sooner rather than later, so I thought it might be worth putting a few feelers out.'

'Good,' said Edward, resisting the urge to punch the

air. This was music to his ears. He could grow to like Paul but only if he wasn't the one thing preventing his little girl from coming home. 'So who are you seeing?' he asked casually.

'A few people at various networks,' replied Paul. 'Though the one I'm really excited about is Bob Chambers.'

'You should be,' exclaimed Edward, impressed. Bob Chambers was responsible for some of the greatest shows ever, on one of America's biggest and most prestigious networks. Edward's mind whirred away. 'I don't know Bob directly,' he said eventually, 'but I know someone who does. In fact, if I were to put a call in to my old friend Steve I reckon I could help swing your meeting in the right direction.'

'Um, oh, well . . .'

'What are you saying, Dad?' interjected Jessica, suddenly wary, having caught the tail end of their conversation.

'Nothing,' said Edward.

'Edward?' said Angelica sternly. 'What are you up to?'

'Nothing,' repeated Edward vaguely.

'Paul?' said Jessica, who didn't believe her father for a second. He had guilt written all over his face.

Paul wondered what to do. He didn't want to be rude and tell on Edward, but at the same time he wasn't about to start lying to Jessica. In the end it was left to Angelica to help him out.

'Edward, what are you up to? We know what you're like, so if you're putting Paul in some awful position you'd better tell us now.'

'Oh, bloody hell,' Edward blustered. 'Since when should a man be questioned all the time in his own house?'

Paul tried not to smile. There was something about Edward that was naturally funny.

'Since that man has never known when not to interfere,' replied Jessica firmly.

'I'm not interfering,' replied Edward, but the game was up. 'Oh, all right. Paul's got a meeting with Bob Chambers and I just thought I might be able to help by putting in a good word with someone.'

Jessica hesitated. On the one hand she would love Paul to get a job out here. It would save them from having to solve some fairly agonizing problems, but if he was going to do it she wanted him to do it on his own. He was talented enough not to need her father's help, but it was up to him. Maybe having worked so hard all his life he might welcome a helping hand for once.

'Christ,' said Edward, laughing at all their stricken faces. 'Anyone would think I was coercing him into becoming a drugs mule or something.'

'Shut up, Dad. It's important to me that Paul doesn't feel like you're interfering. After all, I know how that feels.'

Suddenly, all eyes were on Paul, who could sense it was time to tell it how it was. Time to be honest, even if being honest meant risking being impolite.

'OK,' said Paul. 'In all honesty, it does feel a little like you're interfering. Although I'm sure you're probably only doing it in the hope that, if I get a job here, Jessica will return home quicker.'

Edward tried to look like that wasn't the case, but failed miserably.

'But – and I hope I'm not offending you when I say this – I'd rather you didn't put a call in. You see, if you put a word in and I get the job, I'll feel like that's the only reason I've been given it and I like getting things on merit. I do really appreciate the offer though,' he added hastily.

Jessica was so proud she thought she might burst. However, she and Angelica were also holding their breath, waiting to see whether Edward would respond reasonably.

For a second his expression was so solemn it looked like he might be rather offended. Then his face slowly broke into a broad grin and he stood up and went to shake Paul's hand.

'Well done,' he said, pumping it vigorously. 'You're a good lad and, though it pains me to admit it, you've done the right thing.'

Jessica squealed with delight. Then she ran at Paul, jumped up and wrapped her legs around him, smothering him with kisses.

'Easy, tiger,' said Edward. 'Don't forget, your mum and dad are here, you know.'

Jessica broke away for a second, laughing. 'Yeah well, as Pam would say, pot kettle black.'

'Right,' he said, conceding defeat and turning almost as pink as Angelica had just done.

'Thank you for understanding,' said Paul.

'At last!' quipped Jessica cheekily, before enquiring, 'Hey, are you crying, Dad?'

'No,' snapped Edward, searching in his pocket for his hanky.

'My soppy date is still as soft as ever, eh?' laughed Angelica.

'Oh, shut it you,' said Edward, briskly wiping his eyes

and clearing his throat. 'I'm not bloody crying. It's the grass, it's making my eyes water.'

'Or maybe they're reshowing *Cheaper by the Dozen*?' joked Paul, forgetting who he was taking the piss out of for a second.

Jessica and Angelica looked stunned and pretty quickly Paul realized he may have crossed the line. 'Sorry,' he muttered.

Edward narrowed his eyes and paused, milking the moment just long enough for Paul to think it might be a much shorter trip than originally planned. Then he threw his head back and roared with heartfelt laughter. 'You cheeky bugger,' he said good-naturedly. 'Though don't you dare go spilling any of my less than macho secrets to anyone else,' he instructed.

'Oh, I won't, Mr Granger, I promise,' said Paul, relieved beyond belief.

'And none of that Mr Granger business,' Edward chastised. 'You can call me –' He changed his mind. He wanted to see the look on Paul's face.

'You can call me Bond,' he said, 'James Bond.'

It was worth it. Paul's face was a picture of surprise, so caught off kilter was he by such a brilliantly surreal moment. Angelica giggled and Jessica grinned. Her dad was priceless, and for once his showing off filled her with nothing but affection and pride. In fact, standing here in the hot sunshine with the people she loved, at that precise second she was filled with an overwhelming sense of happiness, hope and pure joy at simply being alive. She went to Paul and kissed him on the cheek and her optimism must have been contagious for Paul found himself pulling her towards him and bending slightly to whisper something in her ear.

'And you never know,' he said, 'maybe one day you'll be Fletcher, Jessica Fletcher?'

'You never know,' she agreed.

Acknowledgements

Huge thanks must go to everyone at Penguin who believed in this book enough to publish it and then made it happen. Particularly Kate Burke, Mari Evans, Anthea Townsend, Karen Whitlock, Debbie Hatfield and Beatrix McIntyre.

Many thanks to my wondrous agent Eugenie Furniss. I am truly grateful for all your hard work, words of wisdom and endless enthusiasm. Thanks also to the uber-efficient and very lovely Claudia Webb.

A big heartfelt and special thank you to Debi Allen, a force to be reckoned with who has championed me through thick and thin. (And I mean that literally. After having Lily I had to wear Bridget Jones support pants on my first job back.) You're amazing, the most hard-working person I know. I'm extremely lucky to have you in my life.

Thanks, as ever, to all my fantastic family. Especially to Mum and Mauro who, after a hell of a year, still managed to come out the other end smiling. Also to Dad, Sally, Imogen, Isabel and Jessica, thank you for all your invaluable advice, time and support. Forget 'the knights of the round table', 'the readers of the rectangle table at Madrid Road' are where it's at. Harry, you have to get a mention too of course, (despite the fact that you haven't even read the first one yet) as do my darling Lily and Freddie. They haven't read it either, though in fairness they probably have more of an excuse.

Thanks to my brilliant, funny, generous and supportive girlfriends. I honestly don't know what I'd do without you. Special thanks to those of you who helped out so much during the really fun no kitchen/washing machine phase of my life. There are probably a few stray pairs of underpants lurking in your machines to this day. . .

Lastly, thanks to my lovely husband Charlie. Even after all these years, you're still my James Bond (though possibly in an Austen Powers type of way). I love you to bits and honestly don't know where I'd be without you.

Win the Bond Girl lifestyle for a day

To celebrate the publication of

From London With Love

we're giving away a fabulous day out in London in association with **secret escapes**, the member only luxury travel site.

The lucky winner will receive

An extended high-speed boat tour for 2 people up the River Thames (to the Bond theme, of course)

Evening cocktails and an overnight stay for 2 at a top London hotel

To enter the competition visit
www.penguin.co.uk/fromlondonwithlove

From London with Love readers can join **secret escapes** for free using this link

www.secretescapes.com/instant-access/penguin

secret escapes